"SEDUCTIVE . . .

We are hopelessly entangled in the intricate web of Piercy's characters. . . . Brings to life the sounds and smells and sights of the often beautifully wild Cape landscape."

The Hartford Courant

"A lively read with a good point to make about the folly of envying rich folks."

Boston Herald

"Enjoyable . . . Piercy is so finely tuned and so accomplished a writer that we root for everyone she wants us to cheer; we hiss her villains quite sincerely."

The Detroit News

"Marge Piercy made me keep reading until I found out the answers."

The Houston Post

Turn the page for more about SUMMER PEOPLE

MEET THE RESIDENTS OF *SUMMER PEOPLE*. . . .

Dinah
A composer who treasures her privacy and her music, she thinks she can never relinquish the tender and passionate life she shared with Willie and Susan—until she realizes she may not have a choice.

Susan
Beautiful, vibrant, and utterly feminine, she begins to feel something's missing in her life. And she thinks one of the glamorous summer residents can give her what she needs.

Willie
A leftist sculptor out of step with the times, he loves both Dinah and his wife Susan—if only he could keep their once-scandalous relationship from falling apart.

Tyrone
One of the "summer people," he's attractive, rich, and absolutely ruthless when it comes to getting what he wants.

Laurie
As Tyrone's daughter, she has a reputation to live up to. But her life has been turned upside down and her father thinks some time on the Cape might help her recover.

Jimmy
Willie and Susan's son has come home to straighten out his life. And there he finds Laurie, vulnerable and available.

Siobhan
A punk artist, always at odds with her mother Susan, she knows that another battle might sever their unstable relationship forever.

Itzak
A world-famous flutist, he has discovered Dinah and her extraordinary work and finds himself helplessly drawn into her exciting orbit.

Also by Marge Piercy:

FICTION

GOING DOWN FAST*
DANCE THE EAGLE TO SLEEP*
SMALL CHANGES*
WOMAN ON THE EDGE OF TIME*
THE HIGH COST OF LIVING*
VIDA*
BRAIDED LIVES*
FLY AWAY HOME*
GONE TO SOLDIERS*

POETRY

BREAKING CAMP
HARD LOVING
4-TELLING *(with Emma Jarrett, Dick Lourie and Bob Hershon)*
TO BE OF USE
LIVING IN THE OPEN
THE TWELVE-SPOKED WHEEL FLASHING
THE MOON IS ALWAYS FEMALE
CIRCLES ON THE WATER: SELECTED POEMS
STONE, PAPER, KNIFE
MY MOTHER'S BODY
AVAILABLE LIGHT

PLAY

THE LAST WHITE CLASS *(Coauthored with Ira Wood)*

ESSAYS

PARTI-COLORED BLOCKS FOR A QUILT *(Poets on Poetry Series)*

ANTHOLOGY

EARLY RIPENING: AMERICAN WOMEN'S POETRY NOW

*Published by Fawcett Books

SUMMER PEOPLE

Marge Piercy

FAWCETT CREST • NEW YORK

I'd like to thank Irwin (Bud) Bazelon and Herschel Garfein for all their help in answering questions and trying to explain the world of the composer to me. At very different points in their careers and with widely differing orientations, each was generous with his time and attention. Caleb Morgan has my gratitude for being clear and uncondescending in demonstrating the electronic options of composers and letting me into his studio.

I would especially like to thank Yo-Yo Ma for his unfailingly good-natured fielding of questions from the philosophical to the minutiae of premieres, and his generosity and patience with a curiosity and informational greed that must have appeared bottomless.

Once again I have prevailed upon the kindness of Elaine McIlroy and Claire Beswick of the Wellfleet Public Library to locate biographies and critical books on music that I needed. My continuing thanks to my bright and hardworking assistant Kathy Shorr, who learned perhaps more than she truly wanted to know about yet another subject while transcribing notes from reading, research, observation and interviews into our family of fat data bases.

Finally I want to thank, as always but never pro forma, my husband, Ira Wood. We share our work from the moment we have the first idea through all the rough and scaly drafts, the traveling and the talking out of problems. All our work is in some sense a collaboration, at the same time that we each have a distinct and quite separate vision, talents and approach. We keep each other on course. I live and work in a network of caring and cooperation that makes the writing both possible and worthwhile.

ONE

Dinah

The noise from outside broke loud and sudden, as if somebody had begun cutting a superhighway through the woods. Dinah's first reaction was fury. Bounding up, she spilled her coffee right into the lap of the black velvet robe Susan had made for her. A chain saw screeched nasally but she heard something growlier under it.

Dinah rose early. Whether she had made love with Willie or Susan during the day or not, she returned to the old house and slept in her own bed. Upon rising, she would breakfast quickly and feed her cats. Except in the stretch the summer people were there or the few times in the winter when the snow was too deep, she would walk around the pond with Figaro, her big orange tabby with a perennial smile like the Cheshire cat, or Bogey, Willie's dog. In her head she would already be working. The rhythms would start. She would hear what she had so far and begin to enrich or simplify. The moment she walked in, she would toss her jacket across the room and start.

One of the reasons she liked sleeping alone was to avoid having to talk to anybody before she set down or played those lines, chords, rhythms, those shapes of sound that moved in her. Music was fragile when it started to coalesce. Silence was the ground.

She stepped into her jeans, pulling a sweater over her tangled curls and headed for the water's edge. Willie came running from the new house—it was a hundred and ninety years old, but so called because it had been built after the house she lived in. He left the door to his studio open, letting the warmth from the wood stove waste itself, and strode across the carpet of pine needles toward the pond. He had not bothered with a jacket. Willie's smooth skin was always warm to the touch. She thought of him as having, like the cats, a naturally hotter body temperature than ordinary humans.

"What the hell's going on?" she croaked in her hoarse morning voice.

The noise was loud enough now so that Susan appeared in the doorway, still scrubbing at her eyes, tousled in a pale green nightgown and peignoir.

"You'll catch your death of a cold," Willie called to her. Voice of honey and smoke. North Carolina in it still. "Bundle up. It frosted last night. Dinah and me'll check it out."

On the dock they stood side by side, blowing steam, staring across the pond of a size she had grown up calling a lake in the Midwest. Willie was a full eight inches taller than Dinah and he always thought he could see farther. "It's the Captain's house," he reported, swaying in excitement.

"Asshole, I can see that. But what are they doing to it?" She took his arm to soften her tone. She wasn't mad at him but at whatever was carving great swaths through the woods and the quiet.

Bogey, who was low to the ground and hairy and cheerful, wagged his tail hard and barked, barked at the trucks and the men. There were only four habitations on the pond, their two houses side by side, then Tyrone Burdock's spread—the big house, the boathouse and other outbuildings considered as one unit—and finally the Captain's house.

Toby Lloyd, who actually had been the captain of a local fishing boat, had lost the house that spring when the IRS landed on him. They were always after the local fishermen, claimed they ran dope in, claimed they never reported their income or their crews' shares. However, the house had been called the Captain's house before Toby was born. It had been in his family for generations, as had most of the land stretching between the pond and the blacktop road a mile away. The Captain it had been named after had died in 1882, but she had still always thought of Toby as the Captain. She had no idea what had become of him.

"Must be those new people who bought it."

Willie and Bogey were eager to go sniffing over, wagging their tails. Willie didn't mind the uproar. He always had the radio or the TV on when he was welding or cooking up his resins. He was a sculptor and worked in a large studio that he and Dinah had built across the yard from his house, a barnlike space with skylights and shingles just beginning to weather a pleasant grey. "I'm going to take a look," he said, whistling unnecessarily to Bogey, whom nothing less than a chain would have restrained from following.

Dinah spat into the pond in the direction of the noise and then swung after his tall lean back. Surprisingly Susan was coming toward them, bundled into her parka. The temperature was close to 40, Dinah estimated, but if Willie was always warm, Susan was always chilly. Even bleary with sleep, she looked lovely, her shoulder length auburn hair tangled in loose waves around her apple blossom skin. Willie and Bogey were forging ahead along the path that skirted the shore of the pond. Dinah waited for Susan, who took her arm and then leaned on her, yawning and sighing.

"What got you up?"

"Mmmmmngh." Susan yawned again, pointing across the pond.

Dinah darkly suspected that it was the glamour of the other side of the pond for Susan that had got her dressed so much earlier than she would normally venture out of bed. Susan liked to have tea in bed and then loll around for another hour or so before she gradually ventured forth. If dishabille had not looked so becoming on Susan, especially in the clothes she made herself, she would have seemed one more brain-damaged housewife unable to tackle her life, Dinah sometimes thought, but Willie and she accepted the slow start of Susan's day as part of her mystique. Often she would not be fully dressed or entirely focused until noon, when she called Willie into the house for lunch and then climbed to her bedroom to work. Susan was more fragile than the other two, more susceptible to mood swings.

Dinah was shorter than Susan by several inches, but she was stronger, stockier. She supported Susan's weight as Susan pushed her way along the narrow path, her long wool skirt catching on the catbriars. They kept having to stop for Susan to pull herself free. Willie had disappeared into the brush, but ahead they could hear Bogey yapping, even through the roar of the machinery that shook Dinah's ear bones. Dinah would rather have walked free and fast, at her customary pace, but she knew Susan liked to walk arm in arm. Dinah could feel herself letting go of her morning like a good plate that had cracked into several fragments irrevocably beyond gluing together.

"Did you hear about your grant yet?" Susan asked her, deciding to put herself together and ask something personal.

"Not yet. Bureaucrats." Dinah meant all the foundations to which she had applied. There was no one "grant" on which she

3

was waiting, for she had applications in to six. Sometimes she spent more time writing proposals than writing music. Not teaching was a weird choice for a composer—one she had made years before almost instinctively, for her music, for her health, but it was hard to get by. As a woman, as a nonacademic with none of the respectability and certification even a bush league college lends its faculty, some years she applied for thirty grants and got none.

"I saw the most exquisite dress in *Vogue* last night. It was simple enough in its lines, but the fagoting . . ." Susan read all the fashion magazines, as the other two read their respective art journals, and Dinah knew it was important for Susan to talk about what was on her mind. She also knew that both Willie and she tuned out Susan's reportage of what was coming to Paris, Milan and Seventh Avenue. All Dinah could imagine of the word fagoting was in the nature of bad homophobic jokes.

A few robins in the rosa virginiana. Not all the robins who lived on the Cape in the summer went south; a small population always spent winters back in the ponds, where the ground tended to stay open. Dinah fed birds all winter; she liked seeing them. "I bet you forgot we have appointments with Dr. Bridey today." Susan pinched Dinah's cheek.

"What?" Dinah jumped. "Today? Are you sure?" But she believed Susan instantly. First, Dinah had put off their annual gynecological appointments this year till they were two months late. They usually went in September. Second, Susan kept their social calendar and if she said they had appointments, they had them. They went in together, for moral support and to pass the time pleasantly while they were waiting and during the long drive into Boston and back. Both women had the habit left over from the years abortions had been illegal of having as progressive a doctor as they could find. Both shared a common superstition on the Cape that all the local doctors had failed elsewhere or would rather go fishing. If that had once been true, Dinah was aware it was long out of date, yet they both trucked into the city together for their once a year Pap smears and checkups. Then they shopped and had supper out together. One of their rituals.

As they approached the far side of the pond, Susan fell silent and her languorous gaze slipped past Dinah to rest on Tyrone's spread, the clapboard outbuildings, the big white porticoed and pillared house that looked as if it had dropped from some dream of Tara smack into the pinewoods. Both their old Cape houses and the studio could fit into Tyrone's house and leave plenty of room for a party. It had been built in the twenties by a businessman from New Jersey who had summered there and got richer by local rum-running. One branch of the sand road that ran past their houses ended at Tyrone's. The Captain's house was reached from the blacktop by a different track.

Susan looked at Tyrone's house as if she could flirt with it, could melt its portico with glances. "He's coming at Christmas," she said half breathlessly. "Poor Tyrone."

"If there's one thing he isn't, that's poor."

"His marriage!"

Dinah grunted. "Number forty-seven down the tubes."

"Only his third wife. Everybody is entitled to a couple of failures. And he's never stopped being a good father to Laurie."

"Anyhow it's the Captain's house under attack." Dinah disliked Tyrone for what were to her excellent reasons, which she ticked off mentally. (1) He was overbearing, manipulative. (2) Once when he had caught Dinah alone at the little beach in between their houses, he had made a heavy droit du seigneur attempt, falling on her as she lay naked. All he had got for his trouble was a punch in the gut, but she had not liked his manners. (3) He had several times questioned her about her relationship with Willie and with Susan in an overly personal way; and he often gave himself leave to joke about it, that it was quaint and old-fashioned. "Monogamy and adultery, that's the way it's done now," he rumbled. "Everyone out here is twenty years behind the times. We were doing that sort of multiple construction in 1972."

When they arrived at the clearing, just by where the Captain had had his vegetable garden, Willie was already in conversation with a young bearded guy in a buffalo plaid jacket—Allie Dove, the middle brother of the Dove boys from Dove Hollow. Dinah waved at him, dragging Susan forward.

Willie turned. He was maybe ten years older than Allie Dove, being forty-eight, with his hair bone white since before Dinah had met him, but he looked younger than Allie because of that smooth boyish skin, his tight lean body and his expression which was always open, interested, wide-eyed. "Hey, this is amazing, Susan, Dinah, looky what Allie and the boys are up to. See how they got it shored up. They're just yanking out the whole innards

5

like sucking the egg from a shell. See, they're pulling down the walls and ceilings, tearing the floors right out.''

Willie loved machinery and gimmicks and novelty. Dinah stared, appalled. "That house is a Victorian. What the hell are they doing to it? Turning it into a McDonald's?''

More, they had bulldozed the Captain's woodshed and toolshed and his chicken house into a pile of old boards. Dinah was glad she'd gotten the last of the chicken shit out of there, because it would be no good mixed with nails and broken glass and smashed wood. Right after the Captain had lost the house, she'd hauled the manure home by boat and let it compost near her garden till she could dig it in. Tyrone had always objected to the smell of the chickens and the crowing of the roosters. Dinah missed both.

It was too noisy to think and Dinah didn't want to take out her ill temper on Allie or his crew. They were glad for what looked like a big job, and it wasn't their idea to gut the old house and replace its insides with high-tech plastic boxes. She turned and started back. Susan and Willie would follow at their leisure. At supper she would hear more than she wanted about what Willie had learned.

A triangle was a highly stable structure, she remembered learning in high school geometry, and so it had proved with them. Ten years they had been together. She wondered if Willie and Susan would have stayed married if she had not seduced each of them and then been invited in, permanently. They had both been discontented, restless. She had been their tenant, living with Mark in the old house. After Mark died, she had bought the house and stayed on alone. When Mark threatened to rise in her memory, she walked faster, practicing the discipline of looking carefully that Susan had taught her. She had always been sensitive to sound, but Susan and Willie between them had taught her to see. Susan was most responsive to color, Willie to light and shadow and texture. Browning bracken. A grey squirrel crashed through the oak boughs in a hurry, chittering at her as she passed beneath. No, at Figaro who was coming to find her and had stopped to eye the squirrel speculatively. He liked to stalk them on the ground. The grey squirrels were big, the size and coloring of her smaller cat, Tosca, who would be curled on her bed or draped on the worktable wondering where she was.

Why did the IRS have to meddle with people who never had much to begin with? Many of the old Cape families should have been rich, because they had owned so much land, lots that today would go for sixty thousand up; but they had mostly lost the land because of back taxes, usually taxes they never paid, might not know about and could not have found the money for, since they subsisted in a barter economy. It was the real estate developers who had made the money, and nowadays, late in the boom, some of the locals had become developers, but most of them just did the work. After twelve years on the Cape, Dinah knew the Dove family, as she knew most year-round people, both the natives and the washed-ashores like herself.

The Captain had been okay as a neighbor. He had been living with Wendy who had two kids, one his, one not, town gossip informed her. Sometimes he had traded Dinah fish for her raspberries or grapes in season. He had always let her have some of his hen manure, as he politely called it, when he had dug enough into his own garden. He was off fishing for days at a time, and if once in a while his buddies got noisily drunk across the pond, that was only once in a while. For two years they had had a goat and she had bought milk from Wendy. One year he had tried geese. If she got stuck, he would come around with his old pickup truck and a winch and chains. When their pump was out one summer, they got drinking water from her. Otherwise they left each other strictly alone: good neighbors.

I am like the cats, she thought, finding Tosca on her writing table with her ears slightly laid back and her tail beating a tattoo of annoyance. I like my patterns. I like to set up my own games and play by my own rules. At least she could keep the windows shut against the encroaching sound. Summer people always said how quiet it was here and then proceeded to destroy that quality, but it wasn't ever really quiet. Gulls mewed. Crows cawed and croaked. Chickadees called and sparrows struck their melancholy repeated phrase. Spring peepers gave a high excited shrilling. The great horned owl hooted all winter. As they mated, raccoons snorted, whistled, broke branches like runaway locomotives. The pond muttered and the wind lashed off the ocean carrying snow. Sometimes at night the surf was as audible as traffic in the city. The builders would annoy her for a couple of months, then depart. It would be her woods and her kind of silence again, the small sounds of animals at their business.

She worked the rest of the morning if not well, then steadily on the Meditation for Flute, Cello and Piano that was to be performed by Kyle McGrath, who was the principal flute with the Boston Symphony Orchestra, her friend Nita who played second cello with the BSO and a pianist who was an old boy-friend of Kyle's. It was scheduled for performance late January in Boston, on the program of a composers group she belonged to—a rough association of mostly men and one other woman aged twenty-five to forty who wanted to get their work out. She had a little grant that would pay the performers and since she would photocopy the parts, give her a pittance. The group rented the hall. Now the pressure was on to get it done. At twelve, Willie brought her mail. He liked to be the one to go to the post office in town. It was a social occasion, a chance to see who was around and pick up local gossip.

The electric bill. Catalogs. An invitation to a reception following a violin recital at Jordan Hall in Boston. A letter from the Department of English at Rutgers, one Professor Bob Sanderson addressing Mrs. Edelmann, a name she had never used. She had been born Dinah Adler and she remained Dinah Adler. It was true that Mark and she had married just before his second operation, to facilitate her position visiting in the hospital and because he was beginning to think about dying and wanted her rights to his work secured.

Indeed, it was about Mark. Received a grant from the Nicholson Foundation . . . ongoing revival of interest in the work of Mark V. Edelmann . . . establishing a chronology and definitive text for the poetry. Hope that you as literary executor will co-operate . . .

Her first impulse was to lose the letter at once and pretend it had never arrived. Revival of interest. Useful as a plastic wombat, souvenir of Melbourne. Still she was Mark's executor and while that had meant only occasional annoyance during the past eleven years, lately the demands for access to Mark's papers had been increasing in intensity, complication and frequency.

She caught a glimpse of herself through the bedroom door, reflected in the mirror there. Her teeth were bared. She looked like a cornered vicious animal. Cet animal est méchant. Il se defend. She could not believe in their interest in him, his ideas, his work. All they ever did while he was alive was throw him in the slammer, insult or ignore him. When he was dying and could

8

have used encouragement, some sense of posterity and continuance, where the hell was this professor? Nor did she want to open those boxes in which the past was stored like a powerful genie of trouble and pain.

She put the letter not in the basket of bills and urgent correspondence beside her computer, but under the basket. Then Susan appeared in her city clothes, a dark green suit trimmed in black velvet that brought out the green in her grey eyes. Susan nudged Dinah upstairs and advanced on her closet. "Wear the maroon wool with the surplice top."

Dinah obeyed, letting Susan pick out the earrings and the panty hose, but she balked at the shoes and put on boots instead. She grumbled about getting dressed up just to take her clothes off for the doctor, but she knew Susan would not enjoy herself if she did not feel they were an elegant couple. Dinah would never look elegant, but she let Susan dress her.

They took Dinah's old Volvo, a once-pricey car meticulously kept up by whatever mechanic was the year's wizard. She did not know what happened to mechanics elsewhere, but two years was the local tenure. After that, they became ballerinas or therapists or divers. They tended to be bright men who got bored. The Volvo sported a terrific tape deck and great speakers, for Dinah never regretted money splurged on sound. However, with Susan in the car, they would chatter the whole way.

"What are you scared of?" Susan asked. "We should have gone two months ago. Do you think something's wrong?"

"It's boring to get pried open." She fended Susan off with a rap about spreading your legs for the ob-gyn lady, but her mind was elsewhere. On what she wasn't thinking about. It did make her anxious. Going to the dentist was nervous-making, but on an immediate level, just like childhood: how many cavities? How much pain? Going to this doctor raised questions about her life she did not want to face. It was an instant bellyache, a tightening in the groin, the cold seep of guilt.

In Dr. Bridey's inner chamber, those issues she was fleeing materialized. "Dinah, don't you think we should consider a sterilization procedure? Instead of taking the pill for two decades? I want you to come off for a year anyhow." Dr. Bridey was a stringy woman in her late fifties, with grey into blond hair like bleached oak. "The laparoscopy procedure is one I can do in my office, under a local."

"I don't want to. Let me stay on just one year more. Just one."

"That's irrational. Unless you do plan to have a child? How old are you?" Dr. Bridey squinted at the chart. "Thirty-eight. I assume not, then."

"I haven't decided," Dinah squeaked. She could scarcely breathe.

"Time will decide for you," Dr. Bridey said with a wee grin. "Okay, Susan, your turn." However, she renewed Dinah's prescription.

Susan, who had been sitting in the next cubicle, must have overheard. At supper in Legal Sea Foods, she said, "Why not have yourself sterilized? It's a silly fear. Do you think you'd be less of a woman?"

Dinah put down her fork, her throat closing. "I haven't decided."

"Well, Dinah, I'm not going to get you pregnant, and I know you wouldn't suddenly decide to have a baby with Willie. That wouldn't be fair."

"Well, it'd make more sense for all of us than doing it the turkey baster way with some random donor, don't you think?"

Now Susan dropped her fork. "I raised two children. I had enough of diapers and rompers and play groups and PTAs. That's not what I want from life, Dinah, and I'm shocked. You're going through some phase. Really! Are you prepared to give up your music, your career?"

"No. It would be hard. That's why I haven't."

"And that's why you won't." Susan picked up her fork again. "I know it's sensible for us to split a half bottle, but I miss the dear old days when nobody thought twice about polishing off several bottles and zipping off home. I must say, sometimes I think the world get drearier every five years!"

"It does seem that way," Dinah said sadly, when she would normally argue with Susan. It was her way to try to be determinedly upbeat, her habit since childhood, since nothing in her life that was problematic or painful or disturbing was more than piffle by comparison with her father Nathan's life. She could feel his heavy gaze upon her now. *Did I survive for this?* Oh, he was on her side with the music, yes, but he would not forgive if she did not bear a child. That he had been dead since she was thirteen did not relieve her of that gaze. A survivor can watch from the grave, she thought, as her father himself had never felt free of the regard of those who had not survived. All her life would be lived with some sense of that gaze, as some people's might pass under what they felt as the eyes of God or history. It was not something she could make Susan understand. History and her father had their expectations of her. It was growing time to fulfill or permanently fail them.

TWO

Laurie

Laurie had had a bad day at work. Manning Stanwyck, who managed the Spring Street Gallery, and the artist whose show they were hanging, Carl Roper, were engaged in a war about what was to go where. In carting the heavy acrylic boards and canvases about, Laurie had pulled a muscle in her back and had a headache besides from Carl's cigars. That she utterly despised Carl's nasty nudes with automatic weapons did nothing for her temper. Sometimes she thought Manning, who was supposed to be a friend of her father's but who had his resentments too, delighted in treating her as a slavey. What on earth was she supposed to be learning? The mentality of a scrubwoman? How to control the temper she had not inherited from her father? She felt unappreciated, underutilized, undernurtured. She also felt subtly tricked. Manning was supposed to be doing her a big favor, for which she was required to be grateful and enduring.

Then to top it all off, one of her absolute culture heroes Sean Corrigan came strolling in and pronounced that Carl had no idea at all how to display his work. It became evident that they were involved, but they were obviously getting on as badly as she was with Tom. She had seen Sean before, of course, on television, at an opening at the Whitney that Tyrone had finagled two invitations to, once when Sean had come along on a gallery visit with a collector who was thinking of buying the work of a friend. She admired his criticism so much she found her hands sweating onto the acrylic. She longed to say something that would make him look at her with those intense blue-black eyes, to see her. It would be so incredible, but by the time she formulated some sentence she could utter, Sean and Carl and Manning had swept

11

off and Manning was motioning to her as to a slow dog, doing everything but whistle for her attendance. At last she managed to blurt out, "Mr. Corrigan, I thought your column on Documenta was brilliant."

"Oh, did you attend the show?"

"No, but . . ."

He turned away with an amused grimace. Her chance to impress him blown. Furthermore when she got out of the gallery finally, exhausted, the fine clear morning air had turned to six o'clock sleet. She could not get a cab to stop for her. Usually she walked to work in the mornings and returned on foot the twenty-odd blocks home from SoHo north and a bit west to her Chelsea duplex, but her back hurt, the slush soaked her Adidas and she shuffled down into the subway in bad humor.

Next week was Thanksgiving, when she and Tom always went to her mother's. She would gladly have forgone that for Tom's parents, but they lived in Santa Cruz and she could not get off the gallery for longer than a day during this busy time of year. She had thought of the job as a kind of toy job, what fun, working in a gallery, meeting other artists, getting inspired to do her own work; but it had turned out to be nothing of the sort. Manning expected her early, late and every day as his girl of all work.

Going to Mother's always began well, with everyone on best behavior, the spread splendid, gradually soured as her mother's blood alcohol level rose and ended every year with Mother crying about her ancient history divorce and the dead end of her life and the lack of appreciation of her only daughter. Then Laurie would go home with Tom and he would take out on her the lack of pleasure of the evening.

One reason she could not quit the gallery (aside from Tyrone having got her the job) was because Tom had been fired eight months before when his publisher had been eaten by a conglomerate, and he had not found another position to his liking. Eight months was a long time to watch soap operas and pretend to be writing a film script. Lately she did not really want to go home at night any more than she wanted to go to work in the mornings.

I need a lover, she thought, not meaning it because the last thing she felt like was spending the effort to know another human being in full vulnerable openness. It seemed just too much work. Even with the subway she had to walk five blocks to her apartment, stopping to pick up deli for supper and a bottle of wine to bribe Tom into being nice to her tonight. Maybe we'll make love, she thought, and allowed herself to fantasize about him in one of his better moods, playful, teasing, maybe even passionate. The supper had been selected with his preferences in mind, even though she knew just about everything she bought tonight was fattening and she had not even walked home. Fettuccini with pine nuts in a creamy sauce. Roast beef. Duck pâté. Ben and Jerry's New York Super Fudge Chunk. Sourdough French bread. A Beaujolais Nouveau. With sleet sticking to her lashes and her sneakers oozing, she nonetheless trudged more cheerfully along her block and up her slippery front stoop. Surely Tom would accept this offering and reward her with a good affectionate evening.

When she came in, dumping her wet gear in the foyer, he did not answer her call. Was he out? Asleep? She carried the food into the kitchen, put it on the black marble counter and stove that stood in the center, called again and looked for a note. Could something have come up? A job interview? At seven in the evening, no way. "Tom!" she bellowed again.

She was not completely disappointed, she realized, shoving the food into the refrigerator much too big for their needs. This kitchen seemed to have been designed for far more than the coffee-making or microwave defrosting they carried on in it. Tyrone had had it remodeled for them—all ash and glass, black and white marble—when they married. No doubt he imagined she would act like one of his wives and "entertain." She felt Tyrone's care for her, as if he had wished her marriage better than it had gone. If Tom was out, she'd just microwave a frozen diet dinner (atoning for her failure to walk home and the lunch she had eaten) and take a long hot bath. She'd stick an old Woody Allen or Hitchcock movie in the VCR, put her feet up and drink the wine herself. Or she'd watch one of those PBS specials she was always taping and forgetting, the programs the VCR watched for her like a hired servant.

She went upstairs to the loft bedroom to change out of her wet clothes and run that bath. The shades were up, the room dark. She switched on the light and then she saw him lying on the bed. There was no moment when she thought he was sleeping. From the instant she saw how he was lying and the way his face was twisted, she knew he was either dead or teasing her, engaged in one of those vicious terrifying practical jokes he visited on her from time to time.

She did not scream. She shut off the light in a reflex of denial.

13

Then she turned it on again and made herself approach him, managing to believe that he was fooling her, that he was playing dead. "Tom!" she said sternly. "Stop it! I've had a rotten day. I brought you take-out, just what you like." Her voice trailed away. She stood over him, holding her breath.

His eyes were open and staring and his mouth was open too, his tongue thrust out. With great difficulty she made herself touch his cheek, gingerly. He needed a shave. His cheek was cold already. Then she screamed.

THREE

Dinah

Dinah stood at the windows that overlooked the pond. She faced east across waters that were a light dusky blue flecked with white, shallow waves the wind scudded into dingy foam on the sandy shore before her. She was lighting Mark's yahrtzeit candle and reciting the mourner's Kaddish in Hebrew. "Yigadal vey-itkadash shemei raba. . . ." The words came to her always in her father Nathan's intonation, the vowels, the accent closer to Yiddish than the pronunciation from Hebrew school. Her father lit not one candle, but every year on Yom Hasho'ah, more yahrtzeit candles than she could count. Her mother always worried that the flimsy wooden house would catch fire and burn down. That day, too, her father always gathered with other survivors for a memorial or some years, a protest. When Nathan spoke, she had felt proud of him and unworthy. He was a frail vessel of history and pain.

She could not say Kaddish in English, because the words would have bothered her. She did not believe in a personal god, only in her duty to light the yahrtzeit candle and say the prayer. Mark had been deeply religious, in that he had believed himself compelled to struggle for justice in the world, to engage in that repair of the world, tikkun, which is commanded to the just.

Susan had gone to a parochial school. Willie had been raised a Presbyterian. Sometimes Dinah felt lonely and strayed in her Jewishness, out here on this sand spit in the woods among gentiles. The damned professor from Rutgers was threatening to

14

come during his Christmas vacation to get his hands on Mark's papers, and she could not justly stop him. Mark had left her his papers, not to rot in boxes but because he believed his work would survive. A candle flickered in a window, visible to the gulls hurrying toward the ocean, a quarter of a mile past the trees on the far side of the big pond.

Outside Willie was chopping wood for all of them, the rhythmic movements of his long body elegant and efficient. How well he moved, always. Susan, up early for her, came out to scatter ground food for the birds and fill the feeders. A chickadee flew down to take seeds from her palm. She had trained them to come to her. Dinah could not help smiling at the sight. Susan's auburn hair escaping from a mauve silk scarf, a long kimono in a peony pattern she had designed wrapped round her, she looked ethereal in the orange light of the low sun, chrysanthemum bronze through the pitch pines. If Willie was elegance in motion, Susan was elegance itself, a beauty Dinah thought had only ripened over the last decade. Dinah herself was a bird of passage Susan had tamed to her hand.

She sat at her piano. Because of the dampness she tuned it frequently. Pianos were as individual as flutes, and this one was decidedly masculine, bearded, stocky, with a tendency to heroics. She called him Chester. She was not entirely satisfied with what she had done with the Meditation for Flute, Cello and Piano. It was still too thin. She would have liked to add an instrument or two, but she was confined by the commission. Which she was lucky to get. So often then the piece would be performed exactly once for an audience of three hostile critics, fourteen superior academics who thought you ought to be writing in their particular mode, a handful of musicians who might or might not be stuck in the nineteenth century and somebody who would be sure to come up afterward to demand what you thought you were doing and what it all meant. She could not think about that. Health lay in concentrating on the work itself, believing passionately that it would ultimately survive and reach an audience who would perform it, listen to it. Truly perceive the movement that was the music. She was making the cello part extra rich for Nita, trying to do it subtly so Kyle could not object. She wanted to show off Nita's deep singing tones. But the piano part was the weak line, those ascending figures perhaps numbing instead of driving into the flute cadenza.

When she rose to stretch and looked out next, Willie had taken

15

off his jacket and his sweater, in the heat of splitting the logs with maul and sledgehammer. He wore a silk undershirt Susan had given him. Susan had discovered that silk long underwear was practical and pleasing. Their winter temperatures never sank below zero and usually hovered in the twenties. Watching his muscles hump and slide under the silk tee, she gloated on him. He was an amazingly good-looking man. Physical strength and gentleness of disposition made for a fine lover. Willie was obviously taking the day off. She should keep that in mind—unless Susan wanted. They communicated their sexual intentions differently, each of them, but usually not by words. Glances, smiles, an inclination of the body.

"No!" she said to Figaro, meeting his golden stare. He was sitting by the door expecting to go out. "You don't understand. Drunk nincompoops with shotguns and chewing gum for brains are running around spraying 000 pellets through the woods. None of us go out. Not today, not tomorrow, not the day after tomorrow. Four more days. Some cats live in apartments in New York City and never go out at all."

Figaro lifted his tail and mimicked spraying the wall, watching her as she charged him. At the last moment he flattened himself and disappeared under the couch. Dinah identified with him completely. She was already suffering cabin fever, and she knew at some point, danger get stuffed, she would go into the woods and walk. It was more than a physical need.

At noon she called Johnny, who had been named Siobhan, pronounced Shavahn by nobody except Susan. Johnny had been in middle school when she had renamed herself. Susan never called her anything except Siobhan. "Hi, Johnny." She realized it was eleven in Minneapolis. "Did I interrupt you? It's me, Dinah."

"Hi, Dee-Di. Naw, I'm up and framing madly for a friend's opening. I'm going to help him hang his show day after tomorrow. What's new in the woods?"

She filled her in, finishing, "Are you coming home for Christmas? I had various ideas for making jolly."

"Home is here, I am home, and no, I can't get away. I'll come in the summer, I promise."

When she entered Susan's bedroom that afternoon, Susan was unwrapping fabric samples that had come back to her, fabrics she had designed for the New York house she free-lanced for. If the colors had turned out as she had imagined, then she would

16

be in a good mood. Susan's designs were vivid, handsome. They were based on what she saw around her, heightened and stylized. Dinah admired one particularly striking pattern of dark, dark green, scarlet and white. "Poison ivy in the fall," Susan said, holding out her arms to Dinah. "You really do like it? You don't think it's too weird, red and green, not Christmassy or chintzy?"

Dinah insisted how much she liked the fabric, again and again, until Susan seemed satisfied. Susan's soft cool cheek pressed against hers with a scent of lemon verbena. It was a Christian Dior perfume, but to Dinah it smelled just like the herb in her garden. Dinah began to melt through her belly, that tightening and loosening at once, but then she became aware Susan was not responding. In disappointment she released Susan and stepped back. How could she break through to her? It was becoming a problem.

"Come look what I found at the thrift shop." Susan adored poking through other people's clothes. It was a bonus when she found old fabrics that gave her ideas, or when she found little presents for herself or Willie or Dinah, presents that did not count as extravagances because they were accompanied by a recitation of how little she had paid for them. "Just two dollars for this scarf! Just four dollars for this blouse!" Now she was holding up a bed jacket quilted of heavy blue satin. "Isn't this adorable? Bed jackets are out of style, but I love them. My shoulders freeze. They're sensational for reading in bed, for proper lolling. Look at this blazer. Come, try it on."

Dinah loved being invited into Susan's room—which is how she always thought of that bedroom, even though Willie slept in it nightly and stored his clothes there. It did not look like Willie's room; the livingroom downstairs was more his province, as was the kitchen. No, this was Susan's room, with pale apricot walls and perpetual June at the windows in a print of pea blossoms and hummingbirds, with a milky green muslin coverlet heaped with pillows of velvet, damask, satin. It was the room of a beautiful woman who fantasized beauty and made beauty. The king-sized bed suggested a canopy, because a tiny print climbed the wall behind it and spread out on the ceiling. In the summer a fine mosquito net hung from a hook mounted there and the big bed became a gossamer tent in a mirage.

Everywhere that Dinah took the time to examine was some object Susan had found or bought or been given or made: a tiny

17

vase of cobalt blue glass Willie had dug up from an abandoned dump with strawflowers from the summer still in it or a tiny clay squatting woman Johnny had made in high school or a swallow-tail butterfly chrysalis Dinah had picked up. Everything was in the right place. It was one of Susan's artifacts, this room, as much as any of her designs for drapery or dress fabric, or her own clothing designs. Susan drank beauty the way nectar was drunk by the hummingbirds she adored, planting trumpet vine, red honeysuckle, cannas for them.

They played try-on in front of the triple mirrors in Susan's room. If she counted the triple mirror as three, Susan's room boasted six mirrors, more than the rest of the rooms and Dinah's house combined. They were high school girls giggling over clothes. They gossiped and drank tisanes and lay on Susan's enormous bed. Both worked as volunteers in the town library one night a week, one of the true nerve centers of local life, and they caught each other up on what they had learned. "The Parkers are reading books on Egypt. I think they're taking a cruise this winter up or down the Nile—I never understand which is up and which is down when a river runs north?"

"Ginger Dove took out *Moby Dick*. I don't think she's read a book since Dick and Jane and see Spot run. Maybe she thinks it's the story of a penis." Susan's grey eyes flashed wickedly as she batted her lashes.

"Hmmm." Dinah frowned. "I remember years ago Wendy kept it out for a whole year until we practically had to send the fire department for it."

"And then Carolyn Rindge. Just when she started chasing the Captain around. After he and Wendy broke up. Carolyn's been taking out books on natural childbirth. Who do you suppose is the lucky daddy?"

"He waited tables in the Inn last summer. Did you think the Captain and Wendy have split for good?"

"For good or ill, it's so. Do you think he makes them read it?"

"Or he talks about it. Fascinating. Do you suppose that's really it? The cause of a run on Melville?" Dinah carried the electric kettle into the bathroom to refill and plugged it in again, letting herself drop back against the heap of pillows, each in a different fabric case.

"Maybe he gives them a test before he'll take them to bed." Susan giggled. "I used to have a crush on my English professor

18

when I was in college, and I'd worry that I didn't sound literary and grammatical enough.''

"Where's Toby living now that his house has been taken and sold?''

"I don't have any idea. . . . I supposed he must have rented a place?'' The kettle was boiling and Susan slid off the bed to make tea.

Dinah could remember her first joy when she had fallen in love with Susan, perhaps a month into the affair that had not promised anything in particular when she lurched into it: the joy of suddenly realizing that more than another bed partner she had a friend, a woman in some ways like and in most ways different from herself, but there for her in a daily and intimate and all-encompassing way. She had someone to gossip with, to mend with, to switch clothes and earrings and all the little silly things she had done with Nita when they were roommates and going to Juilliard, with the other women in the band when she had played in the Wholey Terrors. They cut each other's hair. They talked about which shampoo to use. They discussed whether Susan should dye her hair redder. They worried about their weight and they rated the men they knew. She had female friendship laid on like pure water from the well, something precious and daily and comforting as milk, something as intoxicating and joyful as wine.

While the tea was brewing, Susan drifted toward the dormer window. "Isn't it disgusting? Look at them. Wouldn't it be fun to drop something on their heads? We could stuff them as a fountain. Three hunters peeing in bronze. Let's tell Willie to cast it.''

Dinah looked. Three hunters in bright orange were standing side by side to piss into the pond about a third of the way between the new house and Tyrone's. They came this week to shoot the small Cape deer. In their fluorescent orange shells, they looked like walking neon pumpkins, squat, obese. She decided she would go off to the town where they did their shopping, fifteen miles away, and find a present for Susan. Something that would make her feel cherished. At the florist, she found an amaryllis that was supposed to open apricot, in time for the holidays.

When she got back with the gift, she noticed Willie standing on the pier gazing at the pond. She had become involved first with Susan, during one of Susan's periods of intense discontent and ferment that long ago fall when Dinah had returned from New Mexico to reopen the house, closed after Mark's death. Dinah had taken up Susan with little reflection because Susan was needy and there. Susan had never been with a woman before, but the idea was in the air, something a number of married and unmarried women she knew had done during the past seven or eight years. Dinah had had women lovers. She was moved by something inside a person, as if certain people had a magnet embedded behind the eyes and in the solar plexus, regardless of sex or body type.

She had been in a predatory phase, taking and trying new lovers as she might pick up a new instrument and test its capacities. It was several months after she was thoroughly in love with Susan that she had become involved with Willie, almost accidentally, almost to keep Susan, to bribe him. And found to her astonishment that she liked Willie better in bed than she liked Susan. He was more fun. He was at his best then, the physical Willie. She remained closer emotionally to Susan, who was nine-tenths emotion. Willie was remote on that level. Words were not his means of communication. Touch was.

So she went into his studio and put another log in the stove and gave it a stir. She sat cross-legged on the cot and waited. Willie came in whistling something tuneless, smiled as he saw her. He got the idea at once and began undressing as he walked toward her. He said nothing. Neither did she but she too began to smile. She suspected it would be a feral smile, if anybody saw it besides the two of them. Put the mind out-of-doors the way some people put their cats out. Although his instincts and reflexes were good, he was the least self-critical and reflective person she had ever been close to. But when she put her hands on Willie and lay down to his hot smooth strong body, the good muscles that came from chopping wood three hundred days of the year and from his own work too, when she walked into his body and took him into hers, it was better than words and better than emotion. It was, the way music was. It filled up the void. It pushed anxiety for her life and her work back beyond the lighted circle of her attention. It would be so easy to make a baby, she thought as their bellies rubbed. But Susan had to agree first.

Dinah cooked pasta with their own hot tomato sauce frozen from the summer and a little hamburger. Willie and she alternated cooking. Susan was much neater than the other two and compulsively cleaned and straightened, but she hated to cook. At supper, Willie had news from town.

"Somebody's shooting at the hunters," he said. "Somebody's been shooting over their heads with a rifle. The police have been around asking questions. At first they thought the hunters were drunk. I mean, they were drunk, but somebody is shooting to scare them." Willie ate as much as the two women combined, but he never gained weight. He burned it up. Dinah loved to watch him eat. He ate with real pleasure, never just shoveling the food in, but savoring it without ostentation or self-consciousness. His hands doing any task from slicing bread to making love were strong, shapely, profoundly sexual. He had long fingers but the palms of his hands were massive.

Susan had news too. "Tyrone called this afternoon. He's coming up for Christmas, definitely. He wants us to open his house, turn the water on, get some wood in. He's bringing Laurie. She's extremely depressed." Susan made her grey eyes large and waited for them to beg her for information. Even in winter a sprinkling of freckles lay like paprika on her pale pink skin.

"That jerk Tom left?" Dinah guessed.

"He killed himself! Not intentionally, of course. It was a drug overdose. It turns out that Tom was a cocaine addict and Laurie didn't even know it! Isn't that a ghastly story? She found his body in their bed when she came home from work."

"She must be a little dense," Dinah said. "How could she not know?"

"How could you tell?" Willie asked. "Would you know if I was?"

Dinah laughed sharply. The idea of Willie as any kind of addict was absurd. He no more needed stimulants than Bogey or Figaro did. Natural vigor rose from him like steam from a fine horse that has run well. "How come Tyrone is asking us to turn his house on? He always has the younger Dove boy, Ozzie, working for him."

"Ozzie's working for Allie at the doctor's house—you know, the Captain's," Willie said. "The Doves are making a bundle. Ozzie's getting married on it." Willie was friendly with all the guys who worked construction. They respected him more than many of the other artists. They knew he was a superior carpenter and they saw his sculpture as fine construction too. They had seen too much art to be bothered by abstract shapes or high-tech lines. When Willie and Susan needed a new well, Bud the well-driller had traded them the job for a small piece of Willie's he wanted for his new house.

"So can't Tyrone hire some other kid? How did we get drafted?"

"Dinah, don't be unfeeling." Susan shook her finger with its rings of gold and jade. "A friend in need."

Christmas was not a big holiday for Dinah, but it was for Susan; Dinah had been thinking how to make it especially fine for her. She had tried to reach Jimmy in Seattle, but the number had been disconnected. Now her plans were swept away. Tyrone would take over everything.

"Have you heard from Jimmy?" she asked them, but dubiously. If he was in trouble, Jimmy was more likely to call her than his parents and more likely to ask her to break bad news to them.

"Not since maybe a month ago," Susan said. "I wrote him. I like the children to come home for the holidays."

"I have something you'll like," Dinah promised over coffee and went running across to her house to fetch the amaryllis in a pot. Dinah found them more strange than beautiful, a being from a science fiction planet, but Susan liked them for their out-of-season exoticism, their huge naked flowers without leaves to soften them. "It should bloom before Christmas."

"What color will it be?" Susan flushed with pleasure.

"A sort of apricot pink." Like Susan herself, Dinah thought.

"I'll put it in the bedroom next to my workbench, where I can watch it."

It was the fifth day of deer hunting season. The afternoon before it had snowed lightly. Dinah could no longer endure being housebound. She shut in the cats and did not take Bogey, as any animal would be in more danger than she considered herself to be. She carried a broom, for she meant to sweep any tracks of deer she found or stomp them out with her own. It was one of her little tasks to erase deer tracks before and during hunting season, even though it meant for that period walking with her head down instead of looking around. Dinah had certain religious duties that visited themselves upon her, for instance taking turtles safely out of the road at mating and egg-laying season every year. Feeding the birds even during blizzards and when it was blowing from Canada was another.

At the top of the ridge that lay beyond the pond and the old house, she sat on a fallen pine and listened attentively. Hunters to the west. Shots beyond the blacktop road. Two dogs barking furiously from the dunes. She made her way down off the ridge, bushwhacking through the oak woods. Finding a deer trail she walked on it, destroying the tracks. Two of them, one bigger. Even with her extra effort, she moved quietly. She liked to move well in the woods, not disturbing the other animals more than she must. She liked to see them. She needed to. It was a passion she kept to herself, as she did when she found a fox den or even a raccoon tunnel.

Thus it was that she climbed out of the kettlehole to another slope and saw beneath her a man lying flat on his stomach sighting down the long hollow where the three orange hunters were arguing. He was slight and wearing old fatigues. His hair was black and covered his nape. She crouched and then quietly she worked her way off the ridge through the kettlehole and back the way she had come.

Now she knew who was shooting at the city hunters, but it was not something she was about to share with even Willie or Susan. It was Toby Lloyd, whose house the rich doctor was gutting. She had recognized him lying below her and she had even seen the M-1 rifle in the house no longer his. Toby was exercising his hunting skills on the hunters, although so far he had not killed any. She doubted he would, but she was not sure. It was in any event Toby's business.

Soon she heard voices and hid. Even the winter woods offered sufficient cover if you knew the lay of the land and where the thickets remained impenetrable to a casual gaze. If she made an awkward noise, she might be shot, but she found herself happy, hiding like a deer in the thickets and watching the hunters. She might be a little crazy, and so might the Captain, but the hunters were completely crazy running around spewing beer cans and emptying their shotguns into trees and neighbor's dogs. The light was fading grey and ashy. They walked out of her sight, but she could still hear them.

Once they had made their way out in the direction of the blacktop road, she rose. Willie was cooking his special fried chicken tonight. It was four but dark. She made her way down to the pond by its glint among the trees and then padded along the shore home. Her house was unlit.

She had a sense of someone looking at her through the livingroom windows. It was a familiar sense, one lined with pain.

The last winter when Mark could no longer walk with her, often she had returned from a hike designed to wear herself out to find him sitting without lights watching darkness claim the world, waiting for her but busy, very busy dying. He would have understood her walking over the deer tracks; he would have understood Toby defending the woods and deer from city hunters in their neon gear. Mark had been a deeply political man, fire out of rock, a slight body housing fierce passions.

Dinah walked slowly under the dogwood they had planted outside the livingroom where they could enjoy its white blossoms in May, its berries and maroon leaves in the fall. A spring of blossoming he had not lived to enjoy. Eyes on her, yes. It was Tosca sitting on the wide windowsill waiting for her, watching through the dark. Tosca had an exclusive passionate nature, a patronizing fondness for Figaro, a nodding tolerance of Susan and Willie, but she loved only Dinah, who had saved her as a starving kitten with two broken legs tossed from a speeding car into a culvert. Tosca slept on her pillow and Figaro at her feet.

Once she and Mark had shared that bed, brought from their New York apartment and almost too large for the small Cape bedroom. Only when Mark was too weak to climb stairs had the livingroom become his sickroom. Willie and Susan had each slept in that bed a few times since and nobody else.

She had never replaced Mark as husband, as the one, as the person in whom and for whom and with whom everything was done, not only because such a lover came once in a lifetime, for real love was much rarer than people liked to think. The remainder was friendship, sensuality, affection, domesticity. However, she had come to value that portion highly. She had the energy to put into her music in a far more single-minded and whole spirited way then she had with Mark. Once she had tasted fully her own power in work, she had come to value her solitude, an inner silence on which her imagination could scroll her music in patterns that felt right.

FOUR

Susan

Susan thought that if Dinah had any sense of how to conduct her life, she would take advantage of the coming of the professor from Rutgers and unload Mark's old papers on him. Then she could move her music operation upstairs, clear the livingroom and have a house that looked at least partially civilized. If Susan did not watch Willie and Dinah every day, they would convert both houses to utterly slobby combinations of workshops and pantries. There would have been herbs drying in the livingroom and seedlings started in every window, construction and canning projects sprawling over tables and benches.

She could just imagine what her house would look like if Dinah ever went ahead with her mad scheme to hatch a baby. Who would end up raising that baby? Susan would. No thanks! Two were quite sufficient. She had adored having babies, she had loved Jimmy and Siobhan as infants and toddlers and young children, but somewhere around ten, the joy petered out if mothers would be honest about it. If it started again, she was still waiting.

Susan was using the forenoon to color her hair, while she was alone and undisturbed. Although by policy she was open about the fact that she dyed her hair, she gave it out that she did so because her hair was naturally the color of dead mouse; whereas, as Willie knew, she had been a redhead, and she was covering grey. Now he might know that, but he didn't think about it. She had established her propaganda and it worked. If she let her hair go, she would look ten years older. With men it never seemed to matter. Willie's hair had gone white in his thirties. Tyrone had already been balding when she had first met him. Mark's hair and beard had been streaked with grey.

Mark had nonetheless been a potently attractive man. It was with Mark she had imagined having an affair that year they had lived next door. Even though she knew he was dying, it was of lung cancer and not catching and it was somehow a romantic Keatsian death, the way he brought it off. Even in extremis, he

25

could not help flirting, making eye contact count, putting some spin on a handshake. Here was another artistic couple up from New York, moving to the Cape as they had a few years before: a little colony in the woods.

Maybe she was powerfully attracted to bearded men, although Mark's beard had been long and full, darker than his head hair, while Tyrone's was a neat closely clipped overlay of the pale color his hair must have been. Willie had once tried growing a beard at her suggestion, but it had made him look unkempt and vaguely menacing. She had begged him to shave it off. Yes, had Mark lived, she might have gotten together with him rather than with Dinah. Dinah had been hidden then. Susan had thought of Dinah as a housewife who played strange music on the piano and the flute, who walked bundled up like a curly-headed Eskimo in her parka that winter shuffling through the woods.

Dinah had not mentioned the question of having a baby again, not directly, but Susan could always read her, and she knew Dinah had not forgotten or given up. If Dinah dared just get pregnant and then present her with a fait accompli, she would go through the roof. She must make that clear. She had tried to speak to Willie, but he insisted Dinah had never said anything to him about a baby. If Dinah wanted a baby, she should have had one with Mark at the normal time. By now the kid would be in middle school. Every time Susan thought of Dinah playing with that maddeningly unfair option, she could feel her insides stewing like a pot of hot glue, bubbling, viscous, with a dangerous stench. What a thing to pull on Susan suddenly, what a rotten hat trick.

Susan had paid her dues to womanhood. She had raised two healthy bright kids, with a lot of help from Willie, certainly. He had been a great father. No matter how bored or discontented she got, she never overlooked how much he had given of himself to the children. Further, Susan had helped Laurie through her adolescence. Laurie was a third child to her, closer than her own daughter Siobhan. She knew more about Laurie than Tyrone did, for instance Laurie had been unhappy with Tom—a fact that seemed to come as a surprise to Tyrone. Last night Laurie had called to beg her not to invite anybody else this holiday season, not even people she had known for years. "I'm ashamed. I can't stand to have anyone look at me."

Now it was ten in Seattle. Again she dialed Jimmy's number,

but again a mechanical voice said the number had been disconnected. Again she tried Information, but nothing was listed. Where was he? Had he left Seattle without telling her? Her last letter had not come back, but she had not heard a word from him in two months. He was in some kind of trouble, she was sure of that. The restaurant had been going so well. What was wrong?

Throwing down the blow dryer, she paced, clutching herself. And Siobhan! It was impossible to pry out of her what was going on. She would not even tell Susan if she loved Aldo, the gawky weird playwright she was living with. Now if Siobhan's live-in boyfriend had died of an overdose, Susan would not have been the least bit surprised. Tom had seemed steady.

She finished drying her hair at her bedroom window facing the pond. It was an unexpected blessing that Tyrone was coming for the holidays. She always tried to get to New York a couple of times a winter, but it was still a long dreary time until the summer people started opening their houses. Tyrone had a beach house in Aruba where he was more inclined to go in December than the Cape—a house he had offered them many times, but Willie always said they couldn't afford to fly down there in winter. The pond life was gayer and more civilized in summer. Tyrone would stroll the shore with her, or they would take tea or cocktails together and talk intensely and on a plane she seldom reached with anyone else. With him she was lifted to a beautiful high place, like the view from the terrace of a penthouse where a fine dinner party was just breaking up.

She tried to imagine what she could give him. Willie and Dinah would cart over some of their homemade cordials and preserves, but she knew how silly that was, when Tyrone could buy the best liqueurs and conserves of Europe. Sometimes she had in her treasure hoard, her drawers, her shelves, her closet, a little antique or bizarre or imported folkloric thing, objects to which no price could be attached and thus priceless as presents. She must come up with something like that for Tyrone. Laurie was easy, for Susan would simply knock off work on her designs a day or two early and make some skirt or chemise for her. Tyrone was a more difficult matter; she must put intelligence and creativity into his gift. Then she would wrap. She liked to make her own paper out of reproductions of paintings or drawings, photographs from magazines. Her boxes were each works of art. It took her days, but it made the giving of such presents as they could afford special.

Her hair was dry and looked perfect. She shook it out on her shoulders. It never needed setting, so long as she washed it every other day. She still had a full thick head of hair. Her gaze fell on her hand mirror. Siobhan had bought a dime-store mirror and turned it into a papier-mâché creation, two elongated skinny elephants embracing on tiptoe, while their trunks formed the outside of the mirror. Marvelous thing. Siobhan had been only twelve when she made it and the breach between them still healed frequently. Susan sank onto the bench before her vanity, staring. She was seeing past her face into that sweet intense time when it was always summer and she had presided over the center of a universe of family and friends, her precious children, her husband, her flirtations, other couples they exchanged dinners and child care with, all swirling about the sun she felt within her.

She was only forty-six and in good shape. She could even, she supposed, have another child herself if she were stupid enough to want to. She had had those years and nothing could bring back their joys. She had also endured the immense strain of managing to save money for both children to go to good schools, for although they had got the scholarships that made the whole project feasible, nonetheless their college years had been a savage burden. Willie was no spendthrift, but he thought little about money. It was she who had driven herself to earn at the peak of what she could manage, and now she wanted things easier. She had knocked herself out to get both kids quality educations, and to what point? Siobhan looked like a scarecrow and Jimmy ran a restaurant. Now she wanted for herself. More travel, more time in New York, little luxuries, more interesting friends, some glamour and romance in her life. A decade before she had solved a period of ennui by getting involved with Dinah. It had been a truly daring and outrageous response to boredom, and she had seldom been bored for years. They had made love until she was replete with exhausted languor. Dinah had seemed to her a mad genius of sex whose touch turned her flesh luminous. Sometimes then Dinah needed only to look at her, and her body would melt in response. The scandal merely added fire and spice. The envy of others had acted on her as an aphrodisiac.

Now Dinah was happier piddling around in the sand growing beans and canning peaches than she was pursuing adventure and using what contacts she had in music to enrich their life with

28

people one had at least heard of, who lived out in the real world—people who could tell stories about fascinating events and places. Now Dinah was talking of usurping the role Susan had played so well and long, and she would not have it. It was not fair. Even now, without a child, Dinah paid more attention to the cats than to her.

She hurried to her sewing table. She would start on Laurie's chemise, then find a trinket to surprise Tyrone. Their arrival was the one thing she could summon to bribe herself with, to push on through the grey day.

FIVE

Dinah

Dinah had just played out a passage on the flute she had been struggling with for the past four days and found it finally and utterly delightful when the phone rang. It was her staff contact at the Mass Council telling her she had been awarded a New Works grant. She was very cool on the phone. Then she leapt up whooping. Tosca flattened her ears in dismay. It was some kind of mistake. She had received grants, but never such a big one. The typical commission for a composer would keep her in groceries for a month. How had they made such a gross error as to give her all that money? Usually the significant money was more in performing and in lecturing than in the payment for composing, and recording was something that cost her, rather than providing income. This did not involve her performing and she could live on it all summer if she budgeted carefully. Grants spawned grants, because all granting agencies wanted you to be certified by others first so that they wouldn't be risking anything.

Furthermore it was a commission and therefore would be performed, and by the outstanding flutist Itzak Raab with a chamber orchestra drawn from the BSO at Tanglewood. Raab had gone to Juilliard two years ahead of her. She remembered him in the cafeteria at the table where the best reeds sat, and she had attended the concerto contest where he had blown his opponents into dust. Her flute teacher had been his; twice she had run into him in Madam's apartment. She remembered his intonation and his attack clearly, and vaguely his curly black hair. He had been one of those Juilliard students whom everyone said would make it in the cutthroat concert circuit; and he had, he had.

She ran over to tell Susan and Willie, but their house was empty. Even Bogey was gone. The four-wheel-drive pickup truck encrusted with dust stood at the wide end of the drive next to her Volvo, so they had not gone shopping or to town. They must have gone to Tyrone's to fuss some more. He was due tonight. She made herself coffee in their kitchen—which was more hers than Susan's. They used the same coffee, espresso bought in the North End of Boston, ground fresh in a fancy electric grinder Willie had mail-ordered. She sighed and settled in to wait, hoping they would suddenly appear. If she did not tell someone her good news, it would vanish. Any moment the council would call back and say it was an error. This was not a little commission but a fat plum. It was even faintly conceivable that if Raab liked the piece, he might record it. He recorded often; his records seemed to sell well. He had recorded something by Steve Reich, she was sure. She did not remember if she had it. She'd look later. For now she waited in the kitchen.

Willie had an undying love of gadgets. Theirs was the original electronic cottage, for Willie used a Mindset computer, which he never wearied of telling people was in the MOMA, to play with stresses and run his graphics. She had an IBM, connected to her synthesizers that cost far more than the simple computer. In this small kitchen, she could see without turning her head a Cuisinart, an electric pasta maker, an electric ice-cream machine, a convection oven, a cappuccino and espresso maker big enough for a café, an ice maker, a programmable toaster smarter than most small children. She thought there was nobody from the bridge to the sea with their income level who used more electricity.

It was not consumerism in Willie but a pure bubbling optimism that the new gadget would fulfill its promises, would deliver the labor saving or the improved product or the never-before-achieved-at-home concoction. He liked the idea that people were out there working to make new devices aimed at his happiness. He enjoyed believing in technology.

They lived comfortably, but that was one of the advantages of the Cape; once you owned your land, you could live well on comparatively little. All of them got money in hunks and then nothing for months. Willie would sell some sculpture every summer. Once in a while he got a piece in a show during the winter, in Boston, in New York, sometimes farther afield, in St. Louis or Minneapolis or San Francisco. Sometimes that piece sold. Often it didn't, for Willie liked to create humanoid figures trying to crawl out of coffins, reaching through barbed wire or slats, impaled, raising blocks. He worked a lot with large dangerous constructions of barbed wire and newsprint. Some of them involved tapes of unpleasant noises like screaming and gunfire.

Susan was well requited for her designs. Making clothes just was a hobby. Her fabric designs were valuable, but she could get stuck on an idea whose execution frustrated her and miss deadline after deadline. Sometimes she was too depressed to work and hibernated in her bed for weeks.

When Dinah was in a long dry period between good grants or good gigs, she played with the Moonsnails in the summer. Willie and she worked as carpenters, usually small jobs that regular contractors would not bother with. They were in demand because they did good and careful carpentry, but neither of them took a job unless driven to it. Now why was Willie taking time away from his South Africa piece to act as unpaid handyman for Tyrone Burdock? She finished her coffee and rinsed out the cup. Although Susan seldom cooked, she monitored the kitchen's tidiness. Dinah kept running from window to window to look at the road and then the path, as if that could make at least one of them appear. Susan would be better; she would gush. Dinah had a great need to be gushed over, to prove her good fortune.

The phone rang and she jumped on it. "Jimmy! But where are you?"

"Right in front of the liquor store. Can somebody come and get me?"

He'd taken the bus. So what had happened to his car? "I'll come right away. Listen, could you go into Souza's for skim milk and local eggs while you're waiting, and bananas? Do your parents know you're coming today?"

"I didn't know when I'd arrive. Uh, Dee, if I buy that stuff, I'll have about fifty cents left."

"I'll reimburse you, big spender. Be there in fifteen minutes." She whistled a theme from the rondo of Mozart's Clarinet in A all the way to town. She was not displeased to have a little time with Jimmy first. Find out what was up. Get filled in. In her head the orchestra swelled. Flute was her usual instrument, but she played piccolo, of course, drums, guitar and piano on occasion. Flute was what she played in the Moonsnails—along with some tabla, conga drums, tambourine, occasional rhythm guitar. Not this summer. She wouldn't have to play at the Inn six nights a week. The grant suddenly felt more real. Her fellow musicians would be let down, but they liked the gig better than she did, breathing smoke all evening, drowning out drunks, fending off idiots who fell into the speakers or demanded to sing with the band. It felt like only one step up from waiting tables.

The guys in the band liked it because that was as much music as they ever played and because a fringe benefit was the ease of getting laid. The other fringe benefit was local celebrity far more negotiable in terms of stroking and immediate pleasure than real reputation. So her wind quintet was performed at Helsinki the same summer she worked six nights a week in the tavern. There was more satisfaction walking into the post office or Souza's and having people tell her how great the band was than in a hostile review in a music journal arriving five months later, all of two paragraphs on her quintet.

In another sense the smiling faces in the post office were irrelevant, because the music the band played was not her music and not much good. What mattered to her music happened in Spoleto and Ann Arbor and Lenox and New York and what she did locally was diddling.

She got stuck behind a retiree who drove ten miles an hour along the highway, so Jimmy was outside with the groceries when she pulled up on Main Street. "You owe them two eighteen," he said as he got in. "Lucky they remembered me." His ebullience was a little dimmed. Hard traveling. He had his mother's hair, shock of reddish waves, and her fine pinkish complexion, but he was built tall and lean like Willie and had his brown eyes. He was quite gorgeous and quite conscious of it, the way a woman would be who had spent her adolescence in braces. His own torments had been skinniness and acne. Now his complexion was smooth and a couple of years of weight lifting had given him beauty and confidence.

"Of course they remember." She leaned over to kiss him. After all, she was "from away" in the local vernacular, but he was native, had grown up and gone to school here. He would always belong. In Souza's they would put his shortages on a tab and the liquor store would extend him credit, if need be.

"Home for the holidays?" she asked innocently.

"Sure, I always spend my last dollar crossing the continent because I'm so sentimental. You want to hear it all fast?"

"Let me know what I'm going to be dealing with, kid."

"I thought I'd come back and marry you, before I got in more trouble."

"That's a great idea if you weren't already married. Come on, what's up? Or down. More like it."

"We lost the whole thing. We were making a go of it, but suddenly the money was melting away. Then we caught Jackie cooking the books. Lisa and I started fighting all the time, and then everything fell apart—the restaurant, us, my life. It's all over. My life burned down to the ground and I have to start over. And I don't know how." Jimmy's voice died away. Then he said perkily, "That's all the news from this end. How's yourself?"

"Most small businesses go belly up, no shame attached." Dinah turned off the highway onto the blacktop road that led to the ponds and eventually to the ocean. "I thought you and Lisa were having a baby?"

"We are. She still is, but she's counting me out now."

"So what are you doing here? Why didn't you stay and fight?"

"Fighting's all we've done for months. I don't remember how it was when it was good. I can't even remember why I wanted her. Can we talk about something else?"

"So far it's been a mild winter. I just harvested my last savoy cabbages last week and I've still got arugula and escarole and bok choy. . . ."

"How are they? Is she okay? Her letters have been weird."

"Weird, how?"

Jimmy shrugged. "Weird bitchy. What are you doing with your life, all that. I don't need it. I spend too much time trying to figure out what I'm doing with my life. I feel paralyzed with trying to figure it out. I need to lick my wounds and sleep for about six months."

"When is the baby due?"

"May. It was Lisa's idea anyhow. Look, if she asks me, I'll come back. I'll try again. But I can't sit there waiting for her to change her mind."

Pulling into the driveway between both houses, she sighed. With Jimmy there was always one more layer to peel on the onion. The story would come out gradually. She hoped he wasn't finagling to stay with her. The grant bought her time and the necessity to produce the big piece commissioned under it. No, Willie and Susan were going to have to fit him into their house. Woodsmoke was coming from Willie's studio, so they must be back. "Go on in and say hello. I'll come by around five to start supper. I'll make oyster stew. We can start with ten on the half shell. I know how you miss them. Willie and I went oystering Saturday and there're still two huge bags."

She gave him another quick kiss and ducked into her house. She looked at her morning's work as if it had just arrived in the mail from an enemy. Then she put on her pea coat to walk her sudden agitation away, following a network of trails that led toward the ocean. That was what she needed. To stand on the top of the dunes, gaze at the blue-black, white toothed winter ocean climbing the sky and get sandblasted by the long rough wind, all the smells of the indoor winter blown from her. The winter tides and early storms had already torn away at the dunes and the shelf, leaving the narrow bench of winter beach in a strip along the exposed clay cliffs.

She could feel her mind opening and the nodes of her spine vibrating in resonance. When she was cold and clean through and through, she picked her way across the wide valley behind the last dune, hills and hollows bristling with poverty grass and golden heather, bayberry with tiny grey-green berries the yellow and black warblers ate, rosa rugosa with its big vermilion hips wizened by cold, tiny twisted old oak trees no bigger than beach plum bushes, blueberry bushes nine inches high. As she topped a rise, she smelled woodsmoke. Curious, she bore left on a trail she had not used in years, winding through wild grape into the pine and oak. She could not smell woodsmoke any longer but the trail had been walked lately and was less faint than the last time she had followed it. It did not threaten to peter out. Instead it wound through the woods, skirted a white cedar swamp, then climbed a ridge. Below her was a kettlehole from which the smoke was snaking.

An old house stood there, just two rooms she remembered from exploring it, with an old rounded roof and a stone chimney. Now someone had fixed it up weather tight. Had added a porch, a glass greenhouse lean-to and put up a shed. There are styles in carpentry, signatures that another carpenter will recognize. Toby had built that shed; it was almost identical to the one he had knocked up in his old yard. So this was where he was living.

She became aware he was looking at her through a window. She waved and turned away at once, lest he think she was spying, which of course she was. Exercising her damned curiosity.

She heard his steps behind her on the path and had a moment of indecision that surprised her. She wasn't afraid of him, surely. Why that quiver of unrest? Perhaps because she had spied on him twice now inadvertently, and that was never a wise idea. She had seen him lying on his belly sighting down a rifle at three hunters. She had no idea how loss of his house had affected him, but she doubted it had filled him with joyful goodwill.

She halted and turned. He was coming fast. Toby was of middling height and compact build. He moved quietly and quickly as a bobcat. His hair was dark, but his eyes that met hers steadily as he caught up were pale blue in a face that still had the leathery tan of a fisherman.

"Looking for me?" He was not smiling.

She realized he might have seen and followed her tracks the day she had observed him shooting at the hunters. She nodded and did smile, what she hoped was not a placating smirk. "I had no idea you were in the . . ." she hesitated to call it a shack ". . . little house there. I didn't know whose smoke I was smelling."

He rocked back on the balls of his feet, one hand in his jacket pocket, the other at his side. "We keep passing each other in the woods."

"There's plenty of room for both of us." Then she decided to raise him. "I didn't tell anybody. Why should I? I like the deer better anyhow."

"I don't mind the people who belong here. Only the others."

"Like me?"

"You're from away, but you've never bothered me."

"How come you moved into that little house?"

"My great-uncle built it after he left his wife, because she was temperance, they say. I used to bring girls there, back in high school."

"They're ripping the guts out of your family house."

"I thought of burning it down. But with pitch pines, it's hard to control a burn."

"Well, thanks for not doing it. Although I share the sentiment." She thought of asking openly if he was done testing her, but she decided not to push her luck. She saluted and walked off, almost expecting him to stop her. She imagined a bullet

35

entering her back. But when she reached a switchback and turned, he was strolling toward his shack. The woods were big enough for both of them, as she had said to him. She only hoped he wasn't going to interfere with her pleasure in walking.

At home she called her old friend Nita at once. Nita, who played cello with the BSO, understood the scope and size of her luck. "I just saw an article about Itzak Raab. I'll look for it. Honey, let's celebrate!"

The professor from Rutgers came. Dinah thought of herself as cool and rational, intellectual, against Susan's emotionalism and Willie's immediacy. The first hour with the academic reminded her of how little she was a true intellectual. She did not doubt her own intelligence, but the intellect was not primary for her. It was only part of the whole, the senses, the loud cries of the body, the leap and mutter of the emotions, connection to land and air and water and all the other creatures who flew and trotted in and out of her attention inside the web she shared with them.

Professor Sanderson had no idea who she was, for he announced he was uninterested in music. He wanted to question her and work on Mark's papers. He called it establishing a chronology, but for her it was a breach of privacy.

He was of middling height and weight with sandy hair and the sort of slightly British accent often affected in East Coast English Departments. He dressed in good tweeds and walked briskly. He meant well, for he was truly interested in Mark's poetry, although Dinah could not imagine why. What compulsion had been created in him? What would Mark have thought? Would he have been amused? Would he have been helpful? On a good day, perhaps. She endured his probing the cavity of loss as best she could. His desire to establish exactly which poem had been written in what order and the dating of the earlier drafts which filled many boxes puzzled her. The last draft was the only one that mattered, right? The rest was detritus. Opened cans. Chewed bones. As someone who worked and reworked her scores, she ought to make a bonfire soon.

He stayed in town and walked out to her every day, a walk of two and a half miles each way. She had fantasies of a snowfall that would seal the roads and keep him out, but daily he came with his polite curiosity and his questions and his need to shuffle through the papers. She got little done. When she discovered her music irritated him, she sat in her straight chair playing the flute by the hour. On the piano she ran through versions of her student compositions from her serialist days and her early minimalist pieces where motives changed as slowly as stalactites grow. She had exhausted five or six different musical identities before minimalism, although by the time she came to it, the name was silly, because the composers she admired were constructing complicated richly textured big pieces. After a while she forgot him because ideas for the commission began to coalesce, dimly, furtively. Tomorrow she would give a last polish to the Meditation and send it off.

She moved over to the window and picked up her flute. She had larger ambitions for this piece, something highly textured. It would start with a version of the melody to which she had been saying the Alenu in her head, the flute alone and then joined. She hated the dramatic entrances of the solo instrument in concertos, like a grande dame sweeping into a party late and overdressed. She had five or six of Raab's discs. Next time in Boston, she would pick up more: she would survey his technique. This piece would begin very quietly, a melancholy wail of the flute.

When Professor Sanderson appeared beside her, she looked at him without recognition. "If you want to use the papers, you have to leave me alone when I'm working."

"I thought you were just trying to tune it." He smirked.

She did not kill him. She did not even answer him. She simply got up, ushered him back to the hall and returned to her flute. For Itzak Raab, she ought to cook up some very good soup indeed. Yes, this was where to start. Then she would think hard about structure, shape and scope, the kind of architectural planning of larger pieces that always made her feel as if she were moving mountains and seas around in her head. Musical "ideas"—as if they were ideas. Dances, they were going to be, the sections of the suite. The flute would dance, and around it and with it, the other instruments. This was what her mind did best. Never otherwise did she feel as alive.

SIX
Willie

Willie loved the way they did Christmas. For much of his life, the idea of Christmas had been more compelling than the reality. Beforehand there was the excitement of what he wanted and thought he might get and the attempts to guess or find what he thought others wanted, all the wrapping and the hiding, the buildup to the presents and then afterward a terrible void soon filled with quarrels, broken objects, broken promises, his parents clashing in harsh whispers and harsher silences.

The intricacies of the triangle assured them all of busy times. They opened some presents together, but each of them was entitled to separate time for a private present or two with the others. They had worked out a long time ago that they would go to Dinah's for Christmas Eve dinner. Then they would adjourn to Willie and Susan's to open some presents with the children when the children were still at home, later on just the three of them.

After that Dinah went home and Willie gave Susan her private presents from him. Then he and she would go up to bed. They always made love on Christmas Eve. Willie would have been frightened if they had not, for it would have seemed to him unlucky. In the morning he got up early and went to bring Dinah her presents. They made love that morning. By the time they had breakfast, Susan would be up. When Susan had finally made her toilette and had brunch, she would go to find Dinah and they would share early or midafternoon of Christmas Day. Willie would go for a long walk after lunch, weather permitting, to give them the house alone together. If it was snowing, he would just go to his studio. Then in the late afternoon, the three of them would walk to the Bay. They would all feel cherished, they would feel each relationship individually burnished and their ties strengthened. Christmas, Willie thought, was preeminently a holiday for celebrating his unique family.

The holiday started days before when Dinah and he began looking for a tree. They were technically stealing it, as they did every year. They liked to find a shapely and bushy young pitch pine. Willie had grown to prefer the long needles and the irregular shape of the pitch pines to the symmetrical boughten trees. It had to be a specimen tree, one that had grown not in the woods but out where it got lots of direct sun, but one that had not split into two or more trees, as they often did in good locations. Along the sides of roads or the old railroad cut were good places to search for full trees, or in areas that had been cleared but then not built upon, so that the pines had begun to come back.

Over the course of the last week they had argued their way through five candidates, going back to compare them and finally reaching agreement. The chosen tree was located on land belonging to people from Newton, the Hills, on the next pond over, Bracken Pond. They had a slope that had burned years before they bought it. Several bushy new trees were coming up. They had to be stealthy, because while the Hills seldom came at Christmas, some of the other summer people might be on that pond.

That morning he got up before dawn. Dinah was already bundled into jeans and a parka, stamping her feet by the truck and blowing steam. Willie had thrown the ax and the saw in the back of the truck the night before. The engine seemed uncommonly noisy as the exhaust fumes floated low to the ground in the frigid air. There was little snow in the woods—it had thawed a few days before—and he guessed the temperature was probably no lower than thirty. Still it was nippy. There was a salt tang to the damp air. It was no longer night but that grey time just before sunrise would begin to tint the sky. They drove slowly, but he felt as if they were making so much noise they must be waking everybody for miles.

Dinah was excited. She kept reaching over and squeezing his knee. She was bouncing around in her seat like a kid. Suddenly he did not mind the noise the old truck made. Doing things with her turned into a game, something even more special than it would have been without her. "We should have a song," she announced. To the tune of "Waltzing Matilda" she sang, "Stealing the tree, stealing the tree, won't you come a thieving my Willie with me. . . ."

He cast over the morning's activities, but unfortunately he could not figure in time for a roll in the hay. Her cheeks were pink even in the grey light. She looked like a plump impish baby in the down parka.

They pulled off the road and cut the motor around the bend

from the Hills. Then they hastened single file on an old path that led to the former house site—an old cellar hole where a house had burned twenty-some years before. The tree they had chosen was just ahead, outlined against the pale shimmer of Bracken Pond. None of the ponds had yet frozen over. They were cold as death but clear. The whack of the ax seemed monstrously loud and echoing. He hit it six blows and it toppled. Dinah finished the cut with a saw and then they were pulling it along back through the woods to the waiting truck. They threw it in back, pulled out without turning on their lights and Willie drove as fast as he dared, jouncing and rattling along the maze of wood roads to their own.

Once he pulled into the drive both houses shared, he heaved a great sigh. They let down the tailgate and wrestled the tree out. "I think it grew since we cut it," Dinah said as they got it up on the porch. It seemed to cover the porch entirely.

They always set their tree up in Willie and Susan's livingroom. Dinah had not grown up with Christmas trees and did not own ornaments. She did not put up her own. That made the one they stole and set up together even more special, he thought.

"This happens every year. It won't go through the door."

She offered, "I'll get rope from the truck."

They tied it round and round so that it could come inside, but then it was too tall to stand. They had to cut four inches off the trunk. Willie fetched the holder out of the tiny circular cellar, where it sat on a shelf near the furnace. Then they forced the tree upright by using the holder and only two guy wires to the nearest windows, where there were hooks left over from the last tree that couldn't stand without help. Unlike boughten trees, pitch pines never grew straight, so setting them up took skill.

As happened every year, by the time Willie and Dinah finally had the tree fixed in position and stable, Susan was up. She brought her tea into the livingroom, instead of having it in bed, so that she could admire the tree. As she did every year, she said it was the biggest, the best, the bushiest tree they had ever brought home, and that it would be absolutely a knockout. Soon she would begin to bring the boxes of ornaments down. They wouldn't trim the tree tonight, because Tyrone was arriving and Susan felt they ought to greet Laurie and him, since she said Laurie was in a bad state. Tomorrow would be the great day.

The next morning they had to run over to Tyrone's to put things in order for him, and when they got back, Jimmy was home. It was going to be a grand holiday season, Willie thought. He loved the fuss and the visiting and the decorations. "You should have let us know you were coming," he said to Jimmy.

"Yes!" Susan echoed him. "I mailed all your presents two weeks ago! I sent yours and Lisa's to Seattle. Where's Lisa?"

It turned out Jimmy and Lisa were separated. They'd had some silly fight. Maybe it was the restaurant failing. Willie was sure he'd hear all the details eventually if not from Jimmy, then certainly from Susan, who would not rest until she knew exactly what had happened between the couple. He figured his son would tell him what he wanted to, and that the rest was his own business. Willie always respected his children's privacy; it was a matter of honor to him to trust Jimmy and Johnny and give them room.

Willie was surprised when Jimmy reminded him that in previous years, the two of them had gone out to steal the tree together. Of course. Willie had forgotten that Jimmy had been his partner in the adventure before Dinah. Willie felt a little guilty for losing that memory of his son, but Jimmy did not seem overly sentimental about it. He seemed to remember it more as a joke. "Yeah," he said shaking his head at Dinah, "it was my old man introduced me to a life of crime. First trees. Then cars. Then it was the local bank. That's how it all begins."

This was another of Willie's favorite nights. Sometimes at this season he wished he could slow time down instead of speeding it up, the way he'd often wished as a kid. He wanted this evening to last and last. Jimmy looked fine, even if a little tired and ragged around the edges. Dinah's presence helped there. Jimmy had always confided in Dinah—the kids had used her as a buffer in adolescence between themselves and Susan. Dinah would help both sides calm down. She would state Susan's case to Johnny and Johnny's to Susan. Dinah made each of them sound and thus somehow stuck with being reasonable. She would negotiate a compromise between positions that had suddenly become clear and arguable. Willie had watched the process with relief for years. Dinah would buffer Jimmy's disaster too. Probably she already knew more than he would know for a week or more than Susan would be able to worm out of Jimmy even if she did nothing else all day tomorrow, which he passionately hoped would not happen to screw up his favorite season.

He felt that Jimmy's being home required no fancy explanations. Jimmy would move back in his room and for a while

Susan and Willie would stop fighting about whether she ought to take over the kids' rooms for a studio. She wanted a workroom. She complained incessantly about having to work in their bedroom. He thought she should take over Jimmy's or Johnny's old room, or better yet, since those were small rooms under a slanted roof, he could knock out the wall between and make one decent-sized room. She was unwilling to eliminate either of the kids' old rooms, saying that they wouldn't feel welcome when they came home if their rooms were not kept for them. She would also argue that the rooms were inappropriate in light and size and shape for what she needed. She wanted a workshop added onto the house, or free standing like his studio. She was always comparing her having to work in the bedroom to his having a separate building for a studio.

Someday, he said. In the meantime, take one of their rooms or let me knock the wall down. It's not a structural wall. The conversation repeated itself every month like Susan's periods. Now he couldn't offer that solution, but Jimmy had worked as a carpenter summers while he was going to Dartmouth. Maybe he could put on an addition for her. If Jimmy was really staying, maybe he'd suggest it. Give his son something to keep him occupied.

Now he put all that out of his mind, for this was the night they trimmed the tree. He loved the private times they took with each other, and he loved the rituals they shared, the meals, the holidays. People thought them peculiar but it was at once two separate intimacies he had, two wives, and something more: the three of them together had a strength and a richness he had never found in a couple. It was simply more fun with three lively adults talking and playing. They were polite. Sometimes they had to negotiate who was to be where. Susan would say to him, I'm going over to Dinah's tonight. Other things had been worked out so long ago they no longer needed stating. Susan did not like to stay in the house alone. If he made love with Dinah in the evening, which was not common anyhow, he came home promptly so that he could sleep in the bed with Susan and she would not fret. Dinah did not like anyone hanging around in the morning, so it all worked out. It took attention to their separate and mutual needs, a nice balance of love and respect. He thought of himself as unusually warm and affectionate. There weren't too many men who could keep two women satisfied and happy. This season celebrated that lucky state.

The tree trimmings, too, were special. Susan had found dozens of delicately colored glass baubles at yard sales, in antique and junk shops, in flea markets. Sometimes she drove to Boston the day after Christmas to buy beautiful and expensive ornaments at half or three quarters off. She did not mind standing in line for forty minutes in Lord & Taylor's for the perfect pagoda ornament for the treetop or a spectacular feathered peacock or golden leopard.

Over the years she had collected fabulous beasts, so that the tree was a needled bestiary, a Noah's ark of fantasy, of green burros and glass unicorns, of spotted ducks and fine gold spiderwebs. She also liked little dolls, firemen and wooden soldiers and ballerinas. Among all these were the remains of their early married trees when they had been poor in the city. In those days they had waited till Christmas Eve to pick up a tree free when the local merchants closed. He remembered trees strung with Susan's jewelry for ornaments, her necklaces and earrings. When costume jewelry broke or she lost an earring, she still would recycle her jewelry on the tree.

There, too, were the shell ornaments they had made their first years on the Cape, Johnny frowning with concentration as she drilled little holes in scallop and conch and moon snail shells for the hanger to slip through. It was a whole family history packed into scraps of tissue paper in boxes. Each emerging piece shook memories out of him, glittering in the colored lights.

He loaded the phonograph spindle with Christmas music and the four of them hung the ornaments, one at a time, ritually, drinking hot buttered rum he always made then. Dinah brought the cats over to enjoy the tree. Bogey liked Figaro. The two of them sniffed each other over as if they hadn't met for a month instead of in the yard that afternoon. Then they curled up together in front of the fire. The little multicolored lights shone like chips of bright jelly. Tosca followed every ornament with her eyes. They put only the nonbreakable ones on the lower branches, because every year at a certain point she crept up and began to bat at them. She particularly liked to make the metal bells tinkle.

Willie felt crammed up to his throat with pleasure. This was a time he felt like a rich man. If Johnny were only home, he would have felt himself absolutely sealed in love. There were both his women going back and forth and hanging the pretty gaudy little things, there was his son with hair even redder than

43

Susan's, standing on a chair putting doves and cardinals on the ends of the high branches. When they finished at last and sank, all pleasantly, cozily drunk by now, in the various chairs to stare at their creation while the fire hissed into coals, he thought it a perfect icon of family happiness. His family. Gaudy, unlikely, fanciful but quite, quite real and satisfying. He was the most satisfied man he knew. This was a small town and everybody from the butcher to the postmistress knew their situation, but the Cape also had a history of toleration for eccentrics, economic, social, political and sexual oddballs. They were an old and respected public scandal. He thought he hardly knew a man who didn't secretly or openly envy him.

SEVEN

Laurie

Laurie drove her father to the Cape three days before Christmas. Tyrone had the gift, rare among men in her experience, of relaxing while she drove. It made her feel trusted, competent, piloting the big Mercedes all the way. He chatted with her, played tapes, made and took calls, read papers from his briefcase. He found driving fussy and boring. She drove fast and efficiently. They were at the house in the woods in six hours and ten minutes with Celeste, his new Haitian maid, sleeping in the backseat. All the way she felt as if she were running at the same time she was driving, running full tilt away from New York and everyone in her life.

When they arrived, Willie and Susan were waiting. Laurie felt tired and cranky. She longed to throw herself at Susan and collapse, but Willie was there too. Finally Susan followed her upstairs. While Susan unpacked her, for the first time in days, Laurie cried, letting it all out in gouts of words. Susan held her and kissed her hair and hugged her. Since her parents had divorced when she was ten, every summer when Laurie was with her father and the current wife, Susan stood in for her mother. It was to Susan she had carried her puzzlements, her protests and wounds. Her relief was enormous. She felt as if she had been standing on tiptoe for weeks holding up a ceiling and now she could let it fall. With Susan she need not pretend to control she did not have. She could sob out her outrage, her confusion, her grief. She could let go, because nobody in New York would know. Here in the winter, she was invisible, safe. When Susan finally left, Laurie lay tucked in her bed as countless times before. Exhausted, she slept.

It wasn't until the next morning she saw how nicely Willie and Susan had fixed up the house for them. All Ozzie Dove had ever done was turn on the water and the heat, but they had uncovered everything and put a basket of fruit on the marble coffee table. The house smelled of soup Willie had made and Susan had put milk, butter and eggs in the refrigerator. They could have a decent breakfast. Later she would take Celeste to town to shop. She put herself in order before she came down. She owed that to Daddy. He would not normally leave New York during the brilliant holiday season with all the parties and events and galas except for a week in the sun in their tiny villa in Aruba or for a ski trip to Switzerland. He was doing this for her, burying himself in the woods when nobody else was here and letting her have Christmas alone with him. She owed it to him to hold it together as well as she could until he had gone back to the city and taken Celeste with him.

She dreaded going into town, but there would be almost no one she knew. She could not stand people's eyes on her, pitying, wondering, burning her already scalded skin. She had lost her husband and lost face at the same time, and if she could not sort out humiliation from grief, that was because of the police and people harassing her. She wanted to be quiet. She wanted never to have to speak to anyone again, for at least a year.

The day was something to be got through. Every day was that now. Living reminded her of a bad job, when she was always counting the hours to break and then to lunch and then to quitting time. She owed it to Daddy to try to be stoic, because she knew how much he was doing for her. He was taking heroic measures to save her, as if she were drowning as once in childhood that tenth summer. He was coming after her and bringing her to shore, as he had then. He had saved her life then and he was saving it now, but it was a slow saving. It hurt, as the water being forced from her lungs had hurt then. She was glad when lunch signaled the end of morning, glad when cocktail time closed the afternoon, relieved when supper was served and cleared and she blessed the time the day ended and she could go up to her room and shut the door on the world for eight hours.

At her bedroom window she stared into the darkness. She could make out the crinkly presence of the pond under the stars. The stars seemed to exist only here. She never looked at the sky in the city. Yes, she thought, she could understand nunneries. Once upon a time, she would have withdrawn into one upon the violent death of her husband and taken gladly, gratefully, on her knees with joy a vow of silence. She had the impulse to pretend to develop laryngitis, for the holidays.

Willie and Susan came over every day, but she didn't see Dinah or Jimmy, who was supposed to be home, until Christmas Day. Then she had to help Celeste put a feast together, as if she had any competence in that line. Basically she fussed with the table. In the center she put the really rather striking amaryllis Susan had brought Tyrone as a gift. Laurie spent an hour setting the table and moving objects around the room. Then she went upstairs, put on a dress, took it off, put on another dress, took that off. Finally she put on a loose black Italian wool tunic she felt safe in and black silk pants, because Tyrone insisted on her dressing. She understood his pressure to maintain face. He was so handsome still, she had to make a passable entrance as his daughter. He was both tall and big, an imposing man. Nobody could ignore him, ever. His hair had been blond in her childhood but he had gone bald early. Her mother had told her that virile men balded young, the same remark each of his later wives had made in her presence, so that she assumed it was something Tyrone told them. He had a magnificent head and wore a close beard, as if to balance the weight. His eyes were bold and light blue. He moved like the good all-round athlete he was and never did he rise and knock over a chair, the way she did; never did he drop his napkin or upset his water glass. She wished for the ten thousandth time that she had inherited his grace along with his height.

At least she hadn't gained weight with all this trauma. At least that. Great. She lost her husband, she felt crazy and on the verge of total disintegration, she couldn't face anyone she knew, she was so angry with Tom she could have killed him herself while she could not even yell at him or demand an explanation or say how hurt she was, but at least she wasn't fat. They could put that on her grave. Her life was miserable, she was a total failure as a woman and an artist, but she kept her weight down.

She heard the car arrive, a little surprised they had not walked as they usually did. She crossed the hall to look without turning on the light, to remain invisible. They were spilling out of Dinah's elderly Volvo, their arms full of presents and wine. It had not occurred to Laurie to buy gifts for anyone except Tyrone, whose present she had ordered before Thanksgiving and given him at breakfast: a new neat little two-person sailboat that had won an award for its design and was supposed to be exceedingly maneuverable and able to snatch wind out of a calm. He had been pleased. His gift to her had been the architect's plans and the promise of a contractor as soon a possible. And of course perfume and jewelry. He always gave her some piece of jewelry, this time sapphire studs.

They were jamming the lower hall, getting out of their coats and mufflers, handing over a bottle of champagne and one of those yummy homemade liqueurs they produced, of beach plums or rum cherries. Jimmy, she noticed, was wearing only a light leather jacket instead of an overcoat. His appearance startled her because he had, like herself, grown up. Somehow she had expected him to be the same age as he had been the last summer they had hung out together. It was always startling when the year-round people changed while she was gone. It was like putting toys back in a box and then coming and finding they had secretly gone on with some private game in your absence. However, Jimmy had gone to Dartmouth and had been working on the West Coast for the last three years. He belonged to the real world.

Susan handed her a holly and white cedar wreath she must have made. Really, Susan was amazing with her hands. Just as it was occurring to Laurie she could get Susan to make her something comfortable and chic while she was parked here, Susan gave her a box that she opened to find a perfect midnight blue chemise trimmed in ivory silk. Susan was wearing one of her own dresses, of course, floor length with an uneven handkerchief hem of jacquard floral patterned aquamarine in a heavy silk that hung in thick draperylike folds glimmering. It had a cowl neck but in the back it was deeply cut. Susan still had a handsome back for a woman her age. She seemed to be flirting with Tyrone a lot. Laurie supposed he was more fun to flirt with when he was divorced than when he was getting married. Susan was just having fun. It didn't mean anything. She told Susan how much she loved the chemise.

47

Celeste had just laid out the hors d'oeuvres. Dinah and Willie immediately moved on them. "When we first started the Moonsnails," Dinah was saying to Jimmy, "I said we should call the band Free Hors d'Oeuvres. I figured a sign like that, Free Hors d'Oeuvres at the Inn, would really draw in the tourists."

But Jimmy was not listening. He was looking at Laurie. Not with pity, she noticed. Maybe nobody had told him her disgusting story yet. No, that would be too much to hope for. They couldn't wait to talk about it, the biggest scandal of the year or the decade. He wanted to talk to her, but he didn't have the same look in his eyes that made her avoid Willie, that combination of easy sympathy and hard curiosity.

"Going to stay for a while?" he asked.

She nodded. She was waiting to say she had laryngitis.

"I may, too. I don't know." He grimaced. "I might as well be here as anyplace else right now."

She felt a stirring of dim hope. He wasn't going to ask her about Tom. He was churning with emotional energy, full of some trouble of his own. She took a step closer and decided not to have laryngitis. A man who wanted to talk about his troubles would not have seemed much of a find at a party a couple of months ago, but right now he formed an oasis.

When it was time to go into dinner, she noticed Dinah wince when she sat at the table, staring at the amaryllis. It was a strange-looking flower, but surely it couldn't disturb Dinah. It was odd to see her in a dress, this one black wool and obviously made by Susan. There wasn't much Dinah could do with her hair, which grew out like a prickly bush in kinks, but Susan must have cut it close to her head recently. Dinah wore earrings in all the holes in her lobes, two on one side and three on the other. Around her neck she wore a fetish necklace of carved birds. They looked heavy and primeval.

Dinah was always a presence like a Buddha, squat, full-bodied, a broad, slightly flattened face with piercing, glittering eyes. Tyrone had once said she radiated pure sex, but Laurie thought he was simply reacting to the ancient scandal surrounding her. Dinah had a low cellolike voice, sometimes throaty, sometimes coarse, sometimes caressing. She also had the capacity for sitting without saying a word for endless amounts of time, not fidgeting, not moving, like a woman turned to warm stone. Laurie had come on her more than once in the woods or in the dunes, just sitting, immobile, once with a deer grazing

48

nearby who had fled at her own approach. Dinah would look at Laurie, but sometimes it did not even occur to her to say hello. Laurie thought of her as simple, a true peasant, a dim earthy soul.

Yet if Laurie wanted to impress a certain kind of person in New York, she would mention not her father, not the gallery owners she knew or the artists she had met, but Dinah, who was not widely famous—narrowly but intensely. Only au courant or arty types would have heard of her, but they would be truly astounded that she knew Dinah. An exclusive but potent legend. Laurie found that absolutely weird, because Susan and Willie and Dinah were like family, like aunts or uncles who could fix what went wrong here, who knew what to do when you had friends looking for a summer rental or a baby-sitter or an au pair girl, when you required the roof repaired or the pump fixed. That was mainly Susan and Willie; Dinah was not likely to put herself out. She and Tyrone were not exactly chummy. Was Dinah chummy with anyone? People brought her injured animals and she nursed them back to health. She looked like an Indian through the face, but she wasn't.

It was still kind of gross when she thought about it, looking at them all around the table like regular married people, that Dinah had sex with *both* of them. Laurie always reached a point in any social evening when she would start wondering how they did it, all together, by twos, who chose when and where. How did they arrange it? She really loved Susan, but the cool/warm matronly Susan who tucked her in bed and held her when she cried, how could she have sex with her husband and with this witch? It sometimes made Laurie feel as if the motherly Susan were a front or a trick. Ten years of three of them crawling all over each other. How could Jimmy stand it? How could he grow up with that going on?

"That's a beautiful necklace," Tyrone said, reaching for it. "May I?"

Dinah visibly drew back but suffered herself to endure the examination that brought Tyrone's hand close to her breasts.

"It looks like a fine piece. Do you know where it came from?"

"It was a present from someone I was studying with. His grandmother made it."

"Zuni, isn't it? What an extravagant present! Perhaps he thought of it as something old he had around the house. I met a dealer once in Crete who used to go around to the mountain villages and trade the villagers plastic mixing bowls and nylon blankets for their antiques.''

"Since he teaches Native American culture at a university, he could no doubt assign a dollar value to it. He gave it to me as a bed present," Dinah said blandly, glancing down the table at Susan. "I had a need to study Hopi music." Again she glared at the amaryllis in front of her, its full strange dragonfly head nodding over the china.

"Laurie's going to be living here," Tyrone said. "In the summer with so many people coming and going in the house, she'll need her privacy. I want to remodel the boathouse as a little cottage for her. And I'm looking for a piece of property in town for a gallery."

"You're opening a gallery?" Willie sat up.

"Laurie will be running it. Yes, I think it's time for her to have her own. She's been learning the business in New York."

Jimmy was looking at her with a knowing expression, his lip twisting in an empathetic grimace, but what he was thinking was how Tyrone tried to run her life. It's all right, she would tell him later, he's giving me exactly what I need. What an extraordinarily tactile stare he had. He had become handsome, more than handsome. When had it happened? She had years of memories of Jimmy, summer after summer. He came with the place, like the raft in the pond and the path to the beach. She never even had a crush on him, because he was almost five months younger, which had felt like an enormous stretch in her childhood. He was just Jimmy, skinny, redheaded and freckled, the kid she played with when more exciting kids weren't visiting from the city or renting nearby. Then they both grew up and he was gone.

Celeste was clearing dessert and bringing coffee and liqueurs. Tyrone continued, stroking his beard, "What would be perfect is for the two of you to do the renovation." He beamed first at Willie, then at Dinah. "You do quality work and that's exactly what I want. First the boathouse. Take a look at the plans and tell me what you think of them." Fetching them from the sideboard, he spread them on the table. "Do you like the plans?"

Did they like the plans? Really! Tyrone had had them drawn up by a fine architect, although she was sure nobody else at the table would know how famous and well respected he was. Did they like them! He knew how to make people feel important.

That was part of his charm and she should discover how to do it too. She still had so much to learn from him about how to act with other people. Maybe charm was something she could practice, as she had mastered sailing and studied tennis and backgammon.

"Then the gallery. I have two properties I'm considering. I'll make up my mind this week, I promise you."

"This looks great," Willie said. "I see what you're aiming at. It could be very nice, using the way it goes right to the water."

"No thanks," Dinah said. "I'm doing nothing inessential this year. I have a New Works grant."

Tyrone frowned. "Public works?"

Dinah didn't answer, doing her stone act. Willie hastened to cover for her. "I like the idea. It could be fun. Especially the gallery. I have a lot of ideas about how art should be displayed and I know every gallery in these towns. I can tell you what works and what doesn't, the way they're lit, the spaces for art, the walk-through. Jimmy can help. He's a fine carpenter. And he's done roofing. We wouldn't have to subcontract the roof."

Jimmy shrugged. "Why not? It's something to do."

"I think it's exciting," Susan said. She had not looked at Dinah through the whole conversation and she was not looking at her now. She beamed at Willie and then turned back to Tyrone. "We're delighted Laurie will be living here, I know Jimmy is, and a new gallery! I think that's just what we all need."

"I'd like a dry cleaners," Dinah said, "or a bakery."

Dinah was obviously aware she was being rude. It was like trying to dine with a Neanderthal, Laurie thought, a genuine primitive. The fetish necklace seemed appropriate. Dinah had eaten a hearty dinner and was polishing off a large snifter of cognac. In all the years Laurie had known her, since she was a little girl and they had begun coming to the pond (her mother, Tyrone and her; then Tyrone's next two wives and herself), Dinah never changed. She always seemed to be the same weight and look the same, as if she like the necklace were carved out of something more immutable than flesh.

Now Dinah caught her stare and held it until Laurie looked down, feeling herself blush for no good reason except that staring was rude, but then Dinah had stared too. It made her feel fifteen, and remember how she had had a crush on Willie then, of all people, and how she had hung around his studio. He had encouraged her to start painting and she had shown him and only him her first work, afraid to show Daddy for fear it was not good. Willie was the same age as Tyrone, she supposed, but he never seemed so. Although his hair had been pure white since she could remember, his face was without lines. He was slender, supple, always dressed like a kid, too, in jeans and sneakers. She doubted he owned a suit. He was as ready to listen and respond with disbelief or astonishment or indignation or instant enthusiasm as she herself had been at fifteen. His emotions were close to the surface, not hidden by practice or artifice, not eroded by cynicism or too much experience of the world, she thought.

She had been silly about Dinah then, too, imagining Dinah seducing her in some indefinable way. She remembered with a further rush of blood to her face that she had cast herself in Dinah's way several times, hoping for some cataclysm of unbridled lust. Dinah had done nothing, said nothing, only sent her on her way, yet she felt as if Dinah had read her mind with amusement.

When she looked up again Dinah had slipped from the table. A few moments later she heard the piano from the livingroom. She could not tell if Dinah was improvising or playing; and indeed, when she had occasionally heard one of Dinah's pieces, she had the same problem. It was not harshly atonal like a lot of modern music, but it was odd: repetitive, melodic but circling rather than ongoing. People could have danced to it, but round and round and in place. Like Dinah, it was peculiar stuff.

Jimmy slid over into Dinah's seat across from her. "Do you really want us to make over the boathouse for you? You'd be comfortable with us working on it? It's not necessary, you know." His voice was pitched low enough so that Tyrone and the others would not hear. "Only if it's your desire too."

"It is. I'm glad you're going to help me with a place to live." She chose the words carefully, not to push him into a workman's role. She was being tactful, just the way Tyrone would be. In a way it was too bad he couldn't hear her.

"You're not real easy in company now," he said just as softly. "The evening will be over soon. You can take us all better one on one."

"How did you happen to be here from the West Coast? It's a lucky coincidence."

"It's not a coincidence and if it's luck, it's bad luck, the bottom line from a string of disasters." He forced a grin. "You too?"

She only had to nod. "Me too."

EIGHT

Dinah

Dinah fell in love with Mark Edelmann on the Fourth of July, sitting on a speakers' platform with him as the temperature hit 101 Fahrenheit. She was there as a member of the Wholey Terrors, a self-styled women's liberation rock band famous among their fans for making a hell of a racket and among cognoscenti of that weird area where postmodernism and rock secretly intermingled for being musically interesting. Dinah did not consider vocals her strong point, but she could carry a tune and they could hear her in the back row without amplification, and in the next county with it. She played rhythm guitar, flute, sometimes piano or any extra percussion needed. She was twenty-two, dressed wild and butch in black leather and silver studs, with her brown hair frizzed straight up and out, and was accustomed to groupies of all sexes.

She was seated right bchind thc lectern where she got a fine view of all the speakers' rear parts. Mark Edelmann had a nice tight butt in Levi's, especially considering he was twice her age at least, but it was his rhetoric that made her inner parts stir. He was one fine poet and he wasn't a bad rabble-rouser either. When he returned to his seat beside her, smiled and let his hand rest on her knee, at first she thought it was the heat getting to her. She had never been in love before. She had not had time to bother, with all there was to learn and do. When she felt fussed about someone, she took off on her bike and roared into the countryside. The next day she would be in a different town anyhow.

She went back to his hotel with him without thinking twice, because she felt like it and at twenty-two, she always did what she felt like unless some force prevented her. He talked a lot, in and out of bed. That made him different right away. She was used to other musicians, who didn't, or if they did talk, she could tune out and when she tuned back in, they would still be talking about how their agent screwed them or some new riff or the last or next gig. He expected her to listen. He was talking about Chile and the CIA and international banking. It wasn't a lecture. He kept asking her questions about the band and the music they played. He was curious and he listened when he wasn't talking.

When he made love, he was different too: more specific, more personal. Often she had the feeling with people that whoever they were with was interchangeable with the last five and the next fourteen. They did it this way or that way and she did a certain thing to get them off. They wanted to get off, that was the current phrase, and off was where they went; she was a launching pad; they were the same for her. It was the release, not the partner, that was desired.

Mark was not an experience or a respite from noise but a person who insisted on a romantic overlay she was not accustomed to, a naming and telling and specifying she would have expected herself to find sentimental and old-fashioned, but which, from him, fascinated her. Held her fascinated. Mark Edelmann. He was a poet. So why should that matter? Who read poetry? People read his. People she knew. He was a hero on the campuses. She could reach twenty thousand people at a time and set them screaming, yet her work felt like gauze and his like silver, in their density.

"You're a child," he would tell her, warningly, dismissively, at times in a tone of worship. "But not a girlchild. Not a child of my generation. You have the heart of a boy in the body of a woman."

Oh, her body. He liked that. She was used to men liking her body, for it was in keeping with the taste of the times: chunky, zaftig, an earth mother like the women Crumb drew in his strips. "I'm not a boy. I'm what women are like now. You're a late Victorian, Edelmann. Real tardy."

"The late Mark Edelmann." He had liked that. He was always half obsessed with death, his own and others. Death by fire and death by water ran through his poems, through his language even in bed. "Burn me up, woman," he would mutter. "Stir my ashes."

He was thin and bony, as if he had more vertebrae and elbows than other people. His pale skin made his eyes appear black. His shoulder length honey brown hair was held back by a leather holder in the form of an intricate knot hung with a few beads he told her were lapis lazuli. His darker beard was carefully shaped; indeed she learned it took him as long to trim it to his satisfaction every couple of days as another man would spend shaving. The beard and hair and the studs he wore in his ears gave him a piratical air, but he was clean and careful with his body as a cat. He smoked constantly and had a hacking cough, his long shapely fingers always stained. He hated filters. He found them ugly. He could keep a cigarette between his lips while he drove, while he typed, while he dialed the telephone, while he walked and probably had he desired, in the shower.

The attraction of opposites? He was airy, she was earthy. Yet they both were struck readily into fire, sexual fire, fire of concentration, fire of imagination, fire of creation, fire of anger. She knew herself to be anything but elegant, whereas he was in his person, his writing, his mental routines and habits of thought, of a clean and pared down elegance. His voice moved her right through her guts. His voice vibrated in her like a cat's purr, deep, a marvelous instrument. Till he had to stop giving readings, when cancer had destroyed half his lungs, she never tired of hearing him.

He'd held down a few academic jobs but he had been fired for getting too involved with students, for being too political. Now he was beyond being hirable and made his living off gigs, the same as she did. Both of them had tiny dingy studios in Manhattan where they stored gear they weren't using and camped when they weren't on the road or shacked up with anybody else. She came back to an eviction notice because of the jazz horn player who had been subletting in her absence. She moved in with Mark on Avenue C for a week or so until she could find another cheap flop. She never moved her stuff out until four years later, just after he was released from six months on Rikers Island, was diagnosed as having lung cancer and she took him to the Cape. Sick as he was, they had made him serve time for a demonstration against the neutron bomb.

Still she was gone more than she was with him the first eight months. Then the Wholey Terrors broke up over separatism, forcing Dinah to decide. He was staying in the house of an academic couple who were on sabbatical in England, a farmhouse outside Ithaca, New York, far more comfortable than his little flop in the city. Mark was putting a book together. *Superfluous Bodies*. The house was big for them, comfortable and rambling but chilly. Deep snow hid the ground and ice closed

55

in the Finger Lakes. They had never spent longer than a week together before. They rattled around in the farmhouse and the too ample time, striking sparks of disagreement over the small decisions of the day from when and what to eat for breakfast through the bumpy afternoon until the decision when to go to bed.

He was shocked to find out she had been a scholarship student at Juilliard and while still there, had had a piece performed by a chamber ensemble. "How could you go from writing real music to playing junk?"

"It's not junk, asshole. It's good hard rocking music. We weren't the best musicians, but the stuff was good. We did all kinds of interesting things. We weren't no three chord wonders."

"But you'd been writing real music. Serious music. Not pop. How could you give that up? Was it the money? It isn't as if you sold out for millions and your face on the cover of *Rolling Stone*."

"You really think some music is good and some is bad because it has a backbeat or it doesn't. If you meant it in terms of rhythms or harmonics maybe I could understand. Labeling stuff the classics deadens people. So they go take out a subscription to the Boston Symphony and they expect to hear maybe three of eighty-odd pieces and that's the good safe stuff you pay your money for and it's all certified and it's all dead and stuffed."

"You sound like those idiots who think that all writing is equal, and John Donne and the guy who writes ad copy for toilet bowl cleaners are in the same business."

She got furious with him and would have left except that it was snowing hard and nothing was running, a March snowstorm that knocked out their power for a day. Then she began to enjoy arguing ideas. She wasn't used to it, but she developed a taste and then an addiction. She found out what she thought by defending her at first amorphous but gradually forming ideas against his precision and sarcasm. Sometimes their arguments terminated in screaming and sometimes in throwing dishes. She worried about the breakage; he didn't.

They played too. If he often called her a child, sometimes scornfully and sometimes in what sounded like awe, he also could find his own ten-year-old self, his fifteen-year-old self. They had snowball fights in the yard. With an old sled from the basement, they took turns on the hill behind the house. They took bubble baths together till water shuddered in puddles on

56

the floor. Whooping, he would launch himself at her and they would tussle and roll on the bed tossing the covers across the room. Kneeling naked on the mattress, he would bark and howl. He was ticklish to complete vulnerability and could be dissolved to helpless writhing by her merely poking a finger toward his midsection, threateningly. They made pancakes in the form of naked bodies, sexual organs, words, eating them with maple syrup. Cornell proved a useful source of dairy products and sausage. She met local musicians and began getting seriously into electronic music. She worked lab music briefly and then started playing with tapes, using feedback and delay, mixing the sounds of voice and instruments with natural and mechanical noises. It was the opposite extreme from the band, writing for specific musicians.

She learned he had little understanding of music and a poor ear. He actually preferred the pop music he scorned, or the ersatz stuff from movie scores. Yet he was happier when she was playing music he could not enjoy, because he truly believed in the unbridgeable gap between Culture High and culture low in spite of the fact that he could not always tell the difference when she was practicing flute. Flute was her basic instrument, had been since age seven. It was what she always took with her and what she could always fall back on. For cash, she played the organ Sundays in a church and guitar in a coffeehouse Friday through Sunday nights. He might get a headache from Stockhausen and hum the Beatles when he was truly happy, but he was convinced that only the former counted in eternity.

They were a couple. That was a new and sometimes alarming experience for her. Mark came from a regular mommy/daddy/ two baby family, his father a successful accountant in Philadelphia, his mother a housewife with a busy volunteer life. Dinah had been born in Chicago. Her mother Shirley taught music. Her father, Nathan, had been in Auschwitz. He died of a heart attack when she was thirteen; she could not remember him as ever entirely well. He had been a man of silences, happiest when he was singing or hearing music, especially Baroque music, but not a man who talked much or casually. Once he had been the first violin in a symphony orchestra in Kraków; now he ran a Laundromat. Tenderness came hard to him and sarcasm easy, but there was a gentleness in him she could count on when she was truly hurt, physically or mentally. Shirley was frightened of pain and withdrew behind fussing. Nathan understood pain intimately. But sometimes the entry into his gentleness led through a wall of fire, his temper.

When Dinah talked to Mark about her father, she could almost see the figure building in his mind, sentimentalized, idealized. Years of brutality and pain, witnessing death on the hour, had not made Nathan a saint, but only a complex, once ambitious and thoughtful man of towering emotions who had had his calling, his family, his life, his health, his prime, stolen, stolen forever. After the burning of his family, he was enabled only by the wreck of his once great vitality to make a small leftover life with a wife who would never mean to him what his first wife had, a daughter to replace the murdered son, a strange daughter entirely American, a tough child of the streets of their loud neighborhood who nonetheless could please him in one way utterly. He lamented that he had not the strength, the health, the time left, he had not the money to push her through where he wanted her to go. He had given her what he had to give: the sense that music was supremely important and except for human kindness, perhaps the only sure good, and that her desires were important inside music. He had given her a sense of worth based on her musical ability. He had also insisted she carry on the family.

He had given her a sense that being a Jew was something painful, powerful and radiant she must carry forward. When he talked about the past, it was always in terms of what she must tell her children., He was older than the fathers of her friends, who would sometimes think he was her grandfather. He was closer in age to her mother's father than he was to her mother, but he was ageless. He told her often he felt like a ghost, a revenant. He never stopped insisting that she make music seriously and that she carry on his line. He had less prejudice against women than most of her friends' fathers; he said in Auschwitz the women had been worked like the men, and the few women survivors were just as tough as the few men. He never talked about his first wife, but he did talk about his sister Aviva, who had played the viola professionally in a string quartet, who had been gassed.

Dinah's mother Shirley had been a ringer for Dinah herself: same hair, same eyes, same body. But she was a far gentler longer suffering woman. Shirley taught music in a grade school in a neighborhood two bus rides away. She had a few pupils on the weekend, studying the piano. When Shirley was giving lessons, Dinah slipped out of the house. She could not stand to listen. By the time Dinah was twelve, she could tune the piano and save her mother the fee for the tuner. Dinah was not exactly sure when she had gone from necking with her steady boyfriend Sammy to fucking, but she remembered exactly her fourteenth birthday on which she had been given her first silver flute. Her father had left instructions it was to be purchased from his insurance money. She had begun sex early, she supposed; it had come easily to her. Or she to it. They had clung to the bottom of the lower middle class, working class with pretensions her mother had never had the spare cash to follow through. Without a scholarship, there would have been no Juilliard; but Dinah had been playing for money since junior high.

Shirley's second husband was a retired dentist with whom she moved to Fort Lauderdale. He had come with a hefty income, three grown children, two Cadillacs and a permanent leathery tan. Shirley bleached her hair and they no longer looked like clones. They had not a great deal to say to each other. Shirley worried about her, and her own motto was that the less her mother knew, the less she had to worry about. Dinah was not about to haul Mark home for inspection. Fort Lauderdale had never been her home anyhow, and she had never even worked out a satisfactory mode of address for Dr. Morse.

That first winter and spring of their joining: great fierce winds blew through them. She had had sex with many, mostly men but some women; however she had been most intimate with the musicians she played with and wrote for. She would still find herself working out passages and layers so that she would think, Jeri should come in right there on lead guitar and Sunni should hit the piano entrance percussively. She had little experience of intimacy as Mark, who had been married twice, expected it. She had no housekeeping skills, no preparation for what she thought of as the daddy/mommy roles. In the house of their relationship, it was as if Mark kept walking in and tossing his coat on a chair, only to discover there was no furniture and his coat lay on a bare floor. And she, she was always screaming at him, "I don't see what liking to fuck you has to do with being confused with a laundry service!"

They were unsuited. They were mismatched. But they were not mismated and so they lumbered on, quarreling and making up and breaking things, an uncouth Frankenstein monster with four legs all walking in different directions and two heads talking about different subjects and four arms punching each other, but joined where lovers join, indisputably, compulsively, beyond words and volition joined. It was not that they were even faithful, that first year. Whenever they were separated for longer than a couple of weeks, they both had other people and it did not matter and then it stopped. It was pointless. There was too much noise between them to hear anyone else calling on that wavelength.

She worked her way through electronic serialism and into minimalism where she was writing for spoons and hands clapping and feet tapping while she was with him, but she was never as productive as she had been before she met him or nearly as productive as she would begin to be after his death. Looking back, she thought of the time with Mark as the years when she stopped being a free-form free-floating adolescent; when she was seized and held in place and grew up.

NINE

Susan

Susan had just dropped off the Sunday *Times* Tyrone had ordered in town and truly meant to go home when he popped out of his office to greet her warmly, kissing her cheek. Caress of his beard, curiously animal in his handsome intelligent face. "Dear Susan, it's going to be a mild day, isn't it? I know one is supposed to yearn sentimentally for a white Christmas, but I must say I prefer it green and temperate. Would you have time for a walk, say in an hour and a half? I have a tad of business to clean up first."

She could see the amber monitor behind him flashing lines and boxes of numbers. "That would be wonderful, Ty. When should I come back?"

She just had time to wash and blow-dry her hair. Both Willie and Dinah were in their tunnel routines, oblivious to her as usual. She might as well live with three dogs instead of a dog and two people, for all the company she got out of them when they put on their blinkers and started pulling along on some project. She prided herself that when she worked, she worked, and when she finished work, she let go of her preoccupations and functioned as a fully social being—as anyone could learn to do, witness Tyrone, who certainly was far more seriously plugged into the world than any of the rest of them, yet who could be engaged on an intense human level without her having to sulk or throw tantrums.

Just as she was about to leave, Zee Gildner called—a vigorous widow in her late sixties. "Susan, darling, I am looking at the adult education schedule. I was thinking of taking a class in computers. Everybody should understand them, don't you think? Would you like to go with me?"

"I have no interest, Zee. Willie is always playing with his."

"How about stress management? Embroidering birds and flowers? Swedish conversation? Dancercize?" Zee tried to tempt her, while she seethed, furious that Zee would think her someone who needed such mental pablum.

"Why don't you ask Dinah?" she suggested wickedly.

Tyrone let her choose the walk. She thought of the ocean, her passion, but it would be chilly there with an east wind blowing. Better to follow a trail among the ponds scattered through the woods. Tyrone walked far more slowly than Dinah or Willie, at a pace she could easily accommodate, so that they could go arm in arm and engage in a real conversation.

"It has been hell, Susan my dear, absolute hell. When I think of my daughter married to that drug-happy loser for two years, I could kill him if he hadn't managed to accomplish that himself. Laurie has no proper instincts of self-defense, have you noticed that?"

"You mean she's a little gullible with men?"

"I overprotected her. Certainly that whining drunk who is her biological mother has done nothing for Laurie's confidence or her savvy about men." He stopped to take Susan's face between his hands, dry, warm hands that felt like the finest softest leather. "You know you've been her real mother for years. Without you I don't know how she would have grown up to be as sweet as she is. You were her role model for what a woman should be."

She could feel herself flushing as if steam were rising in her skin. "You're exaggerating, but I do like to know you appreciate what I've tried to do for Laurie. . . ."

"Do you think I've overvalued her sensitivity? That I've encouraged her to remain tenderer than perhaps is safe?"

"Laurie's a very special person, Ty. But what happened to

61

her could happen to any young person now. Jimmy just had the shock of discovering one of his friends was stealing from their business. I do love Laurie, you know. I love her like a daughter, like my own daughter.''

"I know! I know. That's why I feel safe in leaving her here, with you to watch over her. This has been a harrowing episode. Of course it's been that for Laurie, but I can confide in you and you alone, also for me. I've tried not to let Laurie know how shameful and sleazy I've found it.'' He let her go and they walked on, arm in arm through the monochrome landscape.

She rushed to assure him that she understood. He was a deeply feeling man behind his facade, and it was more than facade, because Tyrone was genuine, a man of power and ability. He had inherited money, but he had made his own fortune several times over. He worked in the fray of finance, where risks were enormous and rewards just as generous. Even when he was on the pond with them, over the phone lines he was tied into commodities markets, the rise and fall of currencies all over the globe. He had only to make a call, and thousands of miles away, lackeys bought and sold for him, fought and won or lost on his behalf. Yet such a man could suffer because he truly loved his only child and she was in pain. He could not show that face of tenderness to many people, for he must be strong before his associates and strong before Laurie—but in their special tender friendship, he dared to reveal his pain.

She wanted to reassure him, to ease his worry. At the same time she felt delighted, as if as they strolled, they were moving to grand swelling music. How well turned out he was. Willie went about in jeans baggy with washing, with stains on the knees, ragged at the bottom. He wore tee shirts or an old fisherman's sweater. His idea of dressing for an evening out was to put on newish jeans and a clean sweater. She had bought him beautiful shirts and ties, exquisite Italian silk sports jackets picked up wholesale in New York, and they hung in his closet unworn. He trusted nothing that wasn't just like the last one: the next pair of Levi's, the next L. L. Bean chamois cloth shirt.

Tyrone had on a beautiful Harris tweed with flecks of green and rose in the grey of the jacket, tailored in London of a heavier wool than Americans liked, not the twelve-ounce stuff. Under it he wore a green cashmere sweater just showing the collar of a shirt of fine cotton, with a pale striping. His pants were of an extremely soft pale grey flannel. His boots were Italian and seemed to maintain their high polish regardless of the leaf mold underfoot. Tyrone was always perfect. He had dressed to walk with her, paying her the homage of knowing that she observed clothes. He had complimented her very full skirt. She could wear the high-heeled laced boots needed to set off the tulip hem, because Tyrone walked at a civilized pace. Really anybody would have expected an artist to dawdle and enjoy and a financier to rush along like a one-man battalion on a forced march, but it was the other way round.

"Those are some of the reasons," he was saying, "why I think it wise to keep her out of New York until this scandal has blown over. As it will. Nothing is as dull as last year's sensation."

"That's true in cities, I'm sure, because people have so much to think about and so much to do. Up here, we're always gossiping about what somebody did twenty years ago, for instance that Ozzie is really the Captain's father's son, because Ozzie's mother was having an affair with him. . . ." Susan felt herself blushing again as she remembered that just the night before when the three of them had dined at the house of Burt and Leroy, they had had a wonderful gossip about half the town. Burt was the town librarian, and Leroy ran the Sandspit restaurant and painted. She fell into gossiping often enough, although Tyrone did not know that, bless him. Dinah loved gossip; it did not seem to go with her character, but it was a genuine addiction.

"I'm providing Laurie with a Range Rover to carry her back and forth to New York reliably—she needs four-wheel drive here. I haven't given her a car since college. In New York, they're a nuisance, like keeping a pet rhino, but I can't do without one myself. She's a good driver, better than I am because I grow bored and distracted. Don't you think it's wise to keep judging critically what one does well and what one doesn't, so as not to waste time on what one does badly? Often men imagine because they're good at what they do professionally, they're able in all respects. . . . But, old friend, you'd never think that of me. You've seen what a stream of errors I make with women in my personal life. . . . How I admire you."

"Admire me? How could you?"

"Because you've made an unconventional choice and stuck to it no matter what others may think. That's gutsy. Whereas I've made what seems to be the same mistake three times running. You must think that I'm an idiot with women."

"I don't think that, Tyrone, never." She felt guilty even as she spoke, for she had liked none of his wives, and aside from their blond and slender beauty, had wondered why he had bothered to marry them. "I do think sometimes you're too kind, in a way, I mean that perhaps you've gotten married when, well . . ." She trailed off, embarrassed.

"You think I should have had more affairs and less marriages?" He chuckled. "But a man needs a wife. I need a wife. . . . But I don't doubt you're right that the ones I chose were bad risks."

He was open, guileless with her; no one else was permitted to see him so . . . unadorned. Theirs was a special friendship, as he had often remarked, although she observed it was especially special when he was not married. She always disliked the first two years of his marriages, when he vanished into his infatuation with the new wife and had not yet grown dissatisfied enough to require Susan's sympathy and understanding.

How different it was being with Tyrone in the woods than with Willie. If she tried to talk to Willie about her feelings, she would think he was listening and then suddenly he would burst out, "Look at the flicker. Right on the second branch of that split pine, on the left side." Or, "Hey, a cardinal flower in bloom." He would stare at a grey squirrel chattering on a branch as if it were delivering some personal message to him. He went along pricking his ears after sounds and sniffing after scents and chasing after motions in the corner of his eye, just like Bogey. She swore that he didn't even know what he felt half the time, because he paid no attention. Then he would suddenly wake up one morning depressed and not know why because he was so out of the habit of analyzing or even observing himself. He would rather stare at beech bark than think about her.

Dinah was no better. Dinah could be silent as a tree stump for weeks. Susan would be walking along with Dinah trying to talk and Dinah would hum to herself as if Susan hadn't said a word. Or she would start beating some maddening rhythm on a stick she picked up or on trees they passed and sometimes she would be beating one rhythm with her right hand and one with her left until Susan wanted to beat a third one on her head to shut her up. Dinah would do the exact same thing sometimes when they were sitting at the table. Really, Susan would be there bursting to share her feelings, to talk about something real in her life, and there would be Willie staring at a spiderweb in the corner totally absorbed as a three-year-old in how the light hit the strands; and there would be Dinah like a two-year-old in a crib beating on the table with a spoon. It was like living in a cage with monkeys!

Dinah had the nerve to feel vastly superior to Tyrone on the basis of some bohemian snobbery about the superiority of artists over their patrons, as if it wasn't simply his own sensitivity and refinement that made Tyrone a collector when somebody else with the same amount of money would have spent it all on yachts or Learjets. Yes, here was Tyrone, not wrapped up in himself as well he might have been, not mumbling about finances or money markets or the trade deficit but opening up to her and talking about their lives. How could she help but make comparisons and how could she help but be moved? Tyrone had referred for years to their special friendship, and the passing of time had only made it more important, more necessary to her. She thought they had grown closer since his third marriage had disintegrated.

"I know you'll take care of Laurie while she's recovering. It's only because I trust you that I dare leave her here and go back to the city without feeling I'm abandoning her."

They simply operated together on a different plane of existence than her everyday dreary interactions. It was fine and intelligent, not in the sense of random bombast about art of dry dissection of art theory or Willie's recitation of what he had heard on the radio about South Africa or the Middle East. Rather she and Tyrone shared that high civilized discussion of feelings and intentions and relationships that made life interesting and which for her defined the true best province of human interaction. "I will, Tyrone, I will! You can trust me. I'll do whatever I can for Laurie. I'm delighted that you're creating a new gallery here. Perhaps we can see some of the artists who are getting known in New York. I'd love that."

He took her hand in both of his and squeezed firmly but not too hard. "Ah, Susan. I count on you. I always do."

TEN

Dinah

The first bad storm of the season struck right after New Year's and the woods and the road to town were covered with six inches of snow. Dinah, Willie and Jimmy spent all day digging out. A fine dusting fell on top of the crust. The air grew steely and ice began to skim the pond. Friday the pond stood as a field under a coating of new snow, the treacherous time when the ice looked like solid land but wasn't yet thick enough to bear weight. Monday Dinah flew to Rochester to give a lecture at the Eastman and take part in a performance of her *Celebration for Hands and Feet*, a piece of which she was more than a little weary, but she needed the money.

A gig in academia always reminded her why she had chosen the hard road, although when she had become a minimalist, that in itself would have closed university doors to her. She could remember her own dark feelings as a student, the composing had not always been on a par with theoretical physics in the mathematics and arcane jargon required, that music could perhaps be once again more immediate, more sensual, more accessible and hot. Often by now she forgot that claustrophobic stringency, that pride in rigorous method and meager results, from which she had revolted by going into a rock band instead of a chamber orchestra. It was well to be reminded why she lived from gig to gig and commission to commission, depending between on odd jobs; it was well to remember that her independence had been hard won, painfully maintained but consistently fruitful. She had never run out of musical ideas—what they were called, although of course they were not in any sense "ideas" but shapes moving in her mind, tones, a string of notes. Sounds and silences.

Tuesday the plane into Boston was only two hours late and she caught the last connection to the Cape. The small plane was enveloped in grey matter until it burst free in time for her to see the comma that was Cape's end lying there, a fragile sandbar on the waters. It was the color of a rabbit's coat and furred with grasses from which a winter sun and wind had stripped the thatching of snow already. So small, so beautiful, it took her by the throat as it always did, making a little triumph of every arrival, every homecoming.

By the next day, the remaining snow was thawing to puddles. Dinah burst out of her house. The cats chased each other around the yard. Willie was taking down a rum cherry that had developed ugly dripping knots. He started out in a pea coat and as the morning progressed, shed layer upon layer in the softening warmth until he was wearing only an undershirt. Across the pond, it was quiet. Tyrone had returned to the city. The outside work was done on the Captain's house, the noise of the workmen contained within.

The next week grew gradually warmer. Winter seemed to have come and gone. Dinah felt drunk with the sudden warmth, the soft wet January thaw that blew off the Gulf Stream and felt, not like the real Cape spring which was slow and inch by inch, but as if a ghostly visitation of the tropics touched their faces, a languorous humid fragrant breath. She relished moving around freely in the woods again. She and Susan took a long walk on the old road over the dunes, the badly eroded sand track the original Coast Guard had used to watch for wrecks and drowning sailors. Susan pointed out how much maroon and purple mellowed the winter landscape, the bearberry glinting in the sun, the arching canes of wild roses. The sand was shaded with garnet here and there. The beige grasses wrote with their tips a calligraphy of semicircles. Everywhere the dunes were softly rounded into the shapes of breasts and thighs and bellies, vast gentle planes of flesh. The poverty grass in its dense curliness made Dinah think of pubic hair, grizzled by the winter.

Sometimes they strolled in a miniature desert and sometimes they emerged to stand high over the ocean furiously chewing at the base of the clay and sand cliffs, the winter ocean that came so much higher and tore off chunks of land in every storm. Susan loved the ocean. Dinah could tell she, too, felt high on the clean soft air, glad to be outside to run around without their winter coats. They fell down in a saucer of sand heated by the sun to a temperature that felt more like May than January. Even in the summer few people climbed up here, and now, sheltered from the beach below and the old sand track, their only spies were the gulls who hung over them shrieking scandal.

They did not so much take off as loosen and selectively set

aside some of their clothes. Peaches. Apricots. Peonies, full rich many petaled peonies fragrant and silky. Susan. "It's one of the luxuries of the world to be here, now. Clean air, clean sand, us together." Dinah felt as if the sea were playing a long sonorous note on her bones, a secret vibration, the C far far below the keyboard, the kind of harmonic cloud La Monte Young created. The right harmonics through her body and her mind. Her friend, her love.

Susan arched her long neck. She liked to be kissed on the neck. Sometimes Dinah felt like a vampire and other times she thought of Figaro mounting Tosca, grasping her nape in his teeth, of the kittens Tosca had transported the same way. Susan's perfume filled Dinah's nose and mouth. "What an ear you have, Pretty, my pretty baby, my lady, my angel, what a delicate ear like a peach blossom."

Lately Susan, who had been so passionate in their early years that they had sometimes made love for two hours until both were sore and neither could move, often merely offered herself to be caressed and pleased, returning perfunctory gestures of affection. Oh, she went through the motions and Dinah came with her, but the zing was sizzled out. Today Susan rolled on top of her to suck her breasts and kiss her in those long serpentine movements of the tongue that melted Dinah to warm honey. She was so delighted that she stopped wondering at the change and swam in her delight.

Susan had her seasons and her cycles. Sometimes Dinah understood the causes of a particular trough of depression and sometimes it was mysterious to her, a fault opening in the earth where all had seemed firm in its integrity. Similarly, at times she could reach Susan and draw her out and other times nothing she did would avail. She thought of it as a pane of grey glass behind which her lover sulked. Then suddenly as today the glass was gone and Susan was with her, sensuous, warm, deeply comforting, healing Dinah into the richest silence she knew.

Afterward they sat on the top of the outermost dune watching the waves slide in below, sinuous, cracking the whip of their white backs over the hidden sandbars. Susan brought two yellow apples out of her jacket and bit into one, handing the other to Dinah. She had polished it till it shone, as the afternoon shone. Dinah felt simple with joy. Everything I want is here, now, that's all I want, she thought, just this, just to be alive now. Problems of being a woman composer, bad reviews, the question of offspring, all seemed as far away as Gibraltar across that glittering blue arc. Her life was filled to the top, quivering with light.

Susan stared and stared at the sea, content too, Dinah thought. Susan buried her core neatly in the sand. "Laurie wants to get some mileage on her Rover so she can take it in for the first checkup. She's driving down to New York this week to pick up some things before the buyers move into her condo. Jimmy's going with her. We could go too. . . ."

"To New York?" Dinah yawned, the sun on her face painting her closed eyes vermilion as she lay on the warm sand. "I'm chugging along on my new commission. I have some interesting ideas I want to work out."

"What would a week matter? Or only four or five days. I want to shop the January sales and I want to to see a play—any play. I want to dine in a splendid restaurant with sixteen waiters—Tyrone would take us out, you know he would. He always knows just where to go."

Nothing could sound less appealing. Dinah rose on her elbow looking at Susan. "I'm hot on my work now. Tuesday I have to be in Boston to sit in on a run-through of my Meditation. Why don't you ask Willie? There's always some gallery or museum show he's curious to see."

"I did ask him. He's just like you. He's in the middle of constructing a plastic bone heap and he won't be bothered to have any fun."

Fun, Dinah pondered. Willie was surely having fun if he was working well. She herself evaporated into composition when the flow was on, only to return to her forgotten life hours later with a sense of having been far and high and wide. Susan was a little bored with her designs. She needed some new stimulus. A craftsman in a matrix with two artists may want her work to do more for her and to the world than it can. Yet Susan was more successful as a fabric designer than Willie was as a sculptor.

Susan was shivering, she noticed. It was, after all, January and the sun had slid halfway toward the pines. Shadows spread out to where they sat as the sand began to relinquish its warmth.

"You could go with Jimmy. He's good company and you haven't had time alone with him in a couple of years."

"We wouldn't have time alone. He's helping Laurie. Sure, he wouldn't mind my coming along in the car but once he's in Manhattan, he won't want to hang around with me. He has his own plans. If it isn't Laurie he's after, and I surely hope it isn't, then he's about to look up some old girlfriend. Really, who'd have expected our Jimmy to grow up irresistible?''

"I suspect the keenest Don Juans were lonely nerds in high school. Not that Jimmy was ever that. But do you think he's interested in Laurie?''

"Of course not, Dinah, they practically grew up together. There's no romantic stranger in each other to fall in love with.''

"Was I a romantic stranger to you?'' She helped Susan into her jacket and they started along the dune road toward their own trail home. She wanted Susan to draw near her again.

"Oh, with women, that doesn't matter.''

"You just don't remember. You thought I was dashing and smashing when I got back from New Mexico.''

"Then you hit the road on a whim. You weren't such a home-body. You picked up that grungy pack you used to carry on your back and you were ready for wild adventure. You'd run off with me at a moment's notice.''

"I also wasn't performed then. All I ever did was play other people's music, and I never had the raw talent or the drive to be a virtuoso.'' Dinah liked to play and she played the flute excellently but not superbly, piccolo about the same, and another eight instruments with diminishing mastery. She was still on the road more than she liked, to direct or perform her own music, to coach, to lecture or run workshops. "Pretty, I travel for money and stay home for fun. Here is where I want to be.''

Susan was no longer listening. Instead of going arm in arm, she was walking ahead, tossing her head contemptuously. The pane of glass was back in place. Dinah kicked at the sand, disgusted. Maybe she could get Susan to come into Boston with her when her Meditation was performed. Nita had room for them to sleep over in the house she shared with another woman in Newton. Dinah hoped that a public performance in Susan's presence would glorify her in the eyes of her beloved. She sure needed some kind of help.

ELEVEN

Willie

Just a little after seven as Willie was finishing his coffee, the phone rang. He always shut off the ring upstairs so that if he had an early call—everybody knew he got up at six and had to be caught before he went to his studio—it would not wake Susan.

"Willie?" The voice startled him on first hearing because on the phone Johnny sounded exactly like Susan.

"Johnny, kitten, how are you? It's a pleasure to hear your voice."

"I'm fine, Dad. I've just got a new gallery. It's run by two gay men who are really into new art. They show some exciting stuff from New York and Paris and Berlin."

"Are they going to give you a show?"

"They promised me one in the fall, along with a sculptor. I've really got to produce in the next few months. I have a show in Rochester this August too. I sold two pieces in the group show over Christmas, so I got a new coat. It's leather all the way down to the ground, black leather outside and possum inside. I love it!"

"Every time you get a little ahead, you spend it. I bet you could live and paint for two months on what you put out for that coat."

"It makes me feel good. Besides, what's wrong with working? You always work construction when you need money."

"But maybe I'd get a lot more done if I didn't have to bother with construction. I've taken on two jobs for Tyrone Burdock, and there are times I surely wish I hadn't."

"I meet other artists when I mat and frame for them. . . . I had a postcard from Jimmy. So he and Lisa split?"

"Jimmy's staying here."

"He's gone back home? I don't believe it. What regression!" She sounded delighted. "Is he there? I should say hi."

"I bet he's up. Don't get on his back about Lisa. She tossed him out."

71

"I just think it's a riot he crawled back home to you and Mother. Really! How's herself?"

"Just dandy. How's your boyfriend, Aldo?"

"He just had an impacted wisdom tooth out, so don't ask me how he is or I may tell you."

"I'll fetch Jimmy for you, kitten."

"Willie, don't mention to Mother the paintings I sold. She always wants everything to be a big story. Who bought them, where do they live, she drives me crazy wanting to make a romance out of a business transaction."

While his children were teasing each other, Willie washed his breakfast dishes. He had not answered Johnny truthfully about Susan. Lately he could feel Susan knotting herself up. Actually that was too tactile. No, it was the feeling on a summer's day of the pressure dropping on you, the leaves lolling, the sky getting sulfurous, the congestion of an electric storm about to break open. Summers here were nothing like summers in North Carolina, where he had grown up. The spring and the fall were prolonged here, but summer was pretty much from sometime in June to sometime in September, just as the calendar said. Susan's moodiness was more like the immense thunderstorms of home. A storm took its time building. Then once it started, it took a long while to wear itself out and pass out to sea.

Christmas, the holiday season, had not satisfied her this year, although he did not know what could have been lacking. Johnny hadn't come home for the holidays in four years. She called him every few weeks, always early in the mornings when she knew Susan would not yet be up. Since Johnny had entered high school, she and Susan had been at war. In theory, Susan would have liked Johnny to come home; in actuality, the two of them would be fighting pitched battles every few hours.

Jimmy got off the phone and they scheduled their day. Willie wanted to try to finish the big piece he had been working on while Jimmy checked on their window order and picked up odds and ends they needed. Jimmy would also talk to the health agent again about the plans for the new septic system, and then check again with Tommy Rindge about when he could put it in, ground conditions permitting. The soil seldom froze more than a couple of inches around the pond, and during thaws, often the frost went out of it completely. There was a good chance if the Board of Health approved the system they were proposing, that Tommy and his bulldozer and his German shepherd (who always accompanied Tommy in his work, dashed all around the construction site and barked continuously so that by the end of the day the dog was always hoarse) could get the whole thing in the ground by the weekend.

He did not think about the phone call again until that afternoon when he knocked off work on his piece and joined Jimmy at the boathouse. Carpentry was perfect for brooding and mulling things over. Jimmy was not a compulsive talker. Sometimes they'd just play the radio and work. Willie liked talk programs; Jimmy liked rock. Willie figured he listened to what he wanted all morning, so mostly he gave in and let Jimmy play loud music.

Johnny was probably doing all right. Two pieces sold. Then she wasted the money on flashy clothes. He was surprised how well her paintings seemed to sell. He couldn't like them, no matter how much he tried. He found them ugly, even messy, full of words and images from ads and street graffiti and parts of bodies or inner organs. Still, he was proud that she stuck to her work and took herself seriously as an artist. At least she knew what she wanted to do in the world, and even if he couldn't enjoy her work, she did not seem to lack for places to show. She liked Minneapolis and she had been with the same guy now for a year, so maybe she had calmed down some.

She had always worked, during high school as a chambermaid and then as a waitress, during college in a fast-food place, more recently, matting and framing. She was quick, careful and very good. When he thought of her, he always saw her first as she had been in childhood, with her tousled fine light brown hair, her glasses repaired with tape because she was always putting them on the floor and stepping on them. Then he consciously called her to his mind as she was now, too thin, with spiked blue-black hair and contact lenses that made her eyes green, with enormous skull earrings and bracelets like chunks with holes for her arms, short leather skirts and multicolored jackets teetering on heels that lifted her to his height. It was as if she had made herself up, as he might make a cake out of flour and milk. She had taken a pleasant-looking woman with fine tousled hair and soft sweet face and created from her a comic book heroine, a costume party dominatrix. Yet he knew that as outré as he found her, she was still Johnny and she was not destroying herself as Susan thought. That was part of her image and her image was part of her success. So far, so good. She always had boy-friends. She always had good female friends too. Johnny was more ambitious then he was, than Susan was, far more than Jimmy. He had a secret desire to go out and visit her and see exactly what her scene was like these days, to watch her be shocking and successful in her world, but he knew that Susan would not go and would resent his going. Sometime when Susan went to New York for more than a couple of days, he would sneak off.

He ventured to ask Jimmy, "What do you think is bothering your mother?"

"She just has the wintertime blues. She's bored. Why don't you go to New York with her and stay at Laurie's old apartment before she sells it?"

"Because she's after me to get on with this job. . . ." He gave the wall a kick for emphasis. "And I want to finish off that big piece I've been doing. I'm hot on it. Why go to New York? Run into all those sculptors who patronize me. See work pushed I think is full of shit. See young artists who have one little shtick fussed over like geniuses."

"I think I'll go. I have some friends I need to see."

"You'd better ask Laurie about that."

"She already invited me. To share the driving. I don't have to stay in her place, I have other options."

This was the first he had heard of Jimmy going off. He felt slyly pleased, because he then could take the week off too from carpentry and just do his own work. Jimmy was secretive. Suddenly a plan would surface from him that he had surely been cogitating for days or even weeks. Obviously the conversation was over. Jimmy turned the radio back on and they resumed putting up the joists for the bathroom.

He hated the times when he felt Susan was working up her discontent. He liked peace at the core. He needed that. When she was unhappy, he felt guilty. Lately he had been dreaming of the big stairway at home. It rose gracefully in a coil for three flights, a perfect spiral with a many-paned dome of glass set in the roof over it. The house dated from 1820, and the staircase was a jewel of local architecture. Yet in his dreams he was climbing it in a whine of anxiety, up toward his mother who wept upstairs.

When he had that dream, his father was absent from it, his stern just father who was a lawyer—not a courtroom lawyer but what they would call nowadays a corporate lawyer, one with business interests in real estate and timber. His mother was beautiful in a pale blond lilylike way, with a high girlish voice and the appetite of a dying mouse. Yet she passionately enjoyed hunting. Her father had raised her in fox-hunting country of Virginia to take fences on a good jumper. There was little of that around North Carolina, to her everlasting regret, but she would go off on hunting trips with Willie's father and they would return obviously in love with each other again, a love that turned to irritation and silent battles as the intimacy wore off.

He was the youngest of three. The oldest was a sister Elinor; then his brother Ted and after a space of seven years, himself. Elinor was already at boarding school in the earliest coherent memories he retained. He was the baby, but Mother was his responsibility, making her happy, distracting her. He was in college before he understood her mood swings were caused by drinking. Mother was a quiet functioning alcoholic, and all those headaches and naps were simply when she passed out or was hung over. He felt as if he had escaped her, barely, and only because he had quarreled with his whole family when he was smitten by conscience as by a passionate affair and drawn into the civil rights movement. Once he had fallen in love with Susan, he interposed her between his mother and himself. He had never again seen his mother alone from the day he married Susan.

That did not mean that Susan did not sometimes make him feel just as trapped, as entwined in her rampant needs and moodiness. He would dream then of that beautiful staircase, the huge sculptured spiral of his parents' home that had first taught him about space and light, but instead of the pleasure he had often experienced in its perfect proportions, he was climbing it toward trouble he could not handle, toward guilt, toward a sickening sense of loss and confusion. Then he resented Susan.

He did not want to pay attention to her just now. He had a show scheduled for August in the co-op gallery in the village, and he needed a good breadth and depth of work. He wanted to concentrate on the shapes he could feel in the back of his mind. He wanted to stare at his tools and let his mind move on space sketching out the spidery tensions of metal he would create. He wanted to fix paper against metal. He wanted to finish the work on homelessness he saw as rags and bones and cement.

Let Dinah deal with Susan's problems just now. Why not?

They were always claiming to have some special understanding. Let them understand each other, then. He could not give up a week and risk a lesion of energy by going to New York. It might be exciting for Susan, but it would depress him. He liked to go to New York with a successful show under his belt, a piece sold in St. Louis or San Francisco, an interview calling attention to his work. Dinah was flying. With her new commission, she did not even need the boathouse job. It would have gone far more quickly if she were working along with them too. She was an excellent carpenter and almost as strong as Jimmy. He enjoyed working with her because they were companionably silent, as he often was with Jimmy, but they also discussed news, the political situation and debated issues in their respective arts intensely and excitingly. It was as good as a talk show. It passed the time and stirred him up so that often afterward he had good ideas, even if the shapes that formed had little to do with whatever they had discussed.

He understood why she wasn't helping renovate the boathouse, but he wished she would change her mind. If only the commission could be delayed for six months or if something would come up so she would work with him. It made for some of their best sex, those afternoons in somebody else's house, although of course with Jimmy . . . Still Jimmy ran errands often enough. The smell of sawdust roused him now to no end. Dinah wasn't there.

TWELVE

Laurie

Laurie couldn't decide if she hoped that Susan would accompany her and Jimmy to New York, or if she would prefer Susan stay home. Laurie was a little nervous at the idea of traveling with any man; but Jimmy she had known all her life and who her own age would she be less afraid of? Always he had been there summers, skinny freckled tagalong, the kid she could always fall back on when better company failed, and here he was playing that role again.

Susan could be relied upon to help her pack up and would

protect her from the shadows in the apartment, the fear she had that she would step into it and again find his, Tom's body. Oh, she had seen the coffin but in her mind he was still in their bed, where she certainly had no intention of sleeping. She had slept at Daddy's duplex from that dreadful night until she had left the city. Installing Susan in the apartment she had shared with Tom would reduce its menace, but perhaps Jimmy alone could do that.

The real reason she was uneasy about Susan's coming was that she liked Susan to stay where she belonged, in that vacation world where she was the warm, understanding and beautiful summer mother, not thrust into New York amid her friends and the people she had worked with and the galleries that would not show her and her real angry alcoholic mother in Queens. Susan was too fragile to penetrate the real world where Tom had died mocking Laurie and where she could not survive at present. Furthermore, Susan would expect Daddy to take her out and fuss over her. Laurie doubted he really longed to be hobbled with a guest from the country looking for a New York vacation; if he had time he could spare, she needed it herself.

All week she swang back and forth between wanting Susan to come to make packing easier and wanting Susan to stay here where she belonged, for the cross-patching of her worlds made her uncomfortable. Jimmy did not cause her the same distress because he had left the summer world, if not for New York, at least for some destination people did go off to. Seattle was at least a place of second level reality, like Chicago and New Orleans and Houston. It was respectable if not outstanding.

In the end, just she and Jimmy went. She drove as far as New London before she let him take over, but then he was competent. She resolved to let him drive more of the way on their return. They played the new Sting on the tape deck and gossiped about local kids and kids who used to visit her and what had become of them all, were they gay or straight, had they made it in some way, were they married, had they a baby or had they gutted themselves with drugs or settled someplace. He had picked up volumes of local gossip, especially considering the short time he had been back.

The only time he annoyed her was when he started to call old friends of his in New York. He seemed to think the car phone was a toy. The truth was, she didn't really need it. Daddy was on his all the time. He had decided that it was a safety feature for a woman, and so he had had it put in, but she had not used it yet. Jimmy's response to it was a little embarrassing and she did not care for his tone with the two women he called, flirty and familiar. Perhaps he sensed her disapproval, for after the second call he said no more about old friends and ignored the phone.

That forbearance pleased her. Tom wouldn't have responded to her disapproval by ceasing something; he would have proceeded twice as furiously. After all, it was her car, and she was allowing Jimmy to stay in the apartment she was unloading next week. She was rarely in a position of power vis-à-vis anybody, and it was rather pleasant to feel that Jimmy was on her sufferance and aware of it, from the way he guarded against her annoyance. She realized she had had a normal thought about Tom just then, not illuminated with that ghastly hindsight of disaster like lightning flashing to show the action in a horror film. For weeks she had not been able to remember her husband except in the rictus of his savage end. Now she had had a casual domestic memory that humanized him again, and she was silently grateful.

The answering machine in her apartment was full of messages, most for her but some for Tom—including weird communications she assumed had to do with cocaine. Hers were from friends or acquaintances who had heard and were being nosy. Three of the messages were from Rick Hobbs, whom she had gone out with before she met Tom. It was startling to hear him pushing her to see him. It had not struck her she was single, and there was Jimmy leaning on the marble counter that smelled chlorinated from the cleaning people, listening to the voice of Rick, the last man on earth she felt like seeing.

"Is that an old boyfriend?" Jimmy asked.

"How did you know?"

"The proprietary way he asked after you. Someone you care about?"

"We had a ghastly relationship. We formed this nasty dependency of mutual weaknesses." Now why was she telling him that? He would think her completely neurotic.

"He sounds like he wouldn't half mind having it back."

"Just from three messages?"

"Persistent, too. You have to figure out if you're interested."

In dismay she sat on one of the uncomfortable barstools that were the kitchen chairs. Was it all starting again, that high ten-

78

sion scene of dating and trying to meet men who weren't gay or married or serial killers? She wasn't safe, she wasn't married and above the fray. "I'm not! There's nothing to figure out." Again she envied the woman of an earlier epoch whose husband had died in similarly violent and disgusting circumstances simply withdrawing into a convent—not a harsh one, but one for gentlewomen for whom the world had become a bit much. Retiring with her lap dog and her lady's maid, never having to run a house or think about men again. Not to have to worry about weight or hair or skin or aging or whether some idiot liked her. She had lost years waiting for someone to call who never did, hanging around, not going to a movie, not going out to eat, not going for a walk, because suppose he called and didn't leave a message or called, and when she wasn't there, went out with someone else. The parties she politicked to be invited to because some particular *he* was reputed to be about to put in an appearance; or worse, only that some eligible man might conceivably appear.

"I can't wait to get back to the Cape," she said fervently.

He smiled slightly, leaning his braced arms on the counter. Susan, when she came to New York, was always voluble in her admiration for the way they lived, for Daddy's duplex and her apartment and the furniture and the artworks and where they dined and where they shopped, a sort of chorus of enthusiasm at each demonstration of their taste. Jimmy seemed to take it all for granted. She realized she had no idea on what level he had been living. The restaurant that had failed might have been a neighborhood beanery or Seattle's finest classic cuisine hot spot. If the car phone had made him look naive, he seemed quite in stride at present, asking her if she wanted him to fetch take-out so that they could get started on packing her up.

"Oh, I didn't know you were going to help me. That's awfully sweet of you. I thought you were just coming along for the ride."

"I wouldn't desert you. I'll have a good time anyhow, don't worry about me. I don't require worrying about. Would you rather just go out to eat?"

"I think I would. There's an art deco diner just near here I'm fond of. . . ." She stopped cold, realizing at this time of the evening people she knew would be there. She glanced at Jimmy. Certainly he was handsome enough to provide a reasonable es-

79

cort and his presence would protect her. But could she really face acquaintances?

"If you don't want to run into people you know, we can go downtown and eat Chinese," he said. "That should be safe."

She was startled again at how he read her face. "Let's do that." He was right. She did feel safe as they set out for a cab—she had left her car in the garage under Daddy's building, as parking was impossible on her street. She would not have to face anyone yet. When she returned to start packing, he would be with her.

That evening at ten he walked her to the corner and put her in a cab so that she could spend the night at Tyrone's. Daddy wasn't home yet, but she had her own key, and Celeste had made her bed for her and turned down the corner of the coverlet. Shortly after she had got into bed and started reading *Artforum*, Tyrone came home. He checked in with her, kissed her good night. In the morning he had gone to work before she was up, but he left a note on her breakfast plate.

Dearest Laurikin,

Keep your chin up and march on through this week. If Jimmy is useful, let him stay there, but if you feel crowded by him, we can put him in a hotel. Not to worry. Now remember, only remove the personal things you are concerned about. We have movers scheduled 8:00 a.m. Friday to clear out everything. They will do any gross packing required.

Love, Daddy

When she arrived at her old apartment, Jimmy was out. Never mind. Why should she feel disappointed? She could go through things ever so much more quickly and efficiently alone. The movers had dropped off piles of boxes. Last evening, Jimmy had taped up a row of them for her. Yet she felt exposed as she went up to the bedroom. She imagined that she could smell death, but what it really smelled of was Jimmy's after-shave. She felt all the discomfort she had anticipated. After fifteen minutes of not quite doing anything, she ran back downstairs and decided she would go through her old desk.

When Jimmy walked in around two, he seemed almost startled to see her, although she could not imagine why. It was as if he had forgotten she might be there; or forgotten she existed. Why wasn't she more memorable? It seemed to her she ought to be a much more romantic and sought after woman than any man had yet judged her to be. After all, she was thin, blond, young, reasonably well off and an artist, even if unrecognized. Yet life was always casting her in bit roles, backup, also-ran; even her own husband had kept a private life to himself.

Jimmy made a rapid recovery. Tossing his jacket on a chair, he rolled up the sleeves of his chambray shirt. "Let's start with the hardest part. Otherwise that will be hanging over you."

Together they climbed the stairs, Jimmy just behind her. The room felt smaller and drabber to her than she remembered it. "Celeste was supposed to get rid of his clothes, but I haven't been able to bring myself to look."

"That's the only closet?"

"His half was the right. I was on the left. Then there's a closet downstairs beside the bath. And the coat closet in the foyer."

Jimmy reported that the closet upstairs was cleaned out, as was Tom's chest of drawers, but downstairs, Celeste had missed his gear in both closets. Together they stuffed it into large plastic bags.

"Oh, I forgot. If there's anything of his you want . . ."

"Is there anything of his you want me to have?"

She thought about that. "No. I don't want ever to see his overcoat or his leather jacket or his Aquascutum again."

"Then let's chuck it all."

The phone rang. She cringed. "Unless it's Daddy I don't want to talk to anyone."

But the voice speaking out of the answering machine was female and asking for Jimmy. "Darling, I was out of town. But I got your message and here I am, dying to see you. Do get back to me. How long are you here? It's Kiki and you have my number. . . ."

"Kiki?" Laurie repeated, mistrusting her hearing. "That sounded a lot like the Cathy Porter I went to school with."

"She's kind of a model." He did not elaborate. Nor did he pick up the phone.

"But isn't that Cathy Porter? Her father's a lawyer, a good one. Daddy uses him. Her mother's a Morgan. She came out with her father to visit us a few times on the Cape."

"She doesn't get on too well with her parents," Jimmy said reluctantly.

"Is she an old girlfriend?" Cathy had certainly sounded that way on the answering machine, but when and how could Jimmy have had any romantic contact with one of the Porters? Cathy had never been all that friendly to Laurie, always condescending.

"Barely. I was hoping to borrow some operating expenses from her."

"Oh. I could front you some money if you need it." She thought she sounded very knowing, very cool. "After all, Daddy will be paying you soon. You could get an advance from him. For supplies."

"Willie's handling the negotiations. He gave me strict orders to keep out." Jimmy sketched a line in the air.

She had a sudden intense curiosity about how Willie compared as a father with Tyrone, but she could not think how to ask Jimmy. The packing went quickly. Basically she had to divide up the things she wanted to toss, what she wanted in storage and what she needed during the next six months on the Cape. Jimmy offered to get rid of Tom's stuff, which he carried out in bags. He was gone for two hours. She did not ask him how he had disposed of the clothing and personal effects, appreciating his tact in not volunteering to tell her when at last he returned, his hair slicked down with melting snow.

They were packing up her drawings. She did not trust anybody else to handle them. "I suppose you think I'm some kind of idiot, I could live with a coke addict and not even know it. I just thought he was irritable and had sinus problems."

Jimmy put his hand on her shoulder and squeezed. "No, and I don't feel superior, because I've been an equal idiot. Jackie was cooking the books for months, skimming our profits off, and I never suspected a thing."

"But she was just a business partner. Tom was my husband!"

"Yeah, well Jackie wasn't just my partner either. I mean, we were good friends. . . . In fact, we were involved."

"You were having an affair with her?"

"It wasn't exactly an affair, you know? Jackie was lonely, we were all putting long hours into the business. She needed a little love. That was all. I kept telling her she needed a real boyfriend, one of her own, but since Lisa didn't want to make love every day, what difference did it make?"

more. "And you others make your way round, through the garden. Post yourselves beneath their window, against escape."

Dulcet was stunned. "You . . . you knew they would be here?"

"He's got pages from *Arrivals Macabre* upstairs," Gil told Angorman. Newshield appraised the American.

"Yes, I harbored a very important patron when he was in need. He did not find what he sought in the loose pages he brought, and so left them behind." He smirked. "We would have taken you when you first came, but my aunt's chief servitor got wind of it somehow. He fled, and would have betrayed me. It took us all afternoon to track him down in the marshes. He perished with the Bright Lady's name on his lips, stupid zealot."

He turned back to his men. "You know what is expected. Bear up; within the hour, the Flaming Wheel will be on the wing to the Hand of Salamá. In one hundred heartbeats we will go in at them. Harrowfoot, you will stay here with the remaining men and guard these three."

They took torches and moved out, six to the staircase that led to the guest quarters, behind Newshield, and four more for the garden. That left eight in the dining hall. They waited with unsheathed swords, leaving no doubt what would happen if someone shouted a warning. Gil felt sick to his stomach, angry at himself, very much afraid.

Perhaps the other servants would help? No, not against so many men-at-arms. He felt a split second's pity for the hapless chief servitor, driven to desperate courage by faith in the Bright Lady, run to ground by horsemen and baying dogs.

Something clicked. Short on time, he didn't even stop to look for flaws. "Harrowfoot, you look like a reasonable guy to me." The man, hard-bitten ugly whose midsection had gone to paunch, glared suspiciously.

"I mean, who doesn't want to turn an honest profit?" Gil hastened. Angorman eyed him noncommittally, but Harrowfoot's interest had been piqued.

"What profit is that, witling?"

"Hey, listen, I'm not with these people. Why can't you

"We're both convalescents," he said. "Cracked eggs trying to hatch."

She laughed. It was a gruesome image but one that seemed right at least for her. "We should get the *Voice* and do something nice tonight. A treat. We deserve it."

"Good," he said, nodding. "Step one." A moment later, standing at the window, he whistled. "Scrap that plan. It's snowing as if the sky's ripped open. Actually I noticed headlines about a storm. Maybe we better turn on the radio and find out what's happening. You might want to head for Tyrone's while you still have a chance of arriving."

Already an inch of slush lay in the streets and the other side of the street was barely visible. Quickly she gathered up her things and prepared to flee. When she finally was sitting in a cab, she wondered to herself if now he would call Cathy Porter back.

THIRTEEN

Dinah

Dinah woke to Figaro's baleful glare and his weight on her chest as he hunched there waiting for her to get up and feed him. The room was dark but she had obviously overslept. No comforting greenish glow came from the clock radio that Willie had given her three Christmases ago, a KLH with terrific sound and an external speaker. The lamp beside the bed would not turn on and the air was crisp. The house was not quiet, however, as it often was with the power out, because the wind was shaking it, tearing at the old shingles on the roof, buffeting the pond side. The wind was driving the snow so hard against the eastern windows that she could hear it scratching the glass.

She did not feel like rising. With the furnace out, the house would be cold and damp. She would be entirely dependent on the ineffective fireplace and the tiny stove in the kitchen Willie had installed for just such times; she could not bathe or flush the toilet, for her pump would be off. It would be dark and boring. Tosca showed no desire whatsoever to budge, but dug her claws into Dinah's flannel nightgown to hold her in bed.

The winds were extremely high, gale force her battery operated radio tuned to the weather station informed her. They were predicting at least a foot of snow for the Cape and Islands. The melancholy postscript to the marine forecast was a fishing vessel lost out of Provincetown—caught in the violent onslaught of the storm, perhaps with engine trouble, trying to bring their catch in. She recognized the name of the ship, for one of the crew had been with the Captain, before he had lost his boat to the IRS.

She couldn't grind coffee beans, but she had a can of espresso for just such emergencies, along with a couple of gallons of bottled water. Her propane gas stove worked. She puttered about feeding the cats. For once Figaro did not ask to go out. The storm impressed him, crouched on the window ledge watching it swirl past until a falling limb from a pine thumping the roof sent him under the couch. There was a certain rugged coziness in making do, in carrying out the tasks the lack of power made suddenly arduous.

She had never been good at laying fires, but she finally got one going in the fireplace and one in the wood stove. Tosca claimed the spot between the stove and the wall to bake herself. Dinah gave herself a fast cat cleaning with a wet washrag, standing in front of the stove. Then she got her flute and her score and settled down to work, not in her usual spot in the livingroom by the windows on the pond but in the kitchen, where life would be carried on as long as the power was out. Because the kitchen was dim, she lit a kerosene lantern. Lanterns made her nervous. They seemed so easy to tip and break, spilling fire—Mrs. O'Leary's cow from grade school history.

She worked raggedly, just polishing what she had been doing the week before, not able to achieve the deep concentration she usually took for granted. The storm intruded. Never did she feel so at sea, so aware of being on a narrow strip of sand miles out in the ocean as during a storm. The world was gone except for the jaws that held and worried them. She decided to call Willie and Susan. It felt absurd to use the phone, but at least that did seem to be working. Maybe. She got a busy signal. To see if the phone was still functioning, she tried the library, then realized it was closed. Instead she called Burt, the librarian. He answered in a sleepy voice.

"Did I wake you? I'm sorry. I don't have anything urgent to say."

"It's so cold in here, we went back to bed. We dug the car

85

out and then realized the road's impassable and if we did go to town, we'd never get back. We've given up for the duration.''

"That sounds like the most intelligent response."

She stood at the kitchen window with the receiver in her hand. Still busy. She could not see the new house. Willie and Susan might have vanished. She was dependent on looking out the window at them a dozen times a morning. She read the chronicle of their activities in signs of woodsmoke, curtains drawn or opened, the thuck, thuck of ax on wood. It was a lazy way of maintaining contact while she worked, keeping her in touch without interrupting her concentration. Now the white wall of the storm stood between them.

The phone rang. She jumped on it, absurdly relieved. It would be Susan, with the same impulse that led her to call them. "Hello, am I speaking to Dinah Adler?"

"You are. Who's this?" She did not recognize the man's voice.

"Itzak Raab. I thought I should make contact. I'm delighted that the grant came through. I'm looking forward to playing your piece. I remember your quilt piece I heard at Aspen."

She felt like laughing for the absurdity of it, because it was hard to believe there was still a house forty feet away, let alone a world importantly humming with electricity offCape. "I'm excited about the suite. In fact I'm working on it already. It would be kind of helpful if we could talk at some point about what I have in mind. I'm calling it *The Cat in the Moon*."

"Let's see. I'll be in Boston March nineteenth with the BSO. Can you get in? How far away are you?" The voice was deep, rough and spiky, neutral in its accent. It didn't offer any information about origins, being neither particularly eastern or midwestern, not southern or New York, not European certainly. Bland in its accent as a radio announcer, but that rough voice didn't match. Nita had sent her a clipping from *People* followed by another brief mention in *Vogue*. Young, divorced, recently returned from many years abroad, Raab was getting big attention on the concert circuit.

"Today, years away. If there isn't a storm, I can make it in about two and a half hours by car. Where do you stay?"

"The Copley Plaza. How about breakfast or lunch on the twentieth? Breakfast would give us more time. I have a two-thirty flight out."

"Let's say ten."

"If you'd like, I can send you tickets for the concert on the nineteenth."

"I'd love that." She could stay with Nita, who would be playing.

After she had returned the phone to its cradle, she shook her head as if throwing off water. Would she really meet that voice at ten A.M. on the twentieth of March in a Boston hotel? She hadn't even asked him for his home number or his agent's, to get in touch. She was an idiot. It felt more and more unlikely. After Juilliard she had heard him once in concert, playing the Khachaturian with the Pittsburgh, and once at Aspen where they both had gigs, doing the Telemann C minor Sonata. Then he had gone off to Europe and based himself out of London for years. Only recently had he returned to the States with a large European reputation and that certain glamour required to make it with booking agents. She had some of his records, but she had not heard him live in over a decade. If she had had power, she would have put on the compact disc of his Mozart flute and harp, to make him more real to her.

She felt torn. She was eager to meet someone who played the flute that well. Moreover she wished to please with her work, to mesh with what he would be comfortable performing. Still she feared that any popular performer would try to tone down her work; his early feedback could be dangerous. She wished that the phone had been out, that she had thought of an excuse and begged off, that she had had at least the sense to provide herself with a contact number so that she could pretend to have the flu and cancel.

By one o'clock the snow was slowing; most likely, the eye of the storm was passing over. In a storm of this scope, a hurricane of snow, often a pause interrupted the blizzard before the winds could swing around from the other direction. She could see the new house now, huddled under a thick roof of white. How beautiful the trees were, branches bowed to the ground. Everything was made new and strange. She bundled up, hating the preparation it took to walk forty feet, but needing to see Susan and Willie and needing, too, to share her confusion from the call. When she opened her door, snow piled against it fell into the kitchen. Then she could barely push the door shut from the outside. Besides, she had felt cheated when she had told Susan about the commission, for her thunder had been stolen by Tyrone's arrival, and Susan had not fussed her up the way only

Susan could. Telling Susan about the call was giving her a second chance to celebrate and enjoy.

One of the pitch pines on the shore had fallen, uprooted by the gale with its root ball sticking black and hairy out of a drift. A grey birch was broken halfway up and hung, maimed. Her rhododendrons had taken a beating. Large leathery leaves were strewn over the snow.

It was absurd, an arctic trek in drifts over her boot tops where snow had piled up, barely four inches deep where the wind had scoured it off the rises. She lumbered along, then came into an area where Willie had shoveled a path, now half filled, toward the woodpile and his studio. She headed first for the house. Walking was easy in the rut of path.

"Susan? Susan! Willie?"

Their house was not as cold as hers, because Willie liked wood stoves and the one in the livingroom was big enough to heat the downstairs, with help from the gas oven that was lit. But there was no one in the house except Bogey, who bounded to meet her barking frantically.

Willie was in his studio squatting on the floor staring at a recent structure, a sort of igloo of bones hung with bits of cloth. She fell in and took off her boots before coming closer. Willie had a pair of tinsnips in his hand, and he was looking discontent. In fact he was glaring at his piece.

"What's wrong, love?"

"Do you think I'm repeating myself?"

Some idiot in a review had said that. "They just mean your work looks as if you did it. What are you supposed to do, change your line every year like a fashion designer?"

"Susan says I'm in a rut."

"You're always in rut, Willie bear, which is one reason I love you. But no, I don't think you're stuck. What brought this on?"

"Susan thinks I don't see enough shows."

"She's pissed neither of us wanted to go to New York with Laurie and Jimmy. Have you had lunch? Doing everything is so much work, why don't we all sit down and eat lunch together for once."

Willie looked around vaguely at his digital clock, which was blank. "I'm hungry. It must be past lunchtime."

"It's almost two."

"I thought Susan would be back by now—"

"Back? From where?"

"When it started to let up, she drove over to Tyrone's."

"My god, why? Are you both crazy?"

Willie got to his feet, dusting off his jeans. He gave one last mournful glance at his sculpture. "Tyrone called to find out if his house is all right. There's all sorts of nonsense on TV in New York about the Cape being cut in half, the sea pouring through, roofs caved in. She didn't go during the storm, anyhow. When the snow stopped, she took the truck over."

"I don't think even a four-wheel-drive vehicle can get through the drifts out there, but, Willie, it's just a lull in the storm."

"You think so?" He followed her to the door, stretching. "Maybe she's in the kitchen."

"There's no one in the house. I'm getting worried. When did she leave?" She felt the futility of the question. Willie never wore a watch and all of his clocks were electric.

Willie got into his gear and together they followed the tracks of the truck on foot along the buried road to Tyrone's. "I can't believe she did this," Dinah kept saying. "Going to check on the big house during a storm is just totally nutso!"

"The snow's starting again." Willie was beginning to worry. When anxiety took him, his features drew together in his face, giving him a pinched look. "I didn't think there was any problem. The snow had stopped and I figured if the truck got stuck, she could always walk back. I'd dig it out later on. She seemed so excited about going."

A trip to the house instead of New York, perhaps. "You were just placating her by agreeing, because she's been in a funk."

Willie shrugged. "Why didn't she just go to New York without us?"

"Maybe Laurie didn't insist. Maybe Susan felt she'd be intruding."

Willie grunted. "Jimmy had better keep his pecker in his pants with Laurie. She's high strung and barely treading water now."

"Our Jimmy is not noted for restraint. Nor have any of us set an example of the chaste life."

"Snowing harder," Willie said unnecessarily.

"Yeah." Wading through the snow took too much effort to talk more.

"She was in a backbiting fit today. Kept snipping at me. I thought the fresh air might do her good."

Dinah was panting too hard to answer, plunging through the

drifts. It was rough going and the snow was closing in on them. If it wasn't for the ruts, she wondered it they could find the road. It felt as if night were coming already. Certainly it was getting darker. Still they saw the truck and the tree that had fallen on it long before they could get to it. "Oh God!" Willie moaned. "Let her be all right."

When Dinah caught sight of the large pine, uprooted by the wind and fallen across the old Toyota, her heart clenched like a hand closing on spikes. Please, please, please. The tree had not landed across the cab but across the engine, although the windshield was lost in its boughs.

"We're going to have to cut her out," Willie said. "There are tools in the back if I can get at them. There has to be a saw. We need a saw." He bellowed, "Susan, we're here, we're going to get you out!" No answer.

Dinah shoved at the boughs. "She's alive!" At least now she could make out Susan mouthing at them frantically from inside the cab. Its front windshield was shattered and opaque. Susan was wedged behind the wheel. One door was smashed in but the other, on the driver's side, was simply held shut by the tree. Dinah broke the branches off wildly, trying to thrust her way through the fallen mass to Susan. But it was one thing to break brittle dead branches, another to attack the living green wood. The branches would bend but would not break. She forced her way through and then she was stuck, too, among fallen boughs and had to wriggle back out.

Willie had a saw and an ax, used when they occasionally poached hardwood. They both set to work. Sweat dripped down her back and between her breasts. After a few minutes she hung her parka on a partially severed limb and continued. It was getting darker and the snow was lashing her cheeks raw, clotting in her lashes. Her heart pounded in her throat as much from fear as from exertion. She was wringing wet.

The tree seemed to fight them. Dying it clutched the truck. Her imagination was as overheated as her body. Willie was far cooler and more effective in his attack. That slightly phlegmatic side of him was most valuable at a time like this as he switched off ax and saw with her, each taking turns. Gradually a path through the boughs opened up. She could see that Susan was bleeding. Dinah grew more frantic but also more focused. At last Willie grabbed the door handle and pulled it open. Susan fell out into his arms, crying. Her face was streaked with blood, her poncho spotted. Her hand hung crookedly. Between them they dragged her free of the tree. It was a dim twilight with snow swirling around them. If we can't find our way back, we'll all die here, Dinah realized. Sight was useless. She put her parka back on.

"Can you walk?" Willie was bellowing over the wind.

"I can't feel my feet! They're frozen!"

"We'll get you home," Dinah promised, taking half Susan's weight around her shoulders and staggering onward with the load.

"They'll amputate my feet," Susan moaned. "My feet are dead."

Between them they supported her and went stumbling through the drifts. Susan was sobbing and seemed only half conscious. Obviously she had banged her head. Dinah was still terrified. It seemed to her they made no progress through the snow and the gathering dark. Fortunately the snow was not yet as heavy as it had been during the night, although the wind was gathering force. Her own face felt frozen. Her sinuses ached. Her feet were numb in her boots and her fingers had died. Her eyes teared constantly. Every few steps she stumbled and several times went down, getting wetter.

They went on and on and on. "Are we lost?" Dinah asked repeatedly, and evenly Willie answered, "We're following the truck prints backwards."

They were actually at the house and Willie was kicking open the door before she realized they had come out of the woods, because no lights were on. They staggered with Susan limp and moaning between them into the dark cold livingroom where the fire had long ago gone out, and there they collapsed.

FOURTEEN

Susan

Susan considered her accident one of those ultimately trying situations in which everyone's best and worst characteristics stood out in plain relief. Willie was truly useful but also his withdrawn self. He could not bear to acknowledge she had been

91

in real danger and thus busied himself with incidentals and arrangements.

But Dinah was impossible, her most irritable and imperious. You'd think Susan had had an accident especially to give Dinah a bad day.

"How could you be such a fool! Going out in the worst storm in five years in order to reassure Tyrone? Have you gone completely bonkers?"

Susan was in bed. The power had come back on suddenly as it always did, with the water gushing from the hiccupping faucets, every light in the place blazing in the middle of the night, the radio blasting out, the digital clocks Willie loved all blinking maddeningly 12:00 12:00 12:00 and the phone ringing two minutes later, Burt asking, "Did you get your power?"

At least it was warm. She had been treated for frostbite and her skull had been x-rayed—no fractures except for her wrist. She had been barely conscious, but Dinah had summoned the rescue squad, led in by a snowplow, and Susan had been taken off in an ambulance. Now she was home again tucked into her proper bed with the cushions piled up, five stitches in her forehead that wouldn't show under her hair if she combed it right, her left wrist in a cast, her feet bandaged and what must Dinah do but scold her as if she were an erring cat who had taken a chickadee. Dinah's occasional sternness had wrung tears from her often enough; but no more. She had used to think Dinah's temper was the other side of her passion. "What are the chances of a tree falling on anyone?" Susan asked rather amiably she thought. She was determined to set an example of fortitude and good temper. "One cannot conduct one's life trying to avoid absurd accidents, such as lightning striking and church towers falling on one's head."

"Only an idiot stands under a big tree in the middle of the field in an electric storm, and only an idiot goes out in a blizzard. If someone's life depended on it, if you were on the rescue squad, I'd understand."

"Weren't they sweet? I didn't know Wendy was a paramedic." She thought Dinah looked fetching this afternoon, wearing a finely knit black sweater. Susan hadn't tried making love yet. She wondered how it would go with her wrist in a cast. It would be easier with Dinah than with Willie. Should she suggest giving it a try? She smiled. She was about to give Dinah an unexpected present. She felt relaxed, generous, sensual in spite of her bruises and pains. Everyone had been warm and caring to her.

"She's the best they have," Dinah said parenthetically in her normal voice before resuming her rant. "But to go out in the worst blizzard in five years just to make sure some millionaire's cottage hasn't lost a shingle?"

"When a neighbor asks a favor, I try to oblige. Tyrone has done numerous favors for us." Her gaze came to rest on the Fleur de Fleurs he had given her for Christmas. Who else would give her French perfume? It was just the sort of luxury she needed and constantly missed. Perfume wasn't really a luxury, but something her body required to feel dressed. On the bedside table were the lavender roses he had sent that afternoon, just opening. He knew how to be gracious, which was more than she could say for Dinah. She suspected that Dinah wanted her to be humble and grateful, as if Willie couldn't have rescued her anyway and of course they came after her. It was like thanking somebody for flushing the toilet after themselves or for cutting the bread. Naturally they came after her and she was damned glad to see them, but did Dinah think Susan would not have done the same for her? If somebody went on at great length about their own virtues, it seemed superfluous to commend them.

"Not so numerous as he asks in return. What kind of self-important ass asks you to go check his property at risk to your life?"

"Tyrone is a sensitive caring man and a real friend! If I choose to return his favors with a favor he asks, you have absolutely no right to question my choice! It was a ridiculous accident, a tree leaping on me! Who expects to be attacked by trees? It's as if I were walking down Fifth Avenue and a cornice fell on me." Susan caught sight of herself in the mirror that faced the bed. She looked battered but not impossible, raffish perhaps, waif-like. The bandage would come off soon and the stitches vanish. She saw herself in a large floppy hat. Dark bottle green. How could she hope to find such a treasure out here in the woods. She had never tried to make a hat. That would be amusing. Tyrone would admire it and she would tell him how the bandage had made her think of it.

"Susan, how can you lie there smirking as if you'd done something clever! You almost committed idiot's suicide. Your values have gone whacked. If Tyrone's house had fallen down, what bloody difference would it make?''

''You'd be glad! I'm surprised you haven't burned it down yourself! You hate when anybody lively or intelligent arrives here. You'd like me locked up in the woods all twelve months of the year with no one to talk to but a dog and you and Willie! You'd like me growing moss on my side like some oak. I am not yet ready for a premature retirement to doddering old age.''

''Susan, it wasn't cute. The truck is smashed. You got badly banged up and you're lucky to be alive. Can't you admit it when you've fucked up?''

''It isn't your truck. And you're simply jealous of Tyrone. You think nobody should have more than you have. You resent his style and you want me to pretend he doesn't exist and that he isn't one of my dearest friends.''

''Susan, that's silly. That's the serf touching his cap in the field talking about his intimacy with the grand seigneur. Tyrone uses you. You're more convenient, cleaner and smarter than Ozzie Dove. That's all.''

''Don't try to separate me from my friends, Dinah Adler! You're secretly a very possessive bitch. You simply don't want me close to anyone else. You're afraid you can't compete!''

''Susan, you have a pitiful crush on Tyrone, but his relationship to you only differs from his relationship to that Haitian maid in that he doesn't pay you a salary, but you do it for nothing!''

''Bitch! Liar!'' Susan grabbed the vase of roses and threw it at Dinah, who ducked but was splashed with water. The vase, Victorian marbleized glass, broke into a dozen shards. Susan began to cry furiously. ''Get out of my room! Get out!''

After Dinah had left, she dragged herself out of bed to rescue Tyrone's poor flowers from the mess of spilled water and broken glass. She was not displeased when she cut herself, a minor gash on her finger that bled profusely so that when Willie came running in, he was upset with Dinah as well as with her. He finished cleaning up the mess, put the flowers in a new vase. Her finger stopped bleeding, although she sucked it when he was out of the room. She needed a bit of nice fussing over after Dinah's nastiness.

''What she calls love,'' Susan pronounced at seven when Willie brought her supper tray, ''has become more and more the attempt to control both of us. To make us live just as she finds

94

convenient, without regard to our desires, our tastes, our relationships with others—or with each other."

"You're really mad at her." Willie was eating on the floor, stretched out on his elbow on the beautiful little country knotted carpet she had found at a yard sale, a lamb in a circle of daisies. Very few men his age could sprawl on the floor that way and look as natural as Jimmy would have.

"You bet I am. You don't see how manipulative and controlling she's become, sweetheart. For instance, she won't work with you on Tyrone's renovations. Now we both know that you need that gallery. If she thought of anyone but herself, she'd pitch in."

"I looked at the house on Main Street last week. That space would be great for sculpture. The ceilings are high. With skylights in the roof, the upstairs gallery could be perfect."

"Just what you need. You're getting in on the ground floor, helping Laurie set it up. Why couldn't Dinah see that? Because she isn't thinking about us. She's thinking only about herself. . . . She accused me of being in love with Tyrone! Can you imagine? One of our oldest friends." As she spoke she felt the same hot stab of pain she had felt when Dinah had first accused her. Her eyes burned with a silly desire to cry, from humiliation and the unfairness of it. Really, Dinah was a person she had thought of as knowing and loving her. She was beginning to realize Dinah had masses of unresolved anger floating loose in her—poisonous envy, possessiveness, jealousy—which had been allowed to grow so strong that now Dinah was unable to perceive Susan clearly. Of course she loved Tyrone, but it wasn't romantic love. She had known him far longer than she had known Dinah, in fact; here was Dinah trying to push an older friend from her life. Dinah was behaving just like a possessive husband; but Dinah was not her husband. She had her own husband.

"Why did she say that?"

"Because she's jealous of him, that's it in a sentence. She loves to be the center of attention, and when he's around, she can't be. Don't you think she sometimes absorbs a lot of the attention we'd pay each other? That sometimes she just bumps in between us and we end up all the time worrying about what Dinah wants, what Dinah thinks, what Dinah needs. . . . Don't you sometimes feel you don't get enough of my attention?"

Willie was frowning at his emptied plate.

95

"What's wrong, sweetheart? Did what I say upset you?"

"I was trying to remember how it was before Dinah. I don't think it was so good for us."

"That was years ago, lovey. We're much more mature now."

"I didn't realize how angry you were with Dinah," he said slowly, looking at her with that air of resignation she knew so well.

"She thinks she can dump her anger on me. Because I'm a softer, gentler person than she is, she can just use her loudness and her temper and her strength as a weapon and simply push me where she wants me. I don't like being browbeaten, Willie, and I'm fed up with her attempts. I'm serious." She could feel her love for him strongly tonight. Sometimes that old attraction got lost in the bustle of domestic activity, all the minutiae of problem-solving, of housecleaning, shopping, laundry, cooking, bill-paying, saving and spending, and then Willie was no more sexually attractive than the canister vacuum cleaner or the coffee machine. Then she would suddenly perceive him, as now stretched out on the lamb rug like a domesticated lion, a tall good-looking sweet-natured man with whom she had had two children and with whom she had grown up, essentially. No wonder Dinah fantasized about having children with him.

Susan could feel her desire for him seeping back like sweet red wine, like mulled wine spicy and hot and tipsy. Such a powerful and supple, such an adaptable relationship between them, it had survived not only her having an affair with a woman as compelling and tempestuous as Dinah, but his involvement with Dinah also. A bond, a marriage as strong as theirs, could survive equally well the end of that triangle, if Dinah did not restrain her temper and her overbearing need to control. "Willie . . . come lie beside me here. Let's keep each other company."

FIFTEEN

Dinah

Dinah could no longer enter the new house. Susan would ostentatiously sweep from the room, locking herself in her bedroom until Dinah left. In order to see Willie, she went to his studio or waited for him to come to her. All of a sudden she saw Susan only in glimpses, and she saw Willie by appointment or by descending on him. They didn't eat supper together; she no longer cooked alternate nights in the new house. She could not have imagined that their life together might so abruptly cease, stranding her without an easy opportunity to sue for peace with Susan. She kept expecting Susan to tire of pouting and welcome her with a hug. Nothing had happened that could justify such a radical break.

"I've got into trouble all my life from being opinionated," she said to Willie's back. Willie was trying to get on with a new piece, a great lump of amber plastic with aluminum spokes jutting out. He had put aside the huge bone house almost completed before the storm. Even though Dinah thought the new effort looked arbitrary and ill-conceived, reminiscent of cartoons of mines, her habit of freely criticizing had got her in so much trouble, she confined herself to encouraging noises when Willie asked how she liked it. "I used to get tossed out of social studies in high school for shooting off my mouth. Always I have some opinion burning holes in my tongue. But why does she stay mad at me?"

He was hammering on one of the embedded spokes, trying to flatten or bend it, she could not tell. He did not turn or answer.

She wasn't going to give up. Susan was still speaking to him; in fact they seemed to be getting on fine. He had to help Dinah. He had to make her understand why Susan had withdrawn, and furthermore, he had to make Susan see her. "Why is she doing this now, Willie? I have to know. People don't just stop loving each other on a whim."

"I think she wants you to apologize," Willie said slowly. He got up and sat in a director's chair, pouring himself a cup of coffee from a bright red thermos Dinah had given him.

"For what? Helping to save her life? Not kissing Tyrone's ass?"

"She thinks you want to control who we see. That you're trying to run our lives." Willie was avoiding her gaze, staring into his coffee as if it were full of little swimmers running races.

"But that's ridiculous!"

Willie stared into his cup.

"I don't like Tyrone. But I go along to his house, I cook when we have him over with his current wife. I put in an appearance at his parties."

"Tyrone is an old friend. We've known him for eighteen years, Dinah. You have to understand that when you attack Tyrone, Susan feels attacked too. They've been close forever."

"Let's not rewrite history. It's only since his last marriage broke up that we have Tyrone in our hair all the time. His most recent wife didn't like the Cape, and in fact they spent two summers in Scotland. Am I the only one who remembers life three years ago?"

"That was just for a couple of years. I didn't like her much. Glenda," he said as if pleased to remember her name.

"She wasn't too memorable," Dinah said sourly. "But she did have the advantage that she kept Tyrone offCape."

"See, you can't control your hostility toward him, even talking to me."

"Why should I? Who can I be honest with, if not with you?"

"You're giving way to jealousy. You have to try to control it."

"Willie, he's a rich jerk. If I'm jealous, it's only because Susan makes such a fuss over him." She was dismayed to realize she had now got into an argument with Willie about Tyrone. That was not at all what she had intended.

Willie had finished his coffee and was hunched in his chair glaring sullenly in the direction of his sculpture; now she was put in the position of being a distraction, an interruption. She had always been as careful not to intrude on Willie's work as she had been to keep Susan from intruding on hers. Yet if she left now, everything was worse. What choice did she have? She must abandon the field today and try again tomorrow. "Wouldn't you like to go truck shopping tomorrow? I've been marking ads in the papers."

"Jimmy found an eighty-three Ford. It doesn't have four-wheel drive, which may kill us in the winter, but the price is right. The bed's rusty but the body's in good shape. It's only got fifty-two thou on it."

As she crossed the yard, she felt awkward, runty, cast out. So she didn't like Tyrone; Susan found the Moonsnails unendurable socially. Like Mark before her, Susan found Dinah's playing in a rock band déclassé. Dinah couldn't take that seriously from Susan. She didn't take the band seriously either. After all, she had once been part of a real band. But she had needed a gig to support her without draining the vital juices of her creativity, and the Moonsnails had been precisely that. Susan was shocked whenever she walked in and Dinah was playing a hiphop record, and if Dinah tried to explain why she found the percussion exciting, Susan would think she was trying to excuse bad taste. Susan only liked rock music popular before she left New York.

Maybe she'd given herself license to be too loud about her dislike for Tyrone. But never, never had she taken Susan's attachment to him seriously enough to soft-pedal her opinions. Susan was her lover, not a casual friend she had to be polite to over tea. How had it happened? She was still reeling. When she caught sight of herself in a mirror, she stared, as if to read what had gone wrong. Her face looked like her face, only rumpled and drawn. She saw instead Susan's face, that apple blossom look she wore when happy, the way her face grew hot and ruddy when she was close to coming.

Everything reminded her of her loss, the rupture of her life. She no longer did her laundry in Susan's washer and dryer. It was multiplying. Soon she would have to drive to a Laundromat. She had not used one in so many years, she was vaguely aware the closest was a couple of towns away. All the nearer ones had been shut down for polluting the water table. Under the Cape was a finite aquifer, with salt water bearing in from all sides. Water and land were precious and fragile here. She let her dirty clothes pile up, waiting for Susan to take her back, but now she was running out of underwear. She hated to acknowledge that she was truly thrown out by asking the location of the current Laundromat, but she had no choice. Her last fairly clean pair of socks was on her feet for the second day.

When she finally got back four hours later with her folded laundry, she became aware the moment she walked in that someone was in her house. The kitchen light was on and the rocker moved nearer the table. Susan at long last? Like most Cape people she never locked her door in the winter. Susan had finally come to her senses and returned to her. "Susan?" she called. She felt as if she had grown a foot taller.

Susan was upstairs but did not respond as Dinah climbed the narrow steep staircase. Her bedroom was lit by a gable facing the pond, but the last sun had drained from the east. The room was dark except for her stained glass lamp, made by the Moonsnails' drummer in a crafts phase. It was not Willie and it cer-

99

tainly was not Susan propped in bed with the corduroy bed rest behind him.

"Jimmy." She was so disappointed it was difficult to keep that from her voice, but her fantasies weren't his fault.

"I had a row with Mother about you this afternoon, so I decided to drop in while I'm p.n.g." He was sitting with a cat against each thigh. Animals liked Jimmy. Cats, dogs, horses—all moved toward him.

Persona non grata, she supplied, taking the window seat in the gable. She pulled the thick velvet curtains shut, as the wind was tweaking the old wood. The glass behind her radiated a chill. "Why did you fight about me?"

"Because I'm not prepared to write you off."

"Is she?"

"Sure sounds like it. What went on between the two of you while I was in New York?"

She started to tell him in laborious detail her version of the storm, but he interrupted her. "I can't remember if I ever met Tom—Laurie's husband. I was out on the Coast when they married. What was he like?"

Dinah squinted into a dark corner of her room. "I only met him a couple of times here. He was tall with an arrogant manner." She didn't want to admit how little attention she had bothered to pay him. She was keenly aware of her shortcomings. Her failure to pay attention to most jerks she met socially was seeming more of a vice than a convenience. She felt to herself like a person who has been knocking around cheerfully and has broken everything in sight without noticing. "Are you interested in Laurie?"

"I feel sorry for her," Jimmy said. "But not in any paternalistic way." He crooked his hands behind his head, cuddling up to her corduroy pillow. "She hasn't fucked up her life any worse than I've done to mine. I have a fellow feeling for her of two people who've got a long way to climb before they can see any light."

"Me too," Dinah said sourly. She could not find the tone she frequently adopted with Jimmy, of fondly overlooking his peccadilloes. "How could Susan cut me off this way? How could she just stop caring and slam the door?"

He grinned. "That's what I've been asking about Lisa. And you didn't even make Susan pregnant."

"I guess I'm miserable." Dinah felt as if she had finally

named the weight in her, this vast soggy thing she had been carrying around like a load of wet laundry in her head. She felt immediately guilty. All her life she had said to herself that unhappiness was self-indulgence. Perhaps she was always secretly comparing herself to what her father had gone through so that she felt nothing that happened to her was really bad. She felt a sanction laid on her to be cheerful in minor adversity, with the unsaid proviso that any unhappiness of hers was by definition minor.

"Join the club of the merely human." Jimmy was obviously enjoying her weakened state.

"How haven't I been human?"

"You've felt for years you'd found your own solution. You had it made."

"That's true." Once again Dinah tasted that sharp mustardy disbelief. How could she have suddenly lost what she had treasured? She could see Susan sitting where Jimmy was, so vividly both faces hung superimposed. "I had what I wanted. I still want it!"

"People change," Jimmy said sententiously. "Can we have supper soon? I'm hungry. The level of cuisine isn't so high these days with Willie cooking every night." Jimmy called Susan Mother, but since he had reached what he considered adulthood, around sixteen, he often called Willie by name.

Dinah decided she would cook for him; she had been eating out of cans, an occasional omelet, expecting that the situation would be resolved and she would dine with what had been for a decade her family. It would be healthy and soothing to sit down to a genuine meal.

She realized as she was putting supper together, that she had become accustomed to the range of gadgets in the new house. However much she teased Willie, she was used to tossing the onions in the Cuisinart rather than chopping them by hand. She was used to having a salad dryer. She had trouble lighting her elderly oven with a match. She had not bought a new pan in fifteen years. Hers were chipped and battered. Domesticity was going to be bumpy for a while.

"You're not sleeping with Laurie, then?"

He shook his head. "I'd have scared her out of her skin if I'd made a move. Besides, I have an old flame in New York. Nothing serious, but enough left to satisfy me when I go down there."

"That's good," Dinah said fervently, "because if you think

101

Susan's mad at me, that's nothing to what they'll do to you if you get mixed up with Laurie.''

Jimmy shrugged. "I'll play out that hand if it comes to me, but I'm not looking for it. She's a scared little girl . . . You going to make some music for me tonight?''

Of all of her family on the pond, Jimmy was the one most interested in her music. He had a better ear than anyone else in the family, and he genuinely enjoyed listening to her. That had been true even when he was a kid. It was a bond between them. What she did was far more real to Jimmy than it was to either of his parents. Twice when works of hers were being performed on the West Coast, he had turned up—with Lisa once and once with their bookkeeper. It had been a delight to see him, to share her minor triumphs with her own family.

A mid-February storm shifted to freezing rain as it wound down, crusting the snow with a glaze of ice. Driving was bad and walking was impossible. Dinah was feeling lonely, especially as the light petered out. She missed long talkative evenings by the fire in the new house. At noon she stuck her head in Willie's studio and asked him if she could come by at three, if he thought he'd be finished. He said when he was knocking off, he would signal her.

That didn't happen until four, after she had stopped work an hour before and sat watching his studio across the deeply rutted drive and yard between the houses. She had taken a bath, slipped on her most seductive silky sweater, brushed her hair five times, tweaked her eyebrows and applied bronzy lipstick. Then she added a pair of big metal earrings Willie had made for her years ago, when he had a notion to launch a line of handmade jewelry in local galleries. She was holding tight to Willie. As long as they were still involved, she had her foot in the door, she belonged somewhere.

Just because Susan was temporarily angry with her, why should that ruin her relationship with Willie? After all, she had an independent loving bond with each of them. Susan often withdrew into depression, so why should Susan's alienation affect the pleasure she and Willie took in each other's company? In some ways, as serious working artists, they had more in common with each other than either had with Susan.

She came teetering across the glazed ruts in her high-heeled boots, her least sensible but most attractive pair. Halfway across she skidded and banged her knee, hard. Tears stood out in her eyes for a moment but she soldiered ahead. To complain would call undue attention to how much care she had taken with her appearance.

Willie was sitting backward in a chair glaring at his piece. He had spent the afternoon hammering the spokes awry. Whatever effect he had been aiming for had not been attained. The piece looked more accidental than ever. The big skull igloo had been moved to the back, next to the oven where he softened plastic before bending or molding it. It seemed to radiate powerful anguish, towering over this spiny lump.

She sat down on his couch, seductively she hoped. It had been many years since she had wondered if she was attractive. "You don't look happy," she said mildly, patting the couch. "Would you like a glass of wine?"

"Sure." He sighed and sat down beside her, dropping his arm around her shoulders. "I'm trying something new but I haven't got hold of it yet."

"But, Willie, don't you think you're overreacting to Susan's criticism? She was mad at you because you didn't want to see a show in New York enough to accompany her. She was just getting back at what she felt was disloyalty."

"Susan says you act with her the way men traditionally act with women. That you dismiss her criticism as emotional reactions," Willie said gravely.

"Do you think that's true?" Dinah had the feeling once again things were slipping away from her, plunging downhill. She sidled closer to Willie. Her capacity for seduction had always been slight. She was so busy trying to move closer in a subtle manner she did not hear what Willie was saying until he had run down and was staring morosely at his amber mine, which now looked run over by a truck. She had the sense that Willie had been fulfilling an obligation; he was carrying to Dinah a load of complaint entrusted to him by Susan. Later Susan would ask him if he had told Dinah what she had said to him.

"Willie, Susan has to talk to me face-to-face if she wants to complain. She can't send messages through you. This has to be between Susan and me directly, and you can't let yourself get caught in the middle."

"Oh, great. You've been asking me to squat in the middle. The moment you see me, you ask me what's she's saying, what she's doing, when she'll see you. You keep telling me I have to make her talk to you. Now you tell me to stay out of your quarrel.''

''I've been selfish. I'm sorry,'' Dinah said in a soft apologetic voice she realized she had not heard from herself since Mark died. ''I've been putting you in a bad place.''

''It makes her furious. She thinks I'm taking your part.''

Are you? Dinah wondered. She slid over and sat on his lap, putting her cheek against his. It felt awkward. For a decade she had been making love with this man at least three times a week, and now she felt illicit, embarrassed in approaching him.

Willie responded slowly, as if reluctantly. Then he seemed to get into it. She did not worry much until they were both naked on the couch and she bent down to take him in her mouth. He was flaccid, the soft worm of his penis flowing away from her among his still golden pubic hair. The hair around Willie's genitals and under his arms was still the pale yellow his hair must have been before it turned prematurely white.

She took him in her mouth and tried to bring him to life, but after a few minutes, he stopped her with his hand on her head. She did not have to ask him why, because he was questioning himself. ''I think it doesn't feel right. It's as if I'm seeing you behind her back.''

''After ten years, suddenly it's adultery?''

''I know she doesn't want me to be with you. She doesn't have to say so. I can feel her resentment.''

''But why? Why does she have to take you from me too—after taking herself from me?'' Dinah's eyes began to ooze tears slowly.

''It just doesn't feel right now. It's like something secret.''

She felt utterly defeated, pulling her clothes on as if her nakedness had become shameful. Willie's virtues stymied her. He was simple in the best sense of that word, clear, true, solid, complete. He did not want to cheat on anybody. He didn't want to lie or pretend. Their relationship had been perfectly open; now it was shut.

SIXTEEN

Laurie

Finally Willie and Jimmy had begun work on converting the boathouse to a little house for Laurie. The town was making Tyrone put in a septic tank for the new building, which she thought absurd but there was no getting around it. Fortunately February turned mild and the snow cover melted off. The ground was sandy where the new system was to be. One morning the backhoe arrived to dig the hole. The health agent took another week to inspect the tank in situ, before the hole could be closed and the sand thrown back. Laurie felt enormous relief when the big machine scraped away down the sand road and she was left to herself—except for Willie and Jimmy, who were practically family.

She didn't need the boathouse till summer, so the speed of the work was hardly critical. She was living in the family house, using the bedroom that had been hers since childhood, through all the different apartments of her mother and Tyrone. She was frankly more eager for work to begin on converting the house Tyrone had bought in the center of town into a gallery, but some weird local finagling was holding that up. The town boards kept making demands about parking and zoning that just seemed obstructionist. She let Willie handle it until one hearing when Tyrone was in Japan and she had to go. She really didn't follow the arguments about drainage, runoff from asphalt versus gravel, about congestion and previous use—they all seemed deadly serious—but they were kind to her. Obviously her story was so notorious even the locals pitied her.

She was surprised to watch the four men and the woman on the board chatting with Willie and Jimmy and obviously having some ongoing relationship with the local one-horse lawyer Tyrone was using. She had never thought of the town as active in the winter, having a life of its own. Obviously they recognized her, but she had not even known they existed, local builders and businessmen. One ran a gallery and another an inn. The woman was a retired professor from Smith. Hers was the third case on the evening's docket, following a hearing about horses being kept in town and the case of a man who wanted to expand his boat-repair yard. This was apparently the second time the gallery proposal had come before them, after Tyrone, the architect from New York and Willie had redrawn the plans to meet previous objections.

Beside her, Jimmy murmured a steady commentary on the cases and the personalities involved. This one was the offspring of New York intellectuals who had come to the Cape to drink themselves to death, and had left the boy almost destitute and without the money for an education beyond two years at the community college. Now he was working in a gas station. That one was a millionaire on paper, although always short of cash, a hot developer who had parlayed an old moneyless Cape family's land into a mortgage pyramid to finance his building. That one had been having an affair for the last ten years with the town nurse, who was married to the lawyer. Those two old men had not spoken in thirty years; each spent his time in litigation trying to prevent the other from expanding his business. Here was a Boston lawyer using conservation law to prevent a retired postal worker from building a modest house that would diminish the view of an accountant and his rich wife. It reminded her of going to some gathering with Tyrone and having him fill her in on past histories, affairs, animosities, so that she could conduct herself accordingly. Actually, she seldom conducted herself any particular way, being too shy to maneuver at a party. Tyrone told her those stories to entertain her, and also to show off how much he knew. Jimmy was doing the same.

Jimmy did not care for living at home. She understood, although Tyrone caused her no problems. If she had to live with her mother, she would go out of her mind. Jimmy was spending lots of time at Dinah's little house, where he ate every night. The old triangle had finally broken up, and Dinah was obviously at loose ends. Laurie wondered briefly if Dinah could be interested in Jimmy, even though he was fourteen years younger; but that didn't seem to be the case. Jimmy said she was lonely and he insisted Laurie come with him to dinner at the old house one Wednesday night.

It was not quite as small inside as it looked from the outside, but it was half the size of the house next door where Laurie had been hundreds of times. It was furnished in charming antiques and simple old pieces, with a piano in the livingroom that ran all across the pond side. Probably walls had been taken down at some point. None of the old Cape houses had original rooms the size of this one.

The dinner that Dinah served them was surprisingly good: a pot roast of lamb shoulder in a vaguely Greek style with beans, tomatoes, garlic, lemons served with rice pilaf. It was a better meal than she had had the night before at Susan's. Laurie had always assumed that Susan was the good cook, but now she wondered.

When they moved into the livingroom, a grey cat climbed into Dinah's lap. It seemed to Laurie the cat was trying to stare her down. A huge orange cat with a big head stood on Jimmy's knees and made a digging motion with its front paws. The others seemed to take the presence of animals for granted, so she said nothing, as if she were used to having them nosing around.

"Just the idea of going out and trying to get it together with someone is appalling at my age," Dinah said. "Or maybe it's not my age but *the* age that's awry. In my twenties, I didn't think much harder about fucking somebody than about going out for a beer with them. And all I ever got for my adventures was a urinary infection a couple of times and the crabs once."

"The crabs?" Laurie repeated.

Laurie and Dinah looked at each other in mutual incomprehension. Then Jimmy stepped in. "Body lice," he said briskly. "They live in body hair."

"Yetch! I'm glad we didn't talk about this while we were eating. I'd die if I caught something like that!"

"They weren't that bad," Dinah said gently. "Not like fleas. They just itched. Those dousings with A-1 pyrinate were a ritual of the times. Anyhow the point I was trying to make is that there wasn't any danger then except getting pregnant. I never even knew anybody who had the clap. We were amazingly lucky and we never worried about disease."

Laurie was more appalled than she imagined that Dinah would ever guess. For Laurie, sex had always been rather fraught. Mostly she had gone to bed with men when it was unavoidable, but she could not imagine seeking sex or having that as the primary component of how she related to somebody. It wasn't that she was cold. In fact once she was into a relationship and trusted the man and felt cared for, she often wanted sex with him more than he with her, as had happened with Tom. But she could not imagine walking into a room and looking at some guy

107

and thinking, What a good-looking man, let's fuck. It seemed to her as bizarre as looking at a painting by one of the young painters whose work she admired or seeing a spectacular cloud formation over a salt marsh and saying to it, Do you wanna fuck? What a reaction to an aesthetic frisson! It felt like a short circuit in the brain, two different responses fusing because wires were crossed.

Jimmy was saying, "You just tend now to choose partners from people you know already, because you have some idea how much risk they represent."

"But we meet new people all the time. How do you put someone on hold while you investigate them?" Dinah shook her head. "It all seems weird and awkward to me. I don't think I'm fit for life in these times."

"I never felt I was," Laurie burst out. "All my life I've wished things could be simpler. Plainer. Quieter."

"You might like living here, then," Dinah said seriously. "You can simplify your life far more than you can in the city— if you really want to. It doesn't follow it'll be simple here. You can get as baroque in your relationships as you desire."

"I wouldn't think so, really," Laurie said, wondering who on earth Dinah thought she could become involved with, the plumber? "I want to paint seriously. I want to set up the gallery and make a success of it."

Jimmy built a fire in the fireplace. Now he sat beside it, the warmest spot, with his feet up on a hassock, watching both of them with a proprietary air. He seemed quite pleased with himself and with them. The night was crisp and clear outside, but markedly less cold than it had been. The pond was no longer safe to cross so they had walked around it. The sand road was clear of snow. Dinah insisted that spring was already beginning. "I've had crocuses in bloom on the south side of the house for two weeks already. Early species crocuses. You can see the buds changing on the trees. Willie taught me to notice that. They get furrier, elongated. The twigs brighten on the swamp maples." Dinah's face flattened with sadness.

"Who do you miss more, Susan or Willie?" Jimmy asked her.

Laurie was shocked. "That's a ghastly question to ask! That's like those ghoulish problems kids set each other, would you rather lose your arm or your leg?"

Dinah said blandly, "Tomorrow I have to drive into Boston,

to be there by seven in the evening. I'm staying at my friend Nita's. Either of you want to come along? I'll be returning by late afternoon the next day, unless we have supper there before we drive back.''

"I'll go with you," Jimmy said. "What time are you leaving?"

Laurie was annoyed at him running off, now that they had started construction. As usual he could read her reactions in her face, turning to say, "I have to get butcher block for your kitchenette countertop. I can get it wholesale in Boston." He swung back to Dinah. "I have an old friend to stay with. What will you be doing?"

"I have comps to the BSO—Itzak Raab is playing. I can't take you, because I promised Nita's roommate Giselle. The next morning, I have to meet with him."

"Itzak Raab? You're meeting Itzak Raab?" Laurie couldn't remember exactly what he played, but she knew what he looked like from his picture in *People* magazine and articles about him in the Sunday *Times*. He was certainly a celebrity. Yet Dinah had not mentioned that she was meeting him until just now, and probably wouldn't have brought it up at all if Jimmy hadn't asked what she was going to do in the city.

"I have to talk to him about the piece I'm commissioned to write." Dinah was looking downcast. "I wish I'd never agreed!"

"Why, Dee? It could do your career some good," Jimmy said. "You want him on your side if he has to perform it. Wouldn't you like him to play it again?"

"I'm just afraid he'll ask me to tone down my ideas. Try to get me to produce something easier. Maybe he'll hate what I'm doing and refuse to play it. It could all fall through."

Jimmy grinned. "Go on, I bet musicians are like actors looking for a good part. He wants to show off. Just prove you're giving him a good shot."

Dinah grunted, staring into the fire. "I wish I was only seeing Nita. Suppose we get stuck? There'll probably be a storm."

"I heard a weather report. It's supposed to be almost balmy."

"I'm bound to offend him. He'll find me an uppity woman and there goes my chance. It'd be better if we just talked on the phone and then he couldn't know what I'm like."

Jimmy didn't understand, Laurie could tell. He thought Dinah should jump on the opportunity to sell herself and her work to Raab. Laurie empathized. Before she went to see some gallery owner, she'd have diarrhea for a whole day. She'd walk around the block three or even four times before she could make herself enter the building. If the gallery was upstairs, she'd ride up and down in the elevator for ten minutes. Jimmy couldn't understand because he had an easy confidence in his charm and his person, and because he had no vulnerable art he was trying to usher out into the world. "You'll play some of it for him, right?" Laurie asked.

"It seems like chutzpah to play for a virtuoso who's six times better than me. I'll bring the rough score for the first section."

"So he'll be playing it maybe. Whatever, just keep the emphasis on the music and don't talk too much," Laurie said. "Then you won't keep worrying about whether you're saying the right thing."

Dinah grinned. "That sounds like great advice."

"Wear that black dress Mother made you—you know the one I mean," Jimmy said. "That's sophisticated and sexy and makes you look foxy."

"At breakfast? No thanks."

"Come on," he said to Laurie and stood up, yanking Dinah out of the rocking chair. "Let's go look through her closet and pick out something for her to wear tomorrow. Otherwise she'll go in her jeans."

Laurie did help. Jimmy and she finally found a jumper and silk blouse combination Dinah was willing to wear. Dinah had no sense how to dress for the city; obviously she had obeyed Susan when she had to get dressed up. Laurie was liking Dinah better than before. Dinah wasn't the formidable tough bar dyke Laurie had always imagined her to be. She seemed vulnerable and not as knowledgeable in some ways as Laurie herself. Jimmy was proved right again, dragging her over here. She felt almost comfortable with Dinah.

110

SEVENTEEN

Dinah

Nita and Dinah had been friends since Juilliard, where for two years, they had shared an apartment the size of a shower stall. Dinah's phone bills arrived every month with a half hour phone call each Monday night, from the Cape or wherever she was. Nita always called her Wednesdays. Neither had liked the other's husband, but both had managed to avoid a rift. Nita had married two years after Mark died; her marriage had come apart very soon following Tanya's birth, for her husband was too much of a baby, Dinah thought, to put up with a rival. It was all worth it for Tanya. Tanya, who was just five, was what Dinah imagined when she saw her own child in her desiring mind: bright, musical, mischievous, affectionate, with willpower like a drilling rig that could penetrate to the earth's molten core.

Nita was tall, with glossy black hair she kept in a neat cap, enormous doe eyes and a body that had stayed pear-shaped after Tanya's birth, like the cello she played. Nita was the youngest in a large Italian family from Staten Island, with parents old enough to be her grandparents. Her father had retired on his fireman's pension. He had chronic bronchitis but could not tear himself from the extended family to relocate in a warmer climate. In her own gardening, Dinah was imitating the garden around their home, with its rambling tomatoes and blowsy old-fashioned roses, its grapevines, eggplants, red and green peppers. When she went into Boston, Dinah stayed with Nita in the turn of the century house she and Tanya shared with Giselle and Giselle's daughter Eileen, in Newton five blocks from the turnpike.

Tonight she met Nita at the BSO. Just before the concert, she picked up at the box office the handwritten tickets Itzak Raab had left in her name. Giselle was using the other ticket, as she seldom got to hear Nita. If they weren't both performing (Giselle played in a local chamber orchestra and taught at the New England Conservatory), the other would be home baby-sitting both girls. But Giselle wanted to hear Itzak too.

111

Ozawa started with a brisk Haydn. Then Itzak sauntered out with his flute tucked under his arm to play a shimmering Mozart K313. Nita had asked her if she was going to come back at intermission, but she preferred to wait to meet him until the next day. Giselle urged her to change her mind, but she was adamant.

She didn't get to see Tanya until breakfast time. "I didn't even know you were here," Tanya said, climbing into her lap and lacing her hands in Dinah's curls.

"I snuck in and saw you asleep last night."

"Why didn't you wake me up?"

"Your mother would kill me. So would you."

Sweet face cheek to cheek with hers, snuggly body smelling of soap and banana, from her breakfast cereal. Although Nita was tall and dark and Giselle short and blond, their daughters, Tanya and Eileen, both had smooth light brown hair caught back in barrettes and often passed for sisters. But only Tanya called her aunt. Only Tanya climbed into her lap and hugged her neck and asked her with intense severity, like someone paying a formal call, about Tosca and Figaro. Tanya had been promised a kitten for her sixth birthday, and every week she changed her mind about what color it was to be. "And so dumb bozo Billy didn't repeat when we got to the capo and just kept going while we went back like you're supposed to! Ugh. Was it all a mess. Are you going to take me to the aquarium today?"

"Not today." She always took Tanya to the aquarium every spring. "Next month. It's a date."

"I'm going to have a spotted cat. I saw one on TV."

"It cost a thousand dollars," Eileen said.

"No spotted cats," Nita said. "How could we tell if it was clean? Dinah honey, if you're not going to be late, you better get organized."

"Music was our common language," Dinah said. "Besides sitting and listening the odd times he did want to talk, playing music was the one thing I could do for my father. We weren't even native speakers of the same language. But through music we communicated. That was the way I could touch him, the way I could please him."

"That's at least some connection. Music was part rebellion and part compulsion for me. When I was inside the music, I didn't care about anything else. Who were these two people who called themselves my parents? I was closer to my flute teacher."

112

"Oh, when I was actually playing, I didn't think about my father. It's just that growing up on the streets, you need somebody to give you reinforcement for something so exotic as playing the flute."

"You think growing up in the suburbs it's more relevant? For my parents, it was like I was running back to the ghetto. That was the old folks' shtick—Little Itzak will be a genius at seven and make some money for the family and we can pay the landlord this month. No, I was supposed to be a psychiatrist, a stockbroker. Not a musician, that was too ethnic. Almost embarrassing."

"Short Hills, New Jersey . . ." she mused. It made her think of short hairs. His hair was not so much long as dense, bushy. He had a sharp face built around large wide set brown-black eyes and a long arching, flaring nose, a chin with a marked cleft as if a finger had touched it and left a print. He was only three inches taller than she was but his hair made him seem taller. Performing he always looked tall. Close up he was not lean but solid and strongly built. She thought he probably worked out to keep up his strength on the road.

"My name isn't what I was given at birth. My father had changed Raab to Roberts. I was Ian Roberts. I took Raab back and renamed myself. I did it partly to annoy. And partly because I felt lost. I wanted to be who I really was. I was more at home with my grandparents than with my parents. I was always running off to New York to see them—Avenue A on the Lower East Side. When they turned eighty and my bubba got mugged for the third time, my father finally got them into a retirement community where they died within a year. I still miss them. My problem was feeling rootless. Of course it was easier for them to like me than for my parents. Here I was, a genuine prodigy and a disappointment to my father, who wanted a well-adjusted suburban quarterback. Flute playing wasn't American enough, WASP enough."

"Is it still that way?"

"Is there more coffee?" He turned the pot upside down. "Never mind, I have a coffee machine. It makes better coffee than room service. I'm addicted to caffeine, so I carry it with me—that and five pounds of converters to make it work in Finland and Italy, plugs and transformers. Then you stick the transformer into three plugs in the right combination so you can

113

finally ram it in the wall, and the whole apparatus is so heavy it falls out.''

"I'm so crazy about coffee I only drink espresso from Italian roast beans from a particular store in the North End. I come in and get them every six weeks or so and freeze the beans till I grind them." She felt the chill of depression, as if she had opened a heavy door and a cold wind blew in with the smell of decay. That was what they had used to do, all three of them. If he had changed the subject quickly from his parents, she would like to get it off coffee, fast. "I feel like some ridiculous dinosaur that has overspecialized and eats only one fruit about to become extinct."

She had arrived here nervous and defensive. It had taken them an hour to open up. She had been worried he would try to interfere with what she was writing; he perhaps had been afraid that being a woman she would be incompetent. Then they had had a productive hour looking at the score and discussing it. He had made some useful suggestions. Some she could apply and some she explained her difficulties with. It was a good interaction.

"Twice you said you've never performed music composed by a woman. Does that bother you?"

"No, but I'm conscious of it. I guess I want to see if it feels different. I don't think I'm closed to the idea or scared. But it's interesting. People must have always been telling you no woman has written great music."

"That's what they tell me." Another corn trodden on, hard. That's what she had been taught at Juilliard, that's what she had been told again and again. In 1976 there had been a spate of women's music programs, when her work had been performed, on the radio, at festivals. Special women's programming, so that all those worthy institutions could say, Oh we did that last year, and go on ignoring her work for another decade.

He ordered up lunch, explaining there were no restaurants in the hotel with nonsmoking sections and he could not take a chance on tour of getting clogged up. Planes were bad enough. "To keep my sinuses clear, I sit there squirting myself in the face with water. I don't get any of the spray anywhere but on me, but I've had people move away. They think I'm crazy."

At one point she had thought he was about to make a pass, but then she decided he simply had an ebullient manner. Then she decided he was gay. Then she decided he might not be.

114

Then she decided she had no idea. She had been out of circulation so long, she was unpracticed at deciphering male behavior. She couldn't read signals. She was worse than a twelve-year-old at her first mixed party, because she was sure she seemed sexually knowledgeable while she couldn't even tell what was going on in a man's hotel room. It was like being forced to converse in a foreign language she couldn't remember.

"You perform, don't you? You used to more. I heard you once at Ravinia, outside Chicago."

"I remember that concert. Five years ago. That was when you were still living in London."

"I was back to see my parents. My father was transferred to the Midwest the year before."

"I'm a little embarrassed you heard me. I'm not much of a soloist."

"You were fine. And I remember liking the piece. I started smelling grass when we were looking at the score, fresh cut grass in March, and then I remembered where I'd seen you. Lying on a blanket listening to the Chicago Symphony. Levine did a too zippy Beethoven's Sixth. Right after you played, it started to rain."

"Yeah, great claps of thunder. I felt like I'd caused it by accident. It started to pour and everybody ran for cover. The sky opened up and the water came down like a wall falling. Drops big as cement blocks. That's the Midwest. I could almost get nostalgic . . . I should go now. You have a plane to catch. Where are you headed?"

"Philly. Then Baltimore. Then Atlanta. Then I'm off to Europe." He fumbled in his briefcase for his schedule.

It gave her a rush of memory, for she had spent years on the road. She doubted she could do it now. It was a tremendous drain of vitality. Still she remembered the excitement, the fuss, the exaltation of hot audiences radiating energy back. She felt a moment of strong kinship.

"I should get organized . . ." He rose and stretched.

"Be in touch, then. I'll go back to work." She grabbed her parka off the couch and let herself out while he was staring after her.

"Hey!" he called and stood in the door of the hotel room for a moment, then waved after her and went back in.

* * *

She had base touching to do with her contacts at the council and a couple of foundations. She visited her favorite record shops. She received some freebies, but mostly what would be found in the slender contemporary music bins. *Akhnaten* she got free, but she had to buy the new *Madame Butterfly* and the newest rap record from The Black Plague. Then she met Jimmy and they went to a restaurant supply place and a fancy hardware store to refit her kitchen. "Time to be serious," she said gloomily, "about the fact that I live there and that's the only place I live. Only it is kind of small, isn't it? I haven't much space for dinner parties. Who wants to eat in the kitchen with an unimpeded view of dirty dishes? Since the last ten years have turned me into a good cook, I like to show off now and again. Use it or lose it."

They filled the trunk with a stainless steel steamer, a Dutch oven and sauté pan with cover, a food processor on sale, odd gadgets she found she missed, cheese slicers and garlic presses and basters. "You and Laurie can come to dinner Saturday with Burt and Leroy. You like them, don't you?" She stopped at a Jewish bakery in Brookline for three challahs to freeze. Then they wedged themselves into the traffic on Route Three heading south.

Jimmy said, "If I worked weekends, I could throw another wing on your house. Diningroom downstairs, bedroom for me upstairs."

"What's wrong with the perfectly good bedroom you have now?"

"I'm sick of living at home. The room feels like a shoe I'm cramming my foot in that's too small."

Jimmy's and Johnny's were tiny rooms facing the road and the woods, across the hall from the master bedroom. Susan kept them as they had been when both children lived at home. Johnny had had a huge fight with Susan the summer Johnny insisted on redecorating in purple and black with big silver spiders. Susan mourned every bit of imitation Victorian wallpaper steamed off and every bit of her own fabrics ripped from the windows and the overstuffed chair. "Too much tutti-frutti," Johnny had snarled.

Jimmy nodded. "I want to throw out all the old junk, but every time I take a load to the dump, she starts reproaching me. She's far more attached to my old science projects and my lousy attempts at art photography than I am. It's as if she thinks I'm trying to take my childhood away from her."

116

Jimmy was looking edgy, she thought. "Is something more wrong?"

"I don't like living with my parents. I can't afford a place here yet. The summer people have inflated the prices in town beyond what anybody who works for a living at a real job can pay."

"You have a lot of old buddies around. Move in with one of them."

"I don't want to live with another man. I hate stinko bathrooms and a refrigerator full of rotting take-out."

"You want your wife back. That's what you want."

"I want to get laid. That's for sure. Aren't you starting to miss it?"

"Do you know what I really miss? The routine. Not having to think about who I'm going to eat supper with. Not having to worry should I buy food for one or for two, because maybe one of them will change their mind and see me." If she began telling him what she truly missed, she would be at it all night. She did not think—yet—about sex, but rather she thought of each of their bodies, the noises they made, the smells and textures and taste of intimacy. It was not some *body* she wanted but specifically Willie, specifically Susan. She did not want a stranger. She did not want to put a random body in place of love.

"Dee, I appreciate loads that you aren't pumping me about them. That's heroic restraint."

"I drove your father off by trying to force him to negotiate for me."

"You never had a chance with him once Mother decided it was over. She can always make him feel guilty. She's queen of the guilt-teasers."

"Jimmy, I don't want to get into hating her because I can't have her."

"Sure you do. I'm no masochist and I didn't think you were."

"No, an awful pragmatist."

"What we should do is rent your house for the summer to a rich rock band and then split and let them drive my parents crazy. We'll run off together to some island. Actually I know of a great one in Puget Sound. I even know a house there, up on the rocks. We could still make a profit—it's cheaper than here."

Dinah sighed. "The way things are going, I'll keep it in mind."

When they were unpacking the car, in the dark with the Milky

117

Way splashed overhead, Dinah suddenly shushed Jimmy and held up her hand. Yes! The spring peepers, the little tree frogs with the enormous voices were trilling their piccolos in the marsh. Spring had come. As she passed under the big oak she heard a stirring over her head and realized the tree was crowded with sleeping birds. Either a migrating flock had put down or the first congregation of red-winged blackbirds had arrived. At dawn she would find out. She had a sudden fierce determination to survive her loneliness, survive her isolation, to grasp hard her own life in this place she loved.

EIGHTEEN

Susan

Susan found it difficult having Jimmy home, but deeply satisfying. She felt as if she had made a secret deal with fate whereby she had given up Dinah to gain Jimmy back. He had been too far. It took all day to reach Seattle and the plane fare was expensive. During the time he lived there, she had seen him at most once a year. She had felt bereft.

Although she had married extremely young—too young—she had thought her children would take their time. Jimmy had rushed into marriage after college. She had known it would not work in the long run, although she had been prepared to do whatever she could to help. Lisa was simply a pleasant young lady of no outstanding virtues, and frankly Susan had not understood why Jimmy had married her. Nonetheless whenever the phone rang for Jimmy, she held her breath, certain it was Lisa in her seventh month summoning Jimmy back to Seattle. She could not object to his returning—it was the right thing to do—yet she dreaded it.

She looked down at the yard where Jimmy leaned on a shovel gossiping with Dinah. Dinah was clearly on their land, but Susan managed to restrain herself from ordering her off. It was an absurd impulse, but one she had to fight to control. It hurt to see Dinah, and the pain made her furious. Dinah was deliberately punishing her, but the best course was to pretend she did not notice. Dinah wore an old deerskin jacket Susan remem-

118

bered, could not help but feel and smell. It had been Mark's, and indeed, it was long on Dinah, who wore it with the sleeves rolled back at the wrists. It was jaunty, ancient but still handsome, good washable suede of a weight and drape Susan seldom located. Around her head Dinah had bound a rolled scarf. On her feet were high top leather sneakers. She looked jazzy and ready to dance and prance, in fine spirits—knowing that Susan was watching? No, thinking only of herself, as usual. Susan took care to stay back from the window, where she could see without being seen.

Jimmy was expanding their garden, for the best bottom soil was on Dinah's plot and she had done most of the gardening for both houses. Susan didn't see why Jimmy needed to dig up the yard when it was still winter, cold as could be. Nobody had arrived. It would be months before she could sunbathe or swim or even sit outside and read a book. Spring was when she could arrange the first picnic of the year and Tyrone and Laurie and her own family would go to that spot she loved above Bracken Pond where locust trees grew from an old house site, with lush grass underfoot. She would unpack that special osier picnic basket Tyrone had given her with brown quail china plates and slots that everything fit in, and she would lay out delicacies, some that Tyrone brought from New York, buttery cherry strudel, good French bread. She would prepare that lunch herself, using *The New York Cook Book* she adored. She would bring out one fabulous treat after another. It would be civilized and the sun would be shining and the air balmy and everyone would be talking, really talking to each other. It would come, if only she held on by her fingernails to the icy slope of the long, long winter. What did Jimmy imagine he was doing? They could buy vegetables, that was what stores were for. If they added in Willie's and Dinah's labor, she imagined those Chinese cabbages they boasted about would cost out at five dollars apiece.

Downstairs, Willie was still at the table with a cup of coffee. She had the impression he was usually at work by now. Then she realized he was probably avoiding Dinah too.

"Having her next door is a damned nuisance," Susan said abruptly. It was too early for her to feel hungry, but she poured a cup of his coffee and stirred sugar into it. "What possessed us to sell her the old house?"

"You were afraid she'd leave after Mark died," Willie said reasonably.

"She paid nothing for it."

"Forty-five thousand felt like a good price in those days."

"Too bad she paid it off," Susan said.

Willie stuck his finger in his ear, wincing as he twisted it. "That doctor sold the extra land they bought with the Captain's house. For a lot no bigger than half an acre, would you believe they got a hundred thousand?"

"The old house must be worth two hundred by now. I wonder if she'll sell it." Susan couldn't decide if that would please her, giving them new neighbors and removing the constant irritant of Dinah's presence, or whether the idea of Dinah making that much clear profit would be unendurable.

"Jimmy says she hasn't said anything about leaving."

"Anybody else would have already made arrangements. She knows we sold her the house as a favor. Now here we are out in the woods miles from anyone with her in our yard."

"She likes it here, you know that."

"She never consults anything but her own comfort. We were a convenience, a ready-made family. She didn't have to do any work, she just took over her neighbor's house and children and friends. A life to slip into. Just the thing when you're too self-centered to take the trouble to have children of your own and build your own life." As she spoke, she contemplated how much time Jimmy had been spending over there. He ate with Dinah at least as often as he ate with her and Willie.

"I wonder why she never had a baby with her husband," Willie mused.

"He was a sick old man. Besides, can you imagine Dinah getting up in the morning and feeding a baby? If the baby wanted to be changed while she was working, she'd probably put it outside to yell like a cat."

Willie grinned. "Remember when Jenny Hill handed her a baby that time? She stood there holding the poor kid like a sack of potatoes."

"What is Jimmy doing out there with her? I thought you were going to get an early start on Laurie's today. You know you should finish it up so that she can move in by Memorial Day. Tyrone's planning his usual party."

"I thought maybe I'd take another shot at a new piece I started and then put in an extra long day tomorrow on the boathouse."

"Willie, if you don't get that boathouse done, Tyrone will hire somebody else to work on the gallery."

"Don't be overzealous, honey." Willie's mouth thinned with annoyance. "I'm already subcontracting on the gallery. The problem is getting permits. It's a change of use and there're enormous problems. We had to bring in sanitary engineers to get a septic system the Board of Health will approve. Plus we need five more parking spaces to be legal, but the neighbors object."

She stopped listening. Really, the town was putting obstacle after obstacle in Tyrone's way, deriving furtive pleasure from stalling the plans of a man of his stature. How else could those poor little one cylinder businessmen command his attention for five minutes? She was ashamed of them. She had not the patience for local politics that Willie did. He had always attended town meeting with Dinah and the two of them gossiped about ground water by the hour. He could not expect her to take an interest—she found politics trivial and full of uninteresting personalities and squalid histories.

She worried that Willie and Jimmy were lazing along, content to do a spot of work every other day. They were relying on Tyrone's friendship. It was not fair. Was she the only one in the family who was clear-sighted enough to see where the advantages lay? Yet she knew Willie wanted desperately to be shown in the gallery that was to be. A hundred thousand for a lot. "What do you suppose we could get for our house, with real estate prices soaring?"

Willie shrugged. "Who knows, who cares?"

"We're sitting on a gold mine. Why not find out what it's worth?"

"It's not an investment, it's our home. We couldn't find a better one."

"How do you know?"

"This is silly." Willie put on his jacket and went out. He headed for his studio, defying her good advice. It was time for her exercises, while both men were outside. If spring ever did come, she would need to be in decent shape so that she could wear the new bathing suit she had ordered from Bergdorf's catalog. She had charge accounts at several New York department stores, so she could keep an eye on their lines, what they were pushing. She seldom got to New York to shop, and she disdained shopping in Boston. It was simply not a high fashion town. People wore clothes they had bought ten years before, wore them in restaurants and on the streets. She put in the videotape and started doing aerobics along with the slim figure on the screen. Up and down and up and down and. . . .

She toyed with the idea of producing hand-painted clothes or beadwork of the kind Laurie had brought back from London. Laurie might show them in the gallery. Perhaps it was time for her to put effort into a line of designer clothes, one of a kind originals, yes, wearable art. That would give her a different status with Tyrone's friends. Right and left and right and left.

In summer Tyrone would anchor the raft two thirds of the way down the pond. It was heaven to stretch out with the sun warm on her body, to lie there talking and drinking martinis that Tyrone brought out breathtakingly cold in a silver carafe, talking of the big busy real world. Tyrone would share gossip about people she had met once or twice but never forgotten, the people she had not yet met but had read about and had a chance, through him and through him only, of someday meeting. Warm sun, iced martinis, the water of the pond gently lapping. Such moments were perfection. The rest of her life fell off from them precipitously. It should not be that way. She could remember when her life had seemed as exciting as a good movie. Dinah had failed her. Dinah had settled into a bore.

Sunday just before noon Tyrone called. "It's the first springlike day. It must be seventy. I thought of you and I was filled with envy. I could see you up there among the trees, with the pond before you and the flowers all around your house. Do you know how lucky you are to live in one of the most beautiful and peaceful spots on the East Coast?"

"Of course. Although I have to say in February I envy you. Besides, it isn't seventy here. It's chilly."

"That's my secret fantasy. To live there. To let the city go and just live in peace with myself."

"You should come up oftener, Tyrone. It's good for you. You always manage to relax. You haven't been up since Christmas. I thought you might come for Easter."

"Easter. . . . What a charming idea. Let me see, that's . . . ?"

"A week from today."

"I'll make every effort."

"Shall I plan a dinner? I'd be delighted."

"I'll let you know in the next couple of days. I was supposed to be in Italy, but complications arose. In the meantime, it does

122

me good to know you're there with Laurie. She's been sounding better, don't you think?''

Tyrone's plans swerved about twice more but at last it was settled that he would fly to Nantucket on Friday with a business associate, in his plane. Sunday morning he would be flown over. Monday he would return to New York. He would not have Celeste with him, so the cooking was up to Willie and Susan. She was enormously excited. She had begun cleaning both houses. Now it was time to plan a menu. "Turkey or ham?" She pondered. "Ham! Dinah wouldn't let us have it for years and years.''

"I really would savor a genuine country cured ham.''

"I could get a ham at the supermarket—or better, I know a place that has excellent Dijon ham in Boston. Jimmy can go.''

"I don't want French ham," Willie said stubbornly. "I want a real country ham. I know how we could mail-order a Virginia ham overnight. I have the catalog. I'm going to call that eight hundred number right now.''

It was all coming together in her mind. They would cook at home, then bring dinner over to Tyrone's and serve there. She loved the idea of presiding over the diningroom in Tyrone's house. She would use his china and his silver and set a fabulous table and they would all sit down as one family to a real Easter celebration, the first in years and years. Dinah was weird about Easter. She would go along with Christmas, but she could not stand Easter. Flowers. Susan must get to the florist on Friday. What she would really love would be traditional white lilies. Laurie would not cause her trouble the way Siobhan would have; Laurie would be delighted to have her take over.

As Susan oversaw Alice Dove's cleaning of Tyrone's house and as she polished the silver herself, she was reminded of her wedding. She had created it entirely. She had made her own gown and the gowns of her bridesmaids, although her own mother insisted on ordering hers, not trusting Susan to make one twice as attractive as the local bridal shop. Peach and mauve. How lovely she had been then. She had carried mock orange blossoms. To spite her parents she had insisted the marriage occur in North Carolina, Willie's home, just as she insisted they marry Protestant, not a real marriage to her parents. His parents were very gracious to her. It had been an outdoor wedding in their garden. They had a big house in bad repair with extensive grounds they had gradually sold off to developers.

She could remember just the sense she had now of all her powers coming together, her vision of a perfect occasion, that beautiful civilized moment when all the arts and nuances of living joined in something fine, fleeting but memorable. She had floated across the grass enjoying her own beauty as something she was bringing to Willie—not in the nauseating sense her mother had intended, the very night before the wedding attempting to instruct her on sexual duty in an absurd Victorian vein. Only her own manners and her need for a flawless occasion kept her from correcting her mother's idiot prudery. She wasn't giving herself to Willie the next day as a virgin bride. She and Willie had been making love for a year and a half and she was pregnant, although she did not yet know it. Willie had not been her first lover, but her third. So much for her mother's lecture on submitting to one's husband, delivered even while her mother fretted that her daughter was about to live in sin, since they weren't to be truly married in the Church.

Her mother had predicted to the day she died that Susan would return to the Church. Susan smiled grimly as she laid the silver gently back into its buffet drawers. It was solid silver, weighty in the hands unlike her own silver plate that she rarely bothered to polish for fear it would wear through the plating all the faster. The Church was a dark place she had escaped. Oh, the Protestants thought they had religion but what they had was something comfortable, tidy. Something that kept its place and bothered them little. A place to expose their new clothes and feel pious. There was no odor of sin and sanctity, no great weight of the centuries pressing down. The polite Protestant sects weren't real religions, which was why she liked them. They offered as much religion as a truly civilized person needed. The Founding Fathers had been agnostics. Once she had visited Mount Vernon and had deemed it aesthetically pleasing; it was easy to imagine living a good life there. He had given up a lot for his nation, that man on the dollar bill. If she had a country life as social and as well set up as that one, she would not fantasize a pied-à-terre in New York.

After Alice Dove left, Susan wandered through Tyrone's house. She did not know where Laurie was, but she was out and Susan was left to enjoy. She had been in summer houses of Tyrone's friends who had as much money as he did, where they had simply furnished the space with Bloomingdale's plastic modular stuff or Crate and Barrel tables. Tyrone—actually his

124

second wife, the one who had decorated, Janette—had chosen appropriate antiques and Chinese Orientals, pastels mostly.

Tomorrow morning she would drive to a good florist and get lilics, yes, flowers for every downstairs room. Even the wood of this house was fine oak and maple, not cheap pine. She curled up in a window seat in Tyrone's study, feeling a little presumptuous. His silent computer waited under its hood. The filing cabinets were veneered with walnut. The pond made scaly ripples on the cream ceiling. She imagined she could still smell the pipe he had used to smoke, before he decided it was unhealthy.

When Willie and she had lived in New York, they had never met Tyrone. Willie tended to bring home to their SoHo loft shaggy penniless artists and loud politicoes in those days, but she had encountered Tyrone soon after she and Willie had moved to the Cape year-round. Jimmy was six and Siobhan, five and she was teaching them to swim. Where was Willie? Working in a gallery in Provincetown. She could imagine herself brown with the sun and dressed in some Indian nothing, soaked to the skin trying to get Siobhan to let go of her in the water.

Tyrone had materialized out of the bushes. He was balding even then, perhaps a little heavier than he was now, dressed all in white like an image of vanished elegance. "What you need are water wings," he said. "I've taught my own daughter to swim, so she no longer needs hers. She's six and she swims off the raft we've anchored. Perhaps your son would enjoy the use of it. You can walk over, take the dinghy at my dock and row out."

Yes, typically he had appeared urbane and helpful, bringing her something she had not realized till then she needed. She felt like weeping. Was it for her younger self, carelessly and effortlessly lovely? For the importance and rootedness she had felt as the mother of two young children? They were gorgeous at that age. Adolescence had dealt nastily with both of them. Jimmy had only become handsome again while at college, and Siobhan was still peculiar looking, with her hair dyed patent leather black as if from spite and enough eye makeup to satisfy any clown. She had no idea if her daughter would look pretty if she were hosed down, because when Siobhan came home, rarely, rarely, she put on her cosmetic mask before she ate breakfast. It was her armor.

When Susan heard Laurie on the deck, she barely had time

125

to fly off the window seat and rush into the livingroom. Here was her real daughter. Laurie appreciated her far more than Siobhan ever had, confided in her more fully, enjoyed her company, came to her more willingly for solace. The daughter of my heart, she thought as she caressed Laurie's small fine shoulder. "Tyrone's going to notice right off how much better you're looking. How did you get a tan? It's been so chilly, I've barely ventured out."

"Do I have a tan?" Laurie ran to peer in the mirror over the buffet. "I do! You're right. Thank you, Susan," she burbled, as if Susan were the sun. "It must be from walking with Dinah and Jimmy. They're always dragging me off to the dunes or along the marshes."

"We could take walks together," she said, before she could stop herself.

Laurie did not notice her jealousy. "At least it's clean now, but I hate the smell of disinfectant. I need that tall cut glass vase."

"Right there in the breakfront. I'll get flowers tomorrow."

"I picked daffodils. Smell, how fragrant they are. I never knew they had a scent. Dinah cut some from her garden and then she took me to an old house site on a hill near the Bay. They grow wild there, under the trees."

There were many old house sites on the Cape, but she was sure she knew that one, where once they had made love with the daffodils blooming. Then, when Dinah had truly loved her and not criticized her all the time. It could not have been April. She remembered it as warm, serene. She did not want to remember anymore. Quickly she took her leave.

Saturday she had just finished putting together a cake for the next day, a chocolate gateau with walnut layering, and was looking out at the pond when she noticed a dinghy with a motor on it heading across. Tyrone already? She had taken nearly three hours to put the cake together, but she wanted to do it right. She was too excited to work on the designs she owed Max at Young Ideas, the new one based on the purplish stems of beach plums not yet leafed out, the apricot buds unfurling. She just wanted to enjoy the holiday. Could Tyrone have arrived? She flung her apron off and ran to fix her hair. When she peered out the window of her bedroom through the binoculars she kept there, she saw that it was not Tyrone but a man and a woman. For a moment she thought the woman was Janette, his second wife, but of course she was too young to be Janette as Janette was now, nine years after Tyrone had divorced her.

They were heading right for her dock. She resumed her toilette, sure that they had something to do with Tyrone, perhaps guests he had forgotten to mention, friends of his from New York looking for him. In any event she must change and be appropriately garbed to receive them.

But when she had changed to her casual but smart bottle green smock, she saw Dinah greeting them, with some young man she did not recognize standing in the door of her house. Surely they were not coming to see her? No, she was pointing at the boat and shaking her head and now she was returning to her house. They were a couple almost matched in height and slenderness, both in slacks and sporty anoraks. The man was in his middle thirties, the woman, a few years younger. She was almost more handsome than pretty, extremely fair, white-blond hair cut short and sleek that showed off her high sharp cheekbones, her long neck.

"We're terribly sorry about the motor, we didn't know," the man said in an awkward greeting.

"What about the motor?" She was entirely confused.

"That they're illegal on the ponds. So the young woman there was telling us," he went on.

"Never mind!" Susan said. She could have killed Dinah on the spot. "I'm Susan Dewitt."

"Oh, we found you." The man looked relieved. "Tyrone Burdock told us to look you up. We've bought the house across from you and we've just finished renovating it. I'm Alec and this is Candida. The MacIvors."

"My husband is Dr. MacIvor," Candida said, speaking for the first time. "He's at Deaconess. In Boston."

"Would you come in for a drink? Or coffee? I'll get my husband." It was easy introducing herself. For a decade it had been cumbersome. You see, this is my husband, but there is also Dinah. You want to invite us to dinner and that's awfully kind of you, but there are three of us and we come as a set. She had rejoined society and could meet people as an equal, not as a pariah who had to explain for half an hour in the face of the most banal invitation.

Candida and Alex seemed properly impressed with Tyrone. She enjoyed letting them know how close they were, that he was

127

coming for an Easter she was hostessing. They talked about how wonderful the pond was. Candida loved to swim. She also adored playing tennis. They were going to have a court put in. Did Susan play?

"Oh, I used to. I'd love to play again." She must take lessons at the court on the highway and bone up rapidly. Tyrone was a superb player and between his first and second marriages, they had played every Saturday morning all summer. If there was a court on the pond, he might resume.

She decided to take them to Willie instead of fetching him, so that they could see his studio. Candida seemed puzzled. "I thought you were a carpenter? Or was that somebody else?" she said to Willie, staring at the several large metal and plastic constructions occupying most of the room.

Susan said quickly, "Oh, Willie's overseeing the renovations of the boathouse and the design of a new gallery in town for Tyrone. As a favor. If you want a gallery well designed, who has better ideas than an artist?"

She was delighted with them. What an improvement over the Captain and his drunken buddies and his chickens that crowed at four in the morning and his manure piles stinking. Of course a couple from Boston were not as useful or exciting as a couple from New York would be, but still, they would add to the social life of the pond. They would definitely enrich the coming summer.

NINETEEN

Dinah

The phone rang as Dinah was washing a muddy spring salad, violet leaves and the very first flowers, thinnings from her rows of spinach, turnip and mustard greens, bok choy and lettuce, pinched back sprouts of herb. It was Itzak. "I hope I'm not calling at a bad time. It must be late afternoon."

She could tell from the sound of his voice that he was calling via satellite, that echoey delay. "Where are you?"

"Oslo. Norway. It's after my concert. All Mozart tonight. It's still winter here. What's it like there?"

"It's great. We haven't had a snow cover since late February. I turned over my garden just before we met in March and started planting and putting out seedlings under milk cartons." She stopped, sensing she had told rather more than he had asked for. She knew a few more facts about him by now. She had made a few calls and asked friends, including Nita and Giselle. He was not gay but straight and had been married while abroad to an Israeli, with whom he had lived in London. The marriage had ended badly—that was all Nita knew. She considered him cute but very businesslike. He did not have a reputation for fooling around.

"Sounds lovely. I've been on tour for three weeks and I'm worn out. I have a cold—can you tell?"

"I thought it was just the connection."

"I feel flabby and cranky and lonely and very, very tired of being polite in various languages. How is our piece coming?"

"The first two sections are complete now, I think. I think. Anyhow they're ready to be given a reading. The third section is stuck at the moment so I went on to the fourth, the last, and that's almost together."

"Good. So why is the third section stuck? What's wrong with it?"

"You sounded just like my father." It was the way he had passed over what was done and gone straight to what was left to do. Nathan had never been easy to please. The fathers of girlfriends gave them approval for wearing a new dress or batting their eyes. Fortunately her father saw through the flesh to the spirit. Her real education occurred not in school but with him. He was not satisfied easily, but then neither was Beethoven when she was playing him; Nathan had made her ear acute, self-critical, precise.

"I was imitating my grandfather. I miss them. I just wanted to stay in touch. It's late here. I should go to bed. Tomorrow I'm taking the train to Bergen. They say it's a beautiful trip over the mountains. Maybe the morning after my concert, I'll visit Greig's home. Why not? Wednesday I'll be back in New York. Get our piece unstuck by then. I'll give you a call."

She knew what was inhibiting her in the third section. The relentless rhythm building through it felt too sexual. It was the wrong season in her life and the right season of the year. Tosca remembered her old flings and rolled on her back, arching up her belly and teasing Figaro with soft mrrrs and warbles. Figaro

129

patrolled the garden and brought little furry creatures with their necks broken to adorn the doormat. The raccoons were mating in the night bushes with whistles and snorts and hoarse cries of enraged passion.

Robins hopped in her garden and towhees called from the woods. Flights of geese beat northward over the pond. Some nights ducks rested in her trees, unlikely among the pinecones. Her peach was showing pink tips on the buds. The bright tender new shoots poked up through the thatch of dead beige grass. She had stepped up her walking to burn off the energy rising in her spine like sap in the trees. That morning she saw a doe with her fawn drinking at the pond, between her house and the Captain's. She imagined she was telling a child about Nathan. She imagined she was walking with her child in the woods, a girl with curly hair like her own. This town was a good place to raise a kid, usually accepting of a woman alone with children. Lots of play groups. It wouldn't be as hard here as in the city.

Her dreams were increasingly sexual. She touched herself to orgasm but it felt boring. Years ago she had had a vibrator. She wasted two hours looking for it. Humidity had destroyed the innards. She called her mother in Florida. A dinner party was in progress. The conversation was awkward, almost shy. How are you, I'm just fine, how are you? Is anything wrong? No, of course not. How's the weather up there—cold, I bet.

She took an extra four-mile hike late the next afternoon. She was thirty-eight and relationships had fallen, leaving her naked. If she had gotten pregnant in the winter, at least she would have something. She was thirty-eight and nobody loved her and she had nobody to love. Who was she, outside her work? There she was strong. There she had been commissioned to write for one of the four best flutists in the world. But in her self, she was rejected, with strength and energy burning lonely as a lighthouse on the rocks, whose light only serves to warn off. Of what avail were the physical strength and energy that had—along with passion and willpower and luck—enabled her father to survive Auschwitz? She dug her garden to feed only herself.

When she got back, she was aware at once someone was in the house, but this time she guessed it was Jimmy, as usual. Why had he gone upstairs? Her jeans and socks were damp from a bog of wild cranberries. She wanted to change into something warm and dry before supper. She had put a pot roast in the oven before she left the house. It was Friday. She had begun lighting

130

Sabbath candles as she had during the last year of Mark's life. Jimmy liked the ceremony, so he tended to arrive Fridays for supper.

When she walked into her bedroom, Jimmy was there, in her bed. He was under the covers this time, and as he yawned and flexed his arms behind his head, she saw that he was either naked or partially so.

"What's this?" She stopped where she was.

"Take off your wet pants. I'll warm you up."

"Jimmy, get out of my bed and go wait downstairs. I want to change."

"I need a change too. Come here." He held out his arms.

He was beautiful, nothing short of it, and the response of her body was immediate. His hair was redder than Susan's, his body hair like fox fur. He was in fine shape. She saw all that in a glance as she grabbed a wool skirt from her closet and a warm sweater from her dresser. "Jimmy, we don't have that kind of relationship and we can't. It would be incest." She retreated hastily to the bathroom. She would have liked to warm herself in a hot tub but she did not trust him to stay out. No, he was not her son, but he was the closest she had to one. She was shaken but solid beneath.

When she came out he had put on his pants, but not yet his shirt, and was seated on the side of her bed grinning at her. "You aren't my mother, Dinah. You aren't old enough to be my mother. You'd have had me at fourteen."

"I've been involved with both your parents and I'm not about to have sex with you, too. It's just too involuted and messy."

"Nonsense. It's convenient. We both like it and we're not getting any. It wouldn't be messy at all. I don't know anybody who shows more common sense day in and day out than you."

"Jimmy, your prick is always leading you into trouble you can't handle. Can't you find a girl around here? It ought to be easy."

"You and Willie and Susan all warned me off Laurie. She's under my nose all the time. I've been a tin saint. I haven't even kissed her. Yet."

"What about all the girls you went to high school with?"

"Most of them have babies and they're married or they might as well be. Besides, I like you better. I've always liked you better."

"Better than what? A nice fat sheep? Come on. You can stay

131

up here if you want to, but I'm going to finish putting supper together.''

He slid off her bed, reaching for his shirt. ''All right, sorry if I shocked you. No hard feelings. . . . Hey, remember when Willie and Susan decided I should call you Aunt Dinah?''

''You wouldn't do it.'' She felt giddy with relief as they went down the steep stairs. The moment had passed and he was not angry.

''I'd met my aunt Elinor. I knew it was hypocrisy. You weren't suddenly my aunt. I said to myself, when they fuck up, it'll be my turn.''

She laughed. ''Never mind, it's spring and even Tosca has been in false heat all week.''

''You'll come round,'' he said equably. ''Supper smells great. I drew up plans for your new diningroom. Want to see them after we eat?''

The blessings made a break after what had happened. She had a kiddush cup from her childhood, her best towel to cover the challah. If she was a family of one, she at least felt more connected making a Sabbath. In her solitude she was finding a sense of herself as a Jew, but she was not sure what that meant in isolation. Judaism is not a religion of hermits, she told herself, but of community. To celebrate Pesach, she needed others.

''When you say that Hebrew, are you really praying?'' Jimmy asked.

She nodded. ''But the English equivalent, that is, the equivalent out of my life, wouldn't be a translation.''

''Do you believe in God?''

''I believe in holiness. I experience it whenever I really compose, whenever I play. I think music is holy. It comes through me as if it is.'' She felt as she spoke the resonant memory of that connective force. It was, before her, through her, after her. She was in it. Sometimes of it. It was a vast order, an alignment, a relationship of all beings. She lost her self in it. Her self came back to her afterward like clothes rumpled on the chair put on after lovemaking.

Neither was talkative at supper, but that did not bother her. They were capable of companionable silences. She was running over her guest list. Saturday night was the first night of Pesach, and she had decided to have a seder. She had not done so since the year after Mark died. Always it had been a holiday she loved. Until her mother remarried, she had gone home for Pesach, no

132

matter what was happening in her life. One seder chez the Dentist had foxed that. She was trying to pull together enough people to make it real, odd Jews who weren't already taken. A successful seder would prove to her that she could survive by herself here.

After she had sent Jimmy home, she sat staring at the plans he had drawn. It was true, she had no diningroom and her livingroom was largely occupied by her piano and writing table, her music apparatus, computer and synthesizers. Eating in the kitchen was grim, with company viewing the unwashed pots, the backlash of preparation; in the summer, it was unpleasantly hot. She had a little money now and Jimmy would build with her cheaper than she ever could bring it off in future. The price was buying the materials and working with him. She did not take his pass seriously. It was in his nature to offer himself freely, as it had been her younger nature to leave no sexual stone unturned, no threshold uncrossed. He would begin when the boathouse was finished, starting it while he and Willie were working on the gallery. Tyrone would be subsidizing her diningroom. She felt like a novice skier perched on a long steep slope trying to decide whether to push off downhill. If she was going to have a child, she could not really expect to use Mark's tiny dingy ex-study for a bedroom beyond babyhood. A secret promise. See, Nathan, I am making ready, I am preparing the way.

The phone rang. This time she knew it was Itzak. He would be back in New York. Was he seriously worried about the piece? His voice was normal again, with its own rough bark quality. "I wanted to be back, but I have to say, being here is grim. Eight feet of unanswered mail. Dust balls. The dry cleaner lost a pair of good tails. A heavy metal band moved in next door. The walls throb in and out like a diaphragm. Everybody in the world is having a baby or just had a baby, and I feel superannuated."

"Maybe the heavy metal band will have babies and turn down their amps."

"I think they fuck with their guitars, which are probably sterile. So what are you doing for Passover?"

"I actually thought I'd have a seder this year. With the three other Jews I know out here. What are you doing?"

"Nothing. My grandparents are dead. I always went to them.

My parents are too deracinated to have a seder. Barbecues but no seders. I'm invited to my agent's, but I don't want to go."

"Come up here," she said before she thought twice. Then she thought twice and waited for him to decline. He just liked to kvetch. He must have a lover, a girlfriend.

"Really? Saturday night. I could get out of New York early Saturday morning. I'm not scheduled till Tuesday. Can you put me up?"

"It's not fancy here. But I have a spare bed." In the room where Mark used to write, among the boxes of his moldering papers.

"Are you sure this is all right with you?"

She wasn't sure, but it would be highly impolite to say so. Why had she invited him? Because he obviously wanted to be invited. "It will be rather spare and impromptu. . . . If you have a Haggadah you like, bring it. I'm cobbling this together after years of not doing it."

"What should I bring besides?"

"Good New York Passover macaroons. And if you want other than sweet wine, if you go in for the dry kosher wines, bring a couple of bottles."

"No, I prefer the real old-fashioned sweet stuff. It's part of it."

"Good. . . . If you don't change your mind about coming, let me know which plane to meet." Surely he would reconsider and call it off.

She mentioned to no one that Itzak was coming, until Saturday when it became clear he was on his way. She decided she could tell Jimmy, who had invited himself. He remembered the only seder she had made with Willie and Susan. It had not been a success. Willie and Susan had been appalled by the religious references and the story of Exodus. They had refused to drink the sweet sacramental wine and found the Haggadah reading interminable. They had acted throughout as if it were just too primitive and weird. She had put her desires aside; every year since, Pesach had passed while she glanced at it as into an open grave of guilt.

Burt was coming, along with his lover Leroy, who wasn't Jewish but had been to seders before. Then there was the feisty widow Zee Gildner, whose husband had been an organizer with the steelworkers. In desperation for more Jews she had invited the Hills, a couple from Newton who owned a house on Bracken Pond. They always came up for the holidays, so she had called them in Newton—she owed them although they didn't know it for cutting a Christmas tree on their land. They had a daughter Courtney who was ten and could ask the four questions.

Jenny Hill called to say that Courtney had her girlfriend Molly with her. Dinah asked herself what she had wrought, bringing Itzak together with Jimmy, a gay couple, a bland suburban family with one own and one borrowed child, and the widow Gildner. Itzak would decide he couldn't be bothered playing her *Cat in the Moon* for flute and chamber orchestra. Why had she invited him? Because he seemed to want to be invited. That was no excuse, only a pretext for disaster. She should never have tried to have a seder out here on a sandbar and once launched on that folly, inviting Itzak was a whole higher stage of lunacy.

Then Jimmy stopped by. "Hey, Laurie would like to come. She's really interested. She's never been to a seder."

"Jimmy, this isn't a folk custom put on to amuse the tourists."

"Come on, Dinah, who drove fifteen miles for all the stuff you forgot? I want her to come. She's lonely. Tyrone's only bopping in for Sunday, as it turns out. Don't hurt her feelings."

"I want this to come off right. I need it to work this time."

"Besides, she has good card tables and we can set one of them up. That'll solve the seating problem. We can put it up at the end of your table or just through the archway in the living-room."

"All right. Invite her."

"I did." Jimmy started to saunter off. That was when she told him about Itzak. She hoped the name would mean nothing to him, but Jimmy was more interested in music than his parents. "Holy shit, Dinah. Mother's going to hit the ceiling. She'll swear you're doing this just to spite her."

"Why? I'm sure she's never heard him play."

"Ah, but she's heard *of* him. That's enough. You know Mother loves the famous and the also-rans. . . . So I have a heavy duty rival. From the pictures on his albums, he's a curly headed sweetheart."

"Stuff it, Jimmy. I sleep only with my cats. Bring over that table this afternoon, okay?"

How is this seder going to be different from all other seders? Answer: it could be, kineahora, a complete nightmare.

TWENTY

Dinah

Dinah started cooking in the morning. It was a raw chilly day, so for a while she had hoped that the airport might be fogged in; no such luck. She fetched Itzak, who looked lost. She was sure he was asking himself why he had come. He seemed smaller than she remembered him, huddled in a trench coat beside her in the old Volvo. She had cleaned the spare room cursorily. Mark's papers filled the closet to its ceiling and overflowed against one wall of the room. After a late and hasty lunch, she established Itzak there with a pot of tea and he promptly fell asleep, probably from boredom.

She found herself thinking again of her father. This had been his favorite holiday. For him Pesach bore connotations of the liberation of Auschwitz, the exodus from Europe. Although he was never at home in the States, he had no longer belonged anyplace; all that gave him a sense of home had been burned. Nonetheless he was enormously glad for American citizenship. If he would never feel safe, he appreciated feeling less in danger.

Music was his greatest pleasure, for it did not depend on words. At some point in his youth, he had learned English, but it was his sixth language. He knew Polish, Yiddish, Russian, Hebrew and German better. When he cursed, it was in Yiddish first. She remembered being fascinated as a child by the little differences between her father, her mother and herself. When her mother hurt herself, she cried out Ow! When her father hurt himself, he cried out, Oi! Ai-yi-yi-yi, her father would moan, when her mother would say, Oh, no, it's not fair! They even sneezed differently. Her father's sneeze was far more delicate than her mother's, the sneeze of a small cat. When she was upset, Shirley held herself and drew into a knot. Nathan rocked.

Shirley, doomed to be the second wife of two husbands, Dinah thought. I should talk. I was Mark's third wife. She sought to imagine him, for in her recent loneliness, she had been trying to evoke the sense of lingering presence that a decade before she had fled. He was too distant. The savors of holiday cooking called up her childhood, not her marriage. They had gone to her mother's once, once to his parents', twice to friends. She had hosted a seder in New York before making a last one here for him and friends who knew he was dying. His parents had given them a seder plate from Israel, big and beautiful with an aquamarine glaze.

Silently, secretly she grieved as he was dying. She had not seen Mark's parents since the funeral. In their eyes she had not really been a wife, a true daughter-in-law, because she had produced no grandchildren. Once the funeral was over, the will read, they lost interest in her. They had never been possessive about his papers, for to them he had been a failure.

At six-thirty the guests began arriving as she was arranging the ritual foods. Jimmy helped her set the tables. Laurie volunteered, but she looked so inept handling silverware that Dinah sent her off to the livingroom with Itzak to build a fire. That would keep them out of trouble.

Then came Zee Gildner, enormous in a bright green velvet dress like a stage curtain wrapped around her, carrying yellow chrysanthemums she had obviously purchased from the florist. Dinah felt dismayed, because she knew that Zee lived on a schoolteacher's pension and little else. She also came bearing a well-thumbed Haggadah. "This is what we always used, from when the children were little. It's a good progressive one."

Jenny and Gary Hill arrived with two boxes of Passover matzoth, also Courtney and her girlfriend Molly, both whispering and giggling as they trailed in, and two copies of the Haggadah Jenny's family had always used. "Peeyuh," Courtney said. "It smells like your house is on fire."

Dinah realized that clouds of smoke were floating from the livingroom. Pulling the fire extinguisher off the kitchen wall she raced in. The only fire was in the fireplace.

Itzak and Laurie were coughing madly, flapping at the smoke. Jimmy slipped past them, reached in above the flames and pulled the chain that released the flue. Dinah opened the outer door. Figaro rushed into the yard. Jimmy was shaking his hand. She asked, "Did you burn yourself?"

"I'm just rare, not well done. I'll take some butter."

"Vitamin E is better. Come in the kitchen."

"I'm terribly sorry," Itzak said, tears streaming from his eyes so that he looked sorry indeed. "I never had a fireplace."

"It's my fault for not warning you. . . . Oh, Itzak, did you bring the macaroons?"

"Of course!" He looked relieved to have an excuse to retreat from the smoke. "Upstairs in my suitcase."

"Is the house on fire?" Courtney wanted to know. "Can we go home?" She was a skinny girl who usually lived in a jogging suit but tonight had been hung with a plaid taffeta dress that made Dinah think of Christmas wrapping paper. Her friend wore a corduroy smock decorated with embroidery. The friend was pretty and made faces. Courtney would have sacrificed them all on a pyre, her parents included, for Molly's best-friendship. Dinah remembered, oh she remembered.

Itzak was picking his way down the steps—that short steep flight from the eighteenth century common in old houses here, almost more a ladder than a stairway—no happier than he had gone up. He was holding the white bakery box of macaroons but it was quite flat. "They're a little smushed."

"Don't worry. They'll taste the same." She was thinking maybe she could secretly reshape them in the kitchen.

Burt arrived with the gefilte fish. "Darling, don't say anything. Leroy baked some bread today, he was trying to be nice. I told him to leave it home, but he insisted on bringing it. Could we put it on the table anyhow?"

"Let me freeze it, and I promise the next time I have you over, we'll all enjoy it."

They sat down at the table finally. Introductions had gone well. Nobody paid special attention to Itzak. To the others he was the shmuck from New York who had filled the house with smoke. Laurie knew, but she was used to celebrities and semicelebrities and was her usual shy self. Jimmy was undampened in his customary insouciance, his hand greased with vitamin E and wrapped ostentatiously in a white handkerchief. Maybe things would work out.

The battle of the Haggadahs was on.

Gary: "Blessed art thou, Lord our God, King of the universe, who hast kept us from harm and sustaineth us and sanctifieth us among the nations, Blessed be He."

Zee: "Pharaoh is the same as any other king, dictator or boss who oppresses working people since the class war began. Let us now sing, 'We Shall Overcome.' "

Itzak: "Yatayatayatayatayatayatayatayatayatayata." He spoke the

Hebrew in a dead rush as if compelled to cram it all into one champion flute player's exhaltation.

Courtney: "When do we eat?"(The first question.)

Only Itzak and Burt remembered how to read Hebrew, and only Itzak, Jenny, Dinah knew any of the melodies. She could tell from Itzak's face that like her he found the sound of the eight uncertain voices savaging, "Ma nishtanah halihah hazeh" in eight different wavering keys as unpleasant as brakes squealing. Whenever it was Itzak's turn, he read the Hebrew in a run-together marathon monotone, like an auctioneer selling off a prize bull. It was a high hypnotic supercharged mumble that brought instant glaze to the eyes of everyone else at the table. It stirred ancient unpleasant memories in Dinah, old men making sure, she had suspected at twelve, that you couldn't understand a word they said no matter how well you had studied your Hebrew.

"Did someone in your family read the Haggadah that way?" she thought to ask, for his accent rattling it off was entirely different from the way he spoke Hebrew normally, like an Israeli: from his ex-wife, of course."

Itzak looked surprised. "My grandfather. He never skipped anything, but he managed to get through it all in an hour and twenty minutes . . ."

"How did you ever figure out what he was saying?"

"I didn't have the faintest idea for years. I knew it had something to do with Moses and food, that was it."

Gary: "Who is like unto the Lord our God, He that is enthroned on high, that gazeth down far far below upon the earth; Who lifteth up the poor out of the dust and preserveth the needy out of the dunghill . . ."

Zee: "Why do we eat bitter herbs tonight? We eat bitter herbs dipped in the salt water of tears so that we will remember the taste of oppression and unite ourselves with the oppressed everywhere who are fighting for their freedom. Let us sing 'Solidarity Forever.' "

Itzak: "Gibblegibblegibblegibblegibblegibble."

Courtney: Why do I have to eat horseradish? It burns my mouth." (The second question.)

Dinah was filling her cup too full and drinking it all down each time. It felt appropriate. The wine was so sweet and she forgot how alcoholic it was. Itzak was on her right and Laurie on her left. She had been liking Laurie better lately. She tried

139

to do the right thing. She was the best behaved person at the table. They should have had Laurie ask the four questions.

Courtney: "Can Molly and I go watch TV till this over?" (The third question.)

At some point she realized Burt had taken over and was making it move forward. From somewhere in his present Fred Astaire persona rose a rabbinical scholar who settled points of precedence, danced through the maze of different texts and herded the rowdy guests toward the final goal.

Courtney: "How much do we get for the afikomen?" (The fourth question.)

By the time they were ready to eat, Dinah found herself too drunk to manage. Her head was floating beside the light fixture. Laurie and Jimmy served. Jimmy had been in and out all day and knew what she had been cooking. By the time she had eaten her plate of chicken soup with the matzoh balls in it perfectly light and fluffy, she found herself too dizzy to stand. She drifted up the stairs as the gedempte flaisch mit abricotten was being served and decided it would not hurt if she lay down for just a moment on her bed.

When she awoke, Itzak was sitting on the edge with a cup of coffee. "Your guests are still at the table. I think they've given up on finishing the service. They're finishing each other instead."

"I'm sorry. It didn't work." To her embarrassment a large tear rolled out of her eye. She grabbed for the coffee and drank it down scalding hot. She felt like a large incompetent child. She could hear the babble of voices and the canned roar of the television from below. "Thank you for the coffee! I have to go downstairs. This is embarrassing."

"Tomorrow night we'll eat the leftovers and make a second night seder that works, I promise you. Don't fret." He took the empty cup from her hands and helped her up. His mouth brushed hers as he pulled her against him for a long moment and then turned her toward the door. "Thank you for trying."

Her reflexes were slow. She was just realizing she had been kissed as she picked her way clinging to the railing down the steep flight. It had happened too quickly for her befogged condition. She was not even quite sure what had happened, whether it was affectionate, consolatory or sexual. She did not feel up to sorting it out. Living with Susan and Willie, it had been years since she had had to put together a social evening on her own, and her life with Mark had never followed conventional formulae. "I saved a plate of food for you," Itzak said. "Eat something."

However, when she got downstairs she found people in a jolly mood. The food had been a huge success and Molly and Courtney were watching television in the livingroom, collapsed into inebriated giggles. Jenny and Leroy had formed an alliance of underappreciated spouses and were discussing couples therapy in low voices. Jimmy was selling Gary a sleeping porch, to be added in the fall. Burt was organizing the dishwashing. He had Laurie drying, he was washing, and he drafted Itzak into fetching the dirties and Dinah into putting the clean ones away. Figaro had climbed on the counter and was begging leftovers, stuffing himself until his eyes glazed over while Tosca, glaring from the top of the refrigerator, deigned to eat a few tidbits.

By eleven they were all gone. The coffee was still buzzing in Dinah's brain. Laurie had taken the extra table off with her. The embers of Jimmy's well-made fire smoldered in the fireplace. Itzak and she sat on the couch and stared at it. She still felt befuddled. She could not decide what was happening. Maybe he expected to sleep with her as a matter of courtesy since she had invited him to be her houseguest. She had no idea. She briefly wished she had allowed Jimmy to move in, not as her lover but as her roommate. It would be infinitely easier to handle the situation if they were not alone. Or did she want to "handle" it? Was she curious about him? Yes, but wary. Figaro lay on his back with his white belly exposed, smack in the middle of the hearth rug snoring softly.

"I haven't figured out yet how to live in the States," he said. "I moved back to New York without thinking about it. I went to school there—like you. My grandparents had always been there. So I returned and bought a condo on automatic pilot. . . . I don't like how long it takes me to go in and out of LaGuardia and Kennedy. I don't like my apartment. I don't like never seeing the countryside. I had a little house in Périgord, not fancy. A little stone house in a village that clings to a red cliff. We sold it in the divorce. Now I miss it. I had the use, too, of a friend's house in the Cotswolds, all the years I lived in London. I can't figure out exactly what I need to do with my life to make it more comfortable."

"When did you get divorced?"

"Two years ago."

"What happened? She was Israeli?"

"You've been asking questions about me." He looked sideways at her with a knowing smile. "Caught you."

"I'm someone who likes gossip. It's a weakness of character, but endearing, don't you think?"

"You were checking me out."

"Whereas you never asked anybody about me but just came down here for Pesach thinking I might have fourteen children and a drunken husband."

"I gather that your long ménage à trois has folded its tents."

"Quite. Jimmy is their son, and he still talks to me. But neither of them do."

"I was wondering who the kid was. He's possessive of you."

"He's family, really."

"No one else in the picture?"

"I'm quite clean if that's what you're trying to figure out. And yourself, Itzak? Who are you?"

"I had a life but it came apart. My wife was a dancer who gave that up when she got pregnant, after we'd been married five years. I think we were happy together until then. But she miscarried in her sixth month and they couldn't save the embryo. She was determined to replace it with a real baby. But she couldn't get pregnant again."

"Did the doctors say why?" She wondered if it could be like that for her. Dr. Bridey said that she had already made up her mind not to, because she had waited so long. The women's magazines were full of stories of women who waited too long and proved infertile.

"Every doctor had a different explanation. Our whole life got organized around the effort. When and how we made love, what we ate, all kinds of crackpot diets. She was always taking her temperature and saying, not tonight, or suddenly, 'Now! Right now!' I began to wonder if I really wanted a baby after all. It was like living in a combination sickroom and lab."

"Why did she want a baby so badly?"

"Once she'd stopped dancing, it became the focus of all her energy and all her discontent. It was something she wanted more than she'd wanted to dance, more than she wanted me."

"And you resented that."

"I did. I felt incidental to the great fertility quest. It turned me off, finally. I began to dread going home. I had a long affair with a violinist who was unhappily married too. But we never

142

wanted to live together and when my marriage fell apart, so did our affair."

"What finally broke up your marriage?"

"My wife began having an affair too and she got pregnant by the other man. She decided her luck would be better with him."

"Was it?"

"Actually, yes. She had a little boy while we were getting divorced."

"So you felt betrayed?"

"No." He grinned. "If we're being truthful, I felt relieved. It was off my back. She had what she wanted and I was free to go on my way. But I'm lying a little too, making myself more rational than I was. Sometimes I felt relieved and sometimes I felt like a classic cuckold, that they were both laughing at me. It was messy. Too messy to live with the remains. So I came back to the States."

"What are you looking for?"

"Hot pussy. A nice Jewish girl. Safe sex. A harbor when I put to. What's anybody looking for? All of the above. Someone who won't confuse me with a sperm bank. What are you looking for?"

"I haven't been looking. I've been trying to learn to live my life now that I have it back." She felt slightly evasive, because she knew very well one of his attractions was as a possible father: she was that age, it was that time. How could she help but think that here he was Jewish, attractive, musically talented. Wouldn't Dr. Bridey be surprised if she showed up pregnant? Well, she couldn't do that by impulse, for she was still on the pill.

"Ah, but you were the one who invited me."

She thought, you follow your own star. What else can you do? You do what you know how to do. "Shall we go upstairs? It's late. We've both been up forever."

He could take that either way. She climbed the steps without looking back and entered her own room. He was right behind her. "You have a nice big bed." He caught her around the waist, drawing her back against him. His mouth slid down the side of her neck and his hands moved up over her breasts. Both the men she had been with for any length of time, Mark and Willie, had been much taller than she was. Itzak was closer to her height and it was strangely exciting.

She swung around to face him and their mouths joined, their

143

hips came together. In a way it was more like making love with a woman, with Susan, someone close to her size. Everything was in the right place. His erection was not sticking in her navel but rubbing against her mons. Her breath rasped in her throat. She felt at once loose and juicy, a strong desire to take him and roll him onto the bed and chew on him, curl around him, take him up into her; and a cautious nervous watchfulness. Here she was committed to something she had not really decided to do. You never knew when you took off your clothes with a man exactly what you were getting into, what demons you might be loosing. For years and years she had not been in bed with anyone she had not known intimately, absolutely. In her early life, she had gone to bed with men she had picked up at parties, but she had lost the habit of touching strangers. It felt too intimate to be handling each other in the cold bedroom, to be getting together into her bed. On the dresser Tosca crouched, making little noises of dismay.

They were awkward getting out of their clothes. They each had eight elbows and said excuse me every fifteen seconds. Their bodies at first bumped and knocked knees. It felt very unrehearsed and fumbling. When she saw him sliding a condom onto his prick, she said, "Oh, I'm on the pill."

He gave her a surprised look and went on wriggling the condom over himself. It was as if a cold finger were placed on her nipple. Oh. Safe sex. He was not sure of her. Indeed, how could she be sure of him? Welcome to the wonderful world of the AIDS epidemic. She had not made love with a barrier between organs since high school. It was hard to forget that piece of rubber chafing at her thigh.

When he came into her, he lay still with a great sigh and for a moment she thought he had ejaculated. No, he was still hard in her, she could feel him. He was just resting as if he had climbed a great hill. No, she thought, he was only beginning to climb. Now they were climbing together, very slowly at first, a hill that promised to be high enough, quite high enough.

Because she tended to moan and croon many nonverbal noises while she was making love, she could tell he was not sure whether or not she had come. She had not, she could not the first time. She was too awkward and too curious with him to relax that much, and too tired to concentrate on her own sensations. Before he could ask her—if he meant to—she fell into sleep and its warm waters closed over her head. She was vaguely

144

aware of Tosca arriving in the bed with a flying leap and standing on her hip, hissing once at Itzak to warn him she was not to be had so easily as Dinah, then turning round and round and crawling under the covers to sleep between them, an ineffectual furry chaperon.

TWENTY-ONE

Laurie

Laurie could not understand why Jimmy thought the evening before had been funny or why he was peeved that Itzak Raab was staying with Dinah. Laurie thought it was a nice touch of class. He was cute, although awfully short. She had seen him on television and thought he would be as tall as Daddy. Dinah had knocked herself out doing all that cooking so that by the time the guests arrived, she could only sit nodding out and smiling wistfully. But Itzak had been watching Dinah. He might be interested, Laurie thought, and rather hoped it would be so. Maybe people in music were attracted to each other in different ways than normal people and Dinah wouldn't mind that Itzak was short and he wouldn't care that she was dumpy and fleshy.

In the meantime she had her own life to see to. She had been spending a great deal of time with Jimmy. He had been completely gentle and sweet and companionable with her. Except for an occasional peck on the cheek or squeeze of the hand, he had barely acknowledged their sexes. It had been soothing. He had made her feel at ease and safe.

He had been all of that, and she was sick of it. She had come to think of him as radiantly handsome beyond Tom, beyond any man she had been involved with. Normally, she didn't care much what a man looked like. What use was it, anyhow? Women fell in love with the men they could have. But why couldn't she have Jimmy? He was there, available. His wife apparently had no interest in him. He had made a mistake, but he seemed to have learned from it. She saw young women visit him once or twice, but he paid them less attention than he did his old buddies, especially those who had gone into the construction trades. He was friendlier with Toby Lloyd, who had used to live where the

145

MacIvors were, than any young woman. Willie said that after they finished the boathouse and gallery, he wouldn't take on another job for a year, but Jimmy had decided to go into building and was actively seeking connections.

The false sense of familiarity from their adolescence had made her fail to appreciate how much he had changed—and Tyrone too seemed not to have noticed—but she could see the way women looked at him, gazed after him on the street. She was grateful too how he had run interference for her in town, gone with her to New York, taken her into Boston twice. She sensed that both Susan and Willie worried about the amount of time Jimmy was spending with her, and she resented that apprehension. Did they think her a child who could not say no? During Easter dinner, she was particularly aware how they attempted to interpose themselves between Jimmy and her. Susan had placed them at table as far from each other as they could be, with neither occupying the head or foot. She was stuck between Donald and Willie, with Sally across from her. Were they afraid Tyrone would be annoyed? He never consulted her about his marriages or his affairs. He had planned to spend Easter in Italy with a Contessa Sforzi whose brother was to have been his partner in condo building on the coast of Spain. Something had queered that deal and cooled his romance, but Laurie was still resentful Tyrone had not intended to spend the holiday with her. Only by dumb luck had his plans changed, and he was only with her for twenty-four hours.

If she felt less like the victim of a cosmic bad joke these days, a relic with a Kick Me sign on her butt, it was in large part because Susan and Willie, and even Dinah, but preeminently Jimmy had given her a safe nest in which to recover a sense of herself. Tyrone had been enormously solicitous right after the disaster, but she saw now that he had carried her here because she embarrassed him in New York. Too much bad luck is never welcome at a dinner party. He had removed her to a safe distance, and left her to Susan and Willie. He could hardly blame her if she found other comforts.

Now with Tyrone deserting her again, what to do? She had never had to seduce. The problem had always been getting men to be patient until she could decide if she was serious enough to be willing. With Jimmy she knew she was willing. She imagined waking with him in her room. She imagined breakfast together in the diningroom, the French doors thrown open to the pond.

146

It was warming up. Today, Wednesday, the sun burned off the fog by nine in the morning and the sky was highly polished, an uninterrupted blue slick as a waxed tile.

She looked at herself in the mirror and thought she looked brighter than she had in several years. She had a light tan already from all the walking with Jimmy and Dinah. What had changed most was her expression, but she could not define the difference. Maybe I've lost weight, she thought, but she knew better because she had weighed herself on rising. She had gained two pounds.

Jimmy was already banging on the boathouse. Willie and he were at work most days by seven-thirty. She would have a livingroom facing the pond, opening onto a large deck. Behind would be a kitchenette, a lovely bath and then up a circular metal staircase, her bed in the former sail loft. Compared to the big house, the rooms would not be spacious, but certainly her bedroom would be larger than she had had in Chelsea. Lately she could remember that room without visibly flinching, but the lovemaking there was retroactively tainted by the corpse who had lain in her bed.

Sometimes she regretted Tyrone's decision that she should have her own little house. Her room in the big house had seemed for years her truest home, her continuity with childhood. She didn't really see why, with only the two of them, his houseguests and his assistant, his secretary and of course Celeste, she couldn't simply live on in the big house. Perhaps Tyrone was anticipating what she was beginning to imagine, that she might fall in love again and want privacy.

Obviously Jimmy cared about her. He had put her interests before his own time and again that spring. There was a kind of delicacy in him that was exceptional in a man. But how to break through that reserve? No doubt he was afraid to damage the friendship between them. She had to make the first move, but she had no idea how to begin. Suppose he was simply not attracted to her? Suppose he still saw her as the spoiled sixteen-year-old? She had seldom wished to be beautiful, because it seemed to her beauty had launched her mother into the world unarmed, unfit. When it was gone, a woman had nothing. What was so sad as a former beauty? Now she wished she had the confidence beauty gave. Suppose she made a move and Jimmy drew back, appalled.

Maybe he had a disease and that was why he wouldn't get

147

involved with any of those young women who called on him. But he seemed robust. She could see him on the roof, hammering rapidly and with impunity. In the sun of the morning he had peeled off his jacket, then his shirt, wearing only his undershirt. The sun made his hair flame. She imagined that it would feel more like plumes than like male hair.

If only Willie would be called away or be smitten with a sudden impulse to make things up with Dinah. She strolled over after breakfast to chat with them, but Willie was less friendly than usual. At first she wondered if he was annoyed with her because she had gone to Dinah's party. Jimmy had gone too. Besides, Willie sometimes asked her about Dinah, as if he really wanted to know. Susan never did, although if Jimmy or Laurie mentioned Dinah's name, Susan would stop whatever she was doing to listen. If she had witnessed three of Tyrone's divorces, she would not have believed middle-aged people could be so absurd about relationships. Willie would get a tense woebegone expression on his face that convinced Laurie he missed Dinah.

She felt like saying to him, go on, see her. Let me have a little time with Jimmy this morning. Willie obviously did not like leaving them alone together. If they needed to pick up something at the hardware store, if he did not send Jimmy outright, he would take Jimmy with him even when certainly one of them would have sufficed.

It wasn't until Thursday, when Willie had to meet with the sanitary engineers about the gallery while Jimmy stayed on to finish shingling the roof, that she had a chance to catch him alone. She climbed the ladder, balancing against the pitch of the roof.

"You're not afraid of heights," he said. "I remember. You were the best girl at climbing trees."

"I was." She was flattered he remembered. She had been inordinately proud of her ability. She sat next to him, unable to figure out what to do. "How did you get involved with your wife?"

If he thought that a non sequitur, he did not let on. "The usual way. I was working for a catering service and so was she."

"But how did it start between you?"

"One night late I gave her a ride home. She asked me in. Like that. How most things get started."

"Do you think a woman should be the aggressor?"

148

"Half an hour later, what difference does it make? But you were raised with more rigid sex role expectations than me."

"Because of Dinah?"

He nodded, staring off in the direction of the old house. "Be careful of your step. A roof can be a dangerous place."

She was left to puzzle over that remark, for he picked up his hammer. But the way he smiled at her. It was a knowing and an inviting smile, she thought, but how could she be sure? Why didn't he make a pass at her? She had not been in this situation since school, when she had wanted boys to ask her out who paid no attention. Jimmy paid attention. He had to be interested. He was cautious, viewing her as more fragile than she was.

If only he wasn't living at home! That too was awkward. He was saving money. At noon he accepted her invitation to come in for lunch. As if they were continuing the conversation on the roof, he said, "It's expensive to fly to Seattle. I have to be there while she has the baby, even though she doesn't want me to. I figure it's a last chance. And I want to see the baby."

Now she understood. She was sick with disappointment, but his hesitation was clear and she could not argue with it. "When is the baby due?"

"It's supposed to be next week. I know with a first baby it could be late, but I have to go out and wait. Willie understands, but Susan doesn't. She's convinced if we're not done by Memorial Day, Tyrone will be furious and somebody else will renovate the gallery."

"Really! Don't worry about it. Tyrone's doing it for me, anyhow." She thought she managed to sound quite blithe and sympathetic.

"Maybe you can feel him out about the timing."

"Sure." She felt vulnerable again. If Jimmy stayed in Seattle, what would happen to her? She had become dependent on him. It was more than that. She wanted to be with him. She could hardly beg him not to go to his estranged wife while she had his baby! That would be too gross.

As if he were reading her mind, he said, "Will you be all right here? I don't like to leave you alone. But Willie and Susan and Dinah are all available to you. No matter what happens, I won't stay in Seattle. If Lisa and I get together, I'll bring her and the baby back here."

"Will she want to come?"

"I don't even know that she'll do more than glare at me."

He sighed and took her hand. She felt it was an extremely meaningful gesture, in the context of what they'd been discussing. "I have to get my life settled. One way or the other. You understand."

"Of course," she said fervently and hollowly. "Of course!"

TWENTY-TWO
Willie

When Willie was first out of art school, he found sculpture a lonelier activity than he had anticipated in the scarce and shared studios of college. He had begun working to the radio and had discovered the talk programs, the call-ins. All day long people spoke to him while he worked, and mentally and sometimes aloud he answered them. If only Susan could learn to share that, she would not be so needy in the evenings for the sort of intense chatter she craved. Those voices discussed the news of the day, the issues, reviewed movies, kept him up with sports and the casual scandals of Washington and Hollywood. There was no subject out of current news that any guest mentioned on which Willie hadn't formed an opinion. Sometimes he found Susan touchingly childlike in how little she knew of what was happening in the world.

One reason he missed Dinah was that he used to discuss with her issues that roiled him up, when simply talking back to the radio didn't suffice. Everybody had sore spots. Willie knew that better than most people, because of listening to the call-in shows. Some people got furious if somebody said God damn or mentioned evolution. He got a little crazy about South Africa. It was the nightmare of his childhood played out.

He had grown up in a liberal family, with a father who always said, Remember *they're* human too and they have rights. Separate but equal, maintain the dignity of the races. A gentleman always thinks of the feelings of others. A gentleman acts to protect the weak and succor the needy. Their family treated the colored help well. He loved his Mona, whom he wasn't allowed to call Mammy because that was lacking in dignity. Then in his sophomore year at college, he became involved in civil rights.

150

It had seemed so obviously an extension of what he had been taught, that he could never have imagined his father's response of deep and abiding fury.

It had been a major rebellion. The murderous rage of the white crowds terrified him, but a man could not back down from what was right. He had forced himself again and again to march into that hideous turmoil, clutching a sign with some simple truth carefully lettered on it. He had learned a great deal. He had met other Dewitts, Black Dewitts, and that had intrigued him. One was Jason Dewitt, who was just his age, at least as bright and who wanted to be a lawyer. They were both in a small SCLC-inspired group. He learned they were distant cousins, for the Black Dewitts were another lineage from his paternal great-grandfather. Starting with nothing, they were scrambling into the middle class. Jason's father worked on the railway, as had his grandfather and two of his uncles. A brother and a sister were in the civil service. Another uncle had been in the Black Eagles, flying in World War II. Two other sisters taught school.

The Black Dewitts seemed to him at least as worthy, as cohesive, as gentle as the white Dewitts. He had attempted to convey this knowledge to his immediate family. It was not right to ignore them as kin. It was hypocritical to trace the family tree without that huge branch. He had had the zeal of a young missionary, and the righteousness of one who had been recently beaten in the service of a just cause. His father never forgave him.

Now news about South Africa woke that old mixture of guilt and passion, a sense of a wrong that must be righted and a sense too of a society grown up crooked and people caught in a dense suffocating weave of beliefs and pride and custom. That was what he had been re-creating in his big piece in which the vines all hung with baubles grew into a prison of wires that pierced flesh, an immense nation-tree of barbed wire. Finally he had brought it to triumphant conclusion, but there it stood radiating menace and no one saw it. He had organized a little program about South Africa at the Unitarian Church the winter before. Dinah had helped. She got more excited about nuclear waste and ground water and acid rain, but she had that capacity to listen and be moved by any good cause.

He had never been able to get Susan involved. She sympathized. Her heart was in the right place. It just didn't seem real to her unless she knew the person. She could get passionate

151

about the case of a woman about to lose her children because she had been found unfit by some ramrod judge, or a hemophiliac boy put out of school for having contracted AIDS. She did not read newspapers and tuned out TV news as clutter. When she did pick up the *New York Times*, it was to look for people she knew or had heard of, to torture herself with what was happening in New York without her being there. She was all concrete, he thought. Once he had considered that a difference between the sexes, because for years he had based his opinions of womankind on his mother and Susan; but Dinah was not that way.

He had grown up connected tightly into his family, a sense surrounding him of a comforting web of aunts, uncles, second cousins, great-grand-uncles. His involvement in civil rights had cut most of those ties till he had felt utterly lost. He had been desperate and confused about who he was, where he belonged. The Blacks he met in the movement were often friendly to him, but that friendliness had sharp limits. It was a walled garden in a howling wilderness. The other whites in the movement were just too different, too shrill and rude and noisy for him.

He met Susan by her running into him on her bicycle, and then being stammeringly, profusely apologetic. She had brought him back to her room in an old mansion near campus where she lived in an honors dorm. It was two on a warm April afternoon and nobody was around, including the housemother. She brought him up to her room to tend his wounds, the cuts on his forehead and arm. It had all been so unlikely and she was so radiantly lovely he had begun to make love to her. Perhaps he had a mild concussion. Certainly he had no memory of the accident at all, only of walking down the street and then coming to on the ground with her flower face bent over him.

He would never normally have seized a woman and borne her down on her bed and begun to make passionate love to her, a woman whose last name he had not even learned. He imagined that certainly Susan would not normally have allowed herself to be seized and taken. Perhaps she still felt guilty for running him down. Perhaps it was merely that the strong immediate attraction was mutual. Before she ludicrously smuggled him out of her dormitory at four, he had realized he had fallen into what he most needed, a nest. Susan had the capacity to create home wherever she was, in a motel overnight, in a dorm room. She had immediately centered him, giving him a firm placement.

He had fallen in love with her at once, with a relaxing sense of arriving where he had meant all along to go.

He had realized about himself at around that time, seeing what Susan did for him, that he was a man who must have a woman. There were men, he thought, who went a little crazy without a woman. There were others who would act the same whether they were married or single, whose real life was always with other men in bars or construction sites from which women were excluded. The Captain was like that. But he himself was a man who if he did not make love regularly with a woman and did not have a woman to live with, to make a home for him, was a tree cut off from its roots to wither. There was both strength and weakness in that, but finally he accepted who he was. Susan was as necessary to him as water or air. He grew out of their joining.

In the early years of his marriage with Susan he had tried to talk about that sense of unity at the core, of being almost physically rooted in her, with his brother Ted and with a friend, a fellow artist who had also recently married. What he had learned was that he could not speak of it to other men. They seemed able to feel nothing but contempt for a man who acted and felt deeply monogamous and who was willing to say how much he depended on his wife.

It was a permanent irony that he, who was so thoroughly monogamous in his orientation, should also have been one of the only people he knew who had lived for ten years in a stable and serious triangle. He had thought of himself as having two wives. They were both his and he was theirs.

At times he felt attracted to other women, particularly if they touched him. He could still remember Janette Burdock kissing him once in the moonlight when she was drunk. He sensed that Jimmy's sexuality was different. He wished they could talk, that they could make each other understand, but the deep inhibition of discussing sex with family members stood in the way. He knew that Jimmy's sexuality was more mercurial than his own, could flow in any direction, easily roused, easily satiated. For Willie, only women who touched him were real to him and only the women he mated with, frequently and in full security of possession, could thoroughly excite him.

He was utterly committed to Susan. He would disintegrate if anything happened to her and they were pried apart. But he had grown dependent on Dinah and now he missed her every day, several times a day. It was as if he kept trying to run down a flight of steps where always one step was missing, and he could not seem to learn it was gone.

He understood Susan's fussing over Dinah's presence next door much more clearly than he thought Susan did. If Dinah were dead, if she were in Paris or San Diego, then she would be gone except for memory. They could possess her in absence and remake their memories accordingly. However, there she was under their noses, giving parties, digging up her garden, walking around the pond every morning although now she detoured out to the road instead of crossing their little beach. As the weather warmed up, her music flowed out through the open windows. He could smell woodsmoke from her fireplace. Today he could smell what she was cooking for supper. He could hear her rough laughter and the voices of her arriving guests. Susan could say how she was sure Dinah would simply not make it out there without them to provide her with a ready-made life, but Willie thought all those people seemed to be having a dandy time. Not only did Jimmy come downstairs wearing his best blazer and his good turtleneck but Burt and Leroy drove up. Susan stationed herself at the window and called out as each car arrived. Zee Gildner. The Hills! A subtle war over friends was being fought. Susan, who feared she was losing, had stopped volunteering at the library as if to avoid comparison. "I think I just saw Laurie over there," Susan reported.

Susan kept saying they no longer had to apologize for their weird life, but he felt as if he had lost status in the eyes of other men. If overtly he had been considered peculiar, always there had been an undertone of envy, you old cock, got two women and makes them accept each other too! He never bothered to explain it was the two women who had chosen each other, and that he had managed handily to include himself. Besides, after the first six months, it wasn't that way. In some ways he and Dinah were better suited than Dinah and Susan. If they never noticed that, it was out of loyalty to sisterly ideals from the period each had decided to try a relationship with a woman.

Except for the sound of cars arriving and voices in the yard, Saturday night passed agreeably and quietly. Since Tyrone had let them know he wasn't coming in until next morning, by private plane, Willie had stopped at the market to rent a Paul Newman film that Susan had regretted missing. After a light digestible supper he cooked (flounder, rice pilaf, a salad) they

154

watched it. Willie felt bad about the salad, boughten iceberg lettuce. By this late in April, they always had salad from the garden. He noticed that Dinah did. Her garden was way ahead of his.

About nine, Susan went upstairs. When she came down in the new peach peignoir she had bought recently, he understood she was inviting him. Surprisingly she spread out a quilt in front of the fireplace. Usually she would not make love downstairs for fear someone would look through the window and see them, but tonight that did not seem to cross her mind.

He did not think she came, although she insisted she had, but he did not worry about it. He figured tomorrow or the next day they would make love upstairs, and she would come. The idea of making love by the fireplace had excited her more than the reality, but with Susan, that was often okay. She would remember the scene romantically and remind him of it.

Then came Easter. Susan had not realized that Tyrone would be arriving with his assistant and his secretary. She had not planned dinner for two extra people: the ham had been a little skimpy, as was the cake. She had insisted on doing the cooking herself, with the result that dinner was an hour and a half late. Everything looked perfect and was slightly off: a little dry, overcooked, the sauce floury, the glaze sugary, the pastry chewy.

Susan was upset when she pried Dinah's guest list out of Laurie. She said to Willie, as they were cleaning up afterward, "She only gave a party to compete blatantly with us! I can't believe she's being so shameless. And there's Jimmy and Laurie and Burt and Leroy all eating it up, going from one to the other so they can comparison shop! It's vulgar."

"What does it matter? This was a great dinner." Sometimes he saw Susan as a pot of sugar syrup, fruit compote, something that would froth up and boil over if it was not watched and stirred. She could lather herself over the littlest things. It made her exciting. He felt immensely calm and strong next to her. He saw himself as a noble and powerfully built Percheron next to a delicate overbred lightning fast Arabian. Unlike Dinah, Susan would never be able to manage without him.

"But inviting Itzak Raab. She's always poking vicious fun at me when Tyrone brings home some painter I've read about in *The Times* and I dare to think it's exciting. She's always been so superior about things any normal human would enjoy. It's a kind of puritanism, but it didn't survive wanting to throw something in our faces. She only invited him because she thinks it will put my nose out of joint."

"But we've never even heard him play. What do we care?" Willie knew about Itzak because he had been interviewed on "Fresh Air" on public radio. He didn't remember much, except that Itzak sounded as if he came from New York but had been living abroad for years.

Jimmy, who walked in on the end of the conversation, said, "Don't you guys remember she got a grant to write a piece of music for him?"

"She's always getting some grant," Susan said. "Who can remember?"

Willie felt guilty that he had paid no attention. Their lives had become too chaotic; important information slipped past him.

The next morning as he was working in his studio, he saw the man Itzak walking with Dinah by the lake, a couple of hours later than her usual hike. He had stayed. Perhaps she had other guests? He could not help watching them out of sight into the woods. They were talking intently. Itzak touched her arm, her cheek, her ass. Willie felt a blow in his own belly as if something hard and metallic had entered him. He could not catch his breath. They were lost to him among the trees but he could still see that hand cupping her buttock for a moment as they walked, turned toward each other, closing in like parentheses.

He sat abruptly on his stool. He did not think of himself as jealous, but what he had seen made him feel disemboweled. It was not right! He longed to chase after them and do something to the man. Push him in the pond, stomp on his face, tear at him so that he would hurt as Willie was hurting. How could Dinah let him? She had slept with him. She had taken Itzak into that bed he himself had hardly ever slept in.

He was stunned. He had not imagined she would so quickly let another man have her. He had figured that Susan's anger would wear off and their life would resume together. Partly he had let Susan pull him loose from Dinah so that she would calm down. He wanted her to stop complaining and remaking their history together so that Dinah became ever the deeper villain. He gave up trying to start his new piece that was to be a great shining fishhook impaling a man, and went to work with Jimmy on the boathouse roof. All day he kept glancing toward Dinah's. Twice more he saw them together. He kept waiting for the man

156

to clear out, but that evening, he was still there, and the next morning. He was a strongly built man but short. Willie kept hearing his voice outside, sharp, rasping on his ears. They seemed noisy with each other, talking, talking, arguing, singing at the top of their lungs. They played music together half the day, something Willie could not do with her. He wondered if it was intimate, like making love. They both played flute sometimes and sometimes Dinah played piano and the man, flute.

Finally, finally he saw Dinah take Itzak off in her car. When she returned an hour and a half later, she was alone. The intruder was gone. He knew that before Dinah had come to them, she had had casual affairs. No doubt this was one of them; but suppose it wasn't. It seemed to him he had thought about nothing else for days. He could not see anything, he could not work. He felt as if that initial metal bolt were fixed through him, as if he were the man in his sculpture. His energy, his attention were bleeding away.

He bided his time. The next morning Susan was sleeping turned on her side with her auburn hair falling over her face, snoring softly, sweetly, sounding like a kettle about to boil as he slid out of bed even more quietly than usual and slipped downstairs. He was early in order to watch for Dinah. He dressed in the kitchen, standing at a window. Jimmy still slept upstairs. Jimmy would be pleased, no doubt, if he made up with Dinah, but he felt embarrassed in front of his son, wishing their foibles and emotional turbulence were not so badly apparent. When he had arrived in his parents' house, he would have preferred to remain ignorant of the ups and downs of their marriage.

When he saw her he was ready to take off. Guiltily he felt the house behind him, the windows staring after him. He hoped nothing would wake Susan. He could not bear the fight that would result. He had no idea what he was going to say to Dinah, but he could not stay away. He had to take hold of her and do something, make her look at him, make her talk to him, he did not know. He was hurting and could not focus on anything else.

He ran down the path after her. She was walking quickly, but when she heard his steps, she swung around startled. When she saw it was him, her face closed in and then slightly relaxed. "Is something wrong?"

He could not think what to say. Her face seemed vivid, the dark eyes that always warmed him. Coffee. She looked smaller, rounder, perter than he remembered. She looked like an apple,

157

something to bite, to nibble on. He had no words in his mind at all, only his pain and his delight. He could not think of anything at all to say so he took hold of her by the shoulders and lifted her off her feet to kiss her. She came against him awkwardly and then she kicked him in the shin.

He dropped her and then picked her up again and continued. He said her name again and again. Finally she pried herself loose and fell back against an oak to stand at bay defying him. "Jealous, are we?"

"How could you?"

"What business is it of yours?" Then suddenly she was laughing and he was laughing too. He seized her head between his hands and shook her, cupping her ears. He hugged her again and this time she hugged him back.

"Willie, you're impossible! Have you no shame?"

"I want you. I can't help it."

"You're a pig! You're a dog! You're a jackass!"

He was turning in a slow circle, still clutching her by the waist. Where could they do it? He wanted just to fall on the ground and get into her at once, but it was chilly and wet with last night's rain. He thought of pushing into her against the oak, but probably she would not come and she had to. No, they needed a bed. A bed someplace. If they went back to Dinah's house, Susan would see them. The Captain's house. Those people had left a key with Susan, because she had volunteered to let the tile person in when she came to work on the kitchen and bathrooms sometime in the next two weeks. Everything was done except tiling and painting. Susan had offered to keep track of the work for the MacIvors. They had been overjoyed. He could see the key Candida MacIvor had handed to Susan. It was hanging in the kitchen, on the same peg as the key Susan was proud to have that unlocked Tyrone's house. "Dinah, wait for me. I'll be right back. I love you. Please wait for me."

"What's the matter? You have to take a crap? You suddenly remembered a pot on the stove? You left the water running?"

"Yes, yes," he shouted and rushed back along the path to his house. He ran and ran with his heart bursting. The key was hanging on a peg behind the door, neatly labeled in Susan's round script, Dr. MacIvor residence. He took it and then hovered at the foot of the steps listening. He could hear Jimmy's clock radio faintly playing. No sound from Susan, who would not normally rise for two hours. Shutting the door quietly, he

158

ran toward where he had left Dinah. He half expected her to be gone. She might be barricaded into her house. No, she was sitting on a log about twenty yards farther along the path, giving him a slowly measuring look but waiting. He was almost paralyzed by guilt for the pain he imagined he had caused her, but he had to keep moving toward her through the thick air and the light that seemed bright and icy. The light had turned to heavy crystal. Even the trees looked judgmental.

Then he had his hands on her again. She was warm and solid. Her flesh was more compact and more resilient then Susan's. She felt more animallike. She felt stronger. He was rushing her along the path toward the Captain's house. She did not say anything at all until they had stepped into the clearing. ''Aren't they here?'' She was looking at the key in his hand.

''They went back Monday morning to Boston.'' He knew the tiler and the painters were not about to walk in, because he had the key. The beds must be ready to use, because Candida and Alec had slept there that weekend.

''High-tech boxy,'' she said with disgust as they came into what had been the hall and now was a huge livingroom two stories tall. Of the previous house, only a fireplace and a couple of the old structural beams remained, now suspended in midair. Blowsy white couches like overstuffed beanbags were clumped before the fireplace and again before the floor to ceiling windows that opened on the pond.

The short steep stairs like the flight in Dinah's house had been replaced with circular metal stairs—the same kind Willie had installed in Laurie's. The local supply house had run a special on them and all the builders were using them this year. Dinah was keeping up a sarcastic commentary on the furniture and the construction and the artwork he could barely hear for the blood roaring in his ears. He was erect already and his prick was rubbing on his jeans. He was figuring out where the bedroom would be. He got it right on the first try, a vast king-sized bed onto which he tugged her, falling on her before she could change her mind. He was afraid something would go wrong and she would escape him and disappear.

Dinah was not to be hurried. She did not undress but made him wrestle her, laughing under him, sliding away from him, nipping his ears, his wrists, his cheeks. She did not usually bite him, but she was still angry. In the middle of kissing him she would suddenly turn and sink her teeth into his shoulder. He got on her, something they did not do often because of their discrepancy in weight and size. He did not like to make her feel smothered. This time he was too needy, too harried to wait for her to climb on him. Ah, he was taking her back, taking her back. He determined to make it last. With Dinah there was a point in fucking when he could feel things change, as if he penetrated suddenly to a deeper hotter layer. Her whole body seemed to expand then. She would seem to wrap up and around him, or if she were on top, to flow over him as if her bones had turned electric eels. Then he always knew she would come soon.

Afterward they lay side by side on the awning-striped bedspread recovering. He decided he would say nothing about the man. Why bother? That man was gone and Willie was here, in possession. It was more generous to pretend he knew nothing.

"How are you going to explain this chez vous?" She rose on her elbow.

"I didn't think I would. It would only upset her."

"And we mustn't upset her. Yes, that was how Chamberlain felt about Hitler, so he gave him Czechoslovakia."

He would not argue. He felt too good. "Weren't you surprised I have a key to this house?"

"You're turning into the local concierge for all the summer people."

She was angry still. He tried to think of something to placate her. He could not volunteer to cook one of her favorite meals, which had always worked in the past, because they could not eat together. He would make a promise. "Look, I want things straightened out. I want to work toward getting us all back together again. That's my goal. Wouldn't you rather have that too, than stay mad at me?"

She was silent a long time, then sat up shivering. The furnace was set to come on only if the temperature fell below 40 inside, so the pipes would not freeze in the event of an unseasonable frost. "Yes," she said finally and sadly. "I'd rather have that. But what can you do?"

"Work on her. Gradually. I'm telling you, this fall we'll all make it up and be back together. . . . Now let me give you a massage." She could never resist that, he knew; like a cat, she always wanted her back rubbed.

"We left a stain like a paramecium."

"It'll dry. They'll never notice."

Dinah smiled, one side of her mouth curling up. "Most people notice stains on their bedspreads, Willie."

"So they'll think the roof leaks."

With a sigh she turned onto her stomach letting him straddle her to begin. Her tight hard buttocks bunched beneath him. He swore to himself he would straighten everything out in the fall. He did not have faith he could work Susan around during the summer, but he would keep on it. Eventually his persistence would pay off, because Susan was pulled emotionally hither and yon and would be vulnerable to his wishes at some point, maybe even begin to yearn for Dinah on her own. As he kneaded Dinah's strong back, he thought of a tripod, a three-legged stool, sturdy like the one he used when he was working. His life would once again be set firmly in both of them, his two sweet and spicy and complementary women. His wives.

TWENTY-THREE

Susan

Susan strongly objected to what the government had done to holidays. When Memorial Day was really the end of May, it had been the true beginning of summer. Now it was usually too early, when weather was uncertain on the Cape and a week could make an enormous difference. Willie was looking forward to Tyrone's first party of the season and wanted it as soon as possible, so he did not agree. Often he would seem to assent, to avoid a fight, but he always did so with particularly vague phrases so that she knew he secretly disagreed. It was an irritating habit.

She was even more eager for the party than Willie, but she could gladly wait an extra week for a better chance of decent weather. The shad bloom was just falling from the trees, an impressionist dream of white. Burt brought by smoked alewives, saying the run was ending. Willie had been unusually considerate and placating in the past few weeks, as if worried about her. Or perhaps now that they had settled into a real marriage again, he simply had more time for her. He had been working regularly on the boathouse, without her having to nag him, and it was close to completion. The electrician had finally deigned to come. Jimmy returned from Seattle in time to help Willie with the finish work.

"What happened in Seattle?" she asked Jimmy. "Are you getting back together?"

"We're starting divorce proceedings. That's what Lisa wants."

"What do you want?"

"I'd rather be back with her, but not the way she feels about me now."

He had been there for the birth of his son. Although they had agreed to call a boy Gordon after Willie's father, Lisa had unilaterally changed her mind and named the baby Christopher. It seemed to her, listening to Jimmy, that his time had been divided between the hospital and lawyers' offices. He had seen his lawyer, Lisa's lawyer and the lawyer representing the third partner in the restaurant. There seemed to be legal complications around the bankruptcy.

Jimmy presented her with Polaroid shots of the baby, held by Jimmy or a sullen Lisa. Susan was a grandmother. She found it disquieting that an undistinguished-looking infant named Christopher in Seattle had some claim on her. She hoped that Jimmy would not go around making a big fuss, as she did not find grandparenthood inspiring. She was hardly ready to take to an overstuffed chair and watch TV game shows all day as her own grandma had.

Jimmy was around little that week. He was off with his old buddies, hanging out with the Captain, over at Dinah's and once again spending too much time with Laurie. She began to wonder if she had been wise to wish that he would not go back to Lisa. She remembered that someone had said that the worst fate was getting what you prayed for. She had certainly craved him with his wife and restored to her.

Why did he want to hang around with those losers from high school? Whatever was the point of sending him to Dartmouth if here he was back drinking beer with the good old boys he had palled around with years ago, when she had worried he would get into trouble as so many of them did and amount to nothing? Fishermen, shellfish farmers, carpenters, plumbers, plasterers, the managers of motels and clam shacks. He was even dragging Laurie along to the movies and out to fast food with those yokels. Laurie would feel contempt for him; Tyrone would hear. It

162

was potentially highly embarrassing. She tried to raise the subject with Jimmy twice, but it was as if she spoke in a pitch too high for him to hear. He simply did not respond. It was like yelling at Bogey, except that Bogey would hang his head and whine.

At least Willie was acting more responsibly. Not only had they almost completed the boathouse for Laurie, but he had even taken an interest in the work the MacIvors were having done. Several times he took the key to check on what the tiler had done and the progress of the painters. Finally that work was completed and the MacIvors would be out for Memorial Day weekend. Tyrone had invited them to his party, and she was thinking of asking them along to the traditional picnic she made for Tyrone Saturday of the holiday weekend.

"Isn't it wonderful what the MacIvors have done with that old house?"

"Art by the yard. Ruler minimalism. Something about the place makes me think of a furniture showroom." He shrugged.

Willie thought everyone should furnish a livingroom with antiques or at least old pieces; it was a prejudice of his, on a par with believing that Europeans did not know how to cure ham. Her husband was a creature of his emotions and his prejudices. Her taste was trained in areas where he still relied upon attitudes inculcated in his ancestral home. Mostly she did not mind. Her husband: it was years since she had thought of him that way. All relationships between any two of the three of them had been supposed to be equal. Dinah had a strong sense of what was due her. She was forever cutting a pie into fanatically equal slices, counting chocolates in a box to make sure each got his or her entitled share. A child of poverty, Susan told herself with pity. Dinah would never cease to be a child of want. Now Susan was free of that constant judgmental and measuring gaze.

When she saw Dinah in the yard, she often found an excuse to venture out and say hello quickly. She took a serene satisfaction in being the first to speak in an unfailingly cheery greeting. "Isn't it lovely," she'd say. Or, "Looks like rain, doesn't it?" Nothing Dinah could use to start a conversation but pinning her in place, the neighbor to whom one was civil.

She had recovered completely, so when she caught a glimpse of Dinah in Souza's Market or in the post office picking up her mail, she would go out of her way to greet her. Dinah's face was supremely readable; she was still a child that way, as in so many others. A loud egotistical child. Now a child whose feelings had been hurt. Her eyes enlarged and her mouth turned down. Susan could have laughed out loud. It was such a charade, but it did her good to prove to herself how far she had come since the days when Dinah's frown could make her cry and Dinah's anger could make her shudder and rush to placate, to please.

Today as soon as Susan walked into Souza's, she saw Dinah buying yogurt and local brown eggs. Now she was headed for the meat counter, Susan loitered until Dinah was waiting for Mr. Rimini, the butcher, to grind chuck for her. Then Susan came briskly up to the counter and called to him. "Mr. Rimini, I'm here to pick up my boned chicken breasts!" To Dinah she said in that cheery lacquered tone, "I do hope the weather is fair tomorrow. It's time for our annual picnic on Bracken Pond."

Dinah looked at her uncertainly, obviously waiting to see if she were included, as the picnic had always been a family affair. Susan turned her gaze on the chops laid out under glass. She was acting the friendly neighbor who had no idea what the other person was expecting. Ah, there was an actress inside that had been biding her time all these years. She hoped that Dinah would break down and try to invite herself. Instead as Dinah took her package from Mr. Rimini she muttered, "Too bad. I heard the sky was falling tomorrow. Maybe only the market."

Jimmy went next door far more than Susan liked, and Dinah had begun to chat with Willie in the yard. He let himself be sucked into conversation, as she never permitted Dinah to draw her. He simply lacked the social maneuverability Susan possessed. She decided not to interfere, although sometimes when they seemed to be talking too long and too intimately, she stood at the window fuming. She knew that hidden within was a jagged wound Dinah had given her self-esteem, not in one blow but in hundreds of small contemptuous lessons in how to be a good person like Dinah, rather than a flighty butterfly like herself. She spread out the wings of the new kimono she had made from a bolt of the rayon she had designed for Young Ideas. The dress manufacturer who had bought up most of it was using it for a dress, a Belle France knockoff, but she had made a kimono with enormous sleeves. She made them flutter before the mirror. Suddenly a terrible melancholy blew through her like a wind carrying fog off the ocean.

She could have wept for how passionately she had loved Dinah. Dinah had made her feel precious. Oh, she had been sore with discontent then, bored to disgust with her marriage, tired of being the good mother of two children, no longer small and sweet and lovable and malleable and decorative, but now aggressive, secretive adolescents. Siobhan could have had a wonderful adolescence. Susan hadn't been a ghastly resentful mother who tried to keep her daughter in rompers. She had been as excited as Siobhan when her daughter began to show an interest in boys, began to date. Susan had wanted to be truly helpful and to share her daughter's adventures, an understanding mother as far as possible from the pious repressive attitude of her own mother. But Siobhan had been closed, hostile. Had lied about the most innocuous things. Had met boys secretly, when she could simply have told Susan where she was going. Jimmy had always been taciturn. Her adolescent children walled her out of their intimate lives. She had responded by joining everything in town, PTA, library, whatever. She had stared in the mirror and wanted, wanted, wanted to feel, to know, to experience, to be loved.

Dinah had come back from New Mexico like the hero in a Western riding into town. She had clanked and glittered. Her sexual confidence had been as tangible to Susan as the sun's heat freckling her arm.

Everything about Susan that Willie took for granted was new and splendid to Dinah. Because Dinah was a woman, she appreciated all those fine little touches and gestures and prettinesses, but she was not a rival. Dinah would never have made herself a dress or even knitted a scarf. She had no idea how to shop. She bought gaudy or splendid items on impulse, like a gorgeous suede vest in purple and black, and then put them on with jeans and wore them till they were filthy and spoiled.

I am forty-six, Susan told her favorite mirror, the long one in which she could see herself entire, although I don't look that old. Dr. MacIvor was shocked when he met Jimmy. He said I couldn't be old enough to have a son in his twenties, so probably he thought I was thirty-eight or forty at the most. My skin is still good. My hair hasn't thinned. I keep my weight under control. But who will ever love me the way I want to be loved? I'll die and it will never happen. Oh, Willie loves me the best he can, but he's so self-involved and distracted, and he simply doesn't have the temperament for a grand passion. He's a man of appetites, not of passions.

In girlhood, she had imagined love that would be a wall of

165

compelling emotion like the sound of opera, *La Bohème* or even the musicals she had been fond of when she was a girl, *An American in Paris*. Oh, she had experienced that with Willie in the early days of their affair. It had begun irresistibly. After she had knocked him down, he had swept her off her feet, just as if they were in a movie. It was one of her fantasies come to life. He had been handsome, courteous but unstoppable. If she hadn't been interested, she would never have brought him back to her room, but she hadn't expected anything to happen. She had only hoped something would.

The year before she had had a satisfyingly tempestuous affair with Earl, a young man she had met at a fraternity party, but her passionate nature had frightened him off. He wanted a bland meek girl, which he speedily found. The campus was rife with soft-spoken belles who concealed wills of steel behind a simper. No, Willie had not fallen in love the way Earl had, keeping one hand on dry land so he could haul himself out if the going got rough. Willie had given himself totally.

Slow tears rolled down her face as she flung herself on her bed, remembering how intensely they had longed to be together, how she crept out of her dorm at night to meet him, how they had made love in the grass. She wanted to feel that way again, with love taking her over utterly. Was her life done at forty-six? Was there nothing to look forward to but slowly dying? She could not stand the thought of simply enduring year after year, drinking tea in bed, coming down to the kitchen with Willie already working in his studio, planning dinner parties with no-bodies, hearing Willie gossip about decisions of the selectmen and the Board of Appeals, making designs for fabrics to clothe other women as they lunched with lovers, chattered wittily at cocktail parties, attended openings and were photographed.

How many more thousand times would she stand there brushing her teeth in that bathroom she had created out of a moldy dark room, pale green, the sloping ceiling beams stenciled with leaves, the corner airy with ferns? How often would she peer in that mirror measuring the pores in her nose? How many more nights would she lie awake while Willie snored and dream of slipping out into the night to meet someone, anyone? Is this it? All there would be for her forever and ever until death gnawed her to the bones? Is this all that was going to happen to her, who had so much to give to love?

TWENTY-FOUR

Dinah

The third week in May, Dinah drove to New York with Sal from the Moonsnails. Itzak had invited her to his Sunday afternoon recital. "Four P.M. Horowitz time," he said on the phone. That was when Vladimir Horowitz always scheduled concerts. She would meet him afterward and spend three days with him before he left for the West Coast.

Sal was twenty-nine and would have won a music scholarship had he lived anyplace else, she thought. His father was a fisherman lost at sea. Both his brothers were fishermen too. Sal played just about anything, but he was their lead guitarist. From a family who never "crossed the bridge" over the Canal to the mainland, he had learned everything he knew from records. He was very bright, set up their amps and synthesizers, but he had dropped out of high school from boredom at sixteen and could scarcely read. He was going to New York to visit an old girlfriend he was still crazy for. Dinah would not see him again until they met to drive back, but they sang all the way down.

It was abrupt to hop out of Sal's pickup outside Carnegie Hall, give her name at the box office and be escorted to one of the chairs set up on the stage. The concert had been sold out for several weeks before it had occurred to Itzak to invite her, but sitting on the stage would give her a better view anyhow. She was vaguely aware she should be more dressed up; she hadn't realized she'd be highly visible. She was handed over by the usher to a tall grizzled hard-talking man who was Itzak's manager. She knew his name, of course, but had never got in to see him in the days she had tried. He looked at her jeans, Mark's old jacket, her high leather sneakers and purple silk shirt with a sneer. He looked martyred, he looked bored. A flustered assistant something took her rucksack away backstage.

She did not feel it would be wise to intrude on Itzak beforehand and doubted she would have been let near him in any case. She wondered if she should have come. He certainly pulled out a mixed crowd. She waved to her old flute teacher—his as well.

A good dose of the Juilliard faculty had bestirred themselves to hear him. The audience simmered, waiting: a susurrus nothing like the wind in the pines or the surf battering the shore. Human excitement. The audience burst into frenzy when he strolled out flute hanging from his hand looking like someone who had wandered along, suddenly breaking into a great grin, saluting the audience with the flute. Dinah, who wasn't bad with audiences herself, recognized a master showman. He was not in the line of the demoniacs, or the businesslike, or the monks: his pose was more, Hey, look what we have here, isn't this fun, isn't this super stuff?

If she had had a seat in the audience, she would have disappeared with him into the intricacies of the Bach A Minor at once, but up here on the stage, she could not ignore the great waves of love and sex and charisma that washed through the music and churned from the audience. How could she possibly be meaningfully involved with a man who played audiences as well as his flute? What was real was the commission. The rest was circumstance. It was like standing outside the Lincoln monument and imagining you could camp in it.

The big surprise came in the second half of the program. After the Beethoven with his accompanist Tom, out came a cellist and planted her spike in the floor. Much adjusting of chairs and music stands, assistants flitting across the stage with that air of, If I move quickly and don't look sideways, you can't really see me, and then he announced he was going to play a very new piece of music by a friend of his, and proceeded into the Meditation—whose parts he had asked for on the Cape. She had assumed he was wanting to check out her musicianship. How it sang. Her face was burning with excitement and shock. He played so much better than Kyle it took the piece where she had imagined it, yes, that pattern rising, rising, circling, the hawk pattern with its sharp predatory mournful cry and the piano scuttling underneath, the cello circling it on wide extended heron wings. Oh, this was a bed present indeed, this was perfection. Although if he had asked her, she would have told him to push the tempo there, punch it harder. His accompanist Tom was better than the pianist in Boston, but the cellist lacked Nita's clear singing tone. Nita understood her music thoroughly.

Now the applause made the air itself turn to noise, a medium thicker than water heavily churning. He was beckoning to her to rise, which she did, willingly. To think she had considered not coming. It had been a matter of chance, of Sal planning a trip at the same time. She had accepted Itzak's invitation so casually, she could fall through the floorboards that had suddenly turned to gauze.

She scarcely heard the Mozart. She did not remember leaving the stage. She collected herself only when she realized they were climbing into a limo, bidding farewell to two dozen broad and important men. Itzak had declined a party, dinner. They were going off to his apartment, where he would have Chinese food delivered from his favorite spot. At the last moment a flunkey turned up with her rucksack grasped gingerly by a strap and handed it in.

Itzak had what she thought of as a typical city apartment: a roomy foyer, a large impressive livingroom with a view of the East River, a middling bedroom, a tiny kitchen and tiny bath. It was furnished with a combination of department store couches and storage units and old-fashioned mahogany pieces that had belonged to his grandparents. It reminded her of the apartment she had shared with Mark on the Lower East Side, not rationally, because this was far fancier, roomier, cleaner and cost more a month for condo maintenance than the total rent on that building would have brought her landlord. What was familiar to her was the air of camping in New York, the unpacked boxes filling a closet and lining the foyer, the temporary stratagems for managing, the shelves purchased but not put up, the suitcases never out of sight. Its air of being only passably satisfactory was soothing after the concert. It humanized him.

"Why didn't you tell me you were going to play the Meditation? I mean, suppose I'd screamed or fainted on the stage?"

"I only decided to do it two weeks ago, when the programs were printed already. Why scream? It wasn't satisfactory?"

"You have to be joking. It was superb. Although you know when you get to the part that goes," she began to sing it, and discussion was launched and she forgot to be in awe.

"Besides," he said as they sat down to eat, "a piece belongs to whoever plays it.

> A poem is a costume anyone may put on
> but like the cloak his abandoned wife
> sent to Herakles, it may burn through
> the skin, may char the bones oh quietly
> for truth is the subtlest poison . . ."

He was quoting Mark at her. She was startled, because no one had done so in years and because she had been rereading his poems lately. She had *Intensive Care*, his last book, beside her bed. Itzak must have noticed.

"Do you enjoy his poetry?" she asked cautiously.

"I have been. I hadn't ever read him. Oh, I read 'Skull Dance' in college—I think everybody did. 'Child of Fire'—that's you, isn't it?"

"Nobody in a poem *is* anybody in the normal sense. Poems may start out of an argument or a landscape, but off they go in their own dimension. It's tangential only. Like when people tell you what Bach's A Minor means."

She found his intense beam of curiosity disquieting, because she was not sure what it implied—if anything. She had the sense of a sharp passionate mind meshing poorly with its surroundings. He was fiercely discontented.

Itzak was in a state of deep confusion about his life, which led him to cast about for various stratagems that might reorganize it. Probably going to bed with her had been one of those attempts, along with reading the local real estate ads wherever he was (Should I buy a summer home, to have a place to go?) and calling friends in Boston about whether he should move there. She understood his unsettled state. He was on the road a great deal. His life had changed too much in a short time. Returning to the States had meant dispensing with the network of friends built up during a decade of marriage and living in London. He thought of moving out of the city as self-rescue.

Their sex began to improve as they got used to each other. He liked her body and he liked eating pussy. She began to understand that if she let him eat her to climax, he was more relaxed when they came to fucking. He did not worry as much then whether he would come before she did, and if she came again that was nice, but not critical. He told her once that his wife had lost interest in oral sex when she became passionately engaged in trying to become pregnant. She could feel an enormous wound to his pride and his sexual confidence barely healed over from his marriage, but she did not think it had left him crippled. Only sore.

The next night they went to the Brooklyn Academy of Music to hear the new Glass, sitting with Tom and his wife and going out for a drink with them afterward. Waking beside him the next morning after good music followed by good sex, she thought, I

170

could just stay here and write music and he'd play it better than anyone in the world, and what more could I ask? She felt immediately as if she had wished for life as a harem slave or a bonbon eater. It was silly and sinful to wish for, and besides, nobody was offering it.

They had coffee at their old teacher's apartment. When they arrived, Madam was just finishing with a student, who grew visibly white when he saw Itzak at the door. He dropped music all over the foyer. Itzak saw nothing, greeting Madam warmly and being passionately embraced.

"So, you still look like a street urchin when your piece is premiered at Carnegie? Never will you learn, Dinah."

"Actually, it wasn't the premiere." She was startled how Madam had aged. Her hands had a little wobble. Was that the ravages of a stroke in her face? Dinah felt frightened. The idea of not being able to go back to Madam if she had to was definitely scary.

They stopped at the Greenwich School to hear the Downtown Ensemble play some new German music that night and stayed up much too late afterward talking, making love, talking. Neither wanted to let go into silence.

When Sal, who kept yawning, picked her up, she took over the driving as soon as they hit Connecticut. She realized she had said nothing to Itzak about the renewal of her sexual relationship with Willie. It was a secret. Willie had come back to her, but he could not let Susan know that. Susan would punish him. Furthermore, if Susan realized they were fucking, she would never come back to Dinah. Dinah protected herself as well as Willie as well as Susan by her silence. Her loyalty to both Willie and Susan was old and strong. She did not like to lie to anyone; she did not like to lie to Itzak by omission. On the other hand, who did he see when he was on the road? She did not have the right to ask. The only person who knew everything was Nita, who thought she should drop Willie for Itzak, promptly.

She came back hot on her work. Music felt even more important and central in the universe than it usually did. That hit of applause, no doubt it had pumped her up. The next morning she met Willie at the MacIvors and the connection was as strong as if it had never been interrupted.

It felt awkward, weird, raw to be scampering around meeting once in the boathouse while Laurie was in Boston, usually in the MacIvors' house, a couple of times in the woods since the weather was warming up. They had been in a marriage of sorts for ten years. She would have minded fooling Susan more if Susan were not playing Lady-of-the-Manor-Greeting-the-Peasants. Susan dashed from the house or crossed the street in town especially to greet her with a false club lady sociability. It was an insult to their former intimacy, a mockery of the passion and sweetness they had known together.

Following that first time Willie came after her, Dinah felt ashamed when she saw Susan. She could not even meet her gaze. She felt as if her guilt were so visible Susan must sniff at her and smell Willie on her skin. Gradually the sense of wrongfully deceiving Susan eroded under that maliciously empty manner. As Dinah cooked or washed up, she worked on justifying herself. She had had her own independent loving relationship with Willie. If Susan wanted to dump her, Susan had no right to interfere between them. Deceiving Susan was for her own good, because Susan needed her and just wouldn't admit it.

Over the next week, she got further and further into the third section that had given her such a hard time, and when she was eating, when she was washing up, when she was weeding her garden or carrying salt hay to lay between the baby tomato plants for mulch, music played in her head and she was feeling her way through variations. Regular sex did wonders for her productivity. She got a lot of Itzak about once a month and Willie once or twice a week depending on when they could manage it. She was working splendidly. She woke with music playing in her head. She walked around with it performing. She had parts playing all the time and life just seemed to zip past the hours necessary to get through till she could sit back down to the piece. She was living inside it as if she were a fish in a perfect pond. For three days it rained and she holed up working.

As for not telling Itzak, why should Itzak care about Willie? In the heart of that maelstrom of publicity and performance about Itzak, she could not loom large. Itzak had her to call when he got lonely in Portland or Los Angeles; perhaps the affair would end when she fulfilled the commission. She did not know him well enough yet to understand what she could mean to him, but he was outside the daily flow of her life. The glamour of those moments at Carnegie was alluring but ersatz. The relationship was decorative, external, tangential. Willie and Susan had been essential, daily, her home and family. Going to New York was all very nice and useful to her in managing to hear all

172

kinds of interesting work, but how often could she run off that way? Itzak would suddenly relocate to Vienna or Paris or Copenhagen or Rome. She would not be a major factor in such a decision.

No, she should enjoy the affair with Itzak but not permit herself to take it too seriously. It issued from the good luck of the commission. Like a commission, it was to be savored to the fullest while it lasted, but she would be in trouble if she imagined either would continue or likely recur.

Willie on the other hand had been at the center of her life for ten years. Susan was acting like a major asshole, but that too would pass. Susan had fantasies about Tyrone that weren't going to materialize; the summer would prove that. She would get Susan back. In the meantime, she had not utterly lost Willie after all.

Jimmy came back from Seattle with a sharper edge on him. "It's over with Lisa. She has an attitude about me I can't deal with, no matter what I do." He was washing dishes after supper; Dinah was drying and putting them away.

"You're really getting divorced?"

"Her lawyer thinks she's crazy, but she's going ahead. I did get things settled with Jackie."

"The partner who was keeping the books and ripping you off."

"Oh, it's a complicated mess. Anyhow, we're dropping our suit, she's dropping hers and we settled everything." Jimmy smiled that deprecating half smile of his.

"You're involved with her!"

"Just for old times' sake and to grease the wheels of peace."

"Are you going back?"

"There's nothing there for me. I got everything more or less nailed down on this trip. I wanted to make up with Lisa and bring her and the baby back here, but she won't even discuss it. Another woman with a baby has moved in with her. She has all our friends on her side. She's built a whole life with no room for me. Not a chink, not a crack."

"Did you really try to get through to her? To show her you care?"

"I even bought her a beautiful necklace this woman I know made, with an opal set into the eye of a flying bird. She wouldn't even look at it."

"Jimmy, Jimmy, now what?"

"Everything here is going just fine." He saluted her. "That is, once you let me get started on our addition and once I move in. I can help you financially. I don't like living at home."

"Does Susan give you a hard time about hanging out over here?"

"Mother doesn't know how to bug me. She pulls all her vapor numbers, sighing, giving me looks, acting out distress. I just walk through it. I learned to ignore all those histrionics by the time I was twelve. Susan's fine if you don't let her get to you. She's a good mother, she's always stood by no matter what trouble I got into. She insisted I go to a good college. She managed to find the money no matter what."

"That's true. We had some lean years there."

"She comes through when it counts. For the rest, I just never let her bother me. You always rush in and start interpreting and trying to make it better. That's your mistake."

"But in an intimate relationship—not like mother and son where there's a certain healthy distance you both need—you can't just pretend you don't know what the other person wants. You can't shut out signals and tune out distress."

"I don't see why not," Jimmy said reasonably. "A benign neglect works in most relationships with most little problems. Usually things go away by themselves."

Tyrone called to invite her to his Memorial Day bash. Dinah temporized on the phone, but Tyrone liked to call a person's bluff. It gave him a feeling of power, Dinah thought. He said, "I know you and Willie and Susan are not a ménage à trois anymore, but obviously you're on civil terms. I've seen them chatting with you. Don't be falsely coy. I was disappointed not to see you at the picnic. It wasn't nearly as amusing without you."

"So happy to amuse you," she said. "I'm afraid I'll have to leave it up in the air. I don't know yet whether I'll have company."

"Itzak Raab? I heard you were having an affair with him. Really?"

"I know him. Who are you having an affair with, Tyrone?"

"No one person, my dear. I spread myself around. All right, I understand, you're discreet. Why not bring him? We'll have a delicious spread."

174

"Itzak is in Boise right now. As I said, I'll have to see, but I'll seriously consider your spread."

At noon, she noticed Susan sunbathing in a black and silver bathing suit. Staring at Susan's body offered to the sun, eyes shut as if in ecstasy, Dinah found herself drawn from the house. An oriole flashed from the apple tree, his mate after him, orange and lemon. She stopped on the property line, willing Susan to speak to her. Susan sat up and stared back. Come on, Dinah prayed, forget all this shit and walk toward me. Take one step. Say something real!

Susan abruptly got up and scampered into the house and Dinah went back to work. Itzak called from the Seattle airport. His luggage was lost. His stomach was upset. His accompanist Tom needed a root canal.

That afternoon voices and laughter from across the pond disturbed her. For the hundredth time she wondered if she should buy herself an air conditioner, not to cool the house (which rarely grew hot) but to close out the summer people's noise. Once she had noticed the drone of voices, she could not resume her concentration. Finally at four she abandoned any pretense at working and decided she would not allow Susan to keep her away. Not that she had any great desire to attend a party of Tyrone's, but she resented being made to feel like an exile. She might as well join the noise and have some free and probably excellent supper.

Getting dressed was something of a problem. For years Susan had told her what to wear to parties. She had a pleasant tent of a dress Susan had made for her two years before. That was clean. She was still having laundry problems. She had to drive fifteen miles to the Laundromat, perhaps after the party. Her panties were soaked with sweat. She had handwashed her brassieres, but they hadn't dried yet. The hell with underwear. The dress was so loose nobody would know what she was wearing or not wearing under it, and the afternoon was the first hot day of the year. She had been working so hard until the noise interrupted her, she had not noticed she was hot. Now she decided to take a quick dunk and then throw on the tent dress and row over. That would save her making supper. She'd say Hi to people, eat and drink the best of what was offered and then row home.

TWENTY-FIVE

Laurie

Laurie was lonely for the two weeks that Jimmy was gone. Dinah was away part of that time. Laurie didn't feel at ease with the local people she had met through Jimmy, at least not enough to go off looking for any of them without him. She thought of going to New York with Dinah, but Tyrone was in London and she did not think she would feel less lonely in his apartment. She still felt uncomfortable when she imagined seeing city acquaintances.

Jimmy called her the day his son was born. "Sure, I'm excited. How could I not be set up about it? But it's real and unreal at once. Here I am a father, and I'll have no relationship to my son at all. I'll be the absentee dad."

"Are you thinking of staying?"

"I'm still trying with Lisa. But I'm getting nowhere. Have you any advice for me? Please?"

She cried briefly afterward, partly because she felt sorry for him, mostly because she felt lonely and sorry for herself.

She would have liked to meet his plane, but Susan picked him up from the airport and never thought to ask Laurie if she wanted to go along, although she dropped several hints. She found that she could not talk about Jimmy with Susan. She would have imagined that it would be nice to be close to the mother of the man you had decided you were interested in, that they would have something important in common. However, Susan avoided discussing Jimmy with her, giving the conversation a sharp steer to the right whenever his name began to hover between them. It was embarrassing. Did Susan know that Jimmy was not interested in her, not in that way, only as a friend? Did Susan know that for a fact and thus was trying to protect her by refusing to encourage her folly?

Dinah was less unsatisfactory but didn't really see what Jimmy was like as an adult. Dinah on the subject of Jimmy was the same way many of Tyrone's friends were about her: she was the perennially shy and oversensitive fourteen-year-old just out of braces. They would never take her seriously as an artist or as a person just because they remembered the awkward child they had pitied.

With work suspended, she was still living in the big house, but she was using the boathouse as a studio. The two skylights were in place and functional. What remained to do was finish work on the steps and deck. She had to climb on a cinder block to get in and out. She decided to try some diary paintings, focused on her childhood. She painted more that week than she had in years, if only because there was little else to do. Tyrone would be up soon and fill the house with people.

Jimmy got back just before Tyrone descended with his assistant Donald, Celeste, his secretary Sally and the houseguests. Tyrone brought along a broker and his wife—the Bromleys—who Laurie felt looked down on her, especially since her late disaster, and Betty Gore, the widow of an investment banker and well-connected herself, being a Barrington-Taylor. Tyrone had been having an affair with Betty, rather tepid by all she could judge, since his divorce. He fell back on Betty when he lacked a better option. She seemed to view him as one of a series of interchangeable escorts. Betty drank just a little too much, but she was a quiet and unobnoxious drunk who frequently dozed off. The first day Laurie found her asleep on a towel on their beach at the pond, later snoozing on a chaise longue inside. She claimed the country air made her drowsy. Laurie thought of Betty as the dormouse in *Alice*, except that she was wrong for the part physically, being extremely tall and gaunt, with very large still beautiful dark blue eyes—when they were open. She played tennis decently, and between her first and second naps, she went off with the Bromleys and Tyrone to play on a friend's court.

Laurie had tried for years to be positive and broad-minded about Tyrone's affairs. After all, she found life easier while he was single. When he first remarried, he was almost inaccessible. Still, she found herself wincing when she heard him heartily introduce some new "friend." It was the way he had of saying the word. Did he ever actually have any women friends? Yes, Susan. The sole exception, and she was married.

They had their annual picnic at Bracken Pond, an excursion they had been taking since Laurie could remember. Susan and Celeste divided the cooking this year, although of course Celeste had the day off. She had gone off early that morning with a black man who drove a pickup truck. Laurie wondered where on earth she could have found him. Jimmy told her. Joe was a fisherman, a Black Portugee, so called, one of the descendants of Cape Verdians, just recently broken up with Leroy's younger sister, who of course was white. Celeste had met him when they sent her to buy beer at the liquor store in town. Laurie girded herself for the overpopulated weekend: first the picnic and then the much bigger party Tyrone always threw.

Laurie felt a little out of things. Jimmy was back, but with so many people around, she had snatched no more than the briefest of conversations with him. He was being helpful, serving everyone. Dinah was absent for the first time in years, and Tyrone made a point of saying that he missed her, probably to tease Susan. Laurie was a little shocked that Daddy would go on about Dinah's absence, but sometimes he thought being difficult was amusing, saying out loud what people were thinking.

It seemed to her she could see them sitting on this hill perhaps fifteen times, other years floating like balloons over her head. She remembered her own mother providing the large lunch, always carried in a series of sturdy wicker hampers. Bracken Pond was the next pond over. Like their own, it had only a few houses on it. Traditionally they picnicked at an old house site on a hill in a grove of locusts. Black locusts had been planted widely on the Cape in the reforestation, Willie had once explained to her. Willie was always sharing odd bits of history, because he loved to talk to people and find out whatever they knew. Willie said the forests had been cut down to feed the furnaces for Sandwich glass till the Cape had begun to blow away. Pitch pines had been planted then and people had put in locusts around houses. They not only held the soil but improved it, for they fixed nitrogen, whatever that meant, like giant peavines.

She could still hear Willie saying that. The locusts were not yet leafed out, just beginning to open their intricate airy foliage. The sun leaned hot on her head. She wished she had brought a hat. Soon the locusts would bloom in long sweet white panicles she had painted once, years ago. She still did not know what it meant to fix nitrogen. The image of some hidden underground repair shop came to her mind.

The Hills, who lived on the pond, were out in their Sunfish with a striped sail. Betty had fallen asleep against a tree. Tyrone was talking to Candida MacIvor, who was deeply tanned already and wore a gold bathing suit cut extremely high on the sides, claiming she had already been swimming in their pond. Laurie thought she was crazy. She had stuck her foot in and found it bitter cold. Memorial Day was too early. Laurie wondered how Candida kept her pubic hair from showing, with the suit cut so high. She must shave herself there. The thought made Laurie's flesh crawl.

Jimmy said at her ear, "Maybe she's bald."

"Was I so obvious looking at her?"

"Laurie, that's where everybody's looking."

Jimmy was right. Not only Tyrone, but Willie and Mr. Bromley were gathered around Candida's ten foot long legs shining like bronze, oiled, hairless. Susan and Mrs. Bromley had drawn together protectively. They were both wearing pleasant enough clothes, Mrs. Bromley in tailored linen pants and a linen shirt, Susan in a dress of some gauzy flowing stuff. But Candida MacIvor's legs danced away with all the attention. Laurie felt slightly amused, slightly sympathetic to the neglected women. She was not involved or competing. Jimmy sat beside her. Candida MacIvor's legs meant nothing to him, obviously. Laurie wondered where Dr. MacIvor was.

The next morning was foggy but the sun burnt its way through the overcast by ten. She went to the beach over the dune. The sun was warm enough, although the water was too cold to go in. She never swam in the ocean until mid-July. The pond would be heating up soon and the Bay too. She wondered if she should have bought a sexier bathing suit than her serviceable maillot. She always wanted a suit that dried quickly and that she could really swim in, a suit that would not come off in the water or bind her uncomfortably. Maybe she did not know how to seem sexy to a man. Jimmy obviously liked her, but just as obviously he did not think of her as sexually available. Every man at the picnic had thought lustfully of Candida MacIvor. Laurie tried to imagine herself in that bathing suit. She would have felt silly. She would have felt uncomfortable. It looked as if it would cut into a woman's tender flesh.

She had never wanted to go around attracting men at random, as Candida had done. Why did Candida need that? She had a husband. What did she get out of that buzz of lusting males? Did a woman have to do that to make a point to the one man she did want that she was attractive? Did men only like and want what other men wanted? Like advertising a diet soft drink: this

179

is the one, this is the most popular, all the models in the ads are drinking this one.

She kept hoping Jimmy would come to the beach, but if he did, would he come over the dune as she had, or would he go to the big public beach half a mile south where he would find his buddies? She resolved to find out, as if casually, during the next week. She disliked the public beach, because she hated everybody staring at everybody else, the obvious appraisals, the cold vicious competitive sizing up in the looks of women and men. She hated to feel on display, judged.

At three she went back to dress for the party. She would rather just put on a shirt and slacks, but that hadn't gotten her anyplace, had it? She remembered quarreling with her mother, who would lay out her clothes on the bed. "I don't want to wear the pink jumper, Mommy. I want the plaid skirt."

She had not sufficiently appreciated having her mother make the decisions for her. Now she was tugging on outfits and flinging them on the bed. Her room looked like a thrift shop. Finally she decided she would wear the summer dress Susan had given her. At least that would make Susan happy. Susan had seemed keyed up lately, nervous, a little frantic. She kept wanting everything to be perfect, as if she were the hostess of the universe. Laurie hoped she wouldn't be too dressed up for the crowd, but she need not have worried.

Mrs. Bromley wore a khaki linen safari dress, and Betty wore something similar in beige. Susan and Laurie were twins too, in two versions of the loose gauzy print things Susan had been making, with enormous sleeves and ruffles around the V necks. Candida arrived at three in a white halter dress that when she turned was backless, plunging well below her waist.

Laurie was leaning on the railing of the dock watching the reflections on the water when she heard Candida talking to Tyrone behind her. "Oh, I'm not really a married woman. No woman who's with a devoted doctor like Alec is really married, you know. He's married to his hospital and his practice. I see far less of him than his nurse does. I'm not in his confidence. That's simply the way it is, with an important doctor." It was obviously a rap she delivered to men, a form of flirtation. Laurie considered accidentally pushing her into the pond, but she could not figure how to lift her off the railing. An hour later, Laurie heard Candida telling Willie the same drivel.

Laurie imitated Candida to Jimmy as they sat on the end of

the dock, both their shoes off to dabble in the water. Dinah was rowing toward them in a dinghy. "Did she give you that line too?"

Jimmy shook his head. "She wouldn't waste it on me. I'm not her prey. Neither is my father, but she may not be sure yet."

"Is Dinah coming here?"

"I know your father invited her."

"Do you think Candida MacIvor is really attractive?"

"How do you mean?"

"You know what I mean." She twisted uncomfortably. "The water's still cold." She pulled her feet out.

"I like it like this. I'm going in tomorrow if it stays nice." He took her foot in his hand and chafed it. "I'm always warm."

She felt as if she would pass out. Heat flooded up her leg and she could not look at him. "It's too cold for me," she repeated inanely.

"You have such high arches," he remarked, looking at her foot as he held it. "You're so slender, you must chill easily. You have to be careful."

"I'm not that fragile!"

"Of course you are." He released her foot.

She had to control herself not to run away. Any man she was really interested in could reduce her at once to the early age of adolescence, render her speechless with a touch.

"Did I upset you? I like to tease you. You invite it sometimes, Laurie. I brought you a present from Seattle."

She looked up. "What kind of present?"

"I won't tell you. And you can't have it yet."

"A book?" She tried to imagine what he might have bought for her. Suddenly it seemed very important.

"A real present. But you have to wait. Sometime this week, when you have been very very good." He grinned at her. "Or otherwise, as the case may be. Isn't it more fun to anticipate?"

It seemed to her the air between them was thick with his sensual presence, charged with her desire. Everything he said could have a literal meaning and another meaning if he were interested in her. For the first time in her life, she wished that Tyrone would go back to the city early and take all the houseguests with him. She would not be lonely this week. Perhaps.

TWENTY-SIX

Susan

Susan had anticipated Tyrone's Memorial Day party for days, and then, that morning, she got into a ridiculous quarrel with Willie. She got up early and went to find him. The morning was warm already, the sky a brilliant swimming pool hue, festive, cloudless. He was in his studio working on a piece she assumed was new. He did not encourage her to come to his studio; it was private. He complained she talked too much when she visited, as if he didn't keep the stupid radio chattering. Today was a holiday and she had an image in her head of the two of them eating outside on the picnic table by the pond they hardly ever used—soon it would be too buggy anyhow—and then going inside and making love before she began to think about dressing for the party. Perhaps there would be time to go to the ocean together and see who would be there, the first real beach day of the year.

The trouble started immediately because his response was, "But I had breakfast two hours ago. I don't need a second breakfast. I'm not trying to see how fat I can get."

Was he implying she was gaining weight? She hadn't been walking much, now that she didn't go out with Dinah. Was she heavier? She felt the clutch of anxiety. There was no worse time to fatten up than the late spring, just before she stripped down for her summer clothes. The idea of going to the beach faded away. As her anxiety revved up, she remembered a problem from the day before. "Willie, we have to speak to that woman who did the tiles and the painter, what's his name, the Rindge boy. Candida says that somebody was using their bed."

"That's ridiculous," Willie snapped. He was usually so even tempered she was startled. "How the hell would she know?"

"She says someone obviously was using it. I didn't ask for the details."

"Listen, Susan, we aren't going to get into hot water with local people by accusing them of fucking in the MacIvor house. Probably one of them lay down and took a nap. If she wants to make herself absurd by insisting they used her house as a motel, let her do it. But you stay out of it."

"It is awkward. . . ." Susan felt confused. She had offered to speak to the tiler and the painter, meaning of course that Willie would; now she understood how embarrassing such a conversation could be. She would quietly let the matter drop.

"I'll tell you what I think," Willie went on, sounding harder, louder than she was used to. "I think Candida MacIvor had an affair with somebody and her husband saw signs of it, and now she's trying to say it was somebody else. That's what I think."

Susan saw Candida's nearly naked body flaunted in the bathing suit that had been so inappropriate to wear to the picnic, especially after she had removed the long skirt. Susan felt less enthusiastic about the MacIvors. Alec was on duty for the weekend and Candida was out here by herself, flirting with all the men. She was relieved that Willie did not seem as fascinated as he had appeared at the picnic. She hoped that Alec would be around during the summer. She did not look forward to a lot more of Candida on the prowl.

Willie had eased her out the door before she realized she had failed in her morning's plan. She decided she would stroll over to Tyrone's early and see if he needed help. However, no one was home except his secretary Sally blow-drying her hair and Celeste grimly busy in the kitchen. All the rest were off playing tennis.

Finally she decided that regardless of the water temperature she was going to swim. She would swim the length of the pond to the float that Tyrone had already had Allie Dove tow out and anchor for him. It was a longish swim but she would try it.

She had not swum far past the end of their dock when she realized she was too breathless in the cold. No one was watching. It didn't matter if she turned back. Tomorrow she would swim farther. The raft was unrealistically far anyhow, almost to Tyrone's. She always swam there from his beach. She loved to lie there sipping martinis with Tyrone and his guests. A floating pleasure dome, for the raft had a shade bower at one end for those who had their fill of sun. She would gradually build up her distance. She was always out of condition at the beginning of the season. She resolved to swim every day for exercise, right after she rose.

She decided she would skip breakfast and just have a cup of black coffee and one and only one of the croissants Tyrone had brought her from New York, without even butter or jam. She ate outside. Dinah had no company this weekend. The affair with that violinist must have petered out. Peter out: good phrase for how men's sexual energies waned once a relationship was no longer new and the zest of conquest abated. Dinah would have thought that pun amusing: she would have laughed all the way down to her belly. Dinah loved to laugh. Susan turned her face away from the open windows through which came the sounds of Dinah twidding away on her flute. Tyrone knew she loved a particular kind of almond croissant, with a sweet almost marzipan center, and he had brought her a box of them. Thoughtful as always. Still she had not enjoyed his pointed teasing yesterday about why Dinah wasn't at the picnic.

Da-dum-da-dum-dum, da-dum-dum-da-dum, Dinah kept tootling. It was catchy, but she kept repeating it over and over until Susan saw Dinah as a large woodpecker repeating its maddening cry ad infinitum, like the whippoorwill who had driven one of Tyrone's wives insane crying under their window. Yes, Janette, the one who had looked like Candida. Janette had bought herself an air rifle and practiced with it until they all got really tired of hearing her. She took to firing it out the window at night. Tyrone got rid of her soon after, to everyone's relief.

Susan had opinions about Willie's work; she could see when he was endlessly repeating himself. She could see that Siobhan was just slopping disparate images together in a collage of dissonance. She had never had any idea whether what Dinah did was good. It all sounded pleasant enough. Sometimes it made her think of thunderstorms or waves rolling in or treetops stirred by wind. Sometimes it made her remember feeling sexy or lonely. But after a while when she was listening to Dinah's music, she would begin to daydream and she would come to minutes later with the piece still meandering along.

She had never been musical. No one in her family was. Her mother had sung an Irish song when she was doing dishes, something tuneless and sentimental. "Oh Danny Boy, the pipes are calling," et cetera. Her father labeled it rot. Singing was what the shanty Irish did, cry in their beer and talk about what they would do if they could, he said. She had revered her father when she was little, because he seemed fierce, strong, capable of anything. He would lift her on his shoulders to watch the Thanksgiving Day Parade. They lived in New Jersey then, close enough to New York to see the skyscrapers across the marshes.

Then he moved them to Roanoke, Virginia. Her mother always put it that way: when your father moved us to Roanoke. He had been a mechanic but he bought a franchise to sell VWs just when they were about to become the answer to cheap car prayers.

He moved them into a house with a neat lawn, a white picket fence, and at the end of the driveway, a matched set of white-washed blackfaced grooms holding lanterns. She could remember the point in high school when she had decided they were tacky and tried to get her father to remove them. In high school art class she had discovered her sense of color and line. As if she had converted to a new religion, war was born between herself and her parents. Everything of which they were proudest, the visible signs of their ascent to the comfortable middle class, was a sign of shame to her, a failure of taste.

Perhaps she had left home in hot rebellion not because she had been seeking sexual freedom—although that had followed; not because she had grown bored with being dragged to church and lying in confession—although she certainly had sworn to herself she would never attend Mass again; but because she could not stand to look at her parents' wall to wall green nylon carpeting or the red barn paintings bought in furniture stores to go over the hideous beige couches or the free-form redwood coffee table (exactly the color of a tongue depressor) of which they were extremely proud. She had left home to escape constant rows with her mother about how she would dress, how not.

Susan sighed, the music lapping at her, infiltrating her thoughts, sucking her into its moods. She had noticed early with Willie that he had no taste in clothes, but she had said to herself, I can fix that. I'll dress him. After all, he was an uncommonly tall slender handsome man. Ha. Willie loved the sloppy clothes he wore and he had never let her dress him. To wear jeans and very old Irish sweaters meant to him he was a true artist, liberated from his father's business suits and foulard ties.

The music suddenly stopped. Susan realized she had been sitting with a cup of cold coffee for an hour, gazing at the ripples and watching the minnows flick across the bottom sand that mimicked scales. She felt a gaze on her. There was Dinah only ten feet away, barefoot in shorts and tee shirt. Dinah had beautiful legs, not long and classic like Candida's, but muscular, perfectly shaped: like a powerfully built pony, a horse of the moors. She had crept up, quiet as Tosca who was standing just

185

behind her also eyeing Susan. While Susan stared back, Tosca sat on her haunches and licked daintily at a paw. Dinah went on gawking.

Susan felt herself soften through her belly. Her damned body did not care at all for her ideas and her scruples and her measured resentment. Dinah gazed and her body began to cook, bubbling like hot mud. She could not think of words to say that would make Dinah ridiculous. Dinah's eyes had a way of seeming to turn darker when she stared. Susan could not remember why they were quarreling. It seemed trivial, unnecessary. Those legs could be twined around her. That head could be cheek to her thigh. Her thigh remembered the heaviness of that head, the crisp hair tickling her, curling as her own pubic hair. Slowly all the blood in her body was drawing into her torso and beating between her hips. She was slowly engorging, mesmerized.

She leaped to her feet and ran into the house, clutching her robe about her. She imagined Dinah chasing her, grabbing her. When she turned back at the kitchen door, Dinah was walking toward her own house, Tosca at her heels trotting tail high.

The phone rang. With a feeling of relief, Susan ran to answer it, still shaken. What had come over her? Maybe she should not eat so lightly in the mornings. It was almost noon anyhow. It was Tyrone. She felt as if instinctively he had called to protect her. "Susan darling, do you know where Willie moved the croquet set that used to be in the boathouse? I'm sure he put it someplace logical when they began the work, but I haven't been able to find it, and Laurie has no idea."

"Just a moment, and I'll go ask him."

She ran to his studio. He was wearing one of his protective masks, cooking up a plastic. The studio stank of chemicals. To hear her, he had to lay everything aside and take off the mask. "The croquet set? How in hell do I know?" He turned and stalked back to his work.

"Willie, try to remember," she screeched. "You must have put it somewhere. You have to take responsibility for what you do."

"Tell Tyrone to use his head for a mallet. I'm working! I'm sorry. We can go to the party early and I'll look for it then, okay? Tell Tyrone you couldn't find me or I was molding resins, but that we'll arrive early."

They did. Everybody was upstairs dressing. Celeste greeted them coolly and tried to install them on the deck. Willie thought

186

he'd put the objects stored in the boathouse into the basement under the kitchen. However, Laurie had moved a number of her old paintings down there, standing against the shelves. Willie moved a few boxes, but all he did was get dust on his hands and his shirt.

When Tyrone appeared in a black and white Italian sports jacket, a fine tightly woven linen with a surface like silk, and grey pants in a similar weave, he seemed surprised at the mention of croquet. "Sally found the mallets and all, but the moles have been at the lawn. We must get someone to take care of it. I'll talk to you about it tomorrow."

He smiled at both of them, took Susan's hand, his other palm lightly supporting her at the far elbow as they strolled out on the deck where Celeste and Sally were applying the final touches to the buffet. From the punch bowl reared a frozen swan, perfect because just unmolded, surrounded by a huge flower of cut peaches, pineapples, oranges, papayas and kiwi fruit. The rumaki were hot. The Brie was just beginning to quiver. There were three dips, pale green, pale pink and white with slivers of something black. She assumed the pink was salmon, the green, avocado. Sally had changed for the party into an oversized white dress that looked like the nurse's uniform of a giantess. Sally was a plain English girl with a lovely voice and accent who worked fourteen hours a day for Tyrone. He always had gorgeous receptionists and nunlike secretaries, devout and selfless in his service.

Tommy Lloyd, the Captain's younger brother, and the Captain himself were setting up on the water's edge to open oysters. Willie immediately hurried over to them, as if his first priority at a party had to be to gossip with the help. It would be a wonder if Willie didn't start opening oysters with them.

Betty Gore was wearing a Chanel number. She was always exquisitely if conservatively dressed. Susan always wished she could make more of a connection with Betty, but she was laconic and at her best when they were playing tennis or bridge. Susan thought Betty rather a romantic figure, for she had married a racing car driver, a British viscount, with whom she had had a couple of sons and who had died at Monte Carlo against a wall. Her other marriages seemed much flatter, yet Susan sensed that she truly mourned her last, who had widowed her again. Susan did not think Betty was in love with Tyrone, or he with her, but she seemed, with her many connections in society on both sides of the Atlantic, a suitable companion for him, one appropriate but not threatening, not consuming his attention.

Laurie was wearing the dress Susan had made for her. Susan had begun the habit when Laurie was eleven and pitifully thin and shy. She always made a good summer dress for Siobhan and she began to make one at the same time for Laurie. Once again, Laurie was more her daughter than Siobhan, who had refused from fifteen on to wear the beautiful things Susan made for her.

They must find somebody suitable for Laurie. Why didn't Tyrone invite some young men? Susan hardly thought that Laurie was supposed to take up with his assistant, a rabbity nerd named Donald something who walked around cradling a cellular telephone as somebody else might cuddle a small dog. He was the only man under forty-five, not counting Jimmy, who was as usual immediately at Laurie's side. He was married still and he had just had a son born. Why didn't she think that would slow him down? Fortunately he had just spent five months with Laurie without bothering her, so likely Susan's first guess was correct, that neither of them could stand in as the romantic stranger for the other. She shuddered when she considered the possibility of their involvement. She did not want to deal with Tyrone's reaction to that, not at all. He would think she was somehow trying to crawl into his family through the back door, that she had pushed her son at Laurie. It would cast her in a sort of false mother-in-law role she did not relish. She must bring up with Tyrone the necessity to invite guests who would flirt with Laurie and ease her back into the current of life, toward romance and marrying again.

She managed to catch Tyrone briefly and began to discuss that subject with him, but he seemed a little pained. "I don't think she's ready for anything as risky as a relationship. Let her settle into her new digs. Let her put energy into the gallery. Next year is time enough for such ideas."

"Tyrone, she'll fall in love with somebody. Women always do."

"Now, Susan, you're far more sensible than that, and so is Laurie. She's been badly hurt. She needs time out from men. When she's ready, she'll come back to the city and I'll set her up properly there." He swept forward to greet Candida, who actually looked decent, until she swung around toward the pond and her dress was cut down to her buttocks. There seemed to be several feet of naked back hanging there among all the women

188

in beige and pale pastels, linen and gauze. Her blond hair was up on top of her head in a knot, except for a lock on either side curling along her cheek. The effect was artful, flirtatious. Susan noted that Candida moved rather carefully, not nodding, turning her body rather than her head, so as not to dislodge the hairdo. Betty Gore stood looking at Candida a moment. The sight seemed to make her instantly fatigued, for she went at once to find a chaise longue.

I could wear clothes that extreme, Susan thought; I could bring if off as well as she can. I'm tall and well built. I just never think to wear something that bold and grabby. I've always designed my clothes so you can move well in them. She couldn't dance in that dress or play croquet or even sneeze hard. I don't approve of clothing that hangs so gingerly on the body. It's not real clothing. It's like big flashy costume jewelry that loses its brilliants right away and the catch breaks.

Suddenly she realized Dinah was standing by the food, spearing the smoked salmon that had just appeared. Tyrone had invited the Hills, and they flanked her both talking at once while Dinah steadily ate. Dinah had thrown on a lavender gauze sundress Susan had made for her, a series of four loose tiers, but she had obviously forgotten to put anything under it. Standing on the deck with the light reflecting off the water behind her, that fact was quite clear. Her other concession to the party was to wear sandals and paint her toenails purple, although she was wearing no other makeup. Her hair stood up in a halo of kinks with droplets of water resting on the ends of her curls, as if she had dipped her head in the pond. Perhaps she had. Susan could picture her doing just that.

She could hear Candida flirting with Tyrone, while Sally was chattering to her about ice sculpture, a subject for which Susan felt an indifference vast as the arctic. She recognized that Sally just wanted to talk to someone about something. She looked around for Willie. He was drifting slowly but inexorably along the deck toward Dinah. She had to abort that fast. She wrenched herself free of Sally by a heroic series of non sequiturs. "My husband is a sculptor but I don't think he has ever worked in ice. There he is. That reminds me, I must ask him if he found the croquet set for Tyrone."

"Oh, I found that earlier," Sally called after but she was already fleeing. After him.

Mrs. Bromley caught her by the arm. "Susan. That was such a delightful picnic yesterday."

Dinah had got free of the Hills and was eating oysters as fast as Tommy and Toby Lloyd could open them. They were all laughing heartily together. Dinah was dribbling oyster liquid on her dress. She never shaved under her arms. Susan was sure she could see the little bush of her pubic hair. Willie was at her elbow but Tyrone arrived simultaneously. Now they were laughing too. Toby Lloyd winked at Willie. Candida was left to display her naked back to whoever cared. Mr. Bromley cared. He joined her at once. Mrs. Bromley was talking about diets she had tried and spas she had gone to. She said she understood why that woman had killed Dr. Tarnower. "It had nothing to do with sex, but everything to do with protein overload and vitamin deficiency."

Tyrone, Willie and Dinah were eating oysters while Dinah was talking, probably loudly and dogmatically, waving her free hand so that Susan could see her breasts swing under the loose tent of dress. Willie was leaning over her proprietarily. How dare he act proprietary over Dinah? Tyrone was nodding, nodding again. Now he was set to refute something, admonishing finger tapping the air. What were they so animated about? Mrs. Bromley's voice hissed with excitement, "Without sufficient fiber in your diet, colonic cancer results. Moreover no diet works for a woman our age if our bodies don't think they're getting enough bulk." She leaned close to Susan, saying again and again, women our age, women with our weight problems, women with our metabolic rates, women with our need for calcium and iron. She had Susan pinned against the railing of the deck, trapped between the pond and herself.

Tyrone had taken Dinah's hand and was pointing to the fingers as if using them to illustrate or count. Willie moved closer yet, as if to monitor Tyrone to make sure he didn't keep any of the fingers he was borrowing. Toby kept slipping oysters into her other hand, as fast as she could eat them. Dinah stood there square on her feet the way she liked to plant herself and monopolized the men as if she never dreamed they could both see right through her dress, with the sun dancing off the water behind her. Really, Candida had been outdone. Dinah didn't even look as if she had thought twice about her appearance just as natural and down-homey as could be and no underwear. Everybody wore underwear nowadays; sexy lingerie was in, boned undergarments, silk chemises, tap pants, camisoles trimmed in exquisite lace, bustiers, long line strapless brassieres built like the iron maiden, power shorts for men. Women with large breasts bought brassieres guaranteed to make them look smaller, to squash them in. Nobody had gone around for a decade letting her breasts swing like a cow's udder. It was unbelievable. Mrs. Bromley was explaining why a liquid protein diet was hard on the kidneys. "It's plain murder," she said, "especially for women our age!"

Dinah was just doing this to upset her. It was a way of taking a dress Susan had made for her and perverting it utterly as she stood there eating oysters by the dozen and smiling that strange smile with the lips only that Willie had said was reminiscent of the archaic smile on a Greek kore, those statues of maidens or young goddesses he liked. It was maddening, and Mrs. Bromley, fixing her with a baleful glare, was rattling on about the dangers of saturated fats. It turned out she had not loved the picnic at all, for she found the food unhealthy and fattening. "Mayonnaise is one of the most dangerous substances you can consume! Butter is the second!" Susan decided the woman was both mad and rude, but her own ingrained politeness made her unable to interrupt the tirade. She could not simply make an excuse as she had with Sally, because she could not wedge in a complete sentence.

By the time Susan escaped, Dinah had rowed back across the pond, a cool breeze was springing up, Dr. Alec had arrived from the city for a day off at last and his wife was plastered to his side. It was close to seven with the temperature dropping and the sky ridged with high clouds in ranks like waves coming in from the west. Tyrone appeared at her side and caught up Laurie with his other arm, taking them both into the house where he motioned to Celeste. She brought him a bottle of iced champagne, Roederer Cristal, and four glasses. Sally had followed at his nod.

He made it into a ceremony, all the glasses clinking. "To summer!"

"To summer," Susan repeated. He had called her in, not Candida, not Dinah, not Betty Gore, not anyone else. Just his daughter, his secretary and herself, his family. Not even Willie was included. His best champagne in the fine crystal glasses that were as thin as the first faint sheet of ice that formed on the pond in January, offered to the women who were the closest to

191

him. "To summer." It was a toast, a promise, a summons. The minor disappointments of the day slid from her like discarded clothes. His eyes met hers across the glass and he smiled into her soul, the special friendship between them palpable, caressing, sweet as the mauve twilight filling the room from the French doors. Between all of them was a fine high civilized attention to each other, an attunement, a drawing together. "Oh yes," she said. "To summer!"

TWENTY-SEVEN

Laurie

"Why do I have to wait so long for the present? You make me wonder if there's really a present," Laurie said. She and Jimmy were painting the bathroom, above the line of tile. He had recruited her to help him. Willie was in a panic about having enough pieces for his show the first week in August. Outside it was raining steadily, a sound like gravel on the roof and a lighter sound of drops hitting the pond.

"I could make you wait till your birthday, so cultivate a little patience."

"You don't know when my birthday is. How do you know it isn't today?"

"Your birthday's in October." He leaned down smiling from the ladder.

"How did you know?"

"Never reveal a source."

"When is yours?"

"Come on, you used to lord it over me that you were five months older. Some older woman! My sophisticated Laurie."

"I never will be, will I? New York kids think they know it all. Was I really obnoxious?"

"Only on alternate days."

"Why do I have to wait for the present?"

"Two reasons. I want your attention when I give it to you. It's easier with the house emptied out. Second, I'm not sure Tyrone would be thrilled that I brought you back something so

192

. . . let's just say it's a real present. If he saw it, you'd have to tell him where you got it. And if you didn't, I'd feel hurt.''

"Why would Tyrone mind? Susan's always giving me presents.''

"Tyrone thinks I'm a lowly carpenter. He doesn't know I've taken over subcontracting the gallery, and don't tell him. I know just who to get and they'll come through for me because they're buddies.''

He talked almost as if they were involved already and keeping it a secret from Tyrone—but he had never even kissed her, except a brotherly brush of the lips. Sometimes she worried that her overheated imagination was imbuing his casual remarks with significance he never intended. A present withheld but tendered at the same time reminded her of birthdays, of Christmases, of times Tyrone would promise her a treat if she got above a B average or if she would improve her backhand sufficiently to give him a good game. "Daddy's gone now and so are the houseguests.'' She was sure she would be disappointed. It would be like the presents her mother got her, never quite as good as she had asked for, a knockoff instead of a designer sweater, done in acrylic rather than wool, in polyester instead of silk: things that were almost what she wanted, and thus twice as frustrating, a tawdry betrayal. It would be some trifle in bad taste and she would feel embarrassed for him.

At four o'clock he cleaned the brushes and they ran through the rain to the big house. He followed her in, shaking his head like a dog. "I'll get cleaned up here.'' Without waiting for her assent he went upstairs ahead of her and turned into Tyrone's bathroom.

After all, he knew the house perfectly well. She took a fast shower and put on a clean short-sleeved shirt. She started to put on her jeans and then thought better of it and put on a beige skirt, part silk, part linen. She dabbed a touch of Coco behind her ears and brushed her hair hard. As she was peering critically at herself, she saw him standing behind her in a madras robe of Tyrone's. The box he held out was beautifully wrapped in rice paper with a gold flecked fish pattern, tied with a golden string. Her hand that took the small package quivered.

She was afraid to open it, to be disappointed, to feel embarrassed for him. But he was waiting. The bathrobe was long on him. Finally she eased the string off, tore the beautiful paper. It was in a box from a Seattle jeweler. Inside was a necklace of white gold links. On it was a white gold gull fashioned out of a few zigzags, with an opal for an eye. "It's beautiful! I can't believe you got me this!" She could tell it was real. Oh, Tyrone always gave her real stones, but they were unimaginatively set. This was a piece of art. She hooked the clasp and stared at the necklace against the white of her shirt.

"It needs something black to show it off. Or skin." Casually he reached over her shoulder and unbuttoned her shirt, sliding it back and away. She sat in her camisole with the shirt loose on her shoulders and the necklace against the slight rise of her breasts. "I like it on you," he said. "I knew it was for you when I saw it. I was looking for something that wanted to be yours."

"I really love it," she said. Should she button her shirt? She did not dare. She sat frozen admiring the necklace until he lifted her to her feet. The robe was loosely tied. He was naked underneath. He drew the blouse the rest of the way from her shoulders and hung it on the doorknob, unzipped the skirt and led her forward out of it as he slid the camisole over her head. Most men fumbled at women's clothes, at least in her experience. In a rapid gesture, kneeling and rising, he slid her panties down and then opened the robe and pulled her inside it, so that it closed around their naked bodies. She had a moment's thought that they were naked together and she was committed to his will, and he had not even kissed her yet, when gathered into the robe and feeling his hot sleek body against her, they did finally kiss.

She was enclosed in the robe with him, his body smooth and warm and tight against her and the robe smelling of the Persian leather Tyrone used. Her breath caught in her chest like an opening clasp knife. She found herself squirming against him in a way that would have been embarrassing, except that he was holding her in a grip that did not ease for a moment, murmuring in her hair, "Yes, baby, baby, baby, it's time. Oh, it's time for us." He slid his fingers up into her and began to play with her. It had always taken her forever to come, but this time she came from his fingers. It had been so long, her body was so taut, it hurt a little to come.

He pulled them onto the bed then and put himself into her. She realized he wasn't using a condom and she had not done anything at all. She had gone off the pill after Tom . . . She could not do anything about it.

When they were lying side by side she said sheepishly, "I haven't made love with anyone since Tom died. . . ."

"Of course not," he said. "But I didn't hurt you. Did I?"

"It's just I went off the pill then and I don't have a diaphragm."

He raised himself on his elbow. "We'll take you to a doctor tomorrow, a gynecologist down the Cape. Don't worry about it. Anything that happens is all right, you know, so don't ever worry with me."

They took a bath together and then went out to a fried clam shack that had picnic tables outside. She kept the necklace on under her shirt. It felt different, scary and safe at once, to be with him now. She had not been with anyone as a couple since Tom, and their relationship had been rocky. Jimmy was relaxed, expansive. He did not hang on her, but when he touched her, he was firm, possessive. She felt as if her entire body had changed, growing sensitive. She could not stop looking at him. He was incredibly handsome. She did not know how she had ever managed to keep her eyes off him when he was in her field of vision.

He told her all about the woman who had made her necklace, a Seattle artist he had known when he lived there, about how he went there to find exactly the gift for Laurie, how he had looked through the whole store and found nothing that was perfect. The artist had told him she was just finishing a special new piece and had taken him in the back to see. That was her necklace. It had not been completed for another day, but then he got it for her. The woman had been trying to decide between a turquoise and an opal. He had chosen the opal for her.

"I've never had an opal. It think it's exquisite." She glanced at it tucked in her shirt. It felt a little heavy and almost alive. He had given it to her as a love gift, as a means of taking possession of her. She felt special, planned for, connived for. All the while she had been worried he was not attracted to her, he had been spinning a seductive web. He thought he had caught her, but she knew better.

They went to a movie together, like a couple just beginning to date, like an old married couple. They went to see a bozo comedy and held hands. Then he came back to the house with her. "My parents won't like this. Tyrone won't like this. But I want to be with you."

She lay with him in the bed that had been hers since she was five and given a whole big adult double bed. It had a bird's-eye

195

maple frame that creaked as he made love to her. "Mine," he said as he came into her. "Mine. Mine." Then he laughed against her just after he came. In a way, she thought, he was mocking the rhetoric of passion and possession, but in another way, he meant it. She was thrilled. She felt new. She did not think she had ever felt so sexually alive. She had never wanted a man for a long time before they had sex. Always before she had more or less reluctantly given in. He could have made her try to seduce him; she had almost been driven to that. Instead he had come after her, and beautifully.

She could not sleep, curled with him in her childhood bed, in her old room with the pond rippling outside. The rain had stopped but the night was dark. He slept in her arms, but she was too unused to his presence and too excited to doze off. She could not bear to let go of the day that had just ended, for fear the fragile design it had sketched might dissolve in unconsciousness.

She did sleep because she woke with him in the morning. Willie was making a lot of noise with a saw outside. She was almost afraid to look at Jimmy. Her experience with Tom was that he could go from being passionate to being sarcastic without any action or words of hers having intervened. Jimmy paced to the window, looked out, drew the curtain and came back to bed. "He's starting on the deck early this morning."

"We'd better hurry with breakfast."

"In a bit. He does things at his convenience too. First things first." He put his hand on her belly and leaned for a moment, then let himself down on her, taking the nipple of her small breast into his mouth. She could not imagine so cavalierly making Tyrone wait for her, but Jimmy did not seem to think of his father again until he had finished making love and then eating breakfast. Only then did he go out where Willie was making so much noise with the electric saw.

She went slowly back up to her room to make the bed, much messier than it was when she slept in it alone. Then she sat at her vanity and stared at herself, at the necklace in the middle of the embroidered runner. It was beautiful. She felt ashamed to have doubted his taste. She had not imagined past fretting whether he was attracted to her—or not—to what it would be like to be involved. She had thought it would be as it was, with a layer of sex, of romantic interest. She perceived that she had been wrong.

Now that she was close up to him, he did not seem casual. Would he stay here with her often? Would he find someplace else to take her? If he moved in, Tyrone would probably be furious—she suspected that Jimmy was right about that. Once her boathouse was completed, maybe they could both live there, although it was tiny—still no tinier than the studios many couples in New York shared. She was being premature, but this did not feel like the first time she had slept with Rick or Tom, when each had left her apartment without her having any certainty whether she would see him again.

In midmorning he came up to the house to check that she had made an appointment with the doctor. She had not gotten to it yet. It was disquieting to trust her body to a doctor picked out of a phone book. He made the call for her and then went back to work. "So you don't worry," he said. "Not that it would be a problem anyway. I'll take you there."

In some ways he reminded her of Tyrone, surprisingly. He took charge. She admired that. She washed her hair and reminded herself to ask him if he liked the way she was wearing it. Then she took a couple of magazines and went along the path through the woods to the beach, to pass the time until he could get rid of Willie and knock off work. She did not talk to them but instead left a note saying where she was and that she would be back at four, for she felt a slight discomfort at the thought of seeing Willie before she and Jimmy had worked themselves out more securely. Still it seemed to cast a long shadow for something so recent. As she crossed the dune, she smiled.

TWENTY-EIGHT

Willie

"All you're going to do is force me to move in with her before either of us knows if that's what we want." Arms crossed, Jimmy had his back to the refrigerator door with its magnetic clip of openings and invitations, the formal social occasions of the burgeoning summer.

Willie was hunched over the table with a cup of cold coffee. He wished he had stayed in his studio or at the work site instead of coming home with Jimmy for lunch and barging into a huge fight with Susan, who had been waiting for Jimmy, unable to control herself from the moment they walked in.

Susan was shaking with anger, her hands twisting before her. "I can't understand how you can do this to us! And to her!"

"What do you think I am, a plague? I'm making her happy. It's about time someone did."

"Tyrone is going to be furious!"

"Stuff Tyrone. He parked her out here till the scandal stopped embarrassing him. I didn't seduce a fourteen-year-old. She's a widow of twenty-four." Jimmy glared from Susan to Willie. Willie knew Jimmy was furious with him for hanging back. Working with his son most days, Willie had been feeling close, and Jimmy felt the same. They saw more of each other than either saw of Susan. "You talk about her as if she were feebleminded and I seduced her with lollipops. She's been after me for weeks. I simply wouldn't let anything happen until I knew what was coming off with Lisa."

"Laurie has been after you? You're crazy. I know what state she arrived in. She was broken. You're taking advantage of a young girl who doesn't make friends easily. She's shy. She needs sympathy and a quiet place. She needs to recover, to heal."

"Mother, you're ridiculous. I didn't force myself on her. And I'm a hell of a lot better to and for her than what she's used to. She knows that. Why don't you?"

Willie felt trapped between them. They were both so much more vehement than he ever was, they hemmed him in. The serrated edge on Susan's voice made him deeply apprehensive. He sniffed the air in the kitchen and smelled trouble. Why was she making such a fuss? Okay, he, too, didn't think Jimmy's getting involved with Laurie was a great idea, but given that they had hung out together since they were six, given they were both adults who had been married already, it wasn't as if he or Susan could keep them apart. Tyrone might not be overjoyed but surely expected Laurie to find some guy while she was living on the Cape. Jimmy was a better choice than most. He had a good education, he was clean and handsome, and maybe Laurie felt more secure knowing his family well. Willie was inclined to shrug it off and see how it went.

He could remember when Laurie had had a crush on him, back when she was a teenager built like a bag of golf clubs. She had blushed whenever he spoke to her. Laurie might be shy, as

198

Susan said, but she certainly could telegraph her interest. He had been kind to her, even enjoying her adoration, but she had seemed volatile enough. Willie was willing to believe Jimmy was telling the truth about Laurie showing her attraction plainly and strongly.

Susan however was frantic. Sometimes he thought once she got upset past a certain point, there was no calming down or retreating for her. He wished he could just turn the hose on both of them the way he did when Figaro got into a fight with some summer cat who was poaching on his turf; or the way he'd drag Bogey by the collar away from mischief. If he could just pick Susan up and dump her in the pond, she would cool off and the dangerous moment would go by. If he tried to force his way in between them, he would just draw her wrath. It would end with all of them shouting in a berserk rage. He hated that sense of everything out of control. He didn't want to mix in between them, get riled up, end by saying things he didn't mean.

"There are people one just doesn't get involved with—that one refrains from," Susan was beginning in a high trembly voice.

"What did you ever refrain from that you wanted, Mother? Do tell me. It must have been something really ducky I should try sometime." Jimmy was angry too, bitterly, whitely angry. If Susan flushed with anger, Jimmy grew still and pale with it. "You think I'm not anticipating trouble with Tyrone? You underestimate me. You always have. But you should be on my side, Mother. And you too, Willie. You should be backing me. You both make me sick." He tore out of the room, up the stairs and slammed his door.

Susan was sobbing wildly and Willie got up reluctantly and went to comfort her. "It's a fait accompli. Why not roll with the punches?" He liked the sound of that. In his current struggle with his wife over Dinah, he considered he was letting her wear herself out brawling, while instead of counterpunching, he blocked her wild blows. He ducked and weaved and waited for her energy to flag. His strategy was a good one, but it was lucky he was a patient man. She was taking forever to tire.

"How could he do this to us?"

Willie wasn't sure what Jimmy was supposed to have done. He murmured soothingly. He would really like to get back to his studio or finish up the deck, one or the other. He hated being stuck in an emotional swamp in the middle of the afternoon.

Now Susan was crying and Jimmy was upstairs. It sounded as if he was rearranging the furniture in his room. Willie thought of making love to her, but with Jimmy upstairs banging around, it wasn't feasible. In his head stood the wall he was welding, barbed wire and grey pillars all hung with bits of newsprint and computer printout. He had just had a vision of skulls on the top, skull shapes in all colors. Cobalt blue skulls. Threaded through the barbed wire, acrylic tubes of red and blue, veins, arteries. He would use rods, maybe quarter inch. He reached for a pad to sketch his vision, then froze as Susan fixed him with her liquid gaze.

"If you stop it now, it won't do any damage. You must talk to him."

Willie grimaced. "I'm supposed to tell him to stop fucking Laurie? Why should he lay off until he's ready to? Really, Susan."

"Tyrone usually arrives by the Fourth of July. It must be over by then."

"Maybe it will be. Especially if we keep out of the picture. If it isn't, then Tyrone will just have to adjust to it like anybody else."

"Oh, Willie, don't be naive. You don't understand Tyrone."

"I'd say that's Laurie's problem more than ours." He was tired of thinking about Jimmy and Laurie already. It was really none of his or Susan's business. Kids had to work out their own love affairs. He wanted to clear his mind out and brood on the work he must get done for his coming show.

"You just don't see the whole picture!"

"Susan, you're hurting Jimmy's feelings, can't you see that? For all you know, he's in love with her."

"That's ridiculous!"

He had liked having the MacIvor house for a rendezvous. He had come to think of it as their own, his and Dinah's. He could not help resenting the MacIvors for beginning to use it. Not that they were there all the time, but now he never knew when they would appear. They were not about to call up and inform him. Susan had given the key back—not before he had made a copy of it, just in case they went away to Europe or each broke a leg or something else useful. Fortunately Candida had forgotten about her bed being used. He needed another place to be alone with Dinah. Next door would not do and neither was his studio safe. They made love twice in the dunes above the beach, but Dinah found that risky in the summer, as well as hot. Tourists might step on them at any moment.

"Why can't you just tell Susan? We can't go on keeping it from her forever. She has a right to know." Dinah was lying on a blanket at the old house site on Bracken Pond where they had their annual Memorial Saturday picnic—to which Dinah had not been invited.

"I'm waiting for the right time."

"Wait too long and she'll guess, if she hasn't already. I don't like fooling her. She'll never forgive either of us—and that's not the idea, is it?"

"Dinah, telling her is on my agenda. It's a matter of the right timing. You know how she can get worked up and fly off the handle and blow something up out of proportion." He was thinking of the recent fight with Jimmy.

Dinah knew what he was thinking, because she had Jimmy as a houseguest. "I think everything's going to hell in our earthly paradise. We better start mending our lives."

"Well, haven't you and I done that? The question is where we can meet." The mosquitoes were beginning. Soon making love outside would be an ordeal.

"Is Susan mad because Jimmy moved into my spare room?"

"No madder than she was before."

"Better he should be involved with Laurie than some things he might be doing."

"I suppose you can say that about anything short of murder." Willie shook his head mournfully. "I can't really figure out why this affair exercises her so strongly. Jimmy's slippery and he's a bit of a manipulator but he's hardworking and he doesn't drink heavily or smoke or gamble or take out a lousy temper on women."

"Um," Dinah said noncommittally. "I'm sure Laurie could do worse."

"Why does it make Susan so mad?"

"She doesn't want to be Tyrone's daughter's mother-in-law. How unromantic. How prosaic."

"No, Dinah, you've got that wrong. Susan loves Laurie. She thinks of Laurie as her daughter, she's always telling me that. Are you kidding? She'd love to be part of Tyrone's family. I just think she figures he won't buy it. As far as I can guess, she doesn't want to risk Tyrone getting angry or suspicious that we encouraged the affair.''

"I can't live a life dictated by Tyrone's moods. Do you really want to?''

"Dinah, let's not fight. I've had a belly full of quarrels this week.''

"And I have a houseguest I didn't want.''

"He says he's building you an addition for rent.''

"That's what he says.'' She swatted a mosquito on her arm. "That's the third one I killed. My back is itching like crazy. Did something bite me?'' She turned her fine muscular back to him. Two large red bumps were spaced between her shoulder blades and a couple more on her buttocks.

"You got bitten a few times.''

"That's it. No more outdoor sex until frost kills the mosquitoes.''

"But where will we go?''

"I guess you'll just have to come clean with Susan so that you can walk across the yard to my house, or I can visit your studio the way I used to.''

"I'm working on it,'' he said sullenly. He wanted everything simple again. "I sympathize with Jimmy. If he wants her and she wants him, what business is it of anybody else's? Jimmy had a rough deal out in Seattle. Susan is too hard on him.'' And on me, he thought, swatting a mosquito that had just stabbed him in the ankle. If he didn't make love to Dinah, he could lose her to that musician. He just needed to blur things so that they could all come and go again without it being anything special. With Jimmy next door, that might be easier. But then Jimmy would know he was making love to her. Not if Jimmy was off at Laurie's.

It was all absurdly complicated, but he was sure he could make it work. A tunnel. He imagined a tunnel from his studio to her bedroom. Or suppose he put a shed in the way so that from the bedroom window Susan couldn't look out and see his studio door. A garage. They had been talking for years of building a garage with a room above it. Yes. He would do that and then it would stand between his studio and the house and he could duck into Dinah's with no trouble at all, or she could slip over to him.

He felt so proud of himself for thinking up that solution to his problem that he rolled over on her, starting that round and round motion on her breasts that drove her crazy. "Again?" she asked, coming up for air. "What vitamins have you been taking?"

"I just want you a whole lot. I'm crazy about you."

"I love you, Willie, but I just wish we could get straightened out again. I need for things to be clear and good with all three of us."

"Of course," he said, sliding in easily. When occasionally they did it a second time, it always felt different in her. She seemed bigger, looser, wetter. He was taking his time and driving into her and at the same time he was building a wall and it was rising and rising, the wall of a garage, a garage with a second floor room on top, and it was rising and rising and on the other side of that building, in its shade, he was strolling over to Dinah's and he was in her bed driving into her, just like this, like this, like this.

TWENTY-NINE

Dinah

"I thought you'd stopped nude sunbathing because you're afraid of skin cancer from the thinning of the ozone layer." Jimmy was squinting at her back, Dinah could see in the vanity mirror.

She was clutching a terry robe around herself, pulled down to bare her skin where Jimmy was daubing calamine lotion. "I got the bites taking a dip."

"Interesting stroke you must have, that sticks your ass up in the air."

"More nurse, less wise guy."

"The health agent says to put in a washer, you have to go to a whole new septic system—new holding tank, leaching field, all that. An extra bathroom with a washer—won't that improve life?"

"If Susan wasn't pissed at me, none of this would be necessary."

"If Susan wasn't pissed at me, you wouldn't be getting slave labor out of me, so let's keep smiling through. Tommy Rindge is coming today."

"Tell Willie to keep Bogey inside. Tommy's dog always wants to fight. I better keep both cats in. On such a hot day, everybody's going to be testy."

"Dinah, you're so funny, the way you talk to the cats. Now, people, you say, what's wrong with Shore Dinner today? Now which of you people knocked over my vase?"

"People is any gentle beings you live with. Even men. I'm just used to privacy."

"Do you want to turn into one of those feisty crotchety spinsters who live with their cats and talk to themselves and keep a loaded shotgun in the corner?"

"Why not! Sounds kind of attractive to me."

"There's some weird building competition going on with you guys. I went to see Tommy about the septic system, and he said he'd do it in two weeks or so when he put in Willie's. Willie says to me, Oh, didn't I tell you? We're building a garage with a room upstairs. I'm out and they're expanding."

"That's news to me. Are you sure?"

"Maybe he's sweetening Mother with it. She's always wanted a room to work in, but she has never been willing to take Johnny's or mine. She's always been martyred how Willie has his studio and she has to work in their bedroom."

"Ah," Dinah said. Willie was keeping his part of the bargain. He was softening Susan up with a studio for herself. Excellent! Susan deserved her own space, and ever since Dinah had met them, they had been talking of a garage. They were near enough to the ocean for the winter winds laden with salt to rub the finish off their truck. She felt a tremendous sense of relief. Willie was finally active in turning Susan around.

"I have to go to Tanglewood in ten days," she warned Jimmy. "My piece is premiering there."

"Going to see Itzak Raab?"

"How could I miss him? He's performing it."

When Itzak's name was mentioned, Jimmy projected a fog of disapproval. Like her, Jimmy wanted the triangle reconstituted. They were allies. Maybe the thing with Laurie would work out. Certainly she looked like a new woman, almost pretty lately, with much more to say.

She spoke to Nita the next day. Nita was already at Tanglewood for the summer. "Kyle is jealous, honey," Nita said. "He feels put in the shade, professionally."

"Because Itzak played the piece in New York that I wrote for Kyle?"

"Well, that didn't help matters, as you can guess." Nita giggled, stopped to yell at Tanya to turn the TV down. "But he's got a bug in his ear about what you've written for Itzak. I love the way it starts. But I think there's a mistake in the score you sent me. . . ."

"I'll get my copy. Hold on. You know, I'm still making changes."

Nita kept sending her reviews of Itzak's concerts and records, interviews, articles. Nita was an Itzak Raab fan club of one, a clipping service devoted to his fame. Every couple of weeks an envelope would come with Nita's return address. Inside would be a joke card signed with Tanya's scrawl and Nita's newest tidbits on Itzak.

After she had given Nita the correction, she asked, "Nita, what do you think of it? Can you tell? I'm scared."

"I think it's close to the best thing you've written. It's going to be tough bringing it off on two days' rehearsal. It's going to be a stretch for some of them, the demands you make. Eli and Robby I worry about. And you know how some of those bozos are when a woman conducts."

She found herself kneading her belly with her hands. Was the suite as good as she could make it? The premiere had to be a success. If she had fucked up, if the performance did not come off, she would have blown something really important. Why had she got involved with him? This was too important for her professionally to have taken that risk. For a moment she was furious with herself that she had paid any attention whatsoever to her private life in the last four months. "How is it this year?"

"Giselle's coming down in August. I have the same house I had last year."

"I liked the one you used to get, up on the mountain." Dinah saw herself with Nita and Tanya splashing in the Stockbridge Bowl, picnicking on the grass. Tanya was a baby on a blanket, Tanya was a toddler, then a little girl. Usually Dinah managed to steal away for a week with them.

"That went condo." Nita sighed. "I presume you're staying with me?"

"You still have that convertible bed on the sun porch?"

"The furniture in this house hasn't been changed in thirty

years. The same stain on the kitchen wall, the same sad beds. When are you arriving?"

"I thought I'd drive there maybe Wednesday. What do you think?"

"I'm real curious what happens with Itzak and you. Everyone's gossiping about it, you know that. My roommate says, if you die, can she have him?"

"No, but I expect you to take my cats."

"Don't say that in front of Tanya, or she'll put out a contract on you."

Itzak called the next evening from New York. Tanglewood was on his mind too. She had not been conscious of any great desire to see him. In fact, she had been thinking that now that she was connected to Willie again and expecting to reconcile with Susan, she was not sure she had the time or energy for Itzak in her life. That relationship had been a survival stratagem of the spring, likely to peter out after the premiere. They weren't living in the same state or the same style. His life was out in public, on the road, in the intense glare of celebrity. She was at home in the country, in the woods. Every night in New York, he dropped fifty to a hundred for a meal, take-out or rushing to fancy restaurants. He was used to people staring and murmuring when he walked into a room. His luggage cost more than anything she would ever put into hers. It was a gross mismatch.

"I rented a cottage on the Bowl. I have it for two weeks, but I won't get there until Tuesday. That will give us two days to rehearse. Then I play the Telemann and the Escher with Kyle and the Second Brandenburg with the BSO . . . I've been hoping you can share the cottage with me and stay on."

"I was going to stay with Nita Banuto. She's an old friend of mine."

"Oh, if you'd rather . . ." He sounded desolated. She felt as if she had slapped him in the face. She felt like an idiot.

"I didn't know what your plans were," she said lamely. "I'd just be sleeping on her screened porch." Was she giving in because she really did like him, because she didn't want to hurt him, or because he was potentially important to her career? Was she using him? She had a brief desire to crawl off into a cave and sleep for a month. Maybe he just liked to arrive with a woman instead of wasting energy fighting off pursuit?

"Great!" he said briskly. "We'll share the cottage. It's my

treat, don't worry about it. My assistant took care of the arrangements already. When can you come?''

She ended up agreeing to drive to Tanglewood Tuesday. After all, with Jimmy in the house, her cats would be fed and cared for, her garden would be watered. She felt guilty for having hesitated. They could work on the piece more intensely if they stayed in the same place. That made a lot of sense, as did coming a day early. She would call Nita at once. She perceived herself as pulled between them. When she thought of little Tanya, she felt gypped. Often when she stayed with Nita in the city, she only saw Tanya at supper, and then it was bedtime. At Tanglewood, Dinah had always taken care of Tanya while Nita was rehearsing and performing. It was her time of surrogate motherhood, and now she would be giving that up. Perhaps she had let herself be bribed by what would surely be more sumptuous accommodations—they could hardly be less luxurious. On the other hand, if there was a possibility of a serious connection with Itzak, surely staying with him would promote discovering that or finally dismissing it.

"He wants me to stay with him in his cottage. How would you feel about that? We've always shared your house."

"Because we don't have the money for something fancier. Well, do it," Nita said. "Just don't move to New York. I'd miss you too much."

"Nita, once he performs *The Cat in the Moon*, it's all over. It was just convenience, coincidence."

"You aren't crazy about him, are you? Yet when you got back from New York, you sounded hooked."

"I hardly know him yet. I don't dare take it seriously. I can't believe in it, you know? Right now I'm more worried about my piece than I am about Itzak."

"Well, honey, if it doesn't work out staying with him, remember we have a nice lumpy couch on the leaky screened porch just waiting for you!"

THIRTY

Laurie

Tyrone usually called Laurie once a week, no matter where he was. He was calling this time from Tokyo, where he had gone on business. He sounded rather tired and she did not think he was alone. Again she did not tell him about Jimmy.

She used as an excuse his fatigue and the sense she had that the conversation was being overheard. She suspected that she needed all the time she could steal alone with Jimmy before Tyrone and his entourage arrived and began judging the relationship. It felt fragile, but she wanted to keep it. Therefore, she was not really lying to Tyrone, just waiting for the best time to tell him. She imagined his translator as the woman in the room with him.

He always used the same translator and Laurie had noticed Celeste and the maid before her, Carmella, packing presents, expensive presents, to carry to Tokyo. She had never met the woman but had an idea of her appearance from photographs taken in groups over the years. Tyrone never brought Laurie along to Tokyo, nor his wives. It was always business, but Laurie suspected that there was also a temporary mistress, the lady translator with her downcast eyes and birdlike hands.

After all, Laurie was Tyrone's daughter. Perhaps she was learning to use her charm as he always did. Perhaps she was finally coming to have charm to use. If Tyrone were spending a year in the country, he would find himself some nice local woman to prevent loneliness, to care for him. Maybe she could present the relationship with Jimmy acceptably to Tyrone in some such guise? She did not really think of Jimmy that way, but if she could persuade Tyrone that she did, the relationship might be less annoying to him.

Jimmy worked to exhaustion. She was unused to a man who did physical labor, for Tyrone of course worked tremendously hard but also played hard, since he did nothing more strenuous physically than lifting a telephone receiver. Tom had not had a job the second year they were married. When she dragged herself home from the gallery, he had been bored and demanding.

Although Jimmy did not lack his demanding side, the balance was different. She had moved into the boathouse, which she suspected would always be referred to that way, no matter how long she lived in it. She realized how awkward things would be if she were still in the big house, when Tyrone arrived. Whether he had foreseen such a possibility or not, she understood that a place of her own was vital; once again she was amazed by his acumen.

She was engaged in fixing up the boathouse. She had hung two of her own paintings and some drawings she had bought at a discount while working at Manning Stanwyck's gallery. She shopped for curtains, but she could not find anything that was not ticky-tacky, so she decided to make them herself. That sounded almost sweet. She was still looking for material, wondering if she'd have to go to New York, when she learned there was a place in Hyannis that carried Marimekko fabrics. She found a perfect chintz and decided she would make simple drapes. She loved the idea of being able to say she had done it. That would sabotage her old klutz image.

That afternoon when she got back from the beach, she drove herself and her fabric to Susan's. Susan served her iced peppermint tea and chocolate chip cookies, as they spread out the material they had cut together. Susan could help her with the difficult parts. Susan could make a sewing machine do tricks, and her machine was big and sophisticated. Laurie was generously allowing Susan to make up for being weird about Jimmy and her. Laurie had almost stopped speaking to Susan after she had thrown Jimmy out of the house. Susan ought to be glad, not half crazy, over their getting together. What could Susan want for him that was better than herself?

Laurie felt it was important for her to talk openly about Jimmy around Susan. "Don't you miss having Jimmy home?"

Susan looked as shaken as she always did when Laurie mentioned Jimmy. That was one of the reasons Laurie did it. "He's right next door . . . You spoke to Tyrone Monday? He hasn't called me. Does he know yet?"

"Not yet. He's in Japan, after all. He was full of his trip and I could hardly slip a word in." If she didn't yet have any idea how serious she was or wasn't about Jimmy, at least that was an improvement that would have made her old shrink proud of her

(You want commitment, Laurie, commitment when you do not even know whom you are trying to pry commitment from, and to what? It is the commitment you desire, and not the man, wouldn't you agree? That was her goal-oriented therapist, not the nondirective therapist.)

Further, she doubted if Jimmy had any idea what he wanted from her. Oh, he knew he wanted her, and he had all kinds of sweet ways of showing that. He was more affectionate than Tom had been or Rick. Nobody had acted so lovingly toward her since she was a little girl, back when her mother was happy with her father. "As his mother, don't you think Jimmy is an extraordinary man? The better I get to know him, the more depths I find in him."

"He's like me," Susan said unwillingly. "He's extremely emotional. He covers it up in daily life better than I do—I suppose as a boy, he had to."

Since Laurie had become involved with Jimmy, she found herself feeling strong in comparison to Susan, larger, surer. In reality she was perhaps an inch taller than Susan, but it was as if Susan were hunched over now, protecting her vital organs. Susan had always seemed to her the perfect mother, calm, giving, the woman who could set anything right, who had created a cute homey cottage in the woods. Other people's houses might smell of expensive French scents or of furniture polish, but Susan's house always smelled of cooking, of canning, of woodsmoke. Now she realized she had always idealized Susan. Maybe envying Jimmy for his mother had been unjust to him. Susan was certainly being unfair about their involvement.

It was good for them to work on the curtains together. Laurie was letting go of a piece of her adolescence at last, the idealization of Susan. She could remember when she had stopped imagining Willie was a great artist, in art school when she had learned how out-of-date his work was. Nobody did political work any longer. She had realized then that she had grown beyond him, and she had let go of her adolescent adoration.

That evening she explained some of that to Jimmy, the part about Susan only. He agreed. "All you summer kids were inclined to see her as the perfect Madonna, Our Lady of the Pond. She liked playing that role."

They were lying in her bed up in the loft, with the skylights still open to the long early July twilight. She noticed swallows zooming past. She had loved them since she was a child and her

210

mother told her they ate mosquitos. They were neat sleek birds who moved like nothing else, so she could always recognize them and never be mistaken and feel like an idiot when some knowledgeable adult like Willie corrected an identification she made. Swallows were like robins, guaranteed but not as prosaic.

Jimmy and she were naked, had just made love and were not yet ready to face the problem of supper. Because she had stayed so late with Susan, she had not thought about it; but then Jimmy did not seem to expect that she would.

"I used to feel she preferred the summer kids to us," Jimmy said. "Although Johnny felt that more strongly than I did."

"Susan hates when you call Siobhan Johnny."

"It was a ghastly name to give her. No one can pronounce it. No one can spell it. No one who sees it written ever says, Sha-van, but something tooth-breaking like See-obe-han."

"What made you feel Susan preferred us?" She ran her nail lightly down his satiny back until he shuddered.

"You were all so much better dressed and better educated, just the way she would have liked us to be. I could see her imagining not so much adopting you but getting you to adopt her."

Laurie laughed. "I wanted to be her daughter. I didn't want to be anybody's daughter but Daddy's, but by the time I was in high school, my mother drove me crazy. I never knew what I was coming home to, super mom or this creature who cried and carried on about Daddy and betrayal and her life ruined, like some one-horse soap opera. I was so ashamed of her I was afraid to bring friends home. Yet I felt guilty because she was so needy and she was my mother."

"Is that why Tyrone left her?"

"No. She never started drinking seriously until he married again. Until then, she just kept trying to get him back. I must have been fourteen before I ever saw her drunk. At first I didn't even understand what was wrong."

"That isn't something you ever have to worry about where I'm concerned. I'm a pretty controlled person. I don't need help to feel good or to relax."

"I admire that. I don't understand how I could go from my mother to Tom, from one kind of addict to another, and not even see what I was doing."

"I think until a certain age, we all fuck up in ways we don't understand. Then we begin to take control of our lives. It just takes longer to grow up than it's supposed to."

"I think you're absolutely right! That's what's finally happening to me. I think one enormous thing we have in common is that we both feel as if we made terrible choices that we're responsible for, yes, but that we learned a great deal and are ever so much clearer than most people our age."

"I only hope being clear, as you call it, makes it easier to get what we want and not just easier to see what we didn't get." He stirred, a stretching that rippled over his body. She was proud that she understood that meant he was ready to move now toward supper.

"I hope you don't mind that I was working on the curtains till five. Where do you want to go for supper?"

He suggested a seafood place with a bar where they would run into his friends. That was fine with her. She was accepted as a couple with him. People whose faces she had seen for years in the street now said hello to her. After twenty-four years she had acquired a local identity. It was startling but pleasant. It made going into the post office or Souza's a much more personal experience. On Sunday, the lady in Souza's would hand her *The Times* without her having to ask. In the fish market, the man with the beard would confide what was fresh that day. She was proud that she was acquiring a fund of small talk for such occasions. All her life she had been too shy to function smoothly with people she did not know well; she felt as if this new ability was one more sign of her maturity.

After supper they drove to the ocean and holding hands, strolled along the beach barefoot on the firm sand the tide had relinquished. A wind had risen and combers were building, cracking their long long whips over the hidden sandbars. He insisted she put on his jacket. They huddled at the base of a dune, sheltered from the wind and staring at the line where sea melted into sky, lights of a fishing vessel bobbing perhaps a mile out, the amethyst waves breaking.

"Are you really going to wait till Tyrone gets here to tell him?"

"He's in Japan right now."

"Any excuse. Are you afraid of him? You know, I'm not."

She sighed. "Not afraid. I just don't know how he'll react—"

"On the contrary, we both have a pretty good idea he won't

be overjoyed. He will think of me as déclassé. No surprises there.''

''He's friendly with your mother and your father, after all—''

''Not as equals.''

''Oh, come on, Jimmy, you're practically family. I just think it's silly to give him advance warning so he has time to think up a campaign. Better to have him find out when he's face-to-face with us.''

''Laurie, don't act ashamed of the relationship, and he can't make you ashamed. Understand I am not about to hide in the woods or skulk around. We are together or we aren't. It's that simple.''

She was silent, clutching herself under the jacket that smelled of him, big on her but comforting. She was learning how it was with him. He was not fierce in his daily will the way Tom had been. He did not fight for every detail, the movie they saw, the kind of beer. He had preferences but he attached little passion to most of them. He would just as soon have strawberry ripple as fudge. On the other hand, he was stubborn about what he felt was important. She perceived that he was not going to give her a lot of a room to maneuver with Tyrone. He was not going to let her blur the involvement and gradually sneak it in. He intended to control the content of her presentation. On one hand she felt flattered, because what woman wouldn't prefer that what mattered to her man was the relationship with her rather than the brand of toothpaste she stocked in the bathroom cabinet and which cheese she brought home; on the other, it was frightening, because she could not dissuade herself that being straightforward with Tyrone would cause a fracas. Further, it made the relationship more important than she had fully decided it to be.

''You're shivering,'' he said and drew her up at once. ''The wind's chilly. Come, let's go back.'' He steered her along the twilight shore where the sand glimmered dull grey, toward the parking lot. ''We'll stop for ice cream and map out a strategy. When exactly is he coming?''

Walking barefoot on sand and then on the cracked gritty asphalt that still held a little of the day's heat made her recall every summer of her life, this place where she had been more at home, more important, more confident than she ever could be in New York, in her real life. She never went barefoot in New York. Here she had bossed Jimmy around and sometimes even the

213

children of Tyrone's guests. "He'll be late this year, because of Japan. He said he'd arrive the second week of July. Usually he comes for the Fourth."

"An appropriate time for fireworks." Jimmy stopped to kiss her.

For the first time in her life, she dreaded Tyrone's arrival. She had always cherished any time he could pry loose to be with her. She felt guilty for how little she was looking forward to his arrival this time, for how delighted she would be if he broke his annual pattern and went off instead to England or Sweden. But Tyrone was certainly coming.

THIRTY-ONE

Dinah

An interrupted relationship has its own intensities. Maybe it was the ardent musicality of Tanglewood, the emotional concentration of the place, with all those students wanting a break professionally, all the stars blowing through, isolated from cities, from ordinary life. Maybe it was the season or the mood one or both of them brought with them. Dinah sensed at once things had heated up. When Dinah went from the Cape to Lenox, she was always struck by how different the scale was. The buildings were bigger, the streets, wider, mansions as common as saltboxes at home, the trees twice as tall, the hills, small mountains. Vistas stretched into the distance. It was spacious, and they expanded together to fill it with strong feelings and reactions.

They were not on her turf, as they had been at Pesach; they were not on his, as they had been in May in Manhattan. They were sharing a cottage. Itzak had rented a car. Of course one of his first queries upon seeing her was, "Should I buy a car? But where would I keep it in New York? I could get out of the city much faster with a car. I could get up to see you."

She was getting used to his constant queries, understanding the habit not as a lack of direction but as an openness to all possibilities at this era of his life, when his success as a performer turned all that was theoretically possible into something he might do. Having judged himself a total failure in his marriage, he was all of the time asking himself if he should try any particular option he could envision. He seemed conscious that any one choice shut down countless others and that his alternatives branched away from him in intricate patterns he could not evaluate. Hence the restless questioning.

They went off to their first meeting with the chamber ensemble that was going to play with Itzak. She spoke briefly about the piece she would be conducting and gave out the parts. She cleared out quickly, as today's time belonged to another performance. Tomorrow at ten would be the first run-through. Most of them, she thought, looked bored, testy, reluctant.

Itzak drove them back to the cottage, a modern pine and glass box built against a huge stone fireplace that went up two stories. It was essentially one vast room with a kitchen in a corner and a smaller bedroom. It had a broad deck with two white pines growing up through it. From the deck to the water's edge was no farther than from her door at home to her own pond, but this was even bigger.

He looked terrific. He was a man whose eyes sparkled more against a tan, whose crisp curly hair was set off better against summer clothes. He liked being in the Berkshires; he liked a more out-of-door life than he generally got. This little game of keeping house together briefly was fun for both of them. They tossed their stuff into the bedroom and went swimming at once. They were both inelegant but sturdy swimmers, puffing and splashing but making their determined way across the pond. Then they went back to the cottage and got into bed.

She was kissing him and enjoying his mouth and his hands and thinking casually how he was just the right size for her so that they fitted together without overlap or awkwardness. He was eating her and she was beginning to melt. Then the sex bloomed out from her. She was hot. They were humping each other and it was hot and wordless and molten and she stopped thinking anything. There were sounds in her head, a drone under them sustaining them, a rhythm welling up through them, but no words, no thoughts except that he was inside her in more than one sense. They were almost one animal, one being. She approached orgasm and hung there caught on the verge, caught, and then finally was carried over and exploded in stopped time. It was and it was and it was for her, urgent and then graceful, floating, dispersing. She had to collect herself so that they could go on for him, and she was still so open and grateful that tenderness exuded through all her pores. She could not quite understand what had happened, but it was a sexual event, sui generis; she tried to label it safely, but still her body stirred under his casual glance like a grove of aspens in the wind.

When they had disentangled themselves he lay on his side staring at her in surprise as great as her own. Then he fell asleep. Then she did. When they awoke they were both galvanized by hunger. They had no time to eat anything but a banana and some potato chips to be just in time for a piece of Antoniou that was premiering. They skipped the party afterward and went to bed, both tired from long driving and long lovemaking.

The next morning, they headed over to the grounds early. At home, she missed the company of other musicians sometimes not at all and sometimes as intensely as any other vital thirst. She felt as if she were not only listening to music all day but immersed in a great simmering bowl of it, that her skin was listening, her bones were vibrating to it, her blood was carrying it along in the red blood cells. She argued music at coffee break, she heard music all morning, music was lunch and supper and drinks and the stuff of her dreams at night. When Kyle listened to a mosquito for a moment and identified D over second C before crushing it on his arm, Dinah felt a sense of community with other musicians she never had at home. Walking across the grounds, she heard a soprano practicing lieder overlapping a Brahms sonata for cello and piano overlapping some horns working on a Gunther Schuller piece.

The first rehearsal was difficult. They were meeting in a big rough rehearsal building of perpendicular wood loosely built so that the wind wafted through and cooled them. It was hard to assert herself as a conductor. She had never had conducting fantasies, never stood leading an imaginary orchestra of chairs and cats. She felt she did a workmanlike job when she had to, but as a woman, it was always a matter of having to storm around and demonstrate her grasp of what she should not need to prove at all, her own score. Itzak, of course, already was in control of his part, but he had to help her drag the ensemble along. Nita was an immense support. She had studied her part the week before and played it through. She had played Dinah's music for twenty years.

While Itzak was talking to Ozawa, Nita and she stole away into the formal garden among the clipped hemlock hedges.

"Maybe I am crazy about him. I feel so confused. Where's Tanya?"

"Giselle came up with Eileen to hear your piece, so we're crowded, but we cover for each other. Don't worry," Nita whispered, her bangs falling forward. "If something goes haywire, you can still camp out with us."

Itzak, of course, was much busier than she was, for he had to rehearse the other three pieces on the program and meet with students; after she left, he would be performing with the BSO. He was in residence for two weeks. But she had more than enough to occupy her time.

It was great to argue with composers who still did twelve tone rows and believed passionately that her kind of music was reactionary and formless. She loved to be argued with; usually no one around her understood enough to challenge her premises, let alone judge her output. It wasn't that she needed that kind of atmosphere to produce. As a daily life she thought she was far more productive living in a beautiful place where she could easily get lots of exercise and simply going into herself and her ideas and composing with an independence she would never have if she lived in this kind of simmering musical soup. Still this immersion was great for a vacation.

The second rehearsal things began to come together. She worked the musicians over and over the third section, which was dragging, too soft. She could see when one of them suddenly got it. Robby, the damned viola, was driving her crazy. He was off tempo, coming in late, throwing everybody off. The younger players liked the music better than this guy, maybe fifty, did. She knew Robby was good because she had heard him enough times. He could do it, but he wouldn't—either because he didn't understand yet or because he disliked the music.

But when she was conducting and it was moving right, she felt as if she and Itzak were one body, one mind, one sound. He was good. As a flutist, she wasn't fit to pass him papers. He was not only technically extraordinary, he was extraordinarily expressive. Sometimes when he was playing, she thought she had never seen anyone as beautiful. Then she felt as if there was nothing she did in her life that was probably as truly important as simply pleasing him and enabling him to play. Those moments did not last long, because self-abnegation came rarely to her. She did find herself musing how hereditary such musical talent might prove to be. A child of theirs would certainly be

217

attractive, at least in her lights. He or she would not be tall, would be stocky, muscular, strong; would have curly hair and brown eyes. Itzak was healthy, intelligent. Susan had really been upset by the idea of her having a baby with Willie, but if she had Itzak's baby, maybe Susan would see that differently. Any child of hers would be a Jew, but her father would be pleased by Itzak. A pity Nathan could not have heard him. She kept these little fantasies to herself. She didn't want to terrify Itzak.

Days passed in intense hungers satisfied and sensations clear as the water they swam in. They talked all the time they were not in bed. They argued about the music they heard. They argued about Hindemith, who was undergoing a little revival of late, and whom Dinah liked better than Itzak did. They picked apart their least favorite conductors and described temper tantrums they had witnessed.

Kyle acted like a rejected suitor, although he was gay and never had shown the least personal interest in her. She could tell he was convinced that she had written a better piece for Itzak than for him; that was true, because she had only been subsidized to write a short piece for him for a rather casual reading, while Itzak was getting a suite for a major premiere.

That night was the performance of her piece in the theater, on a program of Debussy, Mozart and Schumann. Her piece was right after intermission. She envied the crowds on the lawn in their beach chairs, with their little floating lights and their picnic hampers, their chaise longues and their blankets sprawled with dozing children. The concert was sold out because it was Itzak performing, the seats crammed on the stage behind little barriers. Supper sat in her stomach hunched on itself like Figaro when he was sulking. She could not exactly remember how to breathe. She marched out onto the stage waiting for the hangman to fix the noose. Along came Itzak, to the crowd's rising crescendo, strolling as into their bedroom. Yet she knew now how he built for performances, all nerves and elbows and static electricity. It was time to start. For a moment she couldn't remember how it went. She had to glance at her own score. She felt disconcerted by all the random strangers on the stage, far outnumbering the little chamber group of musicians. Then she raised the baton and it all came pounding through her.

She was driving them on through it, driving them while the wind ripped along and it was uphill and suddenly the momentum was carrying her, her arms were taken over, the ensemble

218

was together and possessed and over it all the great silver bird that was Itzak was rising into the moon. There it was, just the way she had heard it in her head. Even the late entry of the viola in the same damned place Robby always straggled in did not throw the ensemble off and they churned along.

Sweat was running down her sides under her long blue dress by the time she was facing the applause, which seemed warm, which seemed genuine. It was over. She wanted to do it again. It was too soon. She heard not a note of the last piece, for she was trembling and subsiding.

When it was time for her to leave Monday, he begged her to stay on and she did, for two more days. She called Jimmy, did not get him, left messages on her answering machine to remind him to water the garden and be good to the cats. Then she had to leave. She was taking up too much of his time; they were breaking unwritten rules. Wednesday morning very early she drove out. She felt exhausted with overstimulation. It was a good fatigue, of being well used throughout her mind and body, of being fertilized into fruitfulness. All she could really want was to arrive, finally get home after the five hour drive, and sleep. She wanted to wake energized and start something new and utterly irresistible. She felt full of music, freshened, primed to launch into work while the impulse was fierce in her and while all other needs and hungers were laid to rest—silenced, abolished.

She arrived on the edge of town just after two and stopped to buy groceries. She could feel herself about to commence a period of utter discipline and joyful hard work. A rhythm was beating in the back of her mind, a syncopated march, like an old blues march but with varying rhythms over that base rhythm and she could hear more brass then she usually worked with. She was more a percussion, a keyboard, a reed composer. Then she came to strings. The brass instruments were frequently afterthoughts. Not this time.

She sang one rhythm beating another on the wheel. The two were dodging in and out, they were dancing like stately marsh birds round and round each other, they were flirting and teasing and closing together as once she and Susan and Willie had danced about each other in joy and fruition. Then she swerved off the highway into the maze of roads. Nobody ever found her by accident, for they would have to know just which unmarked sand roads to turn left on and where to turn right and which fork to take, most marked only with a scattering of the names of summer people.

She passed Bracken Pond and came over the crest when she could first see her own pond and the rhythms were intersecting, interweaving. At once she had to slam on the brakes hard and twist half off the road narrowly missing a pine because a big truck was coming at her, driving much too fast through the woods, bouncing with bone crushing thunks off the big exposed roots and the deep puddles and gulches that made driving these roads so interesting. She saw it was Joey Ellis, the lecherous electrician, rushing hell bent from some pond house. He always drove that way. He was a famous menace. He had wrecked three trucks since she had known him.

She went on more cautiously, nothing but a wary silence in her head now. She rolled down the window the rest of the way to give her more chance to hear whatever might be coming at her. What she heard was the sound of machinery.

She turned into the drive she shared with the new house and slammed on her brakes again. Where the drive had been was a large pit. It had a huge septic tank lowered into it and a ditch leading from it toward the new house that an army could have occupied for a month of trench warfare. It occurred to her that she had no idea whether the driveway was on her property or Willie and Susan's; nor until this moment had that ever mattered. The two lots had been arbitrarily separated in the past when real estate matters were much vaguer than the Registry of Deeds like nowadays.

What was she supposed to do with her car? How was she supposed to get anything, including her luggage and her groceries, up to her house? The pit was big enough to contain her old Volvo with room to spare. A hedge of quince ran down one side of the driveway, so she pulled off onto the mangy semilawn that formed the other side, the open side toward Willie and Susan's house, and parked there under the big white oak. Just a few feet away was devastation, where an old arbor had stood with climbing roses in pink and white arching over it. The arbor had been pulled down and lay on its side. The roses had been hacked off at the roots. The entire area had been bulldozed, dug out with a front-end loader and then hastily filled in. A hundred square feet of pleasant garden had been stripped to raw sand.

Carrying groceries, she picked her way through piles of gravel and little stones, heaps of sand, jumping across ditches to a clear place where she could duck through the hedge. Tire tracks scored her lawn and cut right through her iris and daylily bed and across the corner of her cutting garden where broken dahlias sprawled. Beyond her house was a similar pile of sand, of gravel and a pit as big as the other. Into this pit a large concrete structure was just being lowered. That was what she had heard. It landed on the bottom with a great reverberating clunk. Tommy Rindge's dog was barking madly. Jimmy and Tommy's brother were supervising or kibitzing. They did not notice her.

She came into her kitchen, where the remains of several take-out lunches lay on the table in their torn wrappings. Butts were heaped in saucers and china cups. She stepped on a crushed beer can. No cats greeted her. Leaving her groceries on the table, she ran through the house with a growing sense of desolation. Finally a soft mew answered her and she located Tosca under her bed, pretending to be a dust fluff against the wall. She could not find Figaro at all. She went in search of Jimmy.

She had to drag him away from the pit to ask him, "Where's Figaro?"

Jimmy looked vague. He was watching the work over her shoulder. "He's around somewhere. Isn't he?"

"When was the last time you saw him?"

Jimmy caught the rising tone in her voice and looked at her. He tried to remember. "I guess it was a couple of mornings ago."

"He didn't come back for the last two days?"

"He's a big old cat, Dinah. He can take care of himself."

"In a pig's eye. If he was injured by any of these bozos, I will kill the person responsible. And you!"

She fed Tosca in the bedroom, brought the litter box in and shut the door, so that the cat would feel safe. Then she changed into jeans and went into the woods calling Figaro. She was overwound with agitation. Figaro might have decided she was gone forever, chaos had come and run away to try his luck among the foxes, raccoons, great horned owls and hawks as a predator. His would be a short violent life, and she wanted him back.

She was badly shaken by all the devastation that had occurred in the few days of her absence. She had expected a neat little excavation in dead center of her lawn, a narrow trench from there to the old septic system or straight to the house. Whatever had been working in her on the journey was gone. She felt guilty

221

for having stayed the two extra days with Itzak; she felt sorry to be back at all. She felt invaded. She felt like an idiot. She had invited these men with their machines and their carelessness into her house from some weird greed, that since Jimmy offered to enlarge her house, she ought to take him up on it. Something for almost nothing. That wasn't true, as everybody except Jimmy had to be paid and materials were expensive. She had failed to imagine what it would be like to live and work here during the expansion.

She went on calling and calling Figaro, past the MacIvors, where she had screwed Willie about twenty times, along the path toward the dunes. "Figaro," she called.

"Figaro," a voice repeated sarcastically about five feet to her right. "What do you think you are, some half-assed opera?" The Captain was sitting on a log smoking a joint. He had been fishing and had two largemouthed bass on a line.

"I'm calling my cat," she said between clenched teeth and went on, walking a few feet to bellow stubbornly in her coarsening voice, "Figaro! Figaro!"

"Orange cat, isn't he?"

She swung back around. "That's him."

"Good sized? Sort of a belly on him."

She was instantly afraid Figaro was dead. Perhaps Toby had shot him. "Have you seen him?"

"I don't think much of cats. But that one, he runs down rabbits. He takes rabbits all the time."

"Have you seen him?"

"How come you lost him? A cat like that, he doesn't get lost."

"I was away working for a week. In the meantime they started putting a new septic system in my house. Figaro ran away then."

Toby nodded. "I see him now and again. He covers a lot of distance. He visited me last night and we had supper together. I was eating at a picnic table under my tree, and he sat down on the other bench and stared at me till I gave him some fish. But he won't eat clams."

"Thank you for feeding him. Would you mind if I looked for him around your house?"

"I'd rather you didn't. I'll keep an eye out for him. But I don't like people coming to me unless I ask them special."

She would bet he had a garden of weed in. Good cash crop. It was awkward, because she desperately wanted Figaro back

222

and if he was hanging around the Captain's, that was where she longed to go. However, there was no way of quietly looking for a cat. She continued her circuit of the pond until she was hoarse. No Figaro. At least he had still been alive the night before.

She went home and holed up with Tosca in her bedroom. Tosca crawled into her lap and for ten minutes made complaining noises while standing on her back paws with her forepaws against Dinah's face. When Dinah tried to rise to do something about supper, Tosca dug into her shoulder and held on. No way, she said, no way you're leaving me for two minutes again. Dinah went downstairs with Tosca on her shoulder and made her supper preparations in the same state. Even when she was sautéing chopped onions, Tosca rode her shoulder clutching tightly. Finally the Rindge boys were gone and Jimmy came in, ebullient. "Aren't you astonished how much we got done? Now all we have to do is wait for Charley to come and okay the septic system. Then it can be closed up and we can get going."

Dinah served them a late supper—late for people who got up at six every morning. "Jimmy, I can't believe what a mess they made. Half my garden's destroyed."

"You can plant it back. It's just sand, Dinah."

She could barely speak to him. "Jimmy, okay they've dug it all up for the septic system, so I'll go ahead with it. But I don't want anything after that. No addition, no more building!"

"Dinah, you're being silly because your cat's missing. I'm sorry about that. I bet he'll come back tonight or tomorrow. I have everybody lined up for the addition. They're doing it fast as a favor because this is a damned busy season. Besides, if you think it's noisy, it's going to be noisy anyhow, with Willie and Susan having that studio built right outside."

He was right, unfortunately, he was right.

About eight a pickup truck squealed to an abrupt stop outside, while trying to pull into the drive. Only the long July twilight, the mauve light with the birds still hopping around the sand traps looking for the lawn that used to be, kept the battered truck from landing in the pit. Toby hopped out and pulled a box from the back. "Hi, Dinah. Here's your rabbit-killer."

"Toby! Thank you. Is it him?" She took the box and ran into the kitchen. Something heavy and angry was inside. She made sure the screen door was shut before she opened it and Figaro hunched there glowering. He hissed as a general warning. Then he focused on her and gave a loud howl. He sprang from the box and glared around, turned around twice, then ran for his food dish. Tosca climbed down Dinah and ran to sniff his ass and then his nose. They circled each other sniffing and sniffing. Tosca tried to wash his face but he lowered it into his food.

"Look at him put it away," Toby said.

Dinah opened the screen door and pulled him inside. "Toby, I can't tell you how happy I am to have him back. You see what I came home to find."

"A fucking mess," Toby said, snorting. "Is that chicken?"

She drew out a chair, put a plate down. "Have some. I cooked a whole one. Would you like a beer with it? How about some salad?" She was used to cooking for three and had the tendency to make that much. Jimmy ate enough for two anyhow. It was she who had lacked an appetite tonight.

The Captain ate heartily. He finished the entire rest of the chicken, the salad, the rice, the loaf of baker's rye she had brought back. Watching him put it away, she took half a frozen rhubarb pie out of the freezer and heated it in the oven. He and Jimmy competed to finish that. Toby was a slow but methodical eater who simply did not falter until his plate was empty and then all other plates on the table were empty.

Toby thanked her in an almost courtly way, complimenting her on her cooking. Then he took his leave. Figaro did not pay him any attention. He was sitting in Dinah's lap with Tosca intertwined with him. Dinah did not mind that together they weighed twenty-four pounds and cut off the circulation to her right leg. At least something was right. She had to fight the impulse to pack both cats up in the carrier she used to take them to the vet's and drive at more than legal speeds back to Tanglewood. She wanted to flee with them not so much *toward* Itzak, although he seemed in her mind far more civilized and compatible than any other man alive and with no desire to build anything, as *away* from all this — her usually cherished home and life.

THIRTY-TWO

Susan

Tyrone never did call Susan from Japan. Only infrequently did he call from other countries, but she had been sure he would this time, and had tried to avoid being out of the house during the hours she judged likeliest. She had looked up Tokyo time and figured that out, not saying a word to Willie or anyone else. Then she heard from Laurie that he was in New York, and began more strongly than ever to expect to hear from him.

Laurie had not told him. Every afternoon they worked on the curtains together, Susan found that out, approaching obliquely so that she would not make matters worse. Laurie was acting like a teenager with a crush. Every other word out of her mouth was Jimmy, Jimmy, Jimmy. It wasn't a stable or mature relationship but one based mostly on the fact that, as she herself had warned Tyrone, there were no suitable men around for Laurie and she was lonely. Jimmy was on the rebound. Now he was going to get hurt very badly when Tyrone persuaded Laurie to break it off. She wondered if Tyrone would proceed with his plans for the gallery, or if he would simply drop that cold and take Laurie back to New York.

She was the only person who saw the situation clearly, and no one would listen to her. Jimmy was over his head. Like herself, he was intensely emotional under his cool slick surface, and he cared too much for Laurie already. Oh, it wasn't real, but it would hurt just as much. After all, his wife had just had a baby, and she knew perfectly well that Jimmy would go back to Lisa without a moment's hesitation if she would have him. Foolish Lisa, trying to raise a child alone. Too much pride and not enough sense. Susan still expected that Lisa would appear on their doorstep in six months to a year. With Jimmy still married to her and involved with Laurie, that would create a mess that made Susan shudder. Jimmy had agreed to give Lisa a divorce, but after that initial meeting with lawyers, nothing whatsoever had happened. He was still married, and everybody seemed to have decided to ignore that fact as inconvenient. It was simply a situation simmering toward disaster.

When she had visited them last, the restaurant had been a going concern, always crowded. Basta Pasta had been a young people's place, a salad bar and a pasta bar: they had put out ten kinds of hot and cold pasta with many sauces, from meat and clam to pesto di basilico and primavera, additives like cheese and hot peppers. It had been an instant success. In fact Lisa and Jimmy had been talking about franchising the idea. Jimmy simply hadn't a head for business, any more than she had. Jimmy was just too much like her for his own good. They both were tremendously creative, but they couldn't keep books or cost things appropriately. Now he was going to be badly hurt, for he had the arrogance of the young who imagine they can have whatever they want simply because they want it strongly.

She did not think Jimmy was truly in love with Laurie; it was too soon after his loss. He was simply falling in love to feel loved, to make up for his estranged family. Willie as usual refused to understand. At moments, she missed Dinah. Dinah was not as tone deaf as Willie to emotions; if Susan trapped her attention, Dinah could sometimes offer an insight. She would have something to say about the Laurie-Jimmy affair. Susan would have found it a great relief to grab Dinah and pour out everything. Dinah had a way of listening, once her attention was fixed, that soothed Susan, stroking and easing her. Talking with Laurie made her tense. Laurie reminded her of Siobhan, she was being so willful and blind and self-destructive. Susan knew it was a phase Laurie was going through, but it was disappointing to face the same orneriness she had to endure from her own daughter.

She was actually glad when they finished the curtains. Laurie had gone and bought a bland Marimekko fabric. Really, one of her own designs would have been far more appropriate to a house on the pond, perhaps the water lily chintz or that marvelously grassy cotton. Or the dragonflies. Laurie was supposed to be an artist, but she lacked Tyrone's gift for perfect taste. How could Laurie not have realized that one of the fabrics Susan designed would be much more attractive and fitting? If Laurie didn't know where to look, Susan could easily have ordered the fabric for her at wholesale. It was a slap in the face, yet Laurie seemed oblivious. All she wanted to talk about was Jimmy,

226

Jimmy, Jimmy as if flinging in her teeth that neither of them considered her opinion worth taking into consideration.

Willie had finally started a studio for her, after all these years, but she knew it was because she had asked a friendly realtor, Mary Lou, to appraise their house and land. She kept thinking how much money they were sitting on tied up in this one piece of property. Mary Lou casually estimated they could get four hundred thousand for their little spread. Even Willie had been impressed, although he pretended to think it was fictional money. All real estate values here are inflated, Willie emoted. Then he started the studio, a bribe to her not to think of how they might change their life into something more stimulating. She would see. She wasn't in a panic. The summer was upon them and everybody was arriving for the season.

Every morning when she rose, she swam almost to the middle and back, or at any rate out to the point where she was level with a particular big oak she remembered Dinah scaling to bring down Figaro when he was a kitten. When she had begun her morning swims to get into condition for the summer, she used to hear Dinah's flute or piano or sometimes her tape recorder going. Dinah had the habit of recording one line and then writing another line against it. At the time Susan had felt imposed upon by the music, but now with nothing but the roar of front-end loaders in her ears, she rather missed that pleasant rhythmic tinkle she could use to pace her stroke.

It was more satisfying to feel separate from an ex-lover one could locate in a particular room and a particular activity. Since Jimmy had moved next door, she could not even guess who was boiling water in the whistling kettle or slamming the door. Several times she had artfully arranged to be outside cutting a few roses from the surviving bushes only to have Jimmy emerge to get the mail. What was the use of having spent ten minutes arranging her hair and practicing a superior smile, when her son came charging out, "Hi, Mom, I'll get your mail too," jumped in the Ford and tore off to town in a dust cloud. Instead she would face Tommy Rindge waiting, waiting for the health agent to come and okay their holes. His dog would leap upon her with great dusty paws and thrust his muzzle into her crotch. Tommy would try to get her into conversation so he could peek down her dress.

Between Dinah and herself was now a desert, a wasteland, an industrial zone studded with tools and piles of lumber and cement blocks, something no sane person would try to cross in the dark. She rarely saw Dinah. She did not even get a chance to talk loudly to the cats to show Dinah that she was really a warm friendly person, to pick up Tosca or Figaro and fuss them up and kiss them. Dinah was keeping both cats inside. Had Dinah caught on to her game? That was absurd. A person could fuss over a pussycat without meaning anything ulterior.

They had to keep Bogey tied up. After the third time he had managed to get down into one of the septic pits without being able to get back out, Willie had decreed he was to spend the time till the health agent came and inspected on the end of a rope tied to a sturdy red maple on the shore. Bogey howled a lot, but at least he didn't fall down the pit a fourth time, or however he ended up twice in theirs and once in Dinah's cement bunker.

It was infuriating that Dinah should decide to build just because they were enlarging. It was pure competitiveness. Nonetheless, when she did run into Dinah, she made a point of asking about the progress of her addition as if she could not simply look out and see. She liked the stifled look that convulsed Dinah's features on the few occasions Susan managed to make their paths cross.

She was annoyed with herself for her moments of weakness lately when she wished she could talk to Dinah. Once Tyrone arrived, unless Jimmy and Laurie had between them managed to despoil the summer, she would not feel this awkward vacancy. No doubt she had permitted the relationship to drag on so long because having another woman close was convenient, cozy. Whatever Dinah was and wasn't, at least she could be talked to when she could be broken free of her self-involvement. She was a mature woman to whom Susan could confide things Laurie would not understand and Willie didn't know existed.

For instance, when she was younger, every time her period was late, she would convince herself she was pregnant. Dinah would be there to rationalize her fears away and soothe them into small tremors. Now that she was older, when her period was late, she feared menopause. Susan's periods had always tended toward irregularity except while she had been on the pill, so that she seemed to have something to worry about every month. She felt that once she passed into menopause, somehow Willie would know and lose interest in her. She would gain weight. Her hair would fall out. She would pose as a woman, but it would be a pretense because secretly she would no longer be a real woman.

She had no symptoms, no hot flashes, whatever those were. However, her period was late again. Every day she thought ten times that her period had started, and every time she was dry as sandpaper. Yesterday she had asked Willie as if casually, if she looked different to him. He had frowned at her, staring, and then asked if she had cut her hair.

Finally that afternoon the health agent came, spent all of five minutes looking over the plots and departed. By five, Tommy had filled in both holes and finally she could see Dinah's house again from ground level, and once again they had a usable drive. Willie came out of his studio to stand beside her and watch.

"Now maybe *she* can bring herself to stop parking on our lawn."

"What lawn? We haven't had a lawn in two weeks." Tommy had dug a great hole where they had intended the new septic system to be, but he had hit clay. He had filled it in, but now the surface was loose sand.

"Is she going to go on using our driveway forever and ever?"

Willie took her by the arm and walked her into the house for privacy. "Susan, honey, both houses have always shared that there drive." When he got excited, his voice always got more southern.

She almost smiled at the melody while frowning at the content. "That's like saying there's always been slavery. That doesn't make it right. The drive is on our land. She ought to build her own drive."

"If she does, we'll have to. Have you ever looked at our plot? It goes at a very sharp slant. Yes, part of the drive is on our land and so is part of the quince hedge. However, the drive *starts* on Dinah's land. Both lots are parallelograms, not squares."

"Oh."

"So don't say anything. She thinks she's parking on our land, too. She apologized to me twice. But she wasn't. Understand?"

Susan nodded, staring out the window at the disputed drive.

Willie said insistently, "So you're not going to say a word to her about the drive. Right? This addition is costing us more than we ought to be spending. Let's not make it worse."

"I won't say a word." She privately thought Willie was timid about money. She would work harder in the fall. Maybe they'd ask Tyrone to help them find some little pied-à-terre, a small cute apartment in the city, and sell this and have money left over to invest. Willie had been making loads of money remodeling the boathouse and now the house in town. He always seemed to feel that if he did not poor-mouth to her, she would run out and buy something glamorous and expensive like jewelry or furs—she who spent less on herself than any woman she knew in the business.

That evening Tyrone did call, finally. He told her stories about his trip to Japan that would normally have charmed her, but she could scarcely concentrate. Then he started asking questions about everyone on the pond. "Is Candida MacIvor around? And how about Alec? They seemed like such a pleasant couple."

"Tyrone, I have something disturbing to tell you."

"Disturbing in what way?"

"Laurie and Jimmy have got involved with each other."

"Involved. Jimmy." He seemed to by trying to balance some complicated equation. "She hasn't mentioned this to me."

"I don't think it's important," Susan rushed on. "I'm sure she doesn't think it's a big enough matter to bother you with."

"Perhaps . . . But she's moved into the boathouse, hasn't she? I don't imagine that's big enough for two."

"Oh, they aren't living together, Tyrone, I promise you that. It's not anything that important."

"I'll be down shortly. Laurie said you were helping her with curtains. That's sweet of you. She needs to keep busy at small useful tasks. She's a convalescent, Susan, recovering from a violent shock. We must coddle her."

"I know that, Tyrone, but—"

"Of course you understand. I'll see you very, very soon."

When she told Willie it had been Tyrone, he asked at once, "Did he say he's sending the check? He owes us thirty-five hundred on the boathouse, and we need five thousand to proceed on the gallery. I wrote him that. I called twice, but I only got his secretary."

Susan frowned. "I have nothing to do with your business arrangements with Tyrone. You should have said something when I was on the phone."

"You always take his calls upstairs."

"Willie! You sound jealous."

"You know how little I'm the jealous type."

"Umm. Maybe you're changing. We all change, blessed be."

230

She relented. After all, he was finally building her a studio, one reason he needed the money. "He's coming up right away. I'm sure you can catch him then."

She happened to see Tyrone's Mercedes pass from an upstairs window. She had decided to tidy up that afternoon, and she was just dusting Jimmy's room. She was trying to invent a way to get Jimmy to move back—after all, he must miss his things, although he freely came and took what he wanted a couple of times a week. Still, he could not possibly be comfortable at Dinah's, staying in that tiny room that had been Mark's study, a low cubbyhole under the eaves still crammed with Mark's papers in boxes. It was a monument to Dinah's widowhood in a way Susan could never understand.

Tyrone's secretary Sally was driving Tyrone's Mercedes, with him in the backseat, a portable desk on his lap. His assistant Donald was driving an Olds with the maid riding in front, some large piece of equipment occupying the back. The entourage passed, slowing to view the devastation, and then speeded up into the woods—although nobody except that crazy electrician drove the road at a speed above twenty.

She spun from the window. Cleaning lost its appeal. She had things under control. She decided to sketch the lilies she had picked in what remained of their garden. Her designs originated in something seen or remembered or as now directly studied. Then she began altering the proportions and creating a design. Something would click in that initial literal sketch and she would be off. She had a scarlet spray of lilies she had cut, with some buds not yet open over waxy dark leaves. The anthers were dark brown but she played with first gold, then light green, then ivory. That was it. Ivory. She began to bring out veining in the petals. A suggestion of ivory lace over red. No leaves. Scarlet, ivory, something blue. A butterfly, cobalt blue, tiny. Now she had the color scheme. Two small butterflies with ivory dots in their wings. Red antennae. Coming along. Would she mention to Tyrone that she had been hurt Laurie had not chosen one of her designs? Perhaps not the best beginning to the summer, complaining. Unless it would be a way of bonding with him if he was annoyed at Laurie. Best to wait and see.

She would not call yet, no. She would give him time to talk with Laurie. She had gone over yesterday to air out the big house and fill it with what flowers she had. She wished she could slip into Dinah's garden with a shears, but it would hardly go unobserved, as the front-end loader was back playing with sand to make a foundation base and the foundation men were setting up wooden forms. It was annoying, but it seemed as if Jimmy and Willie had coordinated both projects, so that everything that they did, Dinah also had done on the same day. It was not at all cute. It united them in a way she found tacky.

Tyrone called her promptly the next morning, around eleven. She was just back from her morning swim. He sounded extremely annoyed. "I warned you about Laurie's situation, Tyrone," she said placatingly. "I hope you were able to communicate with her."

"What's going on over there? I heard banging and shouting and engines roaring at seven this morning. I had them complete the boathouse before I arrived so I wouldn't have to put up with a high noise level. I come here to get away from the city, not to haul it around with me."

"Dinah's having an addition put on her house. And we're building a studio."

"And you had to wait until I arrive to have it done? I think that's extremely inconsiderate. You had all year to invite the local nailbangers in for a ball."

"Tyrone, that's not fair. Willie and Jimmy were rushing to finish the boathouse so it would be done when you wanted it."

"Why aren't they working on the gallery?"

"You have to talk to them. I don't involve myself in their building, you know that."

"It's extremely inconsiderate to the rest of us on the pond, that's all I can say." Tyrone hung up without even suggesting they go for a walk or get together for coffee or anything.

On one hand she felt mortified. It did seem as if they were making a hideous mess and commotion. She slept in earplugs, to keep out the shriek of the birds in the morning and the clatter Willie made showering and dressing and getting breakfast. She had not really noticed the noise pollution they were creating. Perhaps it could qualify as a nuisance.

But building had been going on at Tyrone's for months, and at the MacIvors for months before that. Their project was no noisier than either of those. She felt wronged. She became convinced, as she sat staring at the sketch that no longer held the slightest interest, that he could not really be upset about the construction. He was furious about Jimmy and felt unable to

232

say to her how little he liked that relationship; therefore he had displaced his anger onto the noise that wafted across the lake to him. In addition to every other mortification, she discovered that her period had finally started, today, when she was already aggravated and tense. She stormed around her bedroom pulling out tampons and pads in a tantrum.

She must speak to Tyrone. She must make him understand that she was on his side, that she had in no way connived at this unlikely coupling and had in fact tried to prevent it. She must remind him how she had urged him to think of a suitable boyfriend for Laurie. She must catch him as if by accident and reestablish that warm open caring bond between them that had existed for years, that had been growing even deeper of late. She remembered again the toast to summer in his office, just the two of them and Laurie, toasting in exquisite crystal and perfectly iced dry champagne the summer that was now upon them. She must recapture with him the beautiful intense glow of civilized friendship that was perhaps the highest form of union possible between a man and a woman, to which were sex added, no marriage could represent a more perfect connection.

THIRTY-THREE

Willie

Willie and Jimmy had been to every meeting of the Zoning Board of Appeals, the Board of Health and the Planning Board for the last two months. They even had developed opinions on all the other pending cases, because they were getting educated in zoning law. They had started being so intimate with the boards because Tyrone wanted that gallery in a previously residential building in town. That involved problems of a legal septic system at a legal distance from neighboring wells and neighboring septic tanks. It meant providing adequate off-street parking. It involved persuading neighbors that a change of use would not mean more traffic and noise.

Their intimacy had flourished because they needed variance after variance and special permit after special permit to carry on with the two additions. Willie was perfectly aware that if he was not putting up a studio that was only quasi-legal, Susan as a complaining abutter would probably have tried to prevent Dinah from putting on her dubious addition. But they were supporting each other, Jimmy representing Dinah and Willie representing himself and Susan, but also helping Jimmy present Dinah's case. Basically their best argument was that their weird early nineteenth century lot divisions made complying with current regulations impossible. The boards were more sympathetic to them than to Tyrone because they were not changing use, not bringing in more traffic, but just rendering both houses more modern, more livable, actually more in keeping with present codes—and, of course, because they were real year-round working residents.

Willie and Jimmy were getting along fine. He liked feeling tight with his son and he was proud of himself that he hadn't let Susan drag him into her quarrel. They enjoyed the hearings and gossiping afterward over drinks with the other builders about board decisions and who was developing what land where. Willie liked to listen to people talk about their fields of expertise. He liked to find out what was happening, so when he was returning from the supermarket and saw a new sand road carved through the woods, he knew that it was a doctor's house on an enormous lot—a house sized like a motel—or that it was a new subdivision pried into twelve odd-shaped lots of three quarters of an acre apiece. Jimmy was friendly with all the younger guys who worked construction. Willie liked going into the hangouts with his son and seeing him greeted and backslapped. They would sit down with Jimmy's high school buddy George who was a local cop and hear about the tourist who had driven through the McBees' living room at two A.M. and whose first words to the astonished family was, Is this the way to Hyannis? They would sit down with Wendy from the rescue squad and hear about heart attacks and crashes.

He had also discovered that talking about septic systems was one of the great universal topics. Everybody had septic problems or had just had them or was anticipating having them. It was better than the weather for an instant conversation. All he had to do to pass a social fifteen minutes was to bring it up, whether in the post office, Souza's, the liquor store, the bank, the Sandspit or in the street. Sometimes they even talked about it from rolled down window to window, two pickups heading in different directions and stopping for a chat in the middle of the street

234

to block traffic with the summer people leaning on their horns before and behind.

Everybody in town knew they weren't pushing hard for the gallery at the moment. Willie didn't like working for people who dragged out payment. He had to front the bills in order to get the supplies and he had to pay the subcontractors. The last person he ever wanted to stiff or make wait too long was somebody he might need the next week to come in and fix his own electricity or pump his septic tank. If he was dealing with a local buyer, he would simply say, I need eight hundred to go down to the lumberyard and pick up the windows. Tyrone was the worst, because he was in Tokyo or Milan half the time, and he was protected by a twenty-foot hedge of secretaries and personal assistants. Willie was not proceeding any further until Tyrone paid for the work on the boathouse and put up money for the materials list Jimmy had drawn up for the gallery. In the meantime Willie was dividing his time between trying frantically to finish enough new pieces for his opening and getting on with the garage-studio.

Basically once the outer walls were up and the roof was on, he could relax and proceed with the rest when he had the time. Susan was satisfied that she was finally getting her studio; she never did much work in summer, anyhow. She was too social. He had full credit from her for having started the project. She had been very affectionate lately. In fact their sex life had improved at once when Jimmy moved out.

However, it would have been a lot more convenient if Jimmy hadn't moved into Dinah's. It seemed to Willie when he started to solve one problem, another popped up. Jimmy's presence there had had the advantage that it put Dinah's house legally back on his personal map. He could reasonably go next door to consult his son. The trouble was that his son was often there to be consulted. He tried to keep track of Jimmy's time with Laurie. Unfortunately for him, they usually spent evenings and nights together. What he could pry out of that was that if he appeared early in the morning, Jimmy was still at Laurie's, Dinah was awake but Susan was not.

It occurred to him he could simply be honest with Jimmy, but that was a theoretical honesty, not a mode of behavior open to him. He could tell himself that he did not want to get Jimmy into more trouble with his mother, but in truth he simply could not talk openly about his sex life with his son. He was more comfortable just quietly dodging around Jimmy as he dodged around Dinah's constant queries about Susan and did she know yet and what was she feeling. Both his women were reasonably satisfied at the moment. The chaos of construction occupied the forefront of their lives and tended to quiet everything else. Afterward he would finally talk to Susan about the situation or she would gradually guess and accept it. Dinah could not possibly have houseguests, including that musician. All things taken into consideration, he was doing okay.

Johnny called at seven-fifteen just as he was about to duck over to Dinah's. "Daddy, exactly when is your opening?"

"August. . . ." He consulted the calendar on the kitchen wall. Susan wrote their social engagements on it. "August tenth is the opening. The show's up for two weeks."

"I think I can make it for your opening. I have to be in Rochester, New York, that week. And I should make an appointment in Boston with a gallery director I've been in touch with. I figure I can come out the day before and leave the day after. I'll stay with Dinah."

"Jimmy's already doing that." He told her the story.

"*Laurie?* That stuck-up skinny twit? Is Jimmy as hard up for pussy as that?"

Johnny liked to be foul-mouthed on principle. He ignored it, as he always did. "She means well and she's crazy about him. She's right on the pond. I can see the advantages, so why the fuss? It just seems natural."

There was a short silence. Then came her voice imitating, exaggerating the little southern drawl left in his. "Jimmy's got into a good relationship with this really nice Irish setter on the pond. I mean, she has good breeding and no fleas at all. It's actually enormously sensible when you think about it. She has an affectionate disposition and she likes to chase sticks. It's a really good thing for him."

Willie forced a chuckle. He was insulted but at the same time amused. She had him to rights. "You think I try to make the best of everything."

"And Jimmy will make anything. A great combo. I bet Mother's in seventh heaven. She always wanted Laurie in the family."

"Actually she's upset about it. She doesn't think it's a good idea."

"Score one for Mother. See you in August, Dad."

236

Willie worked on his new piece all day, the windows open and listening over the radio for the sound of the cement truck arriving. Until the foundation was poured—actually both of them—nothing could go forward. Everything was in place and ready for the truck. The helper, Archie the subcontractor's son, had arrived in the morning and was still waiting for Archie, his partner Steve and the cement truck. In the meantime, the kid had stretched out on the dock sunning himself. In summer, the locals all greeted each other insisting they hadn't been to the beach at all, and if they had a visible tan, they were always careful to explain it came from roofing or carpentry. A pallor was the appropriate look. Nobody would confess to visiting the beaches between June, when it was okay, and September, when it became acceptable behavior again. Unless you had kids, when it was okay. In fact, the Captain brought his two kids to the pond that noon—he must have picked them up from Wendy's apartment in town—to take a dip. Willie saw a little action at the far end of the pond. Tyrone apparently sent his assistant Donald over to where they were swimming to protest. Willie heard loud voices but couldn't make out the words. Donald went back and the Captain and his children stayed put. Tyrone was always trying to keep the locals from using the pond, but after all, Toby had lived on the pond all his life. Every year, Tyrone was at war with somebody who arrived to swim or launch a canoe.

When Willie came in for his afternoon break—the time he paused and had coffee or a beer, went for a swim, sometimes made love with Susan—he found Candida MacIvor in the kitchen. Both women were drinking wine mixed with sparkling water in tall glasses decorated with mint leaves. They were picking at a leftover chicken Willie had planned to recycle from last night's supper for a curried chicken salad tonight. Candida was dressed less excitingly than she had been the last times he had seen her, in a blue romper. Susan had put on a misty green sundress, a color he liked on her, for it brought out the red in her hair. He thought she looked like a piece of ripe fruit, the freckling on her arms and shoulders and back like the seeds in a ripe banana. He longed to take parts of her into his mouth. Candida's presence was an irritant. Maybe she would go soon. Maybe she would leave some of the chicken when she went.

Willie took a beer and prepared to wait her out. She was talking about a dinner party Tyrone had given that had a strong

237

Japanese flavor. Tyrone had brought a chef out from New York for it. Tyrone had found beautiful prints and porcelain in Japan. He had made the most fascinating side trip to a small island where women dived for pearls. He had given Laurie earrings that were large irregular dark pearls.

At first Willie listened idly. Pearls big as thumbnails. A Japanese chef broiling steak at the table. Seaweed wound about rice. It was all pleasant exotic nonsense like somebody telling the plot of a silly movie. Then he saw Susan dragging it into her as if every word would tear wounds. He shook himself and stared again. Susan was riddled by envy. He could feel it. He wondered that Candida could go on prattling. Nervously he began picking at the roast chicken. He did not realize he had bitten into the drumstick until he tasted it in his mouth. Susan was saying the right things, the little exclamations and soft queries that kept Candida chattering, but he did not comprehend how Candida could miss the raw pain leaking out. How could Susan do this to herself? How could she go crazy because some stupid party had occurred to which she had not been invited? She had probably been happy at the time. What on earth could it matter to her that other people were together? It was madness. He said, "Why don't we all go swimming?"

Both women looked at him blankly. "We just had lunch," Susan said.

"It's two," Willie said, leaning over the table hoping to get them both up and moving.

"Is it?" Susan said coldly. "How fascinating. Candida, do have some more of the wine spritzer. Now tell me about dessert."

He gave up and strolled toward his studio. Archie's kid was down by the water with Bogey, tossing a stick. Dinah was hanging panties on a clothesline. Jimmy was sitting shirtless in the shade with Laurie beside him eating watermelon and spitting the seeds away. They were obviously having a contest in who could spit the seeds farthest, giggling together. Willie drifted slowly toward Dinah. In shorts and a tee, her strong legs looked great and the muscles of her back rippled under the thin cotton as her breasts swung, bending, lifting and pinning, bending, lifting and pinning. She waved as she turned back toward the house. Jimmy and Laurie were lying now on their bellies spitting watermelon seeds across a set of lines traced in the sand. Archie's kid had lain down with his hat over his face. From the

238

kitchen in the new house, Willie could just hear the rise and fall of Candida's voice. Dodging Dinah's intimate things, he followed her into the kitchen. It was hot and the pond was still. Dinah's bedroom would be hot, but she had a window fan. He would ask her to turn it on.

With Dinah, when she wasn't thinking about making love, the best approach was not to be talking about it, not to get her in a romantic mood the way he might do with Susan, but to get his hands on her before she thought about it. As soon as she put the empty basket down, he began to kiss her.

Because he did persuade her to turn on the window fan, they had both undressed before he heard the cement truck outside. "Damn it!" he said with a heartfelt moan. He rarely swore, for his family had felt foul language was as vulgar as tracking dog dirt into the house. Years of involvement with Dinah had abraded that reluctance, but when he swore, it was because he felt sorely tried. "The truck's arrived." He reached for his pants and was buttoning his shirt as he half fell down the short steep flight of straight up steps.

Before bursting out of the house, he paused long enough to check himself, fly zipped, shirt properly buttoned. He hoped Jimmy had not noticed the little detail of the bedroom fan. Keeping up appearances, a family compulsion that was part of his breeding. He couldn't help it and saw no reason he should. It was a small nicety.

The cement truck was backing across Dinah's lawn to the construction site. "Those bulvons!" Dinah bellowed from the upstairs window. "Why can't they use the driveway?"

"Too far from the forms," Willie called up. "What's a bull von?"

He rushed to help Archie and Steve, and so did Jimmy. Archie's son woke and sprang into action. Willie would love it if they would also pour his foundation while they were there with the truck. Otherwise they might not get back for a week. He had expected them to start with his, but Jimmy had been downstairs when the truck arrived, and of course, he had directed them to Dinah's site. It was a matter of dumping the cement, spreading it roughly and then as the forms were filled in, leveling the top. He leaned on Dinah's car to wait, wishing he was back upstairs with her. He felt tight and over-sensitized, crammed into his jeans.

Archie and Steve decided to try to pour the other foundation and get it out of the way. "I hate bringing the truck so far into the woods," the driver confided. "Always afraid I'm going to get stuck in one of those potholes."

The truck started to back up the driveway. It was gaily painted red, white and blue from the Fourth of July parade, when Archie's daughter had stood on the cab waving a sign CEMENT GOODWILL AMONG NATIONS. With all the noise, the women had ended their long luncheon and moved out to chairs by the pond. Susan had brought something she was making for Laurie. Lately Susan had been complaining to him that Laurie had become estranged from her because of the affair with Jimmy. Willie said, What did she expect when she had made her objections so vocal. He had no more time to worry about Susan, because the truck was backing up and he and Jimmy were both yelling directions to keep it from smashing into the quince hedge or knocking down the only remaining rose trellis. Willie hated the maddening beep beep the truck made as it backed, one of the most irritating sounds in the world. Archie and Steve were having a beer and a smoke while they waited for the truck to get into position. It was hot and heavy work hauling and spreading the cement. Archie was an immense guy who had once played end for a local team the year they took a championship; Steve was short, blond and bearded, a law school dropout. He had learned the business from Archie.

Suddenly the roar of the big cement mixer and the engine changed cadence and between Willie and Jimmy suddenly the ground shifted and the truck poised and then began to sink into the earth. Willie stared. Was it an earthquake? He thought he must be rising mysteriously into the air beside the truck. A sharp smell of shit arose. "Stop!" Willie bellowed. "Stop!" The truck had broken through into the new septic tank. But the driver could not hear them or could not stop. With a great grinding of gears and groaning the truck continued to sink as the top of the septic tank cracked and then parted. First a giant piece of the lid and then the truck itself broke through into the pit below.

The driver was screaming. His cab was tilted half off the ground. The cement mixer stopped turning. Susan was screaming. Jimmy was screaming. Archie, Steve and Archie's kid were screaming. Bogey was running in tight circles yapping his head off. Dinah was laughing so hard she sat down on her ass and tears trickled down her face.

The driver cut the engine or it stalled out. A terrible silence descended, except for Bogey's frenetic bark. Everybody stopped yelling and gathered in a circle around the half upended cement truck, now embedded two thirds of the way along the driveway. Willie looked at it and could think of nothing whatsoever to say. Dinah blew her nose and kept her mouth shut.

Archie, the older guy, said in a loud disgusted voice, "Where's your phone? We got to get the big tow truck out here fast."

The driver was up in the air trying to get down. He seemed reluctant to jump. Jimmy brought him an aluminum ladder to climb down. "Holy shit!" the driver said, rubbing his chin and his arm where he had banged himself.

There was indeed a smell of shit in the air and there was the immense truck, sunk about a third of the way along and at an angle that suggested it would never fly again. Willie sat down on the grass beside Dinah. He could not quite believe what he was looking at. Steve rubbed his shaggy blond beard, shaking his head and walking a few paces as if he could suddenly swing around and everything would be as it was. "You know," he said suddenly, "the cement is going to harden."

"No shit," the driver said. "Guess what? If that happens, that truck is staying there permanently."

Archie was plodding back. "The big towing rig is off getting a UPS man out of a ditch."

"Did you tell them we're in bad trouble?" Steve asked in a rising whine.

"I told them."

They gathered in a loose prayerful ring around the truck, its front wheels held up like the paws of a dinosaur, a Tyrannosaurus rex in its dotage.

"What would dissolve cement?" Steve asked. "Break it up?"

"A bomb," Archie said. "Dropped from a plane. We can rent one from the Air Force."

"It's a little big for a planter," Dinah said conversationally close to his ear. "Although it's far more striking than a tire of petunias. It lacks something as sculpture, or isn't that your professional opinion?"

He felt like screaming at her, but at the same time it was just too odd to be believed. "I could go to work on it. See what I can do."

He saw Susan glaring at them. He didn't feel like moving.

241

"Come on, Dad," Jimmy aid. "Let's check over the other foundation with a level before it sets hard. We might as well do that."

Willie got up and followed his son. When he looked back, all the women were sitting, Dinah on the grass, Susan and Candida in the lawn chairs by the pond. Archie, Steve, Archie's grangy son and the driver were standing in various positions around the truck, scratching their heads or their asses and staring. Willie wondered if the Board of Health would still accept a Title V septic tank with a red, white and blue cement truck embedded in it.

He glanced at his wrist to see what time it was, if there was hope for the big towing rig, and saw only the band of pale skin on his left wrist. Then he remembered taking off the watch and putting it on Dinah's bedside table. He also saw the layout of the onlookers: Susan was down at the pond with an uninterrupted view of Dinah's kitchen door. He sighed. Then he sighed again.

THIRTY-FOUR

Dinah

Dinah drifted through her days in a despair that was new and bitter to her. She had endured loss and rejection, but never had she been shut out from her own work when the ideas had been fiercely near the boil in her.

Oh, she had an occasional day of work. That was when she went back to what she had composed and worked it over, incorporated notes she had made, stacked up the lines and listened. She never knew when she rose in the morning if this would be a clear day of blessed almost solitude and silence, or a day noisy and overpopulated. Not only did the machines assault her, the yelling, the pounding, the banging, but the workmen brought their ghetto blasters and music she had not chosen invaded her ears until she wanted to slash and maim.

The cats were unhappy. When it was Sunday or when she was convinced no construction was occurring that day, she would let them out. However, she did not trust the trucks backing in or the electric saws running. One day when she thought it was safe to let Figaro out, he returned limping, and nobody would say how his paw had been torn. By the time she took him to the vet's, ran the course of antibiotics and the paw healed, they had adjusted to life inside in the heat of summer. Dinah passed the time painting her kitchen and bedroom. Then she finally sat down to deal with Mark's papers, going through them and boxing them for deposit at a university where scholars could negotiate with the library for access instead of with her.

She had always thought someday she would act the true literary executor, do something appropriate with all of his letters and manuscripts and notes. Now she read the letters for several afternoons while the frame was going up. She rowed her dinghy onto the pond and read until she could stand it no longer. There were letters from his first wife, letters of wild passionate love and then of married business and then of violent reproach. There were letters from twenty other women following a similar curve, without the middle plateau of marriage. There were letters from his son, gradually trailing off to formality and silence. There was a similar arc with the second wife, truncated since they had married and parted quickly. It all felt futile. An expense of great energy into a void.

When she read his poems, she thought of what an extraordinary man he had been, she remembered loving him. When she read the letters, she felt like one of a multitude of buffeted women, selected by chance and denounced at leisure. Then she felt the only reason he had stayed with her was because he was dying. At the same time she identified with him in a new way. Imagine being involved with Jimmy, who was a couple of years older than she had been when she met Mark; then imagine herself ten years older than she was now. It was absurd. What a mismatch. Yet they had been truly mated, fire to fire. Months after his death when she had been ready for relationships again rather than pure sex, she had sought calm, a familial warmth, regular sex and a great deal of mental space. More space than perhaps Susan had ultimately been willing to grant. Was that the flaw? That she had chosen to think about her music instead of Susan, to reserve her energy for her work? Yet Susan had not engaged her mentally as Mark had; as Itzak did.

Tosca liked to go out in the boat. She would stare at the water, then fold her paws into yoga position and contemplate the shores and her beloved. Dinah sat with tears trickling down her face and read in a gathering cloud of mosquitoes. "Tosca, is there any point to this exercise?" she asked the lean grey cat in the prow. "Maybe I should embrace solitude, to minimize the damage people do to the environment and to each other. Is it wrong to think of wanting a child? Would I be as dreadful a parent as Mark was?"

She felt the artificiality of her depression. Were she working on some of the new ideas she had brought back from Tanglewood, she would be happy. Busy was happy. Idle was sad. Elementary chemistry of her body and brain. All this for an addition she did not truly desire. All she wanted was a washer and a dryer, so she wouldn't have to drive fifteen miles each way and hang around the Laundromat for two or three hours every time she needed clean clothes. All she really wanted was to be back in her tight family with Susan and Willie, sharing their lives. This construction was fallout from that initial explosion.

She wondered if Willie had told Susan about them yet. He kept vaguely promising. He implied that Susan knew but not officially. Dinah hoped so, because if Susan did tacitly condone the relationship, then it must mean she was not truly hostile and liked leaving the door that far ajar. It was a way, Dinah told herself, of not letting go entirely. But the months dragged on. She wanted things above-board between them. Open and clear.

She hardly knew if she really objected to sharing her house with Jimmy, since with him had arrived hordes of workmen and carpenters, guys in her kitchen smoking and drinking beer and eating fast food, loud men she was always coming upon and scuttling sideways around like a small wary crab. The new room upstairs would make a wonderful bedroom for a child. She had not said that to anyone. To whom would she say it? Nita knew what she was thinking, but did not believe she would do it. If only delivery really was delivery, by UPS for instance. Send me a baby for Rosh Hashonah, please. Ten fingers, ten toes, any sex. By the time she had begun to think about a baby when she was with Mark, he had lung cancer and he was her baby. But that unconceived but conceivable child was why she had agreed to the addition.

A letter from a freshman at Sarah Lawrence: "I was asleep until I read your poetry. I was frozen and your words thawed me. I was a terrified child, curled up in fetal position afraid to think of love, afraid of life. . . . ." A divorceé in Harrisburg: "Your poems made me hope that somewhere there are men who

244

feel as women do, who have hearts, who shed tears, who can care and connect. . . ." She did not have his letters, but frequently the next letter from the fan, perhaps soon afterward, perhaps many months later, was in obvious reply to a note setting up an appointment. "I'm so thrilled you're giving a reading at Sarah Lawrence. I'd be even more thrilled to have a late supper with you afterward." "Of course I can drive to Wilkes-Barre to see you. And a drink later would be special and wonderful. I can't believe I'm actually going to meet you at last!" Did everybody get what they wanted? Somehow she doubted that. Human relations appeared to her a cesspool.

Tosca decided she had been reading letters long enough and came to stand in her lap and bat at her face. The mosquitoes began to bite beyond endurance. Dinah rowed back to shore and then took a quick dip in shorts and tee shirt.

Her answering machine was blinking with messages. One was a plumber returning Jimmy's calls. The other was Itzak, leaving a Boston area number. She called expecting a hotel. Instead she got his answering machine. As she started to speak, he picked up the phone.

"Dinah! The real estate agent found me a house in Brookline. I came up to see it and took it on the spot."

"You're moving to Boston? Really?" Somehow she had not thought he would choose one of his options, but go on floating them on the air for years.

"Correction. I have *moved* to Boston. I'm in my empty house waiting for my furniture. I have a young man who wants to study with me—he got the phone installed and the electricity and gas connected. I'm here with a chair I just bought on Beacon Street and the suitcases I brought along, my flutes and a sleeping bag my student lent me, waiting for the movers to arrive with all my earthly goods."

The story about the student alarmed her, she could not figure out why. She was surely not jealous of a student, it wasn't that. "What's your house like?" she temporized. "Is it big?"

"It seems huge. But the real estate agent called it a small house. It sits on a good sized lot with two sugar maples and a purple beech, which really is purple, and a hedge out front. It's two stories tall, red brick, with a separate garage, like a cave in the side of the hill."

In her head she saw a detached row house, strait and red brick, sitting in the middle of a flat lot with a purple tree in front of it and privet hedge across the front of a child's drawing. "How many rooms does it have?" She found herself incredulous. Without waiting for him to answer she continued, "Why did you do it? Suddenly buy a house?"

"Why not? I've been hating where I am. I set various things in motion, and this one agent kept calling up with houses. Most of them sounded too big or weird or were beyond expensive into ridiculous. This was three ten and available right now. It had been sold and the people moved into their new condo in Florida when the deal fell through. That is, they wanted three fifty but they'd got the other people's deposit, and I was ready to sign and they needed the money. So. Here I am in my own brick castle."

"Itzak, you've always lived around New York—I mean in the States. I wonder if Boston won't seem too small, too provincial to you."

"I need something less overwhelming. . . . Wait a minute. I hear something."

She held the phone, sorry she had not changed before returning his call. Her wet clothes felt dirty and heavy on her.

"Dinah? It's the movers. I'll call you back when they leave."

Pulling the shades, which she never shut except against the cold, she changed into a sundress. Time to think about making supper. It was too hot to eat. It was too hot to care. Reluctantly she settled down to patting chopped meat into hamburger patties with an egg and wheat germ and sautéed onions added, finely chopped thyme and parsley. She snapped the beans and put on water to steam them. She laid out bagels and condiments.

The student reminded her of Mark. He, too, would always have somebody doing his scut work because they wanted to study with him, hoping his technique or passion or knowledge would rub off. Was Itzak like Mark? She shuddered. No, she did not want to be eaten up by a relationship again, consumed, recruited into a particular man's creativity, no matter how interesting he might be. Willie never stole her energy to feed himself or his work.

She also fretted that Itzak had moved to Boston to be near her, to have better access to a relationship from which he wanted more. Was that true? Or was she caught between paranoia and delusions of grandeur? After all, how much could she mean to him? They had spent a total of perhaps two weeks together. She should have plainly told him that she was involved with Willie

246

again; but it was so confused and murky with Susan, what Susan did or didn't know or condone, she couldn't run about telling others. As an illicit relationship, it was on the silly side, like having an affair with your own ex-husband. Still, had she known Itzak was going to act and not simply go on balancing all his options, she would have told him. Now a guilty common sense informed her that the timing would be distinctly gauche.

The last of the workmen roared off and Jimmy took a shower. He had two guys helping him put the walls up and the roof on, and then he planned to continue with just himself and her. She had been drafted, but she might as well do carpentry, because she was writing no music.

Since Jimmy was involved with Laurie he hadn't tried to inveigle her into bed again, but they could talk bluntly. She told him that she was worried that Itzak had moved to be near her, while she was unsure exactly how committed she was to him.

Jimmy was slathering Dijon mustard on his hamburger. "Do Dad and this guy know about each other?"

"What do you mean?"

"I know you and my old man are getting it on again."

"What makes you say that?"

"Ah, Dinah, you may be a good performer as a musician, but don't ever let any jackass talk you into acting. You're the worst."

"You mean I act a certain way around Willie?"

"You look at him the same way you always did, and that's how he looks at you. It's palpable." Jimmy laughed. "But even if I weren't the perceptive sensitive guy I am, from Laurie's deck I see him scuttling across the yard from his studio and zip, into your house maybe three mornings a week."

"Do you think Susan knows?"

"If she doesn't know, it's because she's not paying attention. If she's paying attention, she knows."

"Jimmy, will we make it up?"

"You seem to have made it up fine with Willie. Mother's harder. She's no good at admitting when she's wrong. She's much less forgiving with women. She has different standards for women."

"Like Johnny."

"Willie says she's coming for his opening. I should give her a call."

"Then remind me not to get back together with Susan till

after that visit. I can't stand to see them together. Talk about two people who bring out the absolute worst in each other.''

"I'd still like to see Johnny. I stopped there when I was on my way east, but she has a live-in boyfriend who did not appreciate my company."

"You have a cold insulting style with each other, but you get on pretty well. You always stick up for each other."

"Johnny can't stand gushing. She breaks out into hives when Mother starts fussing up somebody, her Oh you *dear*, thank you for existing drivel. I don't mind. It's just cheap attention—like scolding somebody or giving advice. All easy forms of concern.'' Jimmy stuck the last burger on a sliced bagel. "The red onions are coming along—very sweet this year and getting big. You never answered whether Willie and Itzak know about each other."

"Willie knows that Itzak exists, sure. Itzak knows I used to be involved with Willie, but I never got around to mentioning we're back together part time." Dinah sat back in her chair. "Does Laurie know you bought that necklace for Lisa?"

"Lisa didn't want it. Laurie did. Lisa didn't want me. Laurie did. Everybody's happy now."

"Are you happy with her?"

"Of course I am. You think I'm just fucking around? When my divorce comes through, I'll marry her."

"You're not in love with her."

"I'm not infatuated. She is. I don't get infatuated. I learned when I was sixteen that's really stupid. It's a form of self-hypnosis that people get high on, but it doesn't have anything to do with the other person. Sometimes, Dinah, you don't give me enough credit for being as smart and sensible as I am. My parents are two likable losers. That's not who Johnny is and that's not who I am."

"Willie lives in a beautiful place. He has two women who love him. He eats well, he's healthy, he makes the art he wants and eventually he sells it because enough other people like his work. Do you really think being on the cover of *People* magazine or wearing a Rolex that costs as much as a car makes anybody feel better than Willie?"

"I love this place. Unlike any of you, I grew up to this and I want it. I want to be somebody in town. I don't want to be on TV. I have hard clear fantasies, things I can have. I'm the real contractor on the gallery and I'm making a place for myself. I'm

248

not going to be a nailbanger. I understand design. I know how to do it right. I'm going to design and build houses that people with money are going to want. It's the only way a kid like me who grew up here can compete with the summer people's money and get me a little piece of land and the good life.''

"And if you're married to Laurie, Tyrone will back you."

"Why shouldn't he? I'll pay off any investment in me better than the stock market. I'm a secure investment, Dinah. He'll figure that out eventually. Susan thought he'd hit the roof, and he's barely paid us any mind.''

"He didn't invite you to that big party last week."

"As I told Laurie, I don't give a damn. Those aren't people I need or want. I don't need to hang around drinking till eight-thirty and sit down to dinner at nine. I have to get up at six. I don't fight unnecessary battles.''

Dinah was still in the kitchen freezing beans when Itzak called back. "They unloaded half the stuff and went off to a motel. They'll be back in the morning. I'm dragging furniture around the house, but I need help. Or maybe I need to get away from this mess. Can I come out the day after tomorrow?''

"Itzak, here is total chaos. I told you Jimmy's living here— my neighbor's son. He's also working on my house. I have carpenters and roofers, plumbers, electricians and I'm going absolutely crazy. I haven't done two full days' work since I left you in Tanglewood. I hate it! I don't live here anymore, I just squat on a construction site!''

"Oh. Then why don't you come in to me? You can work here, once we get things in order. Only the furniture all disappeared into three rooms and there's so much space left. Come tomorrow.''

"Itzak, I have two cats. When I got back from Tanglewood, the builders had let them out and one of them I didn't find for two days. I can't leave them under these conditions.''

"So bring them too. They're nice cats. I like the little grey one, the minx. Bring them both.''

"Really? A refugee composer and two cats?''

"Come camp with me. See what I've done to myself. I'm not sure right now I didn't commit some immense folly. I'm suffering homeowner panic. Did you have a rainstorm last night?''

"No. I wish we had. We need rain.''

"I discovered the roof leaks. Upstairs in one of the bedrooms.''

"The roofs of all old houses leak. You just replace them every twenty years and patch them in between."

"See, you know about houses. You'll explain it all. Can you come?"

"The day after tomorrow. We'll come."

Normally nothing would seduce her into the city in the heat of summer, but she could not resist escaping from the builders for a couple of days. Maybe working. Maybe even working. The huge relief that surged through her gave her a measure of how blocked she had been feeling. Freedom!

THIRTY-FIVE

Susan

Susan could see Tyrone out on the pond. He was sailing the little boat Laurie had given him for Christmas. First he took Laurie out with him; then Candida; then a man with white hair she did not recognize. Susan had the heavy binoculars propped on the sill of a window in her room so that she could steady them.

It was a hideous mockery of what she had looked forward to, the summer come at last, the season she loved, the season she lived for, and she was shut out utterly! Willie treated it as a joke. He pretended indifference at not being invited to Tyrone's, exile from the life at the far end of the pond that was a continual party. By the time she managed a rapprochement, Tyrone would no longer be interested in telling stories about his sojourn in Japan.

Tyrone did not travel as a vulgar tourist. He was met, escorted, feted. He never had to stay in two star compromises hoping for a night's sleep. He was never walking into some random restaurant praying he could make himself understood. He was never cast on his own resources as she had been in Paris years ago, forced into standing in line three times until she was weeping hysterically in the Gare de Lyon frustrated by her inability to get the French official behind the grille to sell her a simple reserved seat ticket to Limoges. He tasted a city as she might pick the finest ripest apricot from a bowl of fruit. He did not rely on brochures and tourist guides, but everywhere he

250

went, interesting people awaited him, eager to share their pleasures.

Willie and Jimmy might as well have conspired to destroy her summer, but they merely bumbled along in their own selfish and thoughtless pursuits, doing casual damage without bothering to notice. Jimmy had the naive conviction he had gotten away with something, that Tyrone had accepted the affair with his daughter without a word of reproach, without a blow struck. She knew better. Tyrone had not begun to deal with what he must regard as a problem. It was on his agenda, of that Susan was certain.

If only she could please him in some way. She thought of bringing him a present, a bouquet of flowers from her garden. Tommy Rindge had destroyed most of her flower garden looking for sand and finding clay. Besides, Tyrone had a cutting garden of his own maintained by Alice Dove. She came by twice a week and weeded and watered. It was in better shape than her own garden this summer. Tyrone had Sally buy flowers in town when he was giving a dinner party. Indeed, what could she give him? His was the largess. She could not afford anything that would be of interest, that might offer him pleasure. In previous years, Dinah and Willie and she had put up conserves, jams, had made cordials out of beach plums, rum cherries, blackberries. Tyrone could buy the finest French and Swiss preserves and Marie Brizard liqueurs. What was the point of going over like an idiot with last year's blueberry conserve?

Far from scheming to run into him, she had stopped swimming at noon. She felt her body was not trim and youthful enough to parade before his guests. She began to swim in the evenings instead. The water was still warm, the air cooler. As long as she swam at a decent pace, the mosquitoes did not bother her. Once she got out of the water, she flapped at them with her towel and ran for the house. She knew she was not swimming as far as she always had. She had trouble telling sometimes how far she had swum.

Her house seemed shabby in the view of all those wealthy people, with its yard torn up and piles of lumber and shingling all over. She felt embarrassed for the mess. They had created a little Appalachia on their shore, offending Tyrone whenever he glanced their way. After delaying so many years on her desire for a studio, why couldn't Willie have waited until fall? On the other hand, Tyrone was unfair. Willie had had to finish the boathouse before he could start anything. Finally it did not matter if

251

Tyrone were fair or unfair, because a summer without him was too bleak to endure.

She felt as if she were trying to make her way and the entire world had turned into a herd of yapping dogs snapping at her feet, leaping on her and barking for attention. Max insisted she come to New York. She was late with some designs. He wanted them and he wanted to talk about color and general plans. Why he needed a face-to-face was more than she could ever understand, but after a while she wasn't real to them unless she appeared. Normally she seized on any excuse to go to New York, but it was two thirds of the way through July, and Tyrone was here, not there. Usually she went down in September, but they were talking about big changes for next year's fall line.

Willie announced, "Johnny's coming for my opening."

"Who is Johnny?" She could not stand that awful desexing nickname.

"Siobhan," Willie corrected appeasingly. "I really look forward to seeing her. I hope the two of you can be a little easier on each other."

"I'm sure *I* at any rate will try to preserve the peace."

After Willie had returned to his studio, she forced herself to put in time on the overdue designs. What she was drawing was beautiful but somehow heartbreaking: those lilies drooped with disappointment and frustration. Graceful arcs of sorrow. Beige and an almost neutral orange, close to rust, a bottle green, a light cream. Maybe the green should be an even darker shade, of lower value and lower chroma.

Whenever she changed colors, she gave herself license to look out. Now they all seemed to be swimming, perhaps eight of them like playful seals bobbing in the slight languid wind. While she watched, a couple waded into the water from a little beach midway between Tyrone's spread and the MacIvor's house. Vaguely familiar looking. She had seen them around town. Tyrone swam rapidly toward shore. A few minutes later she saw Donald hastening along the path toward the swimmers. Tyrone hated other people using the pond. She turned back to her drawing board, as if she might be drawn into the fight simply by watching the tiny figures half a mile away.

Funny that Jimmy had no artistic bent, when even Siobhan did. Willie had said Siobhan had a show scheduled, with a sculptor. If Siobhan would only open up, as any normal daughter would with her mother, they could share that. It would be warm between them and she would feel close to Siobhan, would be able to let out her frustrated affection.

Siobhan was always pushing her away, shutting her out. It had been that way since Siobhan was in middle school and began to be interested in boys. That was a time Susan had expected they would grow closer than ever. She had imagined when Siobhan was born, so tiny, frail, intensely feminine in her arms, that they would be close as she had never been close to her own mother. Susan didn't set herself up as a traffic cop of morals. Far from it, she cared only that Siobhan think about what she was doing and make smart choices.

She had looked forward to shopping for clothes together, to outfitting Siobhan in ways that would flatter her good features, play down her weaknesses. When Siobhan came home from her first parties, Susan had been as excited as if she had been going herself. No mother had ever been less judgmental or more willing to share everything in Siobhan's life, wanting to discuss her girlfriends, the boys she whispered about. From puberty on, Siobhan had walled her out as if frustrating Susan's desire for intimacy made her happy. Yes, there was something perverse in Siobhan. She could take more pleasure in refusing to share an experience than in having it.

Moreover Siobhan simply didn't know how to be popular, how to play boys against each other, how to attract the attention of a boy who interested her in such a way that the boy would think it had been his idea to pursue her. Not only was Siobhan ignorant of all this female lore, she would not allow Susan to teach her. She would disown a boy Susan could tell she had a crush on rather than share that admission with her mother.

She had endured overwhelming frustration all through Siobhan's adolescence, of her daughter simply refusing to see that she, Susan, only wanted to help her, to share her excitement, to share the romance and the silliness of being a teenager again. She saw other mothers making terrible errors forcing their daughters to lie to them, constraining them to a morality in which they themselves did not believe; she saw others making fun of their children's passions and fevers and sorrows. She never did that. She could remember suffering as acutely over Mike McDonough's failure to invite her to his birthday party as over anything in her life since. A thirteen-year-old had almost infinite capacity for feeling rejection and pain. She never forgot that.

Susan sighed deeply, turning from her lilies to watch through binoculars Candida execute a perfect dive off the floating dock. Whenever Siobhan was supposed to arrive, she always imagined things might be different, that Siobhan might go off to her room with her as mothers and daughters did, tell her secrets, ask her advice. She knew her daughter lived with a man, but she had never met Aldo and Siobhan refused even to say whether she loved him. Susan thought of her daughter as icy cold; cold to the spine. She had raised a daughter without normal soft and tender female emotions. Even her beautiful Celtic name she had changed to a man's name, as she had altered her auburn hair to black, tortured like a Halloween wig.

Constantly Siobhan had run to Dinah and to Willie to pour out anger against her mother. Susan knew that was the content of all those long talks Siobhan had with Dinah. Sometimes she even slept at Dinah's, just out of perverse desire to reject Susan and cause her pain, the way Jimmy had moved across the yard. It was too damned convenient for the children, to have that surrogate mother to run to, Dinah who did not give a damn and thus was understanding, oh, endlessly understanding, because finally what did she care about but her flute and her music? As if Susan had opened a box she had laid away in a drawer and forgotten, a present laid aside for the season of its use, she drew out that anger long buried and savored it.

She knew very well she was seeking reasons to stay angry with Dinah, because since Tyrone had withdrawn from her, in punishment for faults not hers, she was tempted to permit Dinah near her again. Dinah would create some counterfestivity, and the three of them, the family they had formed, would whirl round its own center and fill up the afternoons and the evenings with light and sound and activity and affection acted out.

From her window she watched Dinah picking beans and cutting the big purple heads of cabbage. In a faded tee and baggy shorts, she looked shabby. Without Susan to dress her, she had no idea what to wear. Susan felt an odd pang of missing, bound with the memory of Dinah's fleecy hair, its tight curls alive and resilient in her hands as she brushed it. Tomorrow, perhaps tomorrow she would drift downstairs, cross the yard into Dinah's range and let a real conversation begin.

The next day she dressed softly, attractively, pinning the bodice of her loose sundress with a coral flower Dinah had given her years ago, a pin from the twenties. She looked at herself with and without various hats and finally chose a sun hat with a very broad brim and loose weave that cast flattering light shadow on her face. She looped a scarf that matched her dress around the crown. Then she watched for Dinah. But today Dinah frustrated her. Finally Susan wandered outside. Because of the pile of lumber she did not have a clear view next door. Dinah's car was not parked where it ought to be.

Finally she went up to Willie, who had worked all morning in his studio and was spending the afternoon putting up the frame with Jimmy. Jimmy was helping him today and probably Willie would give free labor to Dinah tomorrow. Susan preferred to stay out of the arrangements, pretending she did not know that Willie was helping build Dinah's addition.

"Is Dinah away?" she asked after she'd made idle conversation and stood through a boring story about the Board of Appeals and the gallery permits.

"She's gone into the city," Jimmy said. "To see some friend. I think the building is driving her crazy. She even took the cats."

"Into New York?"

"No, Boston."

"When I say into the city, I always mean New York," she said primly. Dinah often visited a friend who played in the Boston Symphony Orchestra. It was just as well Dinah was gone. Her impulse had been of weakness.

She strolled toward the pond. Today she saw no activity at Tyrone's. Apparently his company of the weekend had left and no new company had arrived. She had observed Candida swimming in front of her own house an hour before. Rather than waste the effect of her outfit, she would drop in there. Candida was proving useful, for she would run on endlessly about what was happening at Tyrone's, giving Susan a window on events there. Candida was good-hearted and rather naive. She would happily repeat everything she heard.

Susan cut across Dinah's land and walked along the path toward the MacIvors. She had not come this way in months, because she would not give Dinah the satisfaction of walking on her land. She had driven around the long way, back to the main road and in on the road that led to that house, or she had walked a mile around the pond via Tyrone's spread, but not since February had she walked this path. Blueberries grew along it and as she ambled, she picked one berry at a time to nibble. Dinah gone was an irritant removed. Maybe Dinah would move into

Boston and sell her house to Jimmy and Laurie. Now she was being as silly as Jimmy. Her step slowed and the heat pressed the energy out of her as she ran over in her head the familiar catechism of questions and imperfect answers about the rupture with Tyrone.

She came out of the woods on the new lawn Candida had had put in. The sliding door was open, only the screen in place. She did not hear voices as she stood peering in calling, "Candida? It's Susan!"

Candida came at once, barefoot. She wore one of those pastel rompers she favored when she was not dressed up. "Come in, come in. We were just having iced coffee."

"Susan, hello. How wonderful to see you," Tyrone said warmly, as if he had only just arrived from his trip.

She felt embarrassed, fearful Tyrone might think she had dropped in to catch him, that she was pursuing him, but he did not seem to feel any such suspicion. He and Candida seemed delighted for company. "I must chat with Willie about getting on with the gallery. Even without the permits, we can repair the roof and paint. As it is, it's an eyesore and totally unusable."

"I'll talk to Willie at once about fixing the roof."

He shook his head. "Don't trouble yourself about it, Susan my dear, I'm just thinking out loud. That's between your husband and myself, and I beg your pardon for alluding to it. . . . Susan, old friend, I have a wee problem of sorts. I have a colleague arriving Friday who has married again and has two very young children. We absolutely must have a reliable sitter for this coming weekend."

"How old are the children?"

Tyrone cast up his eyes. "I don't know. Two, three, that sort of age. Sally will know. Can you find us someone?"

"I told Tyrone I can't help," Candida said. "With us not having children, I never needed anyone."

"I'll try!" She felt illuminated with hope, visited with an annunciation of the return of his favor. She had only to find some teenager who would be responsible and available. "I can take care of them myself if we can't get anyone else. I have to go to New York next week, but I don't leave until Monday morning."

"You don't usually go to the city in the summer, do you?" Tyrone asked.

256

"Never." She explained briefly, slightly exaggerating so that it would sound more interesting, more glamourous than it was.

"Oh, you're a designer," Candida said. "I never knew that. How fabulous. I must have something of yours."

Tyrone said, "Do you have to spend the night?"

"I'm afraid so. I have to be there Monday and Tuesday."

"Then why don't you stay in my apartment? Unless they're putting you up in a good hotel?"

Her heart missed a beat. It lurched painfully under her breasts. "They don't do that. I'll be lucky if they buy me a deli lunch," she managed to say lightly. She dared not reveal how badly she wanted his apartment.

"It's rather closed up. And Celeste is here with us. However, the building's secure, the doorman's on duty. If you don't mind the general air of desuetude, I'm sure you'd be comfortable."

"That's enormously kind of you, Tyrone. I'd be delighted not to have to worry about a hotel. This came up suddenly. I made my airline reservations, but I hadn't done anything about a hotel." She was not flying down, she was driving. They could not afford to blow a couple hundred on plane travel. She did not know why she had said that. She was flustered and trying to seem cool, as if Tyrone offered her his apartment every other day.

"That's all settled, then." Tyrone rose, shaking Candida's hand rather formally. "You see, you did solve my problem."

"No thanks to me. If Susan hadn't dropped in. . . . Well, I was really surprised when you popped out of the woods, Susan. You've never done that before! It was like an apparition."

"You'll call me tonight about the baby-sitter." Tyrone put his arm around her shoulder and led her out with him. Unresisting she floated beside him. She had no desire to sit and chatter with Candida now. She was too happy, too excited. She had no idea where to locate a sitter, but she would call everybody she knew in town, absolutely everybody. Sometimes Zee baby-sat for pin money.

"I'll get right on it, Tyrone, I'll get on it as soon as I'm home. And if I don't find a sitter, I'll do it myself. I promise!" She felt bathed in radiant light. The heat of the day no longer seemed oppressive. A slight but refreshing breeze had risen, riffling the pond. The day seemed delicious as a ripe peach.

"That's terribly sweet. I knew I could count on you, Susan, as ever, as always." He gave her hand a hard squeeze.

She was glad he had taken her with him out of Candida's, giving them a little time together. "Tyrone, I've been miserable being at odds with you."

"Between old friends, what does such nonsense count for?"

"I've missed you. I wanted so badly to hear about your trip to Japan."

"Susan, I won't fool you. It was a business trip. I made money, and that was about the sum of it." He paused, waiting for a reaction.

She stood flat-footed and then realized as she went over his words for the third time that he had made a pun. She laughed.

That freed him to continue. "You know I'm much happier to be here. You find me that sitter. And ask Willie to call me about the gallery roof pronto."

She started to walk around the pond the long way, toward his house, but he stopped her. "I'm off to work now. I have a desk full of obnoxious items to deal with. You need to get on the phone too." He squeezed her shoulder and turned her toward her house, along the path she had come on. Then he gave her a small pat on the behind and strode off.

She was startled so that for a moment she stood absolutely still, feeling the imprint of his hand on her buttock. Never had he touched her so intimately in all their years of friendship, never. He was unfailingly correct. It was not like one of the carpenters trying to pat her fanny. It had been a gesture of affection, yes, but how unexpectedly physical. Just as he had never before offered her his apartment. She had stayed there once with Willie when Tyrone was in town, although extremely busy. This was something new. From exile and separation, she had passed with Tyrone onto a newer higher more intimate level of friendship.

She hurried down the wood path, tripping over a root and loosening her sandal, resenting the time required to stoop and put it back on. She would call the library first and ask Burt. He knew everybody and everything. She had not seen Burt and Leroy socially in ages and she had scarcely been in the library since she had stopped volunteering, but she would chat him up and then ask him for names. The Hills had a daughter. Too young for sitting, too old for a sitter, but they might have somebody they had used. Zee would talk her ear off, but she would ask her too. She'd ask everyone in town!

258

She rushed across the lawn, shouting at Willie, "Call Tyrone. He wants the roof repaired."

"Oh, he does, does he?" Willie growled. "He knows my phone number. He also knows how to sign his name on a check. Let him pay me what he owes me and then I'll start on that rotten mansard roof."

She paused and groaned. Willie wasn't going to screw up the return of Tyrone into their lives. She would make her phone calls and then she would go to work on Willie's attitude.

Even as she was softening up Burt, prior to her request, she kept remembering that private moment when Tyrone had touched her and wondering, wondering what he had meant. Poor Willie. She would cook tonight, once she got the sitter lined up. He would come in from construction and find a sumptuous meal. Then she would go to work on him about the gallery roof.

THIRTY-SIX

Laurie

Laurie found out that in spite of Tyrone's misimpression, Susan was driving to the city, not flying. She asked Celeste where the rest of her summer things were stored; then she arranged with Susan to bring them back. She had begged Tyrone to carry those boxes with him, but he had had too much of his own stuff; more likely, he had simply forgotten in the press of returning from Tokyo, clearing up New York business and packing for the summer house.

Jimmy and she couldn't go because he was working seven days a week, trying to put up Dinah's addition and helping Willie with his garage studio while there was a lull in the gallery. Tyrone was all exercised about the gallery, but she was indifferent. She had always known she couldn't get a gallery together this summer, so there was no hurry. If the renovation was finished by spring, the gallery would be ready for next summer.

She had a great deal to do before then, lining up artists, arranging for shows. She had already decided she would not curate all the shows herself, but would have more than half of them guest-curated by people whose names might draw in the knowledgeable. She would have her hands full with whatever remaining shows she chose to hang.

She liked to talk about her gallery and her plans to Jimmy. Like his father, Jimmy could interest himself in anything, an agreeably civilized wide-ranging intelligence, far less narrow than the men she had been involved with before. Tom had been interested only in publishing, drugs, media and rock music. Rick had cared only about the market, money, expensive cars and basketball. Tyrone, who had led her to expect a broad spectrum of interest in a man, would be astonished how much closer Jimmy came to that ideal than her husband or her former lover had.

She had tried to talk to Tyrone about Jimmy, but he simply would not let her. He was surrounded by guests, his assistant Donald, Sally. She decided he would not take the relationship seriously until more time had passed. He was waiting for her and Jimmy to prove themselves. In the meantime he pretended no such relationship existed. Jimmy spent every night with her in the boathouse, but he went on living at Dinah's—meaning he kept his clothes there, received most phone calls there, ate there half the time.

Tonight they were eating at Dinah's, because she was away and they had more privacy across the pond from the big house. Dinah had left early that morning for Boston, all fussed because Itzak had suddenly moved there and she did not know whether to be glad or sorry. She was carrying him a basket of zucchini, cabbages, early tomatoes, lettuce and beans, as if he must be starving. Laurie found Dinah amusing. She lived by other rules than most people.

"I can remember when Dinah scared me." She gazed at Jimmy across the table of leftovers, more picnic than formal meal. "I thought she was witchy and dangerous—a lesbian who might mesmerize me with a glance."

"Dinah? I can't imagine being scared of her. I used to run to her when I was feeling misunderstood. She always seemed halfway between being a kid and being an adult."

"Because she didn't have children like other adults?"

"No children, she wasn't married, she played instruments alone and with other musicians. She was always running around in the woods like a kid."

"But she was married when she first moved here. Her husband was tall and gaunt, with a beard." She remembered Susan telling Tyrone, "He's a very famous poet," in a tone of awe. Tyrone did not collect literature as he did paintings and sculpture, judging it inherently more subversive and chancier. He had no interest in a dying poet; she however recalled being intensely curious. She had imagined Mark Edelmann falling in love with her and writing her sonnets. She had to write an Elizabethan and a Petrarchan sonnet for her English teacher that year, so she knew how hard they were. Love of her would make them easy for him. She would read them and cry after he was dead, and other men would want to meet the woman who had inspired the poems. Such had been her fantasy at fourteen about Mark Edelmann.

"While she was married she wasn't important in our lives, just the people next door with the sick husband you had to be quiet for. Kids dismiss invalids. We had no idea who Edelmann was. Johnny and I called him Spider Man because he was so skinny and weird looking."

"Dinah's funny about Itzak. She can't seem to figure out how interested she is. I'd think by the time you're her age, you'd know what you want."

"It's more complicated than that." Jimmy nodded toward the new house. "She's involved with my father again."

"She told you?"

"I see him ducking into her house early in the morning."

"Are you sure? My goodness. Does Susan know?"

He shrugged. "I don't think she officially knows, but you'd think she'd guess. Still I don't think she's let herself notice. She's been in a blue funk all summer. I don't know what's eating her. She's sure been moody."

"No wonder Dinah is confused what to do about Itzak. She doesn't seem to know who or what she wants."

"She wants things to be like they were all those years. It might happen. I don't know why Susan is so dead set against her. Susan gets stuck being furious with people. It used to happen all the time with her and Johnny."

"Is Johnny really coming home this summer?"

"Only for a couple of days. She called me yesterday. She's already working on me to stay with you so she can stay here. It makes her nervous to sleep in the same house with Susan."

"I haven't stayed over at my mother's in years. Of course she lives in a tiny apartment, she could only put me on the couch.

261

But I was *glad* when she had to move into that apartment, because then she didn't have a room for me any longer."

"Would you like to stay over here tonight? My room's small, but we can make up the bed in Dinah's room with clean sheets—she stripped it before she left. It's a beautiful room with a nice big bed."

She laughed breathlessly. She didn't know why it should sound exciting to sleep with him in a new bed. Actually she would love it if they could sleep at his parents' house while Susan was away, in his old bedroom. She had a vague memory of having been in that room while they were both of high school age. She wanted to see it again, the room of his boyhood, to touch every old object and hear its story. "Let's stay here. It'll be fun." She liked escaping from the coterie around Tyrone. Since they drew their attitudes from Tyrone, all of them ignored her relationship with Jimmy. That got to her after a while, because she was proud that she had attracted him and that he loved her. She felt as if she ought to be congratulated, envied, not treated to a campaign of calculated silence.

She felt like a woman who had dropped twenty pounds, looked in the mirror and liked what she saw, but no one around her noticed a damn thing. She felt better than she ever had in her life. She felt competent, she felt loved, she even felt pretty. Willie had said to her just the other day, "Laurie, you're positively blooming." She still retained enough of a memory of her old crush on him to have blushed, enormously pleased. It wasn't like asking Tyrone how she looked and having him blandly assure her she looked just fine. Willie had paid a spontaneous compliment: blooming, he had said, like a flower, like a rose, something natural and lovely.

Jimmy appreciated her body. He said she had delicate but strong bones like the best porcelain. He said her hair was spring sunshine. He told her she had an inner strength she was only beginning to explore. Slowly she began to discover how long she had been unhappy, a quiet desperate but almost acceptable unhappiness she had thought of as part of her nature, as someone who never leaves New York will come to take the steady roar of traffic for a given and never know the lack of silence. She always felt second rate, disappointing as Tyrone's daughter. Compared to the golden youthful women he married, she was awkward and shy. Even with the few men who had sought her out, who had pursued her, she had felt plain and apologetic. She had never been among the brightest, the prettiest, the most popular girls in any of the schools she had attended.

She did not apologize to Jimmy, for he had not settled for her. In one version she told herself, she was the princess wooed by the worthy commoner. Only on this pond was she a princess, but here as Tyrone's daughter, she enjoyed a privileged status lacking in Manhattan where she must compete with the prettier and more confident daughters of men richer and more powerful than her father. In another version, he was the beloved she had chosen, who foolishly thought he had seduced her, the prize she had cleverly won. She felt a carefully suppressed anger that neither her father nor any of his attendants, not Sally or Donald or his guests, would give her credit and wish her joy of her choice. Only Celeste acknowledged his existence, calling him when they were both in the kitchen, your man. Do you want to take the rest of this lobster salad to your man?

"Working at the gallery, I was always nervous. I felt as if I was there under sufferance, because Tyrone bought a lot of art from Manning Stanwyck."

"But you know plenty about art. You have good ideas for your gallery. Surely you were overqualified for a job that was mostly hanging stuff on the wall and making phone calls and arranging for caterers."

"I guess I was." Laurie had never thought about it that way. She beamed at him. "But that makes it even more striking, how apologetic I felt in that job, as if I was taking it from someone truly deserving."

"Most of your life, you've been walking around apologizing. . . . I wonder why Tyrone never had another child with any of his wives?"

"I know Glenda wanted a child. They tried, I think."

"Do you want children?" he asked her, as if casually, leaning back in his chair with a knowing grin. "I mean by and by."

"Of course! But not one, like me. I want two or three children. I used to envy you and Johnny, always having each other."

"We didn't always have each other. Sometimes we stuck up for each other, and sometimes we'd sell each other out for a smile from some other kid we had a crush on or wanted to be pals with. They didn't invent sibling rivalry out of some psychology book. Johnny and I were close, yes, but we were also out to get each other, we were always jockeying for favor and space."

"I think a truly wise and caring mother can prevent that."

Jimmy shrugged. "You can't keep the sun from coming up or going down, and you can't keep a little kid from wanting all of his mother's attention all of the time."

"Original sin?" She felt so happy she got up and danced around the table and hugged him. "I love to talk to you. I have better times with you than I ever had with anybody."

"I love you better than anybody else has, or anybody else would," he said, grinning again. "You just have to want to keep me, real bad."

THIRTY-SEVEN

Dinah

Dinah drove to Boston to the regular moans of Figaro. Tosca was curled up in the same carrying case, quiet and at ease. After the first hour of the trip, she suddenly sat up and for ten minutes protested in loud piercing interrogatory mews. Dinah worried about taking the cats into the city. Would Itzak really agree to keep the doors shut and watch that neither of them bolted and was lost? She had been over-anxious about the cats since Figaro had run away. They personified her lost peace. They wanted what she wanted, quiet, a regular schedule, things in their appropriate place and all the others gone away.

She had not told Willie where she was going, because she felt as if being open with him would give him an advantage so far lacking to Itzak, and because she was afraid he would punish her by stopping work on the addition in her absence. Her lie of omission would give her time to make a decision about what she had with Itzak. And maybe she would get some work done. She had to try to be honest with Itzak about Willie, and that hung over her head like a canopy of wet cement.

Itzak's house was two thirds of the way up a steep hill in Brookline. In order to get to the house from her parking space on the street, she had to climb a flight of cement steps set in a rocky slope. The house itself was on a little plateau. Behind it the land fell away, so that the roof of the house on the next street was below them; to the right the land rose sharply to the next lot. His turn of the century brick house was small only by comparison to the Victorians on either side. The purple beech he had mentioned was an enormous full bosomed tree filling half the front yard. The sunny part was planted in browning grass edged with overgrown perennial beds, neglected irises and old-fashioned orange daylilies just finishing.

She could hear Itzak practicing inside. She carried up the cats, her suitcase and the presents of produce and flowers she had brought him, but she did not go in until he finished the Mozart. She was being thoughtful and she was being nervous. Then she rapped on the screen door and called to him. Was this a place she would return many times, a house she would come to love? Or would she never return? She had to get some honesty back into her life, as neglected and weedy as those poor perennial beds. Both cats crowded at the grid of the carrying case, sniffing the air apprehensively and staring out, two yellow and two green eyes with pupils dilated.

He had lost some of his Tanglewood tan. He kissed her and then latched the screen door as she released the cats, who sidled out to move forward like soldiers on point into unfamiliar jungle. He gave her a tour. The furniture she remembered from his New York apartment, the piano his accompanist used huddled in the big livingroom, the kitchen, his bedroom and practice room. He had a desk for his new assistant marooned in a room downstairs with a chair and a telephone. The diningroom was empty and so was the extra bedroom. She had a sense of him as a project like the house she must tackle or refuse. He needed to be taken in hand. The moment she was in his presence she began to feel that sexual energy that had cooked between them at Tanglewood, along with a gust of strong feeling that made her wary. Was this passionate draw something to be seized or fled? Was it sexual programming? She wasn't about to abandon herself to a Wagnerian Liebestod. Wagner had always got her dander up, no matter how she might appreciate his music intellectually.

The house needed draperies, rugs, furniture, lighting. The rooms had been freshly painted, but the fixtures were old. The kitchen and the bathrooms would require complete renovation. The cats disappeared to explore, creeping from room to room, while she unpacked her country gifts for him and hung the couple of things that should go in the closet. Then they sat right down and began going over the suite together, with him reading the flute part and she using the piano as the other instruments.

265

She wanted to show him the changes she had made after the performance at Tanglewood, after their discussions and the feedback she had received. They read their way through, arguing, haggling. Twice she apologetically brought out her own flute to show him what she had been thinking of in the way of attack. By the time they left off, it was midafternoon, the cats were chasing each other up and down the curved stairs and through the empty halls, skidding with their claws on the bare floors, and Dinah was unreasonably happy.

"I'm starving," he said. "I'm not a big luncher except when I'm traveling. Let's go get something for supper. There's a deli, an Indian restaurant, a Greek, a Chinese, an Israeli, a good ice-cream store. We can get take-out or buy groceries. But let's take a walk. I'm curious about my neighborhood. Have you noticed how hilly it is, all the big trees?"

He took her hand as they walked. She had not held hands with a man in twenty years. Mark considered it sentimental. She had gone arm in arm with Susan, but Willie walked at his own pace in a trance of observation. Holding hands was a little confining but it was also cozy, companionable. They stretched their calf muscles tromping up and down the hills. Then they went back to his house and upstairs to his bedroom, where he had obviously made up the bed that morning with fresh sheets in a zebra pattern.

She felt a little shy at first. Then she forgot. It was there again, the pressure, the rush, the depth of feeling that had been stirred up between them at Tanglewood. Her body swelled, elongated, grew more viscous and liquid, a thick golden molten substance beating in waves of urgency. She felt powerfully attracted as she looked at him, his black curls, the fine modeling of his chin, the darkness of eyes that almost absorbed the iris into the pupil, the shaping of the bones of his shoulders, the fine muscling in his arms. He was not a big man, but he was well and strongly built, the same tough stock as herself. Then that observing part of her drowned, and the rhythm that rose in her was a river rushing around them, carrying her forward on its rapids.

He seemed a little shaken but also pleased. "I wondered if it would be the way it was then."

Maybe it had been so many years since she had made love with anyone except Susan and Willie that she had forgotten the intensity of early hot sex; yet she did not think so. Generally sex got better as a relationship improved, relaxed, deepened—

266

that was how it was for her. Chemistry was inexplicable and she could produce no reason her body preferred Itzak—nor was she sure she trusted her body's frenzy. They were the right size for each other, they had a similar high energy level, they were both strongly oral and they both liked to fuck. Yet put that all together and there were overtones, resonances, harmonics that could not be guessed beforehand.

They wandered out behind the house to a view of rooftops and the crowns of oaks and maples. A blue jay scolded from a white birch at the back of the lot beside an old but serviceable picnic table. She felt her emotions churning and splashing around. They had picked up lamb chops while they were out walking and a nice zinfandel. With the vegetables she had grown, she made supper they ate as a picnic at the table. A breeze tousled his hair. His shirtsleeves were rolled up, his arms bare. The dark hairs on his arms rose slightly. Tomorrow was Shabbat, she thought suddenly. She had been lighting the candles, but she had not lit them for or with anyone else since Mark had died. She would get a chicken to roast.

That evening they drove in her car down to the waterfront, where old granite or brick warehouses had been converted into condominiums, with stores and restaurants and offices at water level. Licking ice-cream cones from Atlantic Avenue, they walked out on the piers. "Why do you think you're so much more open to new music than many of the soloists I've met?"

"I like to be stretched. I like something that forces me to learn new ways to play. Besides, maybe I'm grateful somebody's still writing well for flute. Composers who work only with synthesizers and computers are a lot scarier. Don't you think that's the composer's ultimate fantasy? To get rid of the performer who can screw up, who can ham it up, who can give the piece the altogether wrong spin, the batty interpretation?"

"It's a way of controlling performance. I understand the appeal. Years ago, when Mark and I were living outside Ithaca, I got fascinated by electronic music. It was all I cared about." Things kept reminding her of Mark, forcing her to wonder if there was not a lot in Itzak that was like Mark.

"What made you decide to go back to live ornery performers and old-fashioned instruments?"

"One time a storm knocked the power out for two days. I couldn't do anything. It bugged me. I got out my flute and I could play just fine. I also started thinking about all the equip-

267

ment you have to haul around, from when I was in the band, the Wholey Terrors. You need a van just for your amps. Now you know, I'm not pretending I live in the Kalahari Desert and I have to beat two sticks together to make music. I've used tape recorders and delays and feedback, I still use computers and synths. But I also want to write music people can take off with them and play anyplace."

"There's always that pull toward perfection." He was leaning on a parapet staring at the oily black waters sloshing in. "The Glenn Gould trip. Never perform again. Only record the perfect version under controlled circumstances. I can understand that, but I fight it. That's another reason I keep trying to expand my repertoire and another reason I do play new music when I can. Sometimes in your pieces there's space made intentionally for improvisation, so that you are asking the performer to share responsibility and judge the audience and think and feel the music and become totally involved."

"So that there is no ideal performance," she said. "Yes. I want it to be alive and changeable. I'm just enough of a musician to respect performance, to respect the rapport that can create real electricity between the player, the piece and the audience."

"Dinah, sometimes you stare at me and you look so worried. What is it? Do you think I'm pushing you too hard? Is it some professional doubt?"

"No, no! . . . One thing is, sometimes you make me think of my husband."

"You didn't get divorced. He died, right? So is that bad? Or just painful?"

"I loved him. But it wasn't till he died I really could work full steam ahead as a composer. We were involved in some more intimate passionate demanding absorbing way than I've been with anybody else. Maybe I'm scared that could happen between us. Maybe I'm scared that I'll somehow lose myself or my work will suffer."

"How old were you when you met him?"

"Twenty-two."

"How old was he?"

"Forty-eight."

"Don't you think if he overwhelmed you, age had something to do with it? I'm not exactly the overwhelming type. I don't tend to think I know everything, if you haven't noticed. I have more doubts than certainties. And we'd always be apart for long stretches while I'm on tour.''

"I don't know if it was the age difference or that I dealt with sounds and he dealt with words, and words are how people get to each other. But maybe a certain degree of intimacy gets in the way of creation.''

"Do you really believe that? It sounds like romantic nonsense to me.''

"I don't know what I think, Itzak. I'm sorely confused. I have to feel my way.''

"Dinah, I'm not pushing that hard.''

"Maybe I feel pulled that hard.''

When they were back at his house, sitting in the livingroom with the pleasant red and blue tree of life Oriental from his previous apartment—a rug that had belonged to his grandparents—both of them curled up on the leather coach, she said, "There's something else.''

"Why do I think that means, you're going to say there's someone else. Is it that guy who moved in with you? It is, isn't it?''

"Jimmy? Never. I've known him since he was in grade school. He has a girlfriend he'll probably marry, after his divorce comes through.''

"But there is someone else.''

"I've been seeing Willie again. You know, I was with Willie and Susan before I met you. I'd just broken up with them.''

"And the woman? Susan?''

"She speaks to me but distantly, like an acquaintance.''

"What does she think about you fucking her husband?''

He was angry, he was quite angry. His mouth thinned, his voice deepened and hardened. She felt a sense of premonitory loss. Was he about to break off with her? Could she talk him out of it? "Understand, we got involved eleven years ago. We've been family. Their kids have been my kids. When it all came apart, I felt lost.''

"You're saying you got involved with me as an act of desperation?''

"Not at all,'' she said, aware that he spoke perfect truth. "Only that my life has been structured in a certain stable way for a long time and—''

"I don't know that having an affair with a man and a woman at the same time can be described as a stable family setup. And are you saying I interrupted this cozy arrangement?''

"Susan ended it. She got furious with me. She'd been building up resentment toward me for at least a year. But I'm trying to tell you that when I met you, I thought that was all over. Then Willie came to me and we've been involved again. Not the way it was. We don't eat together, we don't have a family life." She decided not to mention that he was helping build her addition. "It is just an affair now. But I can't give up on them just yet. Willie thinks Susan will come to her senses and we'll be close again."

"And where does that leave me? On the sidelines cheering?"

"I don't think it would ever be the way it was with them," she said, aware she was lying about her favorite fantasy. "I feel very connected to you. I'm telling you honestly, I'm confused. Things can't go on as they are with Willie. I have to know what Susan feels. I can't go behind her back."

"So what you want is either to go back to living with both of them or to have this woman give you a license to have a continuing affair with her husband."

"Itzak, you're furious. Yet I told you the situation I'd been in."

"I thought it was pretty bizarre before, but at least it was over. You can't expect me to feel enthusiastic about the way it is now."

"I know I have to straighten it out. I feel as if I'm lying to Susan."

"Why? You haven't been keeping anything from her you haven't been keeping from me."

"This is the first real chance I've had to tell you. It wasn't something I could mention on the phone."

"Why didn't you tell me at Tanglewood?"

"I was so happy with you I was afraid of spoiling it. I didn't know, I still don't know, what I can mean to you. I thought maybe when you had the suite, that might be it. After all, I don't know who you see in New York. I don't know who you go to bed with when you're on tour. We've never discussed these matters." She was sitting there with her stomach turned to lead. She was sure she had lost him, but she could not accept the loss. She had the urge to fling herself at him, on him, so their bodies would argue for her. Inch by inch she moved nearer to him along the leather of the couch.

"I guess we haven't." His voice softened a little. He leaned

270

back against the couch. "Maybe we've both been afraid to ask hard questions."

"Let alone volunteer hard information."

"I guess I assumed we both want one good solid central relationship."

"I didn't set out to get involved with both Susan and Willie. It just happened and it worked that way better than it could with any two of us. No two of us could make it alone—that goes for me and Willie and for Susan and Willie too. We blundered into a triangle and now it has its own history and its own loyalties."

"But is it history or is it now? Because if it's current, there's no room for me. I can't have what I want, so I'd be better off getting out. There's nothing for me in that scenario but disappointment."

"The truth is, I don't know yet. I don't know yet what can be between you and me. We're just getting to know each other. I have my fears about the intensity to deal with. If Willie and Susan moved to Saskatchewan tomorrow, we'd still have serious unanswered questions about the two of us."

"I have questions about you. Can you be honest with me? Can you make any kind of commitment and honor it? Can you be faithful or will you always be harboring fantasies about having a woman too? Can you take living with someone who's going to get more fame and more attention and more money for performing than you get for composing?"

"Itzak." She took his head tentatively between her hands. "Can I stay on? Can we at least try to sort out what's between us this week? Then I make you a promise that when I go back, I'll bring the same rigor to bear on that front." She could feel her hands trembling against his cheeks, smooth, warm, the slight prickle of his returning beard.

He laughed shortly, like a cough, but let her hands remain. His eyes looked into hers with an intensity that made her blink. "You really want to stay?"

"Yes." It came out explosively. She had been holding her breath.

"But if things are good this week, it'll be worse when you leave to know you're going back to him."

"But if I leave now, we'll never know if it would have been good or just not worth the trouble. Besides, this house needs an awful lot of work. I'm good at fixing things up."

"I noticed that," he said dryly, but put his arm around her.

271

"I don't want you to leave. Maybe at least we can settle whether I'm the late great Mark Edelmann returned, or something new under the moon for you. But then you're going to have to decide, Dinah. I'm not your bloody vacation."

THIRTY-EIGHT

Susan

Susan was not tempted to eat out in New York. Instead she shopped at the local gourmet grocery store with its marvelous delicatessen counter half a block long, and found herself spending as much for a full bag as she would have in a restaurant. However, the pleasure of putting her cheeses, her duck pâté, her artichoke salad, her smoked salmon pasta in the giant refrigerator along with a bottle of Chardonnay she had found in a closet and was sure Tyrone would not begrudge her, was keener than she could have derived from any restaurant. It made her able to push away thinking about the afternoon's meeting with Max. They did not like several of her designs. Said she was repeating herself. Fin de siècle wallpaper. That crude bastard. Resolutely she drew herself up. She would not think about it. She would not let his pettiness mar her evening. Mr. di Vecchio, who had far more power and taste than Max, would be there tomorrow when they talked about fabrics for next fall. It would be different with him.

Being alone in Tyrone's apartment was playing house, and funnily enough it reminded her of early adolescence when her parents would go out and by luck take her brothers along. She had loved having the house to herself for a precious evening to play at being adult—not what her parents were, but adults from movies. She would march through the rooms purposefully addressing servants, her husband, her children. She would find the chocolate-covered cherries her mother hid and eat two, pour an inch of her father's rye whiskey into a glass and make up the difference in his decanter with water, go through everybody's drawers. Alas, she had been the only one in the house who kept a diary, and after her brother Jack had got hold of it once, she had never written secrets in it again. She found her older broth-

272

er's condoms and his dirty comic books and a couple of marijuana cigarettes. Her family's dreary house became almost glamourous when it was hers to control.

Now here was Tyrone's home open to her, vulnerable, welcoming. He had given it to her, apologizing because Celeste was not there to take care of her. She had told him she was used to looking after herself, but she did not tell him she was delighted by Celeste's absence, because she was free to exercise her curiosity. She had no wish to rush out to get tickets to a play or to see a movie, to shop, to study the windows of boutiques, her usual New York pleasures. She was accustomed to having his Cape house to explore at her leisure, but it was, after all, only a summer house. He had another house on Aruba he had urged her to borrow, but Willie always said they didn't have the money to fly down. Then he would promptly buy some electric fish scaler.

The livingroom that had so fascinated her the last time held her only long enough to scan his collection of VCR tapes. He must own several hundred movies. She wondered why he bothered, but then perhaps it was an easy way to entertain businessmen he had little in common with, and sometimes their families. When she was trying to work, she had had to resort to babysitting Jimmy and Siobhan with the TV; how much less guilty to pick out a good children's film and plunk them down with it. Children loved to watch a film over and over, she remembered that.

His collection of records and compact discs was scantier than Dinah's. He was visually attuned. Only art books, an occasional best-seller and the latest controversial thesis books about the stock market or the economy lay around the huge room with its view of the East River and the Fifty-ninth Street Bridge. She had been silly to worry about borrowing a bottle of white wine. In the wet bar were stored dozens of bottles of liquor and liqueurs, along with cases of wine. The room had been designed with an eye to showing off art, walls two stories tall with his big Motherwell, his stunning Jackson Pollock, the various paintings and pieces of sculpture that came and went, lights set up to pick them out and set them off.

In one locked case were his pre-Columbian statuettes. He had told her he had begun by collecting them, but as he gained more confidence in his taste and in the market, he had moved into collecting contemporary art and then finally work of younger, just breaking artists. The statuettes belonged to the first period, and the Franz Kline, the Motherwell, the Pollock, the Bultman to the middle period. The strange collages and bright blobs, the distorted figure paintings, fluorescent cartoons by the younger artists she had never heard of were what he collected now. She tried to memorize their names. They must be the pick of their generation. She smiled wryly when she thought how annoyed Willie was that Tyrone had never bought one of his pieces. Really, how out of place one of his shrieking political statements would be in this ambience.

She wandered the room, now lying on the couch that looked away from the room at the river, now trying all the chairs in a conversational grouping. It was time for supper. She would take it, not in the formal diningroom but on the balcony, once she figured out how to get the French doors open. She was still working on it when the phone rang. It was the doorman. She had set off an alarm. She apologized profusely and decided she would eat in the diningroom after all. It slightly overawed her. The table sat twelve without added leaves. The chandelier was glass shards and bronze. It made her think of a crab poised over the table. The diningroom could be a warmer more welcoming room. If she lived here, she would redecorate it. It was too stiff.

If she lived here. This *was* living. It was beautiful, yes, but there was the too careful hand of a decorator everywhere. She would loosen up the color scheme and the placement of objects. She would get more interesting pattern and texture into the draperies. The rooms were too obviously arranged for the benefit of the works of art; she would change that emphasis to make all appear more serendipitous. Tyrone needed her light hand.

Basically the colors in the diningroom were all too cool, too formal. It needed touches of warmth. Everything was beige and celadon and ivory. "Tyrone," she said, "Ty, you must give me a free hand with this room. You want people to relax a little while they eat, to let go. This room doesn't give that message at all."

On the long imposing table she laid two places, as if someone, as if he were eating there with her. She put on a record softly, Handel's *Water Music* she remembered from Dinah's collection. There wasn't much overlap. Tyrone had mostly show tunes, Frank Sinatra, mood music. She wanted background music for dinner with a little more class.

As soon as she finished eating, she carried the dishes to the

274

dishwasher. It would have seemed vulgar to leave dirty dishes in the gorgeous blue sink.

She poured herself another glass of wine, settling the bottle back in the leather padded ice bucket. Glass in hand, she went exploring upstairs. Tyrone had told her to stay in Laurie's room. Reluctantly she had obeyed him, because of the problem of sheets. Laurie's room had only a double bed, while Tyrone's had a king-sized bed and a balcony of its own, above the one off the livingroom. His bed was made up with cotton sheets in a pastel stripe. The coverlet was a light Irish wool, from which she deduced he did not like to lie on the spread. She was always throwing herself down on her bed naked or in her underwear.

She kicked off her shoes and carefully opened the bed, folding the blanket, the comforter and spread neatly to one side. Then she lay down. She expected the pillow to smell of an after-shave Tyrone liked to wear, but it gave up no scent. The sheets were chilly under her. The room had been closed and felt stuffy as a basement although she was high above the river. She wished she could open the doors to the balcony, but she did not want to set off another alarm.

Apparently he did not read in bed except for a couple of catalogs, one from Tiffany's, one from Gumps. He kept a bottle of single cask cognac in the bedside table along with two brandy snifters, a book of Japanese erotic art and a large electrical object that looked like a fan without blades. She examined it and finally decided it was a vibrator. When she plugged it in and turned it on, the padded end oscillated, producing a noise like a vacuum cleaner. Could it really be sexual? The only vibrator she had ever seen Siobhan had once pulled from a suitcase; it had resembled a plastic penis. Yet that had to be what this was. Maybe Tyrone needed some help because his last wife Glenda had been twenty years younger. She wondered what it felt like, but she felt too inhibited. Who could guess what woman it had touched last? She wondered if Willie would ever be willing to try one, but she dismissed the idea. He was too cock-proud to use any device. Tyrone must have an unusual degree of sexual openness, a willingness to experiment rare among men his age.

After all, she was courageous about sex herself. Hadn't she taken a woman lover? Nowadays everybody was in one box or the other. If a woman was with another woman, she would never admit to finding men at all attractive. If a woman was with a man, she pretended she never looked at other women with sexual curiosity.

In his closet at the farthest end two women's robes were hung, one in heavy white cotton terry cloth, one a blue silk kimono. She lifted them to her nostrils. The terry cloth smelled lightly of soap. The other had a faint flowery smell, someone's perfume. She had an excellent memory for scents and in a moment she had placed it: Nina Ricci's Fleur de Fleurs, yes. That was the perfume Tyrone had given her two years ago at Christmas. Was it the perfume Glenda had used? There was something significant in his giving her that very perfume. Perhaps Tyrone himself was not aware of the hidden message some of his choices carried.

His bedroom led into his own bathroom in one direction, and into a dressing room in the other. She saved the dressing room for last. The bathroom was grass green and pale blue, a lively pleasant room as big as her bedroom at home. The basin was grey marble and the window was inlaid with panes of milky green glass. The cabinet was filled with patent and prescription medicines for upset stomach, for sleeplessness, for athlete's foot and headaches. Nothing interesting, except for a couple of left-over women's cosmetics. He must never clear things out.

His walk-in dressing room was a party in itself, all those shoes laid out on wooden racks, his suits in plastic envelopes behind sliding glass doors, his shirts on hangers in their color class, whites together, white on whites, greys, browns, blues. His sweaters were heaped in drawers. His ties were on racks that turned, as in a department store men's section. His socks were arranged by color in two drawers. His handkerchiefs were in wooden subcompartments within a drawer, linen with linen, silk with silk. Even his cuff links were sorted into grids, one pair to each little square.

She imagined walking into such a closet to select what she was wearing to dinner that evening. The Somebodies were coming, The Bromleys from Memorial Day. The far side of the closet was mostly empty. That was where Laurie's boxes were stored, the ones Susan had promised to bring her, so she had a right to be here anyhow. She was dressing for dinner while Tyrone showered. He would not bellow off-key in the shower as Willie did. She had never even heard Tyrone whistle. He was a quiet man when he wasn't speaking, a blessing, although Dinah beat every man Susan had ever known in noisemaking, finger popping, whistling, drumming with hands and random objects from sticks to forks, toe tapping, explosive lip noises, humming through the mouth and nose and outright loud singing, often without words.

Tuesday at four Susan was done with her meetings. It had been a frustrating two days. The year before they had said paisley was dead on its current resurrection, and now they wanted more paisley for next year, mixes of paisley and flowers that she found ill-construed, in what they called jewel colors and brown. They had just rediscovered brown. The new neutral. That and olive. Khaki. Drab. Military colors. Moreover, Mr. di Vecchio too had dismissed half her designs and they had given her a deadline of Labor Day to turn in replacements.

She could conceivably have driven home at once and got there that night, but she had arranged to stay in New York a second night. Indeed, she was weary. Even in the air-conditioned apartment, the street noises were loud enough to make sleeping difficult. What she would have liked to do was to stay yet another day. Why not? She would tell Willie that she had one more meeting. He was wrapped up in his approaching show, only a week away, and busy the rest of the time with building. He would not miss her, and if he did, then he would act more appreciative when she got home.

Before she could feel guilty, she called him at supper time. He was not there, but Jimmy picked it up. "Hi, Mom. Dad's eating out."

"Oh, who invited him?"

"I think he's just picking up a bite in town until he has to go before the Board of Appeals."

"I'll be staying on for a day. One of my bosses didn't get back from Saint Lucia till today, so I have to stick around tomorrow to see him. I'll be back Thursday for sure. I hope your father isn't upset."

"Don't worry about it. Have you seen any good movies?"

"I've just been going to meetings with them and then collapsing at night and going over my notes and my presentation."

"Well, take a little time for yourself. I'll tell Willie you called."

Jimmy could sometimes surprise her by his affection. She hung up feeing agreeably cared for. He was right, her sensitive son: she should take some time for herself. She did go shopping the next afternoon, because going out from the apartment and

277

speaking to the doorman, having him call her a cab was part of the gorgeous routine of living there. The doorman knew her by now and treated her as a resident. The streets were simmering, the air felt like hot glue, but she hurried from air-conditioning to air-conditioning. Her bosses were pushing her around because she wasn't constantly on the spot to defend herself. She would get far more respect from them if she, too, lived in the city. In some ways Willie and she had left New York sacrificing themselves for the children, so they would grow up in a healthy place. Why not return? Moving back would be good for Willie's career; it was essential for hers. She could jump houses and do much better, if she knew the current market. She should be in the center, not out on the periphery trying to second-guess. Tyrone knew hundreds of fascinating people, and soon she, too, would know them. Selling their house would give them a nest egg to invest. Tyrone could easily help them find a small easy-to-keep-up apartment, perhaps in one of his buildings. She was sure he would give them a break on price. Perhaps they could move by Christmas. It wasn't impossible. She just had to start working Willie around to wanting to do it.

Tyrone was lonely. He clung to things that had belonged to Glenda. He was a driven man, frantically busy, always dashing off from one end of the world to the other, but at the core, he was alone. She would never leave Willie, of course not. Willie was a man who simply could not survive on his own. He was profoundly dependent on her. She loved Willie. If she no longer found him exciting romantically, that wasn't shocking after a quarter century of marriage. Moreover, Willie just wasn't growing. He needed to stretch himself. She loved him, but there was no doubt Willie's shortcomings stood out less when he was not the only person she was devoting her energy to. In New York he would wake up intellectually.

She could welcome Tyrone more fully into her life and fit into his, beautifully, warmly. Tyrone had lent her his apartment, as if in an experiment so that she might see what it was like to be here, to live this way, and she had flourished. She had slipped into it as if it were tailored for her. Here during these precious days she had been truly happy. She felt as if she would return home, as she must, carrying with her some of that burnish of beauty and fine taste, some of that fine glow of well polished joy.

She was not leaving New York to rush back to the Cape, but

as a strategic retreat in order to return in strength. Here was where she was going to be living soon. Manhattan was where she belonged.

THIRTY-NINE

Willie

Willie was sprawled on the redwood settee, in conscious contrast to Tyrone, sitting opposite on a lounge chair. Tyrone had his crocodile attaché case at heel, Donald dancing attendance around him. His back vibrated tension and energy six inches from the chair back. He was drinking gin and tonic as was Willie. Why did Willie always suspect Tyrone of drinking mostly tonic and giving him mostly gin during these verbal wrestling matches? Willie could hear his drawl stretching like Figaro just waking up and making himself twice his normal size. He always got very southern when he was being pushed, and Tyrone was trying to push him. His voice was getting more and more down-homey. Like a lot of people where he came from, he had several accents. His parents spoke with a southern rinse to their voices, but not anything like the way northerners put on what they thought was a drawl. But he had also been raised by Mona, and sometimes, as now, he spoke in her accent.

"Surely you're being a little naive about how to handle the local politicoes," Tyrone said, making a gesture of scratching his palm. "Probably a small bribe, either in cash or merchandise. A present to the wife."

"It just don't work that way round these parts."

"I've done business on five continents and one subcontinent, and it always works that way. It's just a matter of finding the correct currency, something the locals want."

Summer people always struck the folks who lived here as being deficient in manners, Willie thought. In a small town you had to have great tolerance and ongoing consideration of each other, or engage in endless bitter feuds. The lady behind the counter in the grocery store, the kid who pumped gas, the plumber who fixed your toilet were all people you would be facing daily for years and whom you often had to count on, people who expressed opinions at town meeting and board hearings, so you responded to them as people rather than as robots or dumping grounds for loose emotions. Anyone you offended would get you back sooner or later. "Parking's one hot issue in town. Traffic makes people's blood boil. The number of parking spaces for a gallery just ain't the same as residential, and that's the current sticking point."

"What are we dealing with, a fisherman, a motel owner and a vendor of souvenir tee shirts? Don't they understand we're offering to bring a quality gallery in, one that will cater to people with real money to spend?"

"Local people would like it better if it was something useful, like a dry cleaners. Everybody would appreciate not to have more cars beached like blackfish in gridlock in town center honking at each other."

"At least you finally managed to put the new roof on."

"It's watertight and yare. You can count on that."

"What other progress have you made? At the slug's pace you're proceeding, is there anything to see yet?"

"We've gutted the top two floors, except for stress bearing walls and structural beams. I'd like you to see the paneling we found on the ground floor under six layers of wallpaper. Oak in unusually wide boards. You should look it over before we touch it. Frankly it ought to be preserved."

"Sounds fascinating. I'll drop by to look at it this week. So some slight progress has been made. . . ."

Willie would not let himself lose his temper. He had done so once this summer, and it had given Tyrone an advantage. He preferred to slow down like a braced mule and let Tyrone wear himself out prodding him. He knew from what Jimmy passed on from Laurie that she didn't plan to open till June. The roof repair and cedar shingling had been the critical outdoor tasks. In truth they could lay off until late fall, although Willie had no intention of dragging the job out that long. It was hot work inside the old Victorian. He'd get cracking when the weather crispened in September and finish by November.

Tyrone had the habit of pushing. He wanted to inspect the work because that made him feel properly in control. Willie had explained to Susan, unsuccessfully, that Tyrone's working life was spent so distant from the reality of people doing physical labor, spent manipulating electronic images of shares and currencies, that he took pleasure in actually witnessing and attempting to boss around men working with visible tools.

Willie wouldn't be hustled. The work was proceeding at a reasonable pace and to hell with Tyrone's antsiness. Willie had his show to hang tonight, Johnny was arriving and tomorrow was his opening. Willie was taking the weekend off plus Monday, until Johnny left. He hardly ever saw his daughter.

Willie had not enjoyed building for Tyrone. He had said to Susan just the night before that Tyrone hadn't got rich being generous with his money, but she wouldn't hear of it. She was still grateful to Tyrone for letting her stay in his New York apartment, although Willie thought she could have insisted to Max that they put her up in a hotel, with them keeping her three days.

Tyrone had finally paid all he owed Willie on the boathouse and had got it through his head that Willie was adamant that nothing would go forward on the gallery until the money was in hand. He was not about to front the gallery for Tyrone. Now if fixtures were to be ordered or lumber picked up, Tyrone wrote the checks with a minimum of haggling. That was how local builders worked, and he wasn't going to make an exception for Tyrone, no matter what Susan said. He was laying too much out for the studio.

Susan had been in a good mood all week. She had even gone blackberry picking with Laurie, who told him privately she had already gone with Dinah and had the scars on her arms to prove it. Then Susan had put up blackberry jam with cinnamon and made a deep-dish blackberry pie, of which he had gobbled three pieces. She should be working on her designs, because several she had brought to New York had been rejected, but he was reluctant to interfere when she was happy. Let her enjoy the summer for a week or two. All the tourists did. The house was a different place when Susan was happy. She had made love with him twice this week. She had gone to town to see the gallery progress, had gone with him to Leroy's opening and then taken off her shoes and walked with him arm in arm along the ocean under the full moon.

Susan had been so forthcoming since she'd come back from New York that he realized he hadn't seen Dinah all week. While Susan was gone, he had eaten there every night and even stayed over once. Dinah was adamant that he tell Susan he was seeing her. She didn't seem to understand she was asking for a storm of blood and thunder. Things were fine. Why make trouble?

Still he was suddenly aware he had not seen her since Susan's return.

When he had walked over to Tyrone's, he had heard Dinah playing the piano, a tape recorder going, too, so that it sounded as if a whole group of musicians were at it. With the shell of the studio up, it was easy for him to hop across the yard without coming into Susan's line of sight. He didn't hear the piano going, so he assumed she was taking a break. He decided to stop by, checking first to make sure Jimmy was off with the truck in town.

Her kitchen was full of tomatoes, green and purple beans not yet frozen, green, yellow and red sweet and hot peppers. She was in the drying closet built into the antique fireplace, laying out herbs on screens that slid in and out of a frame the two of them had built. She did not hear him. When he slipped his arms around her waist, she squeaked with surprise but did not drop the basil.

She sat him down in the livingroom and brought him a beer. "So you've been over visiting our resident millionaire."

"He's been trying to push me around. But when an irresistible object meets an immovable force, what happens? Nothing."

"Guess who he's fucking."

"Donald."

"No, that blond who wears her dresses cut down to her belly button. Candida MacIvor, the doctor's wife."

"How do you know?"

"I'm always in the woods. I see him going in her house when she's alone and I see him coming out. I have a dirty mind."

"You don't know for sure, then. Maybe he just likes to talk to her the way he likes to talk to Susan."

"Always when her husband's in the city, sure. No, I haven't snuck up and peeked in the window. Ugh! Although I saw two red-shouldered hawks fucking in the spring, I forgot to tell you—we weren't speaking." She gave him a minute description of what she had witnessed while squatting in the bushes, the actual act accomplished in fifteen seconds but the story taking five minutes. By the time she finished, Willie was aroused, but Dinah braced her hand flat against his chest.

"So have you talked to Susan?"

"Susan's in a good mood since she got back from New York. Why ruin it?"

"If she's in a bad mood, you say why get her depressed. Now she's in a good mood, don't rock the boat. Willie, I can't go on like this. I need my life cleaned up."

"For Chrissake, Dinah, I'm not something you stepped in. You have a connection with me whether or not Susan ever speaks to you again."

Dinah evaded him, putting the table between them. She stood with her hands on her hips. "But whether I exercise that connection has to have something to do with Susan, honey, any fool can see that."

"Hello?"

Dinah and Willie swung around at the same time. It was Johnny's voice, deep for a woman, husky. She was standing outside the door to the livingroom, open but with the screen door latched. Nobody ever came in that way. Dinah had to move a rocking chair to open it for her.

"I parked and got out, not quite sure was this the old homestead or a strip mine. Even the old rose arbor? I was just moseying around surveying the damage when I heard your voices." Johnny kissed Willie on the cheek and Dinah on the mouth. She looked tall, gaunt, handsome, wearing for traveling a purple halter, black leather shorts and an unzipped sweat suit top for a cardigan, enormous earrings in the form of dice, like proles hung on their rearview mirrors. Willie always started worrying when he saw her, as if anything at all might happen to her.

"I was just looking for Jimmy," Willie said, caught off stride and wondering if Johnny had heard his argument with Dinah. "I thought he was working on the addition here, but he's off with Laurie."

"I'm not your keeper, don't make excuses to me." Johnny swung around to gaze back through the screen door. "You guys have really chewed up the countryside."

"All I wanted was a washer and a dryer," Dinah said bitterly. "How about a beer?"

"I'll drink to that." Johnny plunked down on the couch. "Can I stay here tonight?"

"You'll have to sleep on what you're sitting on."

"How come? Isn't Jimmy boffing little miss vinegar across the water?"

"You work it out with him," Dinah said. "I provide sheets and sympathy."

"Have you checked in with your mother yet?" Willie asked.

"I figured we'd schedule the first set for after you arrived. We need a referee."

"Don't look for trouble, Johnny. Let's make this visit a good one. Don't start with your mother like a kid poking a stick into a hive to see how the bees react. You know how she'll react. Let's be kind to each other." His head rang with old wars, Johnny and Susan fighting about clothing, about school, about drugs and reputed drugs, about the telephone, loudness of music, neatness of room, fights about staying out too late, fights about staying out all night, fights about eating and not eating, drinking and not drinking, smoking and not smoking, fights about boys, about girlfriends, about rudeness, about privacy, about taste, about each woman's vital image of herself.

"If she even said to me Hello, Johnny, my name since I got old enough to choose a name, I'd faint with pleasure." Johnny put down her empty beer.

Willie took that as a signal to rise. The situation was making him nervous, lest Susan realize where they all were. "Then let's go say hello to Susan and get off to a pleasant start. Jimmy should be back soon and then the two of you can negotiate who's sleeping where."

Johnny waggled her long fingers at Dinah. "See you after first blood. I'll bring my stash in."

"How did your show go in Rochester?" Dinah asked.

"I thought no one was going to ask me. As soon as we opened, we sold two big mothers and a little one. My dealer thinks I'll sell most of what I'm showing. Even as I stand here, I may be getting rich—relatively."

Willie knew he should have asked. Johnny needed to tell them her successes, for when she came home she felt instantly a teenager. He had been too worried about Susan to remember. He was angry with himself, even as he kept telling her how proud he was of her, talking excessively to make up for neglect. Behind his eyes dishes sailed through the air, books were thrown, vases broken, shirts torn in two, chairs kicked over. Susan and Johnny always got loud, and they could get very physical. Only Johnny ever reduced Susan to a screaming bitch.

Susan had obviously heard the van arrive or seen it outside, for she was in the kitchen waiting, in a mood of crackling high insult. "I wondered if something had happened to you. I saw your van arrive half an hour ago, but I couldn't locate you."

"I saw Daddy was next door, so I popped in to say hi."

"Next door? I thought you had gone to Tyrone's."

"I was on my way back. I had to talk to Jimmy about the gallery."

"Jimmy and Laurie went to the beach," Susan said. "I heard him tell you."

"I thought he might be back."

"Since when does Daddy need an excuse to be at Dinah's?" Johnny asked.

"Your father and I are no longer involved with Dinah. We've found that our lives are better without her."

"It seems to me you can only say that for yourself," Johnny said.

"I'm speaking for both of us—" Susan began stiffly.

Willie rushed to cut in. "It's a complicated thing, Johnny, please let it alone. You just got here. I want to show you the studio I'm building for Susan. Come on."

That evening Johnny helped him hang his show at the gallery. He had the center of all three rooms, while the two painters showing with him had the walls. The gallery gave him a number of pedestals for the smaller works. The three biggest were freestanding. One piece had to be hung, and that was tricky. They had to unhinge the outer door to get the biggest piece in safely. Jimmy and Laurie showed up in midevening to lend a hand too. Normally Dinah would have been a big help, but she was lying low. Johnny more than filled in. She had a natural instinct for exhibiting.

Johnny slept at Dinah's and spent the afternoon at the beach with Jimmy and Laurie. Jimmy and Johnny might insult each other every other sentence, but they had a mutual trust he liked to know was there. They enjoyed each other's company. He and Susan must have done some things right. He had never been friends with anyone in his family. He had been too close to his mother in childhood and never close to any of the others, lacking the clear-sighted humorous undemanding affection his children offered each other.

Susan and he made love and then she served him an omelet and a salad, telling him she expected they would go out to a heavier meal after the opening, to celebrate. He hoped he felt like celebrating. He always imagined that no one would come, that they would set out the California chablis and the cheese and fruit, and no one would walk into the gallery all evening.

The opening was successful. A lot of local people swelled

the ranks—it looked good at an opening if it was so crowded nobody could see anything. Anybody actually interested in looking at the work would come back during the daytime when the gallery was empty. Willie felt a little guilty about his recent hostility toward Tyrone when it turned out he was taking them out to a late supper at Gilcrest Manor, the local snob restaurant, menus without prices and a wine steward. Tyrone brought along his own guests and functionaries and Willie's family, except of course Dinah. She wouldn't have cared for it anyhow, he told himself consolingly, all that rich food, fawning service and not sitting down to eat until nine o'clock. He had the sense of enjoying and scorning the meal at once, as if thinking of her made him judgmental about things he would have taken for granted in her presence.

Tyrone was giving him the dinner, but said nothing whatsoever about his work. Instead he decided to shine the light of his attention on Johnny, who was stowing away the food at a great clip. Both his kids had had the ability to eat for three. Susan presided from the foot of the table, beaming, savoring the food, the wine, the service, the atmosphere. Willie was glad to see that she and Johnny were making the best of the evening, each walking on eggshells while only offending the other perhaps half the time. Perhaps they were mellowing. Johnny had so far resisted insulting Tyrone. In the past she would have felt called on to make clear that he didn't impress her by saying something as gross as possible. She was growing up, his bright daughter. She would surpass him. That was a reasonable fate.

The mellowness was wearing thin by Sunday afternoon. Susan tried to give Johnny a dress she had made. Johnny said, as she always did, that it wasn't something she would ever wear. "You ought to give it to Laurie. We're roughly the same size, and she wears that kind of thing."

"And what kind of thing is that kind of thing? You mean, something with taste, Siobhan? Something that looks as if somebody made it, as opposed to finding it at the Salvation Army reject pile?"

"Mother, you make the same mistake over and over again of confusing your taste with all taste, you generation's style for all style. I have my own, what suits me!"

Willie got up quietly and turned down the flame on the stove. He was simmering a tomato sauce for spaghetti. If he left it on a low fire, he could slip out to his studio till they stopped fighting. He could not endure to listen, for both were in pain now, both felt rejected, scorned; each longed to justify herself in the face of the other's blind wrong. They were artesian wells of emotion, Susan under the guise of earth mother, Johnny under her punk glaze; each thought the other cold and themselves, hot. If he attempted, as he had used to, to explain one to the other, it would end up with both of them furious with him as well. No, he would extract himself from their fight. He put down the spoon and began drifting toward the door.

"Look, Mother, your problem is trying to control everybody around you. You made up an idiotic name for me and you insist on being the only person in the world who doesn't call me by my own name, Johnny. You've driven Jimmy out of the house by trying to control his sex life—"

"I wanted him to avoid the pain waiting for him. Laurie won't take him seriously for long. Tyrone is going to step in."

"That sad little twat is lucky to get him. She can be a big shot here. In New York she's nothing but the talentless and luckless daughter of a middling successful money man."

"Since when are you so smart about love and marriage? You've never even been able to keep a boyfriend. You've never known how to act around men and you never will!" Susan tossed her hair back in scorn. She was blushing with anger. "You willfully make yourself bizarre and hideous!"

"I'm not hideous. I look like an artist. I look young. You want me to dress like a middle-aged hippie!"

"I'm paid for my knowledge of fabric and style. You've always been jealous of your own mother. Resentful of me. You don't know how to make friends with women or how to get along with men. The only way you can attract attention is by making yourself ridiculous and unpleasant."

Willie sidled past both of them and was opening the door.

"Since when are you the expert? You fucked up your relationship with Dinah and now you're putting pressure on Dad to break off with her, just because you don't want anybody to have a thing you don't have too."

"Your father's not involved with Dinah! These are private matters—"

Willie turned around. He had the impulse to run. Anywhere. Susan was glaring at him as well as Johnny. He said, "I think we should lay off this topic right away. It's a touchy subject. Johnny, shut up now."

287

"It was never private. Everybody in school knew about you guys. So that was the downside. The upside was Dinah herself. How can you pretend Dad isn't involved with her?" Johnny turned toward him, where he stood on one foot at the door.

He took a step toward Susan, then stopped. She was glaring at him. She was staring into him. Her face was red and white in blotches. His throat closed. She opened her mouth but said nothing.

Johnny spoke faster, scared by Susan's reaction. "Of course you knew. But you're making everybody tiptoe all around you. Jimmy knows. Even asshole Laurie knows. Laurie is going on about poor Susan this afternoon and how she really must have guessed but we have to be careful with her, like you're some kind of invalid. It's like when I was fifteen and fucking Allie Dove and everybody in town knew, but you had to pretend it was a big shock." She turned to plead with him, her voice rising into near hysteria. "Why can't you tell Mother for once she's off the wall and everybody knows it!"

"Oh shit oh shit oh shit," Willie muttered, staring at Susan whose jaw had fallen slackly. "Johnny, don't talk about what you don't understand!"

Susan was backed against the stove, where his sauce was simmering. "Willie, what in hell is she talking about?"

"Nothing, Susan, nothing," Willie said.

Johnny said over his voice, "You have to know. Come on, Mother, be honest for once. Stop pretending that because you couldn't keep it together with Dinah, that Dad isn't still with her. It's ridiculous! Dad is fucking her, Jimmy is living there, and you're pretending she doesn't exist. I was embarrassed that she wasn't there last night, really embarrassed for this whole family! It's like you're forcing everybody around you to lie because you want to lie, and I think it's shitty."

"Willie, you goddamned bastard!" Susan picked up the tomato sauce in its saucepan and flung it forward so that it spattered over the room, over Johnny and over him, hot and scalding and burning his arm so he heard himself bellow. Johnny screamed in pain. Then Susan ran sobbing from the room.

FORTY

Laurie

Laurie was summoned on the phone by Dinah and told to bring ice. Jimmy and she were in bed and almost didn't answer. "Something's wrong across the pond!" she said to Jimmy, stepping into her slacks. "Susan has found out."

The atmosphere in Dinah's kitchen was grim and business-like. Johnny's right arm, right shoulder and right breast were scalded, as was Willie's left arm and hand. Dinah was treating them with ice, their stained clothes stripped off. Johnny wore a kimono of Dinah's that Susan had probably made some years before, and Willie, a terry robe of Jimmy's.

"Shouldn't they go to the hospital right away?"

"Second-degree burns. We can handle it. By the time they drive for an hour and then get through emergency room triage, they'll be blistering."

Johnny had obviously been crying, but now she was acting tough. "I'm not going into Emergency and say, my mother mistook me for a pizza and poured boiling tomato sauce all over me."

Willie kept silent, compacted. His face was clenched on itself. He was hunched on a straight chair looking more frightened than angry.

Jimmy said, "I'd better see Susan. She must be locked in the bedroom."

Laurie asked, "Should I go with you?"

"If you really want to." He grimaced at her. "Hang back though."

They crossed the yard among piles of lumber and the garage doors waiting to be installed. The kitchen still reeked of tomato sauce. The stove had been turned off, but the sauce was splashed everywhere. It looked like a scene in a teenage slash movie, blood on the walls, blood on the table, blood on the floor. Jimmy made a pass at cleaning, using a whole roll of paper towels. When he gave up, the kitchen was still splattered with what looked like sticky gore. It turned her stomach. As he went upstairs, she trailed behind him. "Mother!" He knocked on her door. "It's Jimmy! Can I come in?"

"Go away."

"Mother, please open the door. It's just Laurie and me, no one else."

"What do you want?" She sounded stuffed up.

"To make sure you're all right."

They heard the springs creak and slow footsteps. Finally the lock turned and Jimmy pushed the door quickly open. Susan had been crying. Her face was swollen, her cheek reddened and ridged from the coverlet. She huddled on the bed's edge and did not look at them. Laurie was a little frightened by her disheveled appearance, for Susan resembled Laurie's own mother when she had been drinking for hours. Susan had always been well turned out, attractive, together. "Why would I be all right?" she asked rhetorically in a smothered sounding voice. "I have just discovered my husband has been lying to me for months. He's having an affair with a woman he promised me he was done with. My son has been lying to me. Everybody has been laughing at me. Everybody!"

"I'm sure it hasn't been months," Laurie said nervously. "It's been very recent, and we just learned about it after Jimmy started staying next door. Nobody wanted to upset you, Susan. Nobody wanted to hurt you."

"If nobody wanted to hurt me, why am I hurting this way? Why do I wish I were dead?"

"Mother, Johnny shouldn't have stuck her elbow in it. Dad wanted to talk to you about it. Dinah wanted him to. He'd promised her he'd tell you, but he just didn't know how."

"I can see how it would be a problem." Susan stood. She picked up a Tiffany-style lamp beside the bed as if casually and threw it against the wall so it shattered.

Laurie backed away till she was sheltered behind Jimmy. This woman had gone crazy. This woman had become violent. Her own mother at worst was a sloppy crying sort of drunk, not a dangerous maniac.

"Mother, over the years you've been furious with Siobhan many times. You've had terrible fights. Yet you're still mother and daughter. We've weathered a lot of bad scenes with each other."

"I will never forgive that lousy pig bastard for what he did to me. I'm through with him. He lied to me. He lied to me day in

290

and day out for months. He was fucking her while I was in New York and that's where he was every time I called and he wasn't here."

"Mother, everybody lies sometimes. I'm sure you've had to lie to Dad at times. We all do things we don't want to own up to."

"In twenty-six years of marriage, I have never never lied to him about another man. Ever! And I had plenty of opportunities. He made a fool of me." She began to sob again, throwing herself facedown on the bed.

Laurie felt embarrassed. She didn't know where to look. She sidled toward the door. Jimmy sat down on the bed's edge and stroked Susan's tangled hair. "Mom, don't take it so hard. It doesn't mean anything. It's only Dinah. What did he do he hadn't been doing for ten years?"

"It isn't the same! It isn't the same. It's the opposite!" She wriggled away from his hand. "Don't touch me. My own son! You lied to me too. You took his side. You took her side against me."

"I didn't take anybody's side, Mom. You never even explained to me what happened between you and Dinah. I just tried to stay out of the way."

"Not one of you was faithful to me, not one!"

"Mother, what does that mean? That I should have run and made trouble between you and Dad? Siobhan just did that, and look at the mess. I had faith you'd work it out, the two of you."

"There's nothing to work out. Nothing!" She began to cry harder, grinding her face into the pillow.

Laurie crept still nearer to the door. She was appalled by Susan, and she wondered how Jimmy could sit there calmly forcing himself to touch her. Susan's heavy emotionality felt like ugly greasy makeup that could come off and stain hands and clothes. Was Susan crazy? Throwing the boiling sauce over her husband and her daughter, throwing the lamp at the wall. She couldn't conceive of Tyrone acting like a maniac; her own mother cried and carried on, but never had she lost control so completely.

She tried to recall whether Jimmy had ever behaved that irrationally, that violently in the years she had known him. She did not think he had, but she wondered if that wild behavior was somewhere in him waiting to be unleashed. One reason Tyrone had got sick of Janette much more quickly than her own mother, whom after all he had really loved, and Glenda, the most recent wife, was that Janette had a temper she would release freely like a bad dog. But that temper was a trained poodle compared to this ravening beast.

It was a mess, the lives over here, the husband wrapped up in towels and ice in Dinah's kitchen, the daughter too. They did not know how to conduct their affairs properly. They were weird and tacky, as she had thought when she was in high school and this bizarre triangle had begun.

Finally she fled the hot claustrophobic bedroom. She made her apologies to Jimmy, who was too engrossed to notice her escape. Home! She did not go straight to the boathouse but rather to the big house, to consult Tyrone. She found him in his office. Donald had just driven the weekend company to the airport, and Tyrone was dictating to Sally. She had been entering figures on the computer.

She did not bother asking Sally to leave, as Sally had witnessed their life for years. Sally belonged to Tyrone, really, in the same way that a car belonged to him. Laurie thought that she would only quit as one said a car had quit, by breaking down. Laurie felt gently calmed as she sat in Tyrone's office with the amber monitor of the computer lit and faintly humming, with Tyrone's beautiful Chippendale desk on the pastel Oriental before her, with the books in leather bindings and the Japanese floating world prints in bamboo frames, with Sally crisp and cool and sympathetic, but quietly, tactfully so.

Tyrone listened with a grimace of disgust. "They do create messes over there. You would muck around with the son. Such people are fine for a while in their own setting, but then chaos breaks through."

She was stung to defend Jimmy. "He's not like his mother at all. He's very controlled. I wish you would pay some attention to who he is."

"He does decent carpentry. I brought Sampson by to look at the building this week, and they seem to have repaired the structure quite adequately. Sampson by the way remarked that it would condoize well."

"We talked about an apartment upstairs." It felt serene here, as if the air were cleaner and lighter. "What are you doing for dinner tonight?" Celeste was off Sundays.

Tyrone glanced at Sally. She responded, "I made a reserva-

292

tion for you at the Tee and Surf Club. You promised Mr. Sampson you would play snooker with him first.''

''Why not dine with us?'' Tyrone asked. ''You don't want to go across the pond till things have returned to what passes for normal over there.''

On his desk in the basket where notices of shows, of auctions, where catalogs of exhibitions were placed for him to browse through, she saw the little catalog for Johnny's show in Rochester. ''Don't buy one of her paintings, Dad. She's always been rude to me. And she's the one who just had to tell Susan what everyone knew all summer but had the sense to keep quiet.''

He took the catalog, neatly ripped it in two and tossed it into the wastebasket. ''Enough said. Why don't you dress? We should be ready to push off about six.''

That night she did not get back until close to eleven, and Jimmy spent the night across the pond. Monday she elected to go along with Tyrone on Mr. Sampson's boat. She had not been sailing all summer, except for the little toy she had bought Tyrone that they played with on the pond. She had forgot how much she enjoyed handling a nice craft. She had a good time and even flirted with the Sampsons' son, Bob, although she knew he was gay and he knew she knew. It made them a club of two, who understood what his parents did not and Tyrone had not guessed. They bonded quietly apart from their parents, gossiping pleasantly about acquaintances. Bob did not seem to remember her scandal, and she tasted a little nostalgia for New York. When Jimmy arrived as she was taking a shower, she felt almost surprised.

''I packed Johnny off early this morning. I didn't want her to see Susan again. I didn't think any good could come of that. Dad's sleeping on the couch at home. Both he and I thought it would be disastrous if he stayed at Dinah's.'' Jimmy sat on her bed yoga fashion with his bare feet drawn up.

''Do you know how to sail? I went out on a nice little yacht today.''

''Sure I know. Didn't I grow up here?'' He looked pensive, but said nothing more about his family, which she thought extremely tactful. He did ask her, ''Who's this Sampson fellow? Tyrone has brought him by the gallery twice. Does he have an interest in it?''

''Not that I know. He and Daddy had some investment together. He owns a bunch of condos here." She told him that Bob Sampson was gay, so he would not be jealous of her day. They had a fast supper at the Lobster Tent and then took in a movie. By morning she had pushed aside her fears that through him she would be sucked into the whirlpool of his out-of-control family.

Tuesday afternoon she saw Susan walking the path toward the big house. Her impulse was to hide. Tyrone had disappeared into the woods at a brisk clip half an hour before. Dr. MacIvor was back in the city. She did not care to discuss Tyrone's minor activities, but she was always aware. She knew that Tyrone had had a falling out with the Countess Sforzi, was bored with Betty Gore and had become involved with Candida. Candida was eager to please Laurie nowadays and would agree with almost anything she said. Laurie was no longer at all intimidated. She was only a little worried, as Tyrone rarely got involved in anything clandestine. The married women he had taken up with were separated or had arrangements. Candida was exactly Tyrone's type—she really did resemble Janette—and she was available and convenient. Almost the way Laurie had become involved with Jimmy, except he was getting divorced.

She peeked through the window, keeping well back, and saw Sally greet Susan and then manage to dispose of her. Susan stood on the wide verandah looking toward the boathouse, obviously trying to decide whether to visit her. Laurie locked herself in the bathroom, where she could not be seen through a window. She crouched there as she heard Susan's voice outside and her soft rap on the screen door. She heard the door opening. She held her breath, afraid Susan would come in. But she did not. Laurie heard the door shut.

When Laurie dared creep out of the bathroom to peek through her loft window from the bedroom, she could see Susan plodding slowly back around the pond toward her own house. She sighed in relief. Sally had no doubt covered for them all. She felt once again the power of Tyrone cradling her around. Even when he was absent, those he had hired and trained, those who were absolutely loyal to him, like Sally, like Donald, filled in perfectly. She had learned in childhood that perhaps she could not always get what she wanted, but she could always get out of what she did not want. Perhaps in the long view, that was more important.

FORTY-ONE

Susan

Susan felt broken and yet energized. A web of lies spun fine enough to be invisible had trapped her in place. Everyone about her conspired to keep her ignorant; thus she had questioned her own perceptions, her own instincts. Now at the cost of tremendous pain, as if she had been gutted quickly with a razor, she was free at last of hesitation and doubt.

Her marriage was over. Every part of it had collapsed at once, like an old shack hit by a tree. Willie had deceived her, Willie whom she had trusted, whom she had thought she knew as intimately as her own face, Willie had lied to her, not once, not twice, but daily, nightly, all of the time for months. In her heart she had sensed her marriage was over, yet she had doubted her own feelings. She had been weak and sentimental, unwilling to credit what she instinctively knew.

He was sleeping across the hall in Jimmy's room, for she could not stand the two of them sharing a bed. She had been waking exceptionally early. At dawn she lay contemplating the wrinkles of her life in the ripples of light on the ceiling, reflections off the pond that caught on the old uneven plaster. She tossed gnashing her teeth, weeping, utterly desolate. Finally she would reach the point where she must get out of bed because she could not endure her thoughts any longer. This morning she boiled over at eight, much earlier than she had used to rise, back when she had been blind.

When she came downstairs, he was in the kitchen sitting over an empty cup.

"I don't understand why you don't simply move next door." She crossed her arms over her closed bathrobe. "You'd be more comfortable with your lover. I'd avoid tripping over you."

"You know you can't sleep when you're in the house alone, Susan."

"Why, how kind of you to think of me. How extraordinarily kind to fuck and then run back over here. Well, I no longer sleep anyhow, so you may stay over there as far as I'm concerned."

295

She would not look at him. She did not care how hangdog he made himself look, she took pleasure in addressing a shelf over his head.

"Susan, don't cut yourself off from me. Don't destroy everything—"

"You dare say that to me? After what you've done?"

"Dinah won't speak to me either. She says it's my fault for not telling you. I wanted to talk to you, Susan, but I didn't want you to get angry—"

"If you don't get out of the kitchen, I'll do without breakfast and lock myself in my room."

"Susan, this has been going on for three days! We have to talk. We have to sit down together. . . . Maybe we should go to a marriage counselor. Burt says there's a good therapist named Amy Roget—"

"Who else have you told in town? Are you proud of what's going on?"

"You won't talk to me. Dinah won't talk to me—"

"I'm leaving the kitchen. When I know you're out of the house, I may come down again." She swept out and locked herself in the bathroom. She turned on the water, tossed in bubble bath. She would deny herself no small luxuries. She regretted flouncing out of the kitchen, for she had far, far more to say to him. The best solution to the current situation was to have Willie move next door and Jimmy move back. She did not want to be in the house alone, certainly not. Every little sound of the night would terrify her. Every raccoon in the trash, every pine bough rubbing against a gutter would become a prowler. She had not seen Laurie around for a couple of days, so perhaps that was winding down.

She had forgiven Jimmy. He was right when he said he had not wanted to make trouble. With Willie lying to her, Jimmy had been in an impossible position. She prided herself on being just, as well as wronged. Jimmy had come out well, and so for that matter had Siobhan. Siobhan had told her the truth, and Susan had to be grateful. She tried to call Siobhan, but she got only the answering machine with what was supposed to be an amusing message. Aldo's voice said, "We're probably in bed or drunk, so we can't come to the phone, but you can leave a message. If you're lucky, we'll even call you back."

Although her first impulse had been to hang up, she had left a message. She did not know if Siobhan had gone straight back to Minneapolis or to some other destination. Susan must take advantage of the fact that Siobhan had cared enough to tell her the ugly truth. She would thank her. Susan would apologize for making a scene in the kitchen, explaining how upset she had been. It would represent a breakthrough between them, no thanks to Willie.

She was going to be clearheaded, she was going to be efficient in the pursuit of a decent life for herself. She ate a muffin with tea and called Mary Lou, who had a real estate license. "Mary Lou, how are you?" She planned to chat the obligatory five minutes about the weather, the tourist season, the traffic in town, the latest accident on the highway.

Mary Lou forestalled her. "Oh, Susan, I hope you're all right. If you want to come over and talk to me about it all, I can kick the old man out this evening and send him to a movie."

Were her troubles all over town? She felt her face heating in embarrassment. "Actually I was calling you in a professional capacity. I'd love it if you could drop by and formally appraise my house."

"Oh, Susan, you're not thinking of that already, are you? Charlie and I went to a wonderful marriage counselor."

"Amy Roget?"

"Are you going to her too? Isn't she wonderful?"

"No, I'm not. Could you discuss selling the house, Mary Lou?"

"Of course, Susan, and I'd be pleased to handle it for you." Mary Lou's voice changed to her professional chirp. "We should be able to get a good price for a pond house. Would tomorrow at four be okay for you?"

As Susan made a note of the time on her calendar, she reflected that Amy Roget must know the secrets of every couple in town, but not hers. She did not seek reconciliation. She did not want to sit pretending to believe his excuses. She did not want to present herself in a therapist's office to explain the wriggling mess of their relationships. She could not endure some young shrimp lecturing on the give-and-take of marriage and somehow twisting things around so that it was her fault Willie had ruined their lives.

She needed desperately to see Tyrone. She had called several times, but he was always out or on another line. Sally had the habit of protecting him from everyone, even from her, so she decided she would simply stroll over at five. If he was still working, she would have a seat and wait for him. She had plenty of time, after all. She had no house to clean, no supper to prepare, no social calendar to arrange. She had resigned. She couldn't possibly concentrate on redoing the fabric designs until her life had settled into the semblance of a new order. She could work extremely fast when she had to, and obviously, she would have to. But first, she needed a lawyer, she needed plans. She needed Tyrone's advice and help. She had seen him through three divorces. He could be considered an expert. She needed his help in the move to the city.

Had Tyrone also known about Dinah? She doubted it. Laurie would probably not have told him anything potentially scandalous about Jimmy's family; it would be too stupid for her to do so. Tyrone had no contact with Dinah. Willie and Tyrone had been at odds all summer over petty details of the gallery project. Tyrone was the one person she was certain had been as ignorant as herself. She found that oddly comforting. Further, why would the MacIvors have known? They did not meet Dinah socially. So Willie had not polluted all her friendships. She still had room to maneuver, even here.

She felt detached and elegiac as she strolled along the shore. Soon she would leave. She would move to Manhattan and perhaps return only as Tyrone's guest. It felt terribly sad, something once beautiful that had decayed. It was that time in August when everything was fraying, wearing out, showing dirt. The pond no longer held the pristine waters of June. Here and there plastic cartons lay on the shore. A little froth of pollution danced in the shallows. The leaves were beginning to dull into brown. An occasional bright leaf of rum cherry or poison ivy predicted the fall. The grass had faded to straw. Only a few mummies marked the blueberry and blackberry bushes.

Leaving a marriage, even one that had so signally fallen to pieces, was departing from a large part of herself. She walked more slowly. The heat felt woolen, oppressive. Usually close to the ocean some breeze stirred, but this afternoon the air was thick as the stuffing in a pillow. She had come to Willie ripe but oh so young. Why had she married him? He had been the wrong choice, but she had been stubborn at top volume, ignoring her family's protests as knee-jerk anti-Protestantism. Now she wondered if they had not seen in him something that had disturbed them, if they had not anticipated her disillusion, her pain.

He was not a brilliant man, as for instance Tyrone was. She

had always felt he was not quite as bright as she was, but for a long time she had not minded. Now she minded. What he had done was so egregiously stupid, she found its clumsiness as obnoxious as the infidelity itself. What kind of nincompoop would tell himself that he could be putting it to the woman next door, and his wife would not notice? A man with even minimal sense, who felt compelled by midlife crisis to have an affair, would have conducted it in some discreet way so that half the world wouldn't gossip about it.

Nor was he immensely talented. Tyrone had never bought a piece of his. Willie maundered along stuck in a time warp making ugly cages and wire monstrosities festooned with newsprint, a kind of naive pottering, as if everybody didn't know art wasn't supposed to be political any more than dress fabric was. In short, he was no bargain. He had no more ability to earn money than she did. He had been an excellent father to the children, she would give him that, which was perhaps why their marriage had endured as long as it had. He was good with children and animals, great, but she was neither a dog nor a four-year-old. He was no good to her.

She wanted to be scrupulously fair. They should sell the house and divide the money. She would take her half and go to New York and he might do as he pleased. Probably he would move in with Dinah. After all, Dinah was enlarging her house. She had a moment of deep suspicion that Dinah was still intending to have a baby, that all this was to get a baby out of Willie. She would be furious if Dinah was pregnant. Was there a chance? No, Dinah was just getting back at her by fooling around with Willie.

The children could not reasonably object to her plans. Jimmy would soon return to Seattle or settle locally. If he continued with Laurie, she had a trust fund; if not, then he would save enough working in the building trades to buy land. He could build far more cheaply than other people, the same way he and Willie were handling these additions, by general contracting and doing the carpentry. It wasn't as if she were selling the house from under her children. Jimmy had moved out. Siobhan might as readily visit her in New York as here. Although she had never been able to take their rooms from them, now that she was selling the house, she felt less sentimental. Everything in her mind seemed clearer, she thought, harder.

As she walked through the hedge of old lilacs onto the lawn

of the big house, she felt she was coming to Tyrone today as an equal, someone alone, in control of her life. As sensitive as he always was, he had to observe the changes in her. It was five-thirty, giving her confidence that he would be detaching connector by connector from the elaborate harness of his days, preparing for his before-dinner cocktail and relaxation ritual. Smiling calmly, walking slowly to emphasize her control, her serenity, she strolled onto the verandah of the big house, going directly to the French doors into the livingroom, knocking lightly and then walking in like any other expected guest.

Sally came rustling to meet her, looking sightly alarmed. "Mrs. Dewitt, is he expecting you?"

"No more than usual, I'm sure. How are you, Sally? You look well tanned and healthy."

"Thank you. I'll tell him you're waiting."

But Tyrone came to the door of his office. "Ah, Susan. I was just knocking off. Do have a seat and Celeste will bring you a martini. I'll join you momentarily." He motioned her onto the verandah. Celeste appeared shortly. Susan sipped her very cold martini and stared at the pond with an odd, light detachment. This was the place she had lived for the last eighteen years. Now she was preparing to leave it. Emotionally she felt distant already. This was a place with which she was almost finished.

Tyrone strode out. Instead of sitting beside her, he leaned against the railing facing her, looking into her face. "How are you bearing up?"

"Surprisingly well. I suppose subliminally I knew things were very bad. I was shocked when I learned he had been deceiving me, but I knew all along that something was radically wrong."

"Just so you can talk it out. I know I'm a poor one to give advice, with my broken marriages behind me, but you and Willie have been together far longer than I managed with any of my wives."

"Too long. It's quite dead and done with."

"Susan, that would be exceedingly foolish. Don't let pride talk so loud you can't hear your heart—or your common sense."

"You've had to cut your losses. Why be surprised I want to cut mine?"

"My dear, I'm only thinking of what's best for you. Life is not always kind or just, but we have to soldier on. . . ."

"I'm not giving up—far from it. I'm making quite rational plans, believe me. I have a real estate woman coming tomorrow to appraise the property. I intend to put it on the market and split the money with him. I think it would be good for my career and for me to be in New York.''

"The city is dreadfully expensive, Susan. Half of what you could get for your house and land . . . um . . ." He pulled out a small calculator. "Say two hundred, two fifty, your share. With that, you can't afford anything livable in Manhattan. Would you find Staten Island attractive? Or New Jersey? Perhaps you opt not to buy anything, but to take the money and invest it for income. Invested with a return of ten percent, you'd have, let's say after taxes take their bite from the sale price, perhaps twenty K a year. That won't pay your rent.''

"I was hoping that you might know of some small condo in one of your buildings.''

"I don't own anything myself. I've simply bought shares in various holding and management companies. I'd never care to be a landlord, Susan, it must be rather trying.''

It was the tone of voice that she found less than pleasant. He was talking to her distantly, politely. There was none of the caressing intimacy in his voice she was used to. What had happened? She held her face still and tried to keep the whine of disappointment from her voice. "My demands alone, Tyrone, are rather modest. A studio. A place I can eat, sleep, create my designs, come home and curl up with a book and have a friend to dinner. I need nothing elaborate. I'm not as naive about my prospects as you imagine. I simply want artistic and intellectual stimulation, friends, a chance to pursue my career. And peace of mind.''

"I don't know how much peace of mind you can expect to find by moving to the city, Susan. You're used to living in a beautiful and easygoing place. You're a gracious part of that place for many of the summer people who come, and you enjoy each other's company. But I don't know if you'd see . . . quite so much of them if you lived in the city. People do tend to be rather caught up in their little circles.''

He was giving her a warning, that was why he sounded cool, that was why he was not sitting beside her on the rattan couch but standing against the railing, keeping his distance. He did not want her to move to New York; but, why? Surely she had made clear she understood that lending his apartment was a discrete instance and that she in no way expected to stay there, even while looking for a place to live. Tentatively she said, "My

301

work centers on New York. I have rather a lot of acquaintances there. I wasn't expecting to be dependent on anyone in particular.''

"But you have expectations based on being a guest there, a married woman coming up to the city for a day or two, who entertains so beautifully here and whom everyone wants to visit with on their holidays in the country. You see, that gives you a particular position, one you relish and might not finally enjoy relinquishing.''

She had lost status in his eyes, as if Willie's affair had tarnished her. "You think I'm foolish because I didn't see what was going on under my nose.''

"No, my dear, you haven't a suspicious nature, that's one of your charms. I simply feel you're being foolish now, yes, a little silly in how you're overreacting to what, after all, is nothing new. You can't allow a man every freedom for ten years and then be surprised if he still feels he can exercise a little of that freedom, now can you, Susan?'' He beamed at her as if his little précis of her life would turn her mind around.

Sally brought the phone out to him and he embarked on a lengthy call with Los Angeles. She realized she had been effectively dismissed. Celeste did not appear to refill her drink and she was left to listen to an incomprehensible call he was taking with his back to her, as if to create artificial privacy for himself. She took the hint and picked herself up. She paused in front of him and tentatively waved good-bye. He favored her with a big smile, waved but kept on talking.

She felt tremendously disappointed. He didn't understand, he didn't understand at all. He liked the way things were set up just fine. He actually expected her to eat her shame and stay with Willie. Was he right that her summer friends would drop her in New York? A woman of a certain age alone, working for a modestly middle-class living. Would it even be middle class with only her earnings to counter higher expenses? Was that his point? Perhaps she had assumed that Tyrone would assist her in finding a place to live, that he would share his resources with her to some extent. She had supposed that he would welcome her presence in his life in Manhattan, that she would help him there much as she did here. She felt exhausted as she walked home even more slowly than she had come.

She could not relinquish the images of her new life in the city, but she obviously had to win back Tyrone to her side. Had Laurie given him some lurid version of events? Something had caused him to withdraw. But she could get him back. Earlier in the summer they had had that coolness over Willie's bungling of the gallery permits, but it had not lasted. Instead they had ended up closer than ever; instead he had lent his apartment to her. This coldness, too, would thaw. He would come to see how advantageous it would be for him to have her nearby.

Of course! He wanted her nearby in the summer. He had come to depend on her. He found the prospect of summers here without her presence on the pond worrisome, but his anxiety expressed itself in coldness, in being judgmental with her. He was used to her being his interface with local people and feared managing without her. She had to find some way of reassuring him, making him see she could still come. His house was large. She could take over Laurie's boathouse. She could live in the apartment in town over the gallery. There were a hundred solutions. How foolish she had been not to understand that naturally he would think of her decision as it might impact on him. She had given him credit for being a little more mature and together than perhaps any man really had to be. She began to walk more briskly.

However, when she got back to her house, she could scarcely force herself to enter. Obviously Willie had been cooking. He had set the table for two, but his place was used. He had left grilled salmon, rice, a salad on the table for her. At first she thought she would simply ignore the food, but then she realized she had no desire to scrounge a meal for herself. A great deal of figuring and hard planning lay before her. She had resumed swimming after supper, scrupulously exercising to tighten her body in anticipation of the more critical eyes of acquaintances in the city. If Willie wanted to make supper for her at the same time that he cooked for himself, she might as well enjoy the perks of his guilt. It had been long enough building.

FORTY-TWO

Dinah

Dinah stood arms crossed before Willie, who slumped in the sagging center of her old couch with his head in his hands. "Telling *me* how sorry you are isn't useful," she said in a cheery tone of voice intended more to annoy than to soothe. "You have to talk to her, not to me." Dinah had to keep her emotional distance from him in order to keep her physical distance. She had been refusing to go to bed with Willie until he told Susan, and now everything was in smelly pieces.

"She won't talk to me. While you were in Boston Friday she had Mary Lou over to appraise the house. She wants a divorce."

"She's royally pissed off." Dinah paced, a little crazy from being interrupted during her work time. "You should concentrate on getting through to her. Buy her a necklace. Bring home champagne. Seduce her, Willie. There's got to be a way."

"She won't even look at me. Every time I'm in the room with her, I feel guilty. I don't know why. I don't think I did anything wrong. I want to talk to her, but she won't listen."

"Complaining to me is getting you further into the hole." She knew that Willie felt that she was insufficiently sympathetic, but she was angry that he had temporized until Susan found out. Dinah was also annoyed with herself for not insisting more vehemently. Since she had got back from her week with Itzak, she and Willie had been fighting. She had not felt she could march over and confront Susan without doing more damage than good; she had been convinced that Willie had to be truthful. Now they were stuck with the consequences of his avoidance. "Willie, you have to sit down and really talk with each other. You have to figure out what the two of you want."

"I want her back. I want things the way they were before."

"It doesn't look as if either of us can have that. Moreover, it seems to have suited you and me better than it suited Susan." She needed to be practicing. She had a gig in Hartford that required her to perform. She was working on her *Five Vegetables for Chamber Orchestra* which she hadn't played publicly in four years. As she practiced, she rewrote. She had a rule that pieces written in one of her old styles, she left alone, but that anything more or less in her current idiom, she was free to fool around with. The concert was the first Sunday in September, but here she was still reworking the music. The "Vegetables" filled her with delight; the frustration was her own eroded technique. She kept imagining how Itzak would make it sound. She wasn't being paid much, but it was something. She found Willie's misery hard to focus on, with a chamber orchestra playing full tilt in her head. At the same time her indignation was suspect. She was part of the problem. Perhaps since Willie kept delaying, she should have blurted out the truth to Susan. Or abstained from Willie, as she finally had recently.

"Why can't it be the way it was? I was happy. I was working well. Everything felt good."

"To us. Maybe I have to go talk to her. But you need to do some serious thinking." Even as she spoke, she could not imagine Willie making lists of pros and cons and weighing a decision. "You have to figure out, is it more important to you to be with Susan or to live here? She wants to move to New York. You may have to give up even being friends with me to keep her."

"I don't want to move to New York and feel like a failure. What the hell would I do there? I like living where I know everybody. I know what counts locally, the right and wrong of every issue. I feel about water table issues and solid waste and acid rain, about why we have to worry about an accident at the nuclear power plant across the Bay. There's not all that fake one-upmanship. Nobody judges you by the last review you had in *The Times*—if they bothered reviewing you."

"Susan lives for the summer people. Now she wants to live like them."

"Mary Lou discouraged Susan from selling with the addition only begun. Mary Lou said as it stands, it would bring down the value of the property, but if I finish it, it'll raise the value. Maybe Susan will put off a move till I finish. I could take months."

A resolution had formed in her under the suite playing in her head. "I'll go talk to her. I'll straighten things out if I can, and if I can't, I'll at least know I did everything in my power."

Willie sat up as if he would protest, but then he sighed. "Maybe you should. Things couldn't be much worse."

As Dinah marched off toward the new house, he shambled

bent over toward his studio, as if stooping his shoulders could make him less visible to Susan. Why hadn't he told Susan before Susan found out? Why hadn't she forced him to tell Susan? Why had she let things drift so long? At least she had been able to say to Itzak, with whom she had spent Thursday and Friday, that she had put the relationship with Willie on hold until her life was straightened out, and that Susan finally was read into the whole picture. She could promise him some resolution. He had become much more real to her since he had bought the house in Brookline. She felt his presence even on the days when they did not talk on the phone. The better the sex, the easier the communication, the more emotionally entangled she felt, the more she sometimes longed to flee an involvement that frightened her almost as often as it satisfied her.

The week before, she had been offered a position teaching for a semester at U. of California, Santa Cruz, replacing a colleague who had just been in a near-fatal accident. She had to tell them immediately, because school opened in September and they were up a tree. She had promised to call back Monday. Normally she would have declined politely, but she needed the money; after Tanglewood, she had expected a commission or two, but so far, nothing had materialized. She kept just missing grants. The addition had pauperized her.

She was a touch irritable. She had not been working well and she had not been sleeping well, two activities on which her strength and vitality were based. Without work, she felt lost. Without sleep, she was crabby and ill at ease in her body. She slept well in the city, which was topsy-turvy. Here she worried. She felt fussed over everything in her life. California had a certain appeal—it was far from Willie, Itzak, Susan.

As she stopped outside the screen door to the kitchen, where she had cooked hundreds of meals, she felt the bitter drag of nostalgia for their old communication. Yes, Susan was demanding. Yes, Susan wanted to gossip when Dinah wanted to work. Yes, Susan had been emotionally draining. But for years, when Dinah was perplexed, she had Susan to unpack her. She wanted to go to Susan and talk about Itzak, talk about Willie; that was the last thing she could do. It was a huge loss that they should be alienated. She had been able to discuss Itzak a little with Johnny. Johnny understood why Dinah feared being consumed in a relationship with a man she really cared for who was also involved in music, but Johnny, like Jimmy, was Willie's partisan and thought she should stick to him and let Itzak go.

She would have bet her best flute that Susan had watched her cross the yard, but the kitchen was empty. Her tentative rapping on the doorframe brought no response. Boldly she walked in and bellowed, "Susan!" until she heard steps approaching.

"I heard you, of course," Susan said with cold precision, stopping in the doorway. "But I couldn't believe you'd have the gall."

"One of us had better before it all goes down the tubes."

"That's where shit belongs, isn't it?"

"You're shredding your life, Susan. Willie's your husband. You've been together twenty-six years and raised two kids. He did break off with me when you ordered him to, but after all, he wasn't mad at me. He missed me. Are you telling me you never do? I miss you every day."

"I guess that shows who was getting something out of whom." Susan crossed her arms. She wore a bronze and green dress that fell in loose folds from the shoulders. Susan was deeply tanned but looked as tired as Dinah felt. She was not sure if she could really smell the perfume Susan was wearing, or whether her memory was tickling her nostrils with its ghost.

Dinah had a moment's urge to take Susan in her arms and soothe her. "Are you really lost and stuck in your anger? Can't I help you find your way out?"

"I'm not angry as a form of spiritual exercise. I'm tired of being saintly and giving. I'm sick unto death of picking up everyone's lives after them. I'm angry because I've been hurt!"

"Susan, listen. We can come back from this. We can still save our lives together. Nothing irrevocable has yet happened—"

"You're crazy! You've been fucking my husband all summer, and that's nothing to get riled up about? You're kidding me."

"I've been fucking both of you for ten years. Did you think I'd stop loving Willie or Willie would stop caring about me? We were divorced by fiat." As if casually, Dinah took a seat at the table. Sitting face-to-face might discourage dramatics. "I still care for you. That's real."

"You never cared for anybody in your life. You just like to go around wrapped in a blanket of music, and you don't want anyone to bug you."

"I do get terrifically involved in music. But that doesn't

mean I don't care about you and Willie, that I don't worry about you—''

"You're both stifling me. I can't live the way I want to with the two of you hung around my neck.''

"Susan, you're making a gross mistake. We're on your side. We're the ones who are.''

"You two have had things your way, you with your music no one can stand to listen to and him with his cages of starving children no one wants to look at—''

"Oh, you don't understand my music, and that's my fault, is it?'' Dinah was furious. That was the kind of insult the most banal critics put out. "How much time have you spent this summer listening to Bach, to Mozart, to Schöenberg? Do you 'understand' them? Or is it just that you object to music that asks more attention than easy listening?''

"We've been living like peasants, onions and garlic hanging from the rafters, canning tomatoes, making preserves, digging potatoes while life passes by, while the real world goes on.''

"No, you want to hang out at Tyrone's, pretending to be rich. Hoping some diamonds will fall off the table, and you can slip one in your pocket. Over there, you're just a servant without livery, Susan. They'll use you when it's convenient, but they won't love you. They won't consider you their peer.''

"You never could stand for me to have friends you can't overawe.''

"Susan, Susan, you've given yourself leave to blame Willie and me for your life not being what you want. You're bored with designing fabrics. You're facile and it pays decently, but you need something more demanding. You wanted to be a designer. Why not try it, now?''

"I'm sick of you, and you tell me I have a problem. Talk about self-serving!''

It was a certain glitter in Susan's eye that made Dinah realize Susan was enjoying the confrontation, enjoying her anger. Dinah stood. "I can't reach you, so let's forget it. I give up. But I also inform you that I won't be involved with Willie either. That was a stopgap measure to hold on to what we had. So your husband is your husband only. You're alone to work out with him whatever the two of you can, with no help and no hindrance from me. I thank you for not throwing anything.'' She stalked as far as the door, then turned. It felt dreary. She looked Susan in the eyes, her hand on the door handle. Even at this last moment, a hint of softness would stay her.

Susan snorted a fake laugh. "Don't you think it's a little late for that resolution, staying out of Willie's bed?"

"No. Anytime we part like this is too soon. I still love you. You've never been able to be close to another woman the way you were with me. Maybe you can only open up with a woman if she's your lover and you trust her with your body." She wondered if she embraced Susan, if Susan would soften.

"That's typical of your complete egotism. I have no trouble whatsoever making friends. I've been getting quite close to Candida this summer."

"Close? You don't know the second thing about each other." She was tempted to tell Susan that she probably knew more than Susan did about Candida, including who she was having an affair with, but it occurred to her she couldn't be sure Susan wouldn't repeat that to Candida. She had no legal right to walk across the MacIvors' land, simply the habit of years of trespassing. "Look, standing here trading insults is too sad. Are you telling me you have no regrets?"

"Regrets! I have thousands. All the years I've wasted here. All the years burned up freezing beans and picking blackberries and smoking salmon. My God, I can live in a place where you can walk to the store and buy anything in the world. The two of you are so self-satisfied and so boring, finally!"

"Ah, Susan. What can I say? Have a nice life. Good-bye."

As Dinah trudged across the yard, dodging the piles of lumber, Willie motioned to her from the door of his studio. She shook her head violently and kept walking, her vision wavering with tears. If she could be transported back a year, two years, however many years it would take to predate Susan's long anger, could she conduct herself enough differently to keep Susan? It was pointless to ask. Nobody was offering a ticket into the past. It was blown, it was gone, it was past. She had to deal with her own problems. She snuffled her tears back.

She had to decide about Itzak and her fear and her desire. It seemed to her as she plodded through the hot heavy afternoon blurred by the saltwater prisms of her lashes, that she could easily turn and live as a celibate hermit. Kick Jimmy out to move in with Laurie. Cut her losses on the addition. Rip out her phone. Let the mail molder at the post office. Hole up and write music and the hell with the pesky lot of them. The hell with everybody.

309

Maybe she'd take that job in California for five months. Jimmy could rent her house. She'd take the cats along; that would be part of her conditions for filling in on a month's notice. The truth was, teaching turned her on in prospect; in reality, she did it well but hated it. It was the opposite of composing, talking about what was not the province of words, which is why she had never gone the academic route, making neat and orderly what was mysterious. But what the hell, for five months, wouldn't it be worth it to fly off and leave her life untenanted, abandoned? Be paid for escaping the mess she had made. She would brood on it, seriously. Even the consideration of that job was proof her life had irrevocably changed its course.

FORTY-THREE

Laurie

Laurie said, "But, Daddy, you don't understand. Bob Sampson is gay. Going out with him has no point."

"How dreary. No, I didn't know." Tyrone grimaced, sitting on the rail that ran along the deck. Candida was lying out on the raft, at least two hundred yards offshore and well out of earshot, but they spoke softly anyhow.

"Besides, you know I'm practically living with Jimmy."

"The summer's almost over, my dear. I'm proud of you, do you know that?"

She was startled, for she had been bracing herself for a lecture on how foolish her attachment to Jimmy was. "Why, Daddy?"

"Because of the recovery you've made. You were dealt a dreadful accident, one that was scandalous, embarrassing, one that would have been difficult for a woman of twice your age and four times your experience to handle gracefully. You've made the most of this time out of the city. I thought you would need a year, two years, to recover your poise and your momentum."

"Jimmy has really helped. He's given me a great deal of confidence."

"Confidence is not a gift anyone can give you, Laurie. People can aid you in its development or interfere, but only you yourself

310

can make it happen. I'm sure you'll always be grateful to him for being there during this period, but the strength is yours."

His finally talking about Jimmy with her and his praise of her confidence made her dare to take a personal tone with him also. "Daddy, isn't your relationship with Candida a little unusual for you, also? There you are dodging through the woods to see her. Meeting her on the raft."

"I haven't been as subtle about it as I thought, have I?" He smiled and took her arm, steering her inside through the French doors. "It's addictive, but I'm aware it's a bad risk. As I said, the summer is drawing to a close and the fall provides a natural quietus to many activities."

Nonetheless at dusk she saw him swimming out to the raft. Candida and he were both excellent swimmers. Alec was not. The little pavilion on the raft with the air mattress inside offered privacy for them to meet when Alec was around and the MacIvor house was off bounds. The raft was a great place to make love, floating on the bosom of the pond in the soft warm night. She and Jimmy had used it a couple of times before she had realized Tyrone had the same idea. Tyrone had been in New York most of the week and was off to Boston tomorrow, so she excused his eagerness to see Candida in spite of Alec's presence. August was Alec's vacation, so he was always here.

The next day Jimmy came over early at three, very upset. "This guy named Sampson came by today while Willie and I were working on the stairs and told us we should finish them and then stop. He said he's buying the building and he's going to turn it into condos. What about your gallery?"

"Jimmy, he's crazy. I haven't changed my mind. I suppose Daddy talked to him at some point when he was feeling discouraged about permits, but he's off the wall, absolutely."

"Let's go see Tyrone right now."

"Daddy's in Boston on business. He won't be back until late tonight. I'll catch him in the morning. I'll wake early and have breakfast with him."

Jimmy was truly anxious. He wasn't interested in supper or in making love, but went back to Dinah's at nine. She sat up watching a stupid baseball game that went into extra innings between two random teams. The Mets were her team. This was the Blue Jays playing the Red Sox. She watched because she was disappointed in the evening, annoyed with Jimmy, bored. She did not enjoy sitting in the boathouse that suddenly felt tiny, but she could not think of anyplace to go. She and Jimmy had seen all the movies. Tyrone always said the locals had nothing to do in the winter but drink. She could not remember how she had spent the previous winter. She had been too numb to care. Probably she had been totally engaged trying to figure out whether to fall in love with Jimmy. In the morning she'd talk to Tyrone. Of course he hadn't sold her gallery.

At breakfast he said, "I was waiting until the negotiations were settled in New York. I told you I'm proud of you. I mean to show it. You don't need a dry run operating a summer gallery in a resort. I'm bringing you into a new gallery on Prince Street. The space is excellent. Your partner will be Sean Corrigan. . . ." Tyrone paused, smiling.

"Sean Corrigan! He'd never agree!"

"He already has."

"Daddy! I can't believe it. He's really willing?"

"Eager, my dear. You have a shot at establishing an important gallery for breaking artists. He has excellent contacts, but you'll have to ride herd on him financially. You'll be the real manager, the business side, the one ultimately in charge. You'll be the partner with the lion's share, so you can learn to roar, softly but whenever appropriate. . . . Does that please my brave daughter?"

Sean Corrigan was a youngish art critic with a big reputation. He was extremely good looking, gay of course but friendly enough to women and someone she absolutely admired, although when she had met him at Manning Stanwyck's gallery, he had paid her no attention. Not only was he an arbiter of taste, but he was someone people would kill to be seen with. It was unbelievable. "Are you sure he'll do it? Really, that he'll share it with me?"

"No question." Tyrone handed her a sheet of computer runoff. "Here's his address, his public and his private numbers. He's expecting you to call him, so summon your nerve and catch him this week. I thought we might have him up Labor Day weekend."

"Daddy, what about the gallery in town?"

"I can unload it at a tidy profit, which I mean to pump right into your Prince Street gallery. You'll make that into a place people want to be seen, where people fight for invitations to openings. Everything is to be done correctly, from the begin-

312

ning. That's what I've promised Sean, and that's what I'm promising you."

"Mr. Sampson is buying the house in town?"

"For a hundred more than I've put into it. He thinks he can clear twice that."

She could see herself, wearing one of those new asymmetrical slit sheaths, presiding at Sean's side over a perfectly catered opening not even worrying if *The Times* would cover it, because of course they would. Sean was a man who conferred status simply by his presence. It was an incredible coup. At the same time she was frightened. Would she be good enough? Would she know enough to keep up her side? "Daddy, this must be horrendously expensive."

"It's an investment, my dear. You'll make sure it's a sound one. I have faith in you."

Laurie felt as if she were going to cry, but she did not, as that would have distressed him; and she wanted only to please him. She felt humble and proud at the same time, humble before her father who sought to find what was best for her and counted no cost exorbitant. Nobody understood him the way she did, because nobody else knew how kind and generous he could be. What incredible faith he had in her to be sure she could carry off such a grand enterprise.

She was rushing to the boathouse bubbling over to tell Jimmy, when she realized that he was not exactly going to rejoice in her news. So, he'd build the condos for the new owner, what did that matter? She imagined taking him to New York with her. What would he do in New York? Get a job as a carpenter? Well, he could work in the gallery too. After all, he had run a restaurant in Seattle. One that had failed. But that hadn't been his fault. The bookkeeper had been embezzling money. Would he mind working under her? As the kind of assistant of all work she had been in her last New York job. Well, she had done it. Why shouldn't he?

Still, she had the sense that she was going to have to conceal her joy, and that was irritating. She would have liked to celebrate, but she did not think that Jimmy was going to want to celebrate this news with her. She would have to play it softly, give him the news in stages, over time.

Jimmy was extremely upset and called Willie. The two of them talked forever, as if they hadn't spent the day together. The only supper she got was fried clams and that not until nine. If

313

Susan hadn't been Jimmy's mother and hadn't been weird lately, Laurie would have run over to tell her. She felt annoyed with Susan for making such a fuss and tearing up everything. It rendered Susan useless. That was a nuisance, because ever since she could remember, she had always been able to count on Susan when she was happy as well as when she was unhappy. Susan would have given a party for her, made an occasion. Now Laurie had this great news, something splendid and special, and with her own boyfriend, she had to conceal the best part.

She ended up confiding in Candida. After all, Candida was closer to Laurie in age than she was to Tyrone. She was eager to please. Grasping that Laurie was thrilled about the prospect of her own New York gallery with a man whom Candida had never heard of but quickly understood she should have, Candida offered to take Laurie out to lunch in Provincetown.

They ate outside at a table under an umbrella, watching the yachts and fishing boats enter and leave the harbor, drinking wine at one, which felt almost decadent. They both ate chef's salads. The Chardonnay made them quickly giddy. "I'm so unhappy with Alec," Candida said. "I'm bored out of my mind. All he talks about is urinary tract problems and the politics of the hospital. He gets narrower and narrower."

"Why don't you leave him?"

"I think about it."

"Well, why don't you?" Laurie felt calm and superior, in control of her life. She wanted to help Candida, who was six years older, but impulsive, confused. "After all, you don't have children."

"He didn't want to at first. Not till he was set up. Now we're having so many problems, I don't want to. I'd feel stuck."

"If you left him, how would you manage to live?"

Candida looked shocked. "Of course I'd have a settlement. And besides, I have a trust fund. I'm not dependent on Alec. Really! How could you think I'd be so mercenary as to stay with him because of money?"

"Of course not. I really do understand your hesitation. I was devastated when Tom killed himself, I mean by accident, if it was by accident. And we hadn't been getting along at all. It was ghastly. Yet I hadn't thought of leaving him. It's hard to give it all up even when you're unhappy."

"Exactly," Candida said, clasping her hands before her. "Before I met your father, I didn't know how nice a man could be. He's so different from other men, so much deeper and more cultured.''

"The older I get, the more I appreciate him," Laurie said, delighted to find someone to discuss Tyrone with. Maybe Tyrone would marry Candida. She would rather like that. Candida was not as sophisticated as Glenda or Janette, both of whom had made her feel rather the ugly duckling. Candida was gorgeous, but she lacked polish. She dressed a bit like a tart. Laurie doubted if Candida knew how to entertain properly, but she could teach Candida and so could Sally. Candida would not be half bad as a wife for Tyrone.

"Jimmy seems very sweet," Candida said. "He did a beautiful job on your cottage.''

"He's a darling. Did you know I practically grew up with him? I've known him since I was six.''

"Oh, he's your childhood sweetheart," Candida said, as if that explained everything. "That's sweet. I never had a childhood sweetheart. I started dating when I was in junior high, but I wouldn't care to face one of those beef-brained jocks again.''

Jimmy lay limply on her couch as if he had no more strength. "Sure, the permits will be easier for condos, because there's enough parking in the yard for six cars. It was a rooming house before.''

"But what does it matter which you're building?''

"Sampson won't use us. He likes Techmasters. They're fast and sloppy and cheaper than we are. Because they cut all the legal corners and whatever illegal ones they can hide.''

"Darling, I'm sorry too. I was looking forward to the gallery there. But the permits didn't come through, and Tyrone couldn't carry it any longer. You have to understand.''

"Why aren't you upset about losing your gallery? What are you going to do for work now?''

"But I'll have a gallery. He promised me that. If I don't have it in that old house, it will be somewhere else.''

"You're awfully trusting for someone who just had the rug pulled out from under you.''

"Tyrone is somebody you can trust, Jimmy. I will have a gallery, if not in one place, then someplace else. I know I'll have one by next summer, as he promised." Carefully she did not say where. She was keeping quiet about New York until a better moment.

"I've got to get Willie and finish up the addition on the old house so I'm free to take another job. Damn it." He sat up scowling. "I was using the gallery renovation to move into building. Now I'll be back to having to work for somebody else. Nailbanging. It's slowing down my plans."

She wanted to tell him that he wouldn't be doing that long because they'd both be going to New York, but she did not want to make promises until she had talked with Sean Corrigan and knew that he was willing. She still couldn't believe her luck. She had to call him, but she was fearful. She had been a tweeny at Manning Stanwyck's gallery when she had met Sean. It felt presumptuous to call him, particularly on his private line, as if she were pretending to be someone important, but she could not let Tyrone down. He had told her to be brave, and she must be.

While Jimmy was working on Dinah's addition, she did call Sean and left a message on his answering machine. She tried again two hours later. Then she had to dress. She was having supper with Tyrone and his guests.

As they were sitting down to the cold lobster bisque, Tyrone said to the table in general that Sean had called him just before, and he would be spending Friday of Labor Day weekend with them. After that he would be staying with friends who had a house in Provincetown. She was so excited she lost the flow of dinner table conversation. Tyrone had to nudge her under the table to bring her back. It was really happening. He had done this for her. She could hardly pay attention to anybody, with her head simmering. She could see herself walking into Elaine's with Sean, into clubs so of the moment she had no idea what they were called, parties she had not only never been invited to, but so far out of her ken as never even to have heard about. She had to start calling her New York friends and letting them know she was coming back. Returning victorious. She would throw a party to demonstrate her new status. But where? At Tyrone's? That was always possible, but still, she needed an apartment.

"Daddy, I need a place to live."

"Of course. I already have Sally working on that."

Sally said to her softly, "I'm making calls. Saturday I'll fly down and look things over. When I find some possibilities, you may want to pop in to check them."

In eleven days she would meet Sean as her houseguest. She had to have her hair cut at once. Was there anyone here who

316

could do it? Should she go into Boston? Perhaps it would be safer to get it done in New York, if Rafael wasn't on vacation. It was hard to sit here chattering with so much to do.

FORTY-FOUR

Susan

Susan felt remote from her recent life, removed enough to see it whole and tiny in the distance, spread out behind her as she turned for a final survey. She could even afford to remember how much fun it had been in the early years with Dinah. Dinah had been crazy about her, a wonderful lover who adored her body just as it was, passionate through thick and thin. Susan smiled, approving that she was able to joke. She was going through her cupboards and closets, ruthlessly discarding for the local thrift shop clothes that were out of style, shabby, tiresome, too country. That blue Indian shift belonged to her first year with Dinah, when she had actually been persuaded to play in a group with her, beating on a tambourine and prancing around the little stage of the local tavern.

Even supper had turned from chore into event. Willie and Dinah egged each other on in foraging, seeing what they could turn up in the woods, shell fishing, what they could barter for. Willie had wakened up too, from a marriage that had grown stale. Having another woman involved with Willie made him exciting to Susan, proving there was something to him. It justified her attachment. No doubt adding Dinah to the marriage had postponed its demise, but to what end? Susan should have left years before and returned to New York. She would never wear this corduroy jumper there. Out with it!

Willie and she had left at a time half the couples they knew were moving out, some to the West Coast, to Vermont or Maine, to Boston, to upstate New York. Rents had surged, and as the drug scene shifted from soft drugs to the hard expensive habits, the street scene grew nastier and more violent. People were beginning to talk about health and fitness, clean air, fresh food. When their building changed owners and services were cut to force the rent-controlled tenants out, they joined the exodus from

Manhattan without hesitation. They moved to the Cape where they had shared a house during August with another couple. It was a place they knew, they thought. In that era, prices had not taken off. They bought the two houses side by side—the old house to provide income as a rental unit—for a total of sixty thousand. Both had been in dreadful shape. Besides raccoons, no one had been living in the old house, which lacked central heating and required a new well. For the last thirty years, the new house had belonged to a mad old lady who kept chickens inside. To get rid of the smell, Willie had to rip up the kitchen floor.

Odors clung to the old wood anyhow. Sometimes sitting at her vanity she thought she could still smell the bottle of Opium that had been broken in a fight with Dinah two years before. The day was unseasonably cool, making it easy to work upstairs. The sky had clouded over. The air, palpably dank, smelled of the sea. Here was a prom dress she had made Siobhan in high school, which Siobhan had never worn, refusing to go to her own prom, spending the night getting puking drunk with a girlfriend. Would Siobhan have grown up less weird in the city? Frankly she doubted it. Out with the children's castoffs. She felt distant, let down by both her children.

She thought of Willie and herself as a couple picked up like paper on the wind of the zeitgeist and dumped where its energy faded. Here they had washed up and here they had stayed. Similarly, just after the height of the women's movement, she had become involved with Dinah when half the women she knew had already tried out affairs with other women. Only she had taken ten years to figure out she had made a mistake. Out with the long black dress with the patchwork top in which she had gone out with her two companions for hundreds of gossipy suppers. She had enjoyed the scandal for a long time, childishly no doubt. Out with that absurd purple pantsuit she had thought very au courant some forgettable winter.

Out with all her long underwear. Nobody wore long underwear in New York. Buildings were extravagantly heated, so women wore the ghost of lace, wisps of satin and silk. She had to break through to Tyrone. He was acting frightened of her. She wondered what ghastly exaggeration he had heard about her argument with Siobhan and Willie. He must have been shocked by what would sound like a complete loss of control. She had to allay his nervousness, set him at ease with her, for she needed

318

his help to move to New York. It had been a silly mistake to have brought it up quickly, bluntly. She should have let him suggest it himself, for it followed logically from her situation, and had she allowed him to take the lead, surely he must have stumbled upon it as a solution. Her mistake had been presenting him with her plans as projects, as demands. Men hated that sort of approach. They liked to feel in control. That was less true of Willie than most, and perhaps her technique had grown rusty. With Willie it was better to ask for what you wanted, as loudly as possible, in order to get his attention. She could remember when she had thought his equanimity a virtue, for her own father had a temper she and her mother tiptoed around. "Let sleeping dogs lie," Susan's mother was always warning her. If she could enlist Tyrone's help, she could make her move.

She must get her relationship with Tyrone back on course, smooth his fears away, reestablish the social connection, quickly before Labor Day took him back to the city. She had to work fast, for it was late August. She was amused how abruptly Tyrone had reacted to the news she was leaving Willie, by stopping work on the gallery. All along, he must have been throwing work Willie's way out of kindness to her. Laurie did not seem disturbed. Laurie believed that Tyrone would keep his promise of a gallery; Susan thought that Laurie's confidence was surely not misplaced.

Willie too wasn't as bothered as she would have expected. She said to him, "Now you can deal with that stupid mess in the yard and we can get the place cleaned up to show." His priorities were different, as he demonstrated, not by arguing with her, but by going ahead and doing just as he pleased, as he had all the years of their marriage. He was making a new cage of suppliants waving long gawky arms.

Every afternoon instead of the studio, he was working on Dinah's addition with Jimmy. She complained to Jimmy, who defended their actions. "Dad has to help me. I can't take on another job till it's done, and I need one. It's just finish work. Let Dad alone to help me polish it off."

She argued, but neither wanted to help her sell the place. Willie imagined if he dragged his feet, she would forget everything and life would stagnate on. Willie started on her whenever he caught her in the kitchen: "Susan, let's go pick rum cherries and make cordial." "The bluefish are biting in the harbor, think I should try my luck from Fergie's boat?" "It looks like the beach plums are ripening early this year. We oughtn't to let the tourists get them all.''

Enticing her with his homely little tasks, as if she were not sick to death of cobbling a life out of beach plum jam and smoked bluefish, how quaint, how cottagey, how dull. Let him play with Dinah, who had disappeared again. Willie was excited because some French dealer who had seen one of his pieces had invited him to submit slides for an exposition in Paris featuring work of social significance. That was Willie. Socially naive and stuck in 1973. It would cost three hundred dollars to ship a piece, and he wouldn't make a cent. He kept bringing her these little pieces of news, these picayune tasks, as if he were Bogey catching chipmunks and bringing them partially chewed to lay at her feet. She saw herself taxiing off to openings, shopping smart boutiques, breaking into designing, there in the hot heart of fashion.

She was winnowing her possessions, finding little enough to save. She would end up with perhaps three suitcases of clothing worth carrying into her new life. Four times that amount would be dumped at the thrift shop to disperse among the matrons and teenagers of the village. If she still lived here, she would be amused next winter to see her old dresses in the grocery store and at the movies. Sometimes she still picked out items she had discarded five years before turning up at a party or an art fair. This was a backwater in which useful or semiuseful items might bob for a decade round and round. She would be gone.

In midafternoon Candida dropped by. ''Alec is rather a bore when he's around twenty-four hours a day. I had to get out, so I thought I'd steal away to have coffee with you. Your house always feels so cozy and friendly. I think you have the sweetest kitchen I've ever seen. It's like something out of a painting.'' She waved toward the dried red peppers hanging from the beam. Actually they were two years old and dusty, since Dinah was the one who cooked hot dishes.

Susan smiled and let it pass. Candida was a darling, but she did not live in New York and thus could not help Susan find an apartment or additional work. ''Is Tyrone hip deep in company? I haven't seen him all week.''

''No company this week. He went off to New York for three days. Now he's back and caught up in some complicated investment. He's putting a lot of cash into it at the outset, whatever it is. He says that's one reason he had to give up on the gallery in town.''

Everybody kept offering her explanations, as if she cared, as if she wouldn't rather have Willie free to clear up the mess in the yard. "I must ask him what he's doing." Actually she would never press Tyrone about business, as he preferred to talk about personal matters with her. But Susan did not like Candida to have the impression that she knew more about Tyrone than Susan did.

"Alec and I are really getting in each other's hair. We fight about the stupidest things, who didn't put the milk back in the refrigerator and who left the wet towel on the coffee table. And who's responsible that we spend so much and save so little. It just goes on and on!"

"If you're not happy with him, why don't you leave him?" Susan asked. Candida was sweet but wishy-washy. Unable to commit to action. "It's your best years that you're wasting, and no one will give them back to you."

"That's true, isn't it?" Candida seemed struck by that remark. She nodded, nodded again. "Nobody will give them back. Oh my!"

Susan felt crisply decisive. After Candida left, she hurried upstairs to resume her sorting. She was discarding hunks of her past, folding them cursorily and stowing them in shopping bags. One of her new habits was to stay out of the kitchen altogether while Willie cooked supper. He then ate, leaving her half the meal. She did not dine at six-thirty with Willie, but waited till after her seven o'clock swim and sat down to supper at the civilized hour of eight. I may still be *in* the country, Susan told her reflection, trying on a green tunic and discarding it, but I am no longer *of* the country. She must change her hair, lighten it, have it shortened. Get it done by someone versed in current styles. Betty Gore's hair was always impeccable.

By seven she had every shopping bag in the house jammed full and was bored with the game of throwaway. It was a mild evening, still damp but no colder than the day had been. She hesitated, wandering to the gable window. The woods, the shores were dark, but the pond was still dull silver. It wasn't prime swimming weather. All the way down the pond in the twilight she saw someone on the deck outside the big house. Through her binoculars she watched Tyrone dive in. Good. She swam every evening. Lately she had noticed him paddling around in the evenings also, although he came only as far as the raft anchored near his end of the pond. She would go all the way to the raft tonight and join him. It would be a relaxed intimate setting. She would say not a word about her plans but draw him out, get him to discuss himself. Her skills with men were blunted after years with Willie. Her edges had worn dull, but she felt alert, primed. She would charm him back. She desperately needed his help.

She changed into her suit and ran barefoot to the pond, sliding gently into the water and wading out, kicking off and settling into a steady pull. She had not managed to go as far as the raft all summer, but generally turned back when she grew level with a large oak on the right bank that marked the boundary of the MacIvors' land, but she did not doubt her ability to reach the raft. After all, she could haul out and rest there. She did a side stroke, keeping her head up so that her hair would not get soaked. In previous years she knew she had swum as far as the raft, she remembered doing it.

It was a long distance for her, but she pushed herself along steadily, fixing her mind on her goal. She would not mention Willie. She would not bring up New York. She would open with Laurie's situation. Since Laurie had been almost a daughter to her, she had the right to worry aloud about her, perhaps discuss what he might be planning to acquire for a gallery now that he had given up on the old Victorian in town. She had something to add there. Mary Lou had told her about a piece of property on Commercial Street, suitable for a shop or a gallery and coming on the market in September. With that parcel, there would be no problem with permits. She would once again demonstrate her usefulness, and then they would move on from there. Her legs felt heavy, her arms ached. Could it be much farther?

She liked to swim quietly, gently, not splashing or beating the water unnecessarily. She never did the crawl, for it was a messy stroke. She liked the ladylike side stroke, with its feeling of gliding, kicking gently underwater as if she were a dancer. If it was not the fastest or the most efficient stroke, she thought it by far the least unpleasant. The pond spread around her, the water thick and cool as mercury, heavy tonight and resistant. It seemed to take forever to reach the point where she usually turned, and then she must swim on.

Yet she was still enjoying the feeling of pressing on with her life, moving decisively through the problems, the decisions, the changes that resisted her as the water of the pond resisted, and yet she crept steadily, gracefully onward. She felt in full possession of herself. She could almost pity Tyrone, because she was going to get round him, but what she proposed to manipulate him toward was as good for him as for her. Her conscience was clear and cool. He had her pigeonholed, his country friend, Willie's wife, but she was beginning a campaign to work her way out of that limiting category in his life. The special intimacy between them only required being reknit, extended, till it suffused both their lives in the city as well as here. She had to make clear that she had never expected the relationship between Laurie and Jimmy to last; that she maintained a crisp laissez-faire attitude toward that unlikely bonding. Tyrone could make her new life easy for her with a few words to subordinates, to business associates.

Finally she made out the dim shape of the raft before her. It was bobbing. Perhaps the wind had come up. Little wavelets rippled out from it to slap her face. She grabbed the edge, resting. She was exhausted. Her heart stumbled painfully. She thought to call to him to pull her up, but did not at first see him. She feared he had already swum back to his deck. Damn! It would not make sense to rest here, then swim on to his dock. It would be just too weird to drag herself out of the pond exhausted and stagger into his livingroom in her wet bathing suit. She would have to abandon her plan until tomorrow. Then she saw his back. He was under the canopy that covered half the raft, protection against sun and wind. He was lying facedown on the air mattress making a sort of animal noise. For a moment she thought he was being sick. Grunting into the mattress. She called, "Tyrone?" She pulled herself up with a great heave onto the raft and lay there panting. "Tyrone?" she gasped between breaths.

Even as she spoke and his head whipped around and another face appeared from under him, turning toward her, she realized he was on top of someone, a woman, he was fucking someone here. She froze. She could not move. The woman screamed and the two bodies broke apart flailing wildly while the raft dipped and sloshed on the water.

"Oh my God," the woman said. Susan recognized Candida's voice.

He extricated himself and hopped up, covering himself with a towel. "It's you again! You're a pest, you know that?"

"Tyrone! I'm sorry. I'm so sorry!" she said, wringing her hands.

"Are you spying on me? You must be crazy!"

Candida was trying to pull on her wet bathing suit, yanking on it. Susan heard something rip.

"I didn't know!" Susan began to cry. She was hideously embarrassed and all she could think to do was to slide off the raft at once into the water. She forgot to start swimming. Her hands lay limp at her sides. She fell into the water. She was so startled that she sank over her head and down, down, staring into darkness, her feet brushing weeds, before she realized she was in the water and was headed for the bottom. She kicked her way to the surface and came up again sputtering just beside the raft. "Tyrone," she said again, "I'm sorry. I'm sorry. I didn't know."

Alec was calling from shore, "Candida? Candida! Is that you? Are you all right? Candida!"

Candida was still trying to pull on her bathing suit. It had ripped in front from her tugging.

"Shit!" Tyrone said. Susan heard a great splash that must be him diving off. As she swam aimlessly, frantically away, she could hear behind her much churning of the water. She assumed Candida was swimming toward her house and Tyrone toward his. No one came near her. She was exhausted and let herself rest for a moment, rocking idly. Then she stroked slowly back toward the far end. It was dark now. Tears filled her eyes, blinding her in the dimness. How could he be fucking Candida? He had recognized Susan and he had been furious. Nasty. He hated her. He called her a pest, and he would never forgive her. It was a mess, it was a mess, it was all a mess. Everything was spoiled. Everything was in ruins. The tears stopped up her nose till she had to gasp for breath through her mouth. It all felt disgusting.

She was spent. Her arms and legs were weary pushing against the water. Even her blood felt cold. Her thighs were pulling her down. Her flesh had soaked up water and grown heavy. She was tired trying to make her life work right. Everybody was betraying her, everybody. She kept seeing Tyrone grinding away on Candida, his bare ass white and ridiculous and bony, pumping up and down mechanically. She could not stop hearing him making those ugly noises that sounded like vomiting, those grunting pig noises. Even Willie never sounded like that. There he was grinding away on a woman barely older than Laurie. Of course, he was always marrying fair haired women around thirty, one after another, like a dog with only one trick. He was banal, foolish. Having an affair with Candida right in the middle of her pond. He had ruined and vulgarized everything. There was nothing special between Tyrone and herself. Nothing special at all. He was about to marry another young wife and disappear into infatuation for several years, and she could rot here for all he would care. He would not help her out of her dead life.

How could he bring himself down to that level? How could he make such an idiot of himself? How could he turn out to be so boring? Bouncing away. She kept seeing him and it hurt. Why could he never turn and look at her, why could he never turn and want her? Why all these silly women one after the other? The first wife, who had become a drunk; the second, who had been a shrew; the third, who had been a spendthrift and unfaithful. Now vapid Candida who was going to bring a scandal down on his head.

He had called her a pest when she had been going to meet him to make things better between them, and now it was all ruined. He had accused her of following him. Of spying on him. He must have seen her use the binoculars through her bedroom window. He knew she watched him and he despised her. She had destroyed everything when she was only trying to get back what had been good, and now even the past was changed and sickened.

She stopped fighting the water. She stopped pushing on it with her heavy exhausted aching arms and legs. It let her in like a goose down comforter. She was angry and hurt and she could not see in the darkness which way to go. She could not even tell where her shore was. She felt blocked on all sides, suffocated. The water was splashing into her mouth. She was too tired to keep her head above water. She was too tired to fight the water. She was too tired. The water came round her soft and comforting and warmer than the cold dank air. She had to lie down, let go and lie down and down. She would show them. She would make them all sorry for what they had done to her. She would show Dinah and Willie and Siobhan and Jimmy and Tyrone how vile they had been. She was quitting. The mess of living was theirs to clean up. She was going to lie down where it was warm and dark, she was going to drift slowly deep down into sleep and forget all of them.

FORTY-FIVE

Dinah

"Pass the fusilli," Tanya said.

Seeing Itzak's face, Dinah laughed. "She has a great technical vocabulary for pasta and for music, considering she's only six in October."

"I'm six already," Giselle's daughter Eileen said importantly. "I was six August seventeenth."

"Even if you're older than me, it's no good having a birthday in August," Tanya said. "You have to be at Tanglewood and not home, so you don't get to have a real party."

In some ways being there with Itzak interfered with Dinah's wooing of Tanya, her favorite, but she was interested and nervous also to see how he was with the kids. There was no way she could judge his potential as a father by watching him eat Nita's fusilli, she realized, but studied him nonetheless. It was important to her that he fit in with Nita and Tanya; maybe she and Nita should have paid attention to their dislike of each other's husbands the last time around.

"This is one of the best ways to eat zucchini ever," Itzak said. "Dinah is a volcano of zucchini. She appears out of the country every time with a backseat full. She arrives with one dress and forty zukes."

"You get no sympathy from me. The more she brings me, the better I like it. But she never brings me enough tomatoes. Ever notice she's stingy with her tomatoes?" Nita wrinkled her nose at Dinah.

The first time she had brought Itzak over to the house in Newton, everybody had been stiff and proper, but by now they were at ease. They ate too much, drank too much wine and after the girls were in bed, got started reminiscing about Juilliard, which was boring for Giselle but enthralling for the rest of them. Here Dinah was, reliving her entrance audition, here Itzak was with sweat breaking out on his forehead as he described switching teachers in his second year. Then his first teacher, whom they all knew, actually struck him in the face and burst into tears of outraged betrayal.

Both Nita and Giselle said they were jealous of Dinah, because Itzak was bringing her to Scotland in early September to join him there. She would overlap with his time at the Edinburgh festival by a couple of days and then they would have a week of vacation before she came back and he set about a series of concerts in England.

"Aw come on," Dinah said. "It'll rain the whole time."

"Better to get wet in Scotland than broil in Boston," Nita said. "Maybe I'll go out to your house that weekend. Tanya would love it."

"So would the cats. Do it."

Even on the way home in the car, they were still reminiscing. When she met someone else from Chicago, they had a few routines they might go through together, but if they did not come from the same neighborhood, that was the end. But with flute players who had gone through Juilliard, a year of remembering aloud would not touch the labor, the drama, the passion. Relationships with teachers were more intense than those with lovers, and never had she known before and never would she know again the fierce direct competition, open, raw, unmitigated by politeness or pretense. Of course Mark or Susan or Willie could not share such reminiscing, any more than they would have enjoyed Nita's sly anecdotes about the BSO or Itzak's gossip about other orchestras, other conductors. Itzak, Dinah, Nita and Giselle each made a living quite differently, yet all in the same extended world.

"It was a nice evening," he said as they climbed the steps of the Brookline house. As they opened the door, Figaro and Tosca were sitting on the stairway at human eye level, where they could glare together at the humans who had abandoned them. "You were relaxed. I like an evening when I figure you're doing something else besides worrying if you should be with me."

"Itzak, have I been that bad? I fuss about commitments."

He always checked his answering machine when he came in. He sat on the couch to listen and she curled on his lap. A call from Aspen, worrying about next summer already. Most concert arrangements were made through his agent, but a few places called him directly, either because they knew him or because they were angling for something special. Then Jimmy's voice came on. "Dinah, something may be wrong with Mother. We don't know. It's nine-thirty and I'm at the new house."

She hit the button, backtracked and listened again. "Something wrong? What does that mean?"

"Call and find out."

"It's midnight. Jimmy and Willie get up early." She frowned. "I'll call my house." All she got was her own answering machine. She left a message for Jimmy, feeling silly. She was not about to call Susan in the middle of the night to ask her if she were feeling ill. She would call in the morning. Something wrong. Had Susan flipped out? She had been tense enough, violent with Siobhan and Willie. She remembered their burns.

At eight she called first her own house, then the new house. Susan and Willie's line was busy. Itzak was reading her a review from the *Globe* with sarcastic comments about the critic's ear and musicology, when the phone rang. Itzak always let the machine answer, but as soon as she heard Jimmy's voice, she picked it up.

"I've been trying to reach you since I got your message," she began apologetically.

He interrupted her, speaking in a flat tone. "Mother's dead. She drowned in the pond last night. They just pulled the body out."

"What?" she barked out, but she had heard and did not let Jimmy finish his repetition. "She can't be drowned! She can't be!"

"The pond's big and deep enough," Jimmy said. "You know she was swimming every evening. It was dark. We can talk about it when you get here."

"Is there something you're not telling me?"

"When are you coming?"

"Hold on." She turned to Itzak, briefing him. "I have to go."

"Of course. We'll both go. I have appointments to cancel and I'll throw some things in a bag."

"Jimmy," she said into the phone and then a wall fell on her. She dropped the phone and went down on her knees, moaning. Itzak picked up the phone and spoke into it. She got up and grabbed the phone from him. "Jimmy, she can't be dead. What do you mean she's dead?"

"I have to try Johnny again. See you in a couple of hours."

She was slashed open. Susan. Never to talk to her again,

never even to see her across the yard. Her anger had dried like blood all over her face. Anger was a luxury she had indulged in, a vice, and now Susan was gone. They would never make peace. There was no tomorrow for them in which to say the soft words, to give the small presents of attention and solicitude, to touch and bless. Her hands opened and closed helplessly in her lap.

She had abandoned the hope that Susan and she would be lovers again, that they would twine their lives together, that their days would be warp and woof of the same rug. But as long as they were neighbors, she had assumed they would be friends again. They would share meals and stories and seasons. It could not end in silence, in raw estrangement, in emotions cut open and exposed like metal wires in an electric cord sliced through. All summer long, Susan had swum every evening a fixed distance and back. She could see Susan swimming into the darkness away from them, in anger and spite away.

"I loved her," she said to Itzak, who was kneeling beside her. "I loved her! How could she die?"

"You had already lost her, Dinah. She was already dead to you."

"There was always a chance to be friends again, to sit in the kitchen and drink coffee and remember together. Now she's really lost, still angry at me. She'll never stop hating me."

"Where she is, she doesn't hate anyone." Itzak pulled her to her feet. "Come. Get yourself together. We should go. What you can do is to be useful to your friends. What I can do is to get you there and help you."

"Are you sure you want to go? I can fly."

"And leave your car here? And the cats? Besides, if we're a couple, we should act as a couple. I'm going with you."

"But you hardly know any of them."

"Don't worry about me. Either we're a couple or we aren't," he repeated.

"I let her down. She was so needy and so lovely, Itzak, that maybe we did all just take and take from her. She had to be loved more than anybody had time for. Now she's dead." What will Willie do? she thought, but stopped herself from saying it. Her bathrobe was wet on the chest from her tears.

She wanted to rush back to their last scene together, back to the table, sit down again and find the right words. Find the words to say, Susan, I am still your friend. Susan, if we can't be lovers, say you forgive me whatever you feel I did and I'll forgive you for ending our life together. Let's kiss like friends if we can't kiss like lovers. Let's touch noses lightly like cats and sniff each other's joys and troubles. Susan, Susan, Susan, don't leave us, don't shut me out. Susan, you can't die on me in raw angry silence! The unsaid words ran down Dinah's face in salt.

FORTY-SIX

Willie

Willie had been sitting outside with Toby drinking beer and chatting about fish and the weather and the coming exodus of the summer people. All of the time he was watching for Susan to come out of the water, thinking that she was taking an awfully long swim tonight, when he heard a woman scream. Willie stood on the pier and called till he was hoarse. Then they took the dinghy out to search for Susan.

Out on the pond, when Toby rested his oars so they could listen for a swimmer, for an answer to their shouts, they heard loud voices. "That's the MacIvors fighting again," Willie said. "Maybe that's who was screaming."

By the time they had circuited the pond, it was after nine. Willie was beginning to feel a cold stone in the bottom of his chest. When they got back, she would be home. They had missed her in the dark. She would be tossing things around upstairs or in the kitchen eating. He told himself that and yet he was scared.

When she was not in the house, he called Candida to ask her if she had seen Susan. It took a long time to answer the phone, but he remembered they had been yelling at each other, and let it ring. Finally Alec picked it up. "And who the hell is this?"

Willie stared at the phone as if it had given him a light electric shock, but he was too desperate to be stopped. "Have you seen Susan?"

"Susan? Your wife? Why would I see her?"

"Please, could you ask Candida? She was swimming in the pond. I heard somebody scream. Did Candida see her?"

"Ask her yourself." Alec dropped the phone and it clonked

and clonked. "For you, bitch," he said loudly. "One of your boyfriends."

"Hello?" Candida said thickly. She sounded as if she had been crying. "Oh, Willie. . . . Susan? How would I know?"

"She was swimming in the pond. She hasn't come back. I'm worried about her."

There was a long silence. "I think I did see her. Near the raft."

"Near the raft? She never swims that far."

"She did tonight." Candida hung up.

Maybe she had swum all the way across the pond. He called Tyrone. Sally answered. "No, Mrs. Dewitt hasn't been by in several days. Mr. Burdock is engaged right now. He's on another line. I'm afraid he can't help you, as he's been here all evening working with me. He's talking to Tokyo, and frankly I do not expect him to be free any time soon."

Laurie's phone did not answer. He ran out on the pier and again shouted and shouted, with Bogey yapping at his heels. "Find Susan," he said to the dog, who stood wagging his tail and looking hopeful. Could Susan have decided to disappear as some obscure punishment for him? But where could she go in a wet bathing suit with the temperature around sixty? When he got back to the house, feeling foolish and frightened at the same time, he called the police.

Just after dawn, it was Toby who figured out where to find her. He remembered where his uncle had come up after going through the ice one February. Jimmy's high school buddy George, now a cop, hooked the body and drew it up.

It could not be, it could not be. Willie had the sense of having taken a wrong turn. He could still go back and fix it. He could still make it come out if he could only remember the way back and do it again. The medical examiner finally came. The body was taken away to the funeral home in town. He could not think of it as Susan. Susan was somewhere else. Susan was still in the house or in the pond.

He went upstairs and flung himself on their bed. Lately she had made him sleep in Jimmy's old room, but he had known that was only temporary until he could get around her. He should never have let her take up the habit of swimming after dark. But she had not been speaking to him for the last two weeks, except for an occasional sarcastic remark or bitter complaint. He should have got through to her. It was his fault for hanging back. He had been waiting for her anger to ease up. He lay moaning on her bed, inhaling traces of the perfume she enjoyed. Every so often Tyrone gave her perfume. Willie didn't like her to use too much of it, for he liked the natural smells of her body. Now the dying scent of the perfume from the pillows made him want her so intensely he thrashed to and fro.

When he cried, it was only a dry heaving. He could not actually squeeze tears from his eyes. His father had not been able to endure a boy's tears and had taught him to suppress them before he was ten. Now his eyes felt dry and hot, his lids itched, his sinuses were swollen with the urge to cry, but he could not. He could not force out a drop of relief.

He was being consumed with a dry flickering white fever of remorse. Grief was a thing that burned him. Grief took him over and used him up. He went on, burning and burning, a pain that was fierce and yet endless. Susan was taken from him. Taken stupidly. Taken by the pond he had loved. It was a thing that lay blue, freckled with sunlight on the short chop and yet it was evil underneath. She had wanted to leave here but he would not agree. Then the pond took her, the pond killed her.

Jimmy was dealing with the undertaker. When Willie could feel anything beyond the pain, he felt what a good son Jimmy was, how oddly tender Jimmy could be. When Jimmy returned from town and hurried upstairs to check him out, he rolled over and began to tell him so. "Because I appreciate you. Because you're the best son a man could have. You come through for me time after time. . . . We have to call Johnny."

"I left a message on her answering machine."

"No, Jimmy, you didn't!"

"Just that it's an emergency."

"We have to call Dinah."

"She's on her way."

"Tyrone."

"He left for the city this morning, I am told."

"We can reach him there."

"Maybe." Jimmy walked to the window, looked out. "I actually saw him leaving. *After* I called. Laurie was driving his Mercedes, with him talking on the car phone. They went by while we were waiting for the medical examiner." Jimmy spoke softly but bitterly.

"Tyrone is always zooming off. He probably meant to go to

New York this morning anyhow. He has some million dollar deal on tap." He buried his face into the pillow again.

"Laurie didn't say anything to me last night. She only said she'd have to go to New York sometime before Labor Day, not this morning."

Willie could not care about Tyrone. He did not want to make arrangements and talk to undertakers. He just wanted Susan back. If he had Susan, he would not care if she did not speak to him. He would not press her to make love. He would be happy just having her in the house. The room was pretty and very much like Susan: Her little blue glass vases. Her jewelry box standing open with its jumble of necklaces like a child's heap of painted shells and pebbles. Her mound of pillows wearing velvet and satin and patchwork and lace. Her drawing table held a half-completed design just as she had left it, wild roses in plum, olive leaves, blue hips. The entire room was a dress thrown down still warm from her body: surely she must rise and put it on. Surely she must appear here where everything spoke her name.

The green silk tunic and the straight black pants she had been wearing were tossed on her vanity bench. She must have put on her suit in a hurry, for she was extremely neat and fussy about her clothes. Even when they were about to make love, she would pause and hang the blouse she took off. Never again. It could not be. Why had she rushed out in such a hurry and gone off to drown? Had she been in despair? He knew that the distance between them had hurt her as much as it had hurt him. She needed him, she always needed him. She had pretended to think lately about leaving, but he knew she was rooted in him.

"Dad . . . Dad!" Jimmy stood over him, frowning with worry.

"Sorry. I didn't hear you."

"I told the undertakers we'd have a viewing tomorrow night for friends of the family and the cremation the next morning. . . . I need to tell them what kind of minister. Do you want a minister and a funeral?"

"A minister? Do we have to have one?"

"People usually do, but whatever you want, Dad. Please sit up and look at me. It's hard to talk to the back of your head."

"Can't we discuss this later?" He wanted to tell Jimmy to do whatever he felt like with the thing that had come out of the pond, an object like one of those rubber inflatable women, a caricature of his wife. It wasn't Susan. He wouldn't leave this

333

room. He would stay here where she seemed to linger, her scent, her clothing. It was almost like touching her. If he had not been talking with Toby, maybe he would have heard her. Maybe she had called to him. He still did not know if that had been her screaming. Had she hit her head? The medical examiner had not thought so. Had she had a cramp? He had been sitting and gabbing and drinking beer when he should have been swimming after her.

"Dad, we have to arrange the funeral. We have to let people know. Mother was raised Catholic, so should we get a priest?"

"She hadn't been in a church in thirty years. You can't do that to her. She told me she wanted to be cremated." He remembered also that she had told him, they were in bed and fooling around, that if she died before him, she wanted him to eat her ashes. Remembering that made him feel ill. He sat up. She had also suggested scattering the ashes from an airplane. "She wanted the ashes scattered on the Cape from a small plane."

"How are we going to do that?"

"The Captain can fly a plane. He'll help us."

Jimmy looked dubious. "Johnny will like that touch. But if you don't want a priest, what about a minister?"

"She didn't like churches. She wasn't a Christian. She said she was a pagan. She said she was a Druid."

"I don't think they have ministers, Dad. Maybe we should just have a memorial service and friends can get up and say something."

"That sounds better," Willie said.

"Great," Jimmy said with a loud sigh of relief and went directly to the bedside phone.

Willie realized he did not want to overhear that conversation. He pulled himself off the bed and stumbled downstairs. He remembered his uncle Jasper's funeral, with the widow weeping throughout; his aunt Maryellen's, when his grandfather had fallen asleep during the eulogy. He would have to call his parents. There had been little contact since a bitter fight some six years before when his damned brother Ted had been stupid enough, after a visit during a tour of New England, to act the tattletale to his parents about his living arrangements. Since then they had sent each other Christmas and birthday cards, but there had not been a phone conversation. He hoped they would not come north for the funeral, but he must give them that option.

334

Someone was banging on the screen door. Without curiosity he shuffled across the kitchen to open it. Behind him the phone was ringing, but it stopped, so he assumed Jimmy picked it up. Candida was banging on the screen door, which somebody had latched. He never latched it. He stood aside for her to come in. A moment later he looked hard at her because even in his absorption, he noticed her eye was puffy and darkening. Her left cheek and her throat were bruised.

"What's wrong?" he asked her, with a great effort at speaking.

She began to cry at once, putting her hands over her face. "Alec found out I've been seeing Tyrone. He beat me up. Tyrone has run away to New York. I don't have anywhere to go! I don't understand what happened with Susan, but I'm terribly terribly sorry!"

He had trouble following, but she was a mess and needed help. She was crying full throttle on his shoulder, and that was something real to be dealt with. He could pat her back and make comforting noises and put a pot of coffee on. Alec was a fool to beat her. He had never wanted to hit Susan, ever. Sometimes he withdrew from her and sometimes he argued with her; usually he waited her out. All chances gone now, wrongs never to be straightened and made right.

Partly he had been raised a gentleman, who would never raise his hand to his wife or any other woman, although the civil rights movement had made him quite aware of the lie of that tradition. Partly he could never imagine wanting to cause Susan physical pain, for she had seemed fragile to him, flowerlike, after all these years still with a flush and bloom on her. A doctor was supposed to heal pain, not willingly and brutally to cause it. He felt a fierce despisal of Alec MacIvor, who used his wife badly and sent her out bruised and weeping, who did not understand that losing a wife was losing your center, your core, the motive power of your life.

Candida was settled in the livingroom with ice on her face when Dinah arrived with the curly-headed musician. The phone rang every time Jimmy hung it up. Dinah put her arms around Willie and cried. He was wracked with sobs, he shook, but his eyes would not moisten. After a moment she pulled free of him. She seemed shy about touching him. He guessed she felt guilty too. They had all failed Susan. They had all let Susan lose herself in the pond.

335

Dinah was weeping on and off, but she was dashing around, electrified like Jimmy to make things happen. He would have liked better to sit down and mourn together. He did not give a damn about the undertakers or the friends who had them to dinner or people Susan used to work with in the library or the PTA. They would all survive her death just fine. He was bleeding silently and invisibly all of the time.

Dinah took charge of the memorial service. She went off to her house to work on it. Johnny called, crying on the phone, and promised to come the next day. He had not slept at all. The air felt thick. His body was oversized and heavy. It moved poorly. Dinah made a big fish chowder for everyone from cod Toby brought by. Zee baked a blackberry pie. Leroy dropped off fresh baked bread. Willie realized he had not eaten since supper the night before, except for a piece of stale coffee cake.

After supper he went upstairs to Susan's room again and lay on the bed. When he woke up it was lighter, which puzzled him until he realized from the clock and the sun that he had slept from eight in the evening until nine the next morning. Susan was gone. That was why he was in her bed. She was not with him and she would never again be with him. It was permanent, this sense of being gutted like a fish. At first when he stood, he swayed. He felt drugged. He could hardly focus his eyes.

Downstairs, breakfast was set up, everything clean and put away. Candida was waiting at the table. Her right eye had been blackened and the bruises on her throat were lurid, but she seemed calm. He figured out from her chatter that it was she who had cleaned up the kitchen. Dinah was going with her to her house, to protect her.

He stayed in the kitchen. He did not know what to do with himself. He did not feel like going to his studio. He felt broken. His work seemed absurd. Why would he want to build a cage with hands sticking out? Susan had called the piece that. She was right. It was meaningless. What was he to do with the half-built garage in the yard? What was he to do with the rest of his life? Susan dying had taken half of himself along. She could not be utterly gone, suddenly, like that. How could he get through a day without her? He had always thought she was the one dependent on him. I can't go to Minneapolis, he had told Johnny, because Susan doesn't want to go (nor did Johnny want her to come) and she can't sleep when I'm away. He had thought of Susan as unable to manage without him. He had thought she

336

could not survive in the house, in the woods, without his protection and help. Now he saw he was the one who could not manage alone.

Dinah appeared and took Candida off with her. Johnny called from Logan to give him her time of arrival in Provincetown. He could not imagine driving, but Jimmy had gone off with Toby to town, so he must fetch his daughter. He was halfway to the airport before he realized that he was looking at a gas gauge on empty and must fill the truck's tank.

When Johnny got off the plane and saw him, she started to run. She hurled herself into his arms and burst into tears. When she could speak, she blew her nose and asked, "Are you okay, Dad? Are you okay?"

"No," he said honestly, but he was feeling a little better being with her. "I'm kind of busted."

"What happened, Dad? How could she drown right in front of the house?"

"She swam all the way to the raft and the way I piece it together—it was after dark—Tyrone was humping Candida MacIvor. Susan must have heard them and tried to swim back. She died from being too damned polite, I guess."

"Who is Candida MacIvor?"

"You met her at my opening. She's married to a doctor who beat her up."

Johnny shook her head. "My friends are dull compared to life here."

"I liked it when it was dull." They were standing in the parking lot. Johnny took the keys from his hand and got into the driver's side. He took the passenger's seat gladly. He felt good about being with Johnny because he thought she must feel as guilty as he did. They had both been cut off from Susan, they had both quarreled with her. An image came to him. He remembered Tosca had got tangled up in a fishing line hung with sharp barbed hooks, and she had simply crouched there and waited to be discovered, not panicking, in a kind of numb abiding despair. He was caught in just such a barbed net that seemed to hurt no matter which way he pulled, but if he waited patiently in his despair Johnny might help him. They were both murderers and victims, they were complicitous and lost. Maybe she would stay for a while.

She did not take him home but to the Bay, where they parked at the end of a wriggly sand road and walked over the dune and along the pebbled shore. Out on the waves lavender-blue under a huge thickening swirl of rain clouds, terns were diving and streaking away. "I can't believe the last time I'm ever going to see her, she poured tomato sauce on me. I know I should have kept my mouth shut. I always used to swear I would, but then she'd get at me, and I'd have to hurt her. And now it's stuck there."

He put his arm around her shoulders. "For me it's stuck with her furious with me, threatening to sell the house in spite. And me hiding in my studio and skulking around, scared to confront her. I was just waiting for her anger to wear itself out, the way it always did. It would have. I know she would have forgiven us all and we would have carried on."

"She wrote me a letter how my telling her was for the best and she was sorry she lost her temper. So she was already coming around. What's happening with a service? Are we getting some minister in a tie and grey suit?"

"Dinah is taking care of a memorial service."

"Good. Because she's really family. We have to make it beautiful, for Susan. For us. There shouldn't be anything we say or do that isn't real and doesn't mean something. Nothing at all!"

He stirred. "You're right. I should talk to Dinah about it."

"What are you going to do, Dad?"

"I'm kind of empty. I don't know what to do."

"Come back to Minneapolis with me. You've never been. It'll be good for you. Why not?"

"Maybe I will." It sounded like something to do. He could remember that he had wanted for a long time to visit his daughter. It was a thing he had wanted, back then; it would be nice to look forward to. Maybe what he needed more than anything else was someone in his family to tell him what to do, to give him some mandated activity beyond the funeral.

"I want you to get to know Aldo and see my new work, I really do."

"Right," he said nodding, and from that moment on, he took it as settled.

FORTY-SEVEN

Laurie

Laurie was proud of herself, the way she packed in under an hour and slipped behind the wheel, ready to go. Loyalty to her father was like a bright fierce rush in her veins, a blast of early invigorating fall air galvanizing her into decisive action. Tyrone was right in his confidence in her and she was proving it. She drove, alert but fast, the radar indicator perched on the dash. Tyrone was deferring the appointments he had in the country, setting up others in the city.

The night before, when she had come in with Jimmy, her phone had been ringing with Willie almost hysterical. On the door had been a note from Sally asking that she drop by the big house no matter what time. Jimmy had hurried off to see what had happened at home, and she had slipped off to find Sally and Tyrone waiting for her. The situation with Candida had blown up, and something was clearly wrong with Susan, with Toby Lloyd and Willie screaming all over the pond and now the lights of police cars on that shore. This morning the phone call had arrived as Tyrone was already packed for a strategic retreat to New York. He had turned white. She had not seen him as disturbed since Somoza fell, queering some coffee speculation. His reaction scared her. It was time for them to pull together as a family, for her to show every bit of the strength he had been praising in her. Carefully he watched her to see if she was with him, and she jumped to prove herself. A trap of scandal and potential danger was seeking to close on them, but they would break free.

Around New Bedford, he caught up with himself and poured them each a cup of coffee from the thermos in the basket Celeste had packed. Sally had stayed behind to field inquiries and problems. Donald was already in the city, dealing with the decorator refurbishing the gallery.

"It's not as inconvenient as it might have been a week ago," Tyrone said. "It wouldn't hurt to put in an appearance at the gallery and have a look-see."

The sense of sudden death and scandal mixed was overly familiar. She could not bear it again. But she must. Brave, he had called her. "Daddy, do you think she killed herself?"

"Don't be absurd. She may have gone beyond her depth and her distance. I know she was spying on me. I don't know what was in her mind. Indeed, whether she imagined she could parlay that knowledge into something she wanted, such as assistance in finding housing in the city, or whether it was simply prurient interest, we'll never be sure."

She didn't want to believe anything like that of Susan. "Couldn't she just have come upon you by accident?"

"On the raft? I don't believe it. This is only for your ears. My opinion is that the woman was suffering some sort of menopausal depression, a wild veering to and fro and loss of control."

Laurie saw the kitchen dripping with tomato sauce like thick blood. "That's it—a complete loss of control!"

"Exactly." Tyrone sighed. "It's a great pity, and I, for one, will miss her. She was like an aunt to you when you were younger. Women sometimes become a little strange, Laurie, in their middle years if they're unhappy."

She suspected he was referring to her mother. She pretended not to understand. Her eyes burned for a moment. She blinked rapidly and thought of Sean Corrigan, of the gallery that was to come on Prince Street, of all Tyrone was risking for her. Others were unreliable: Tom, Susan. "What will we do about the funeral?"

"One of us will return for it, of course."

She understood she was likely to be sent. "But what about Sean Corrigan? He was going to visit us Labor Day weekend."

"Tranquillity should be restored by then. We can slip back and enjoy a quiet weekend with our guests."

"You're more worried about Alec MacIvor than you are about the situation with Willie and Jimmy."

"I've nothing to be ashamed of with the latter. Alec MacIvor has good reason to be hostile. I'm truly annoyed with myself." He screwed his face up, ran a linen handkerchief over his dome. She saw that he was speaking the truth: he was angry with himself. "It was a foolish entrapment. Quite, quite over, I promise. You must think your father has faltered this summer, but if I was slipshod in my personal involvements, I was brilliantly aggressive, if I may boast a little, on more important fronts. On the

340

Japanese front, I made a killing, Laurie, giving us the stuff of which the best galleries are made.''

It was great of him to level with her. They rarely spoke of finances, so this was in the nature of a confidence she truly appreciated. It was just like him to judge himself harshly for a little affair. "Daddy, you don't have to apologize to me about Candida. I liked her. I think she genuinely admired you and cared about you. She was very unhappy and she made herself more than available.''

"Ah, what's put on your plate, courtesy may force you to taste, but nothing requires you to finish.''

"Besides, Daddy, if Alec has thrown her out, the scandal is over and she's free.''

"A divorce can be nasty and expensive. I don't wish to be locked into negotiations between them. But I sincerely doubt one more argument is about to end that marriage. The kindest gift I can give them is to absent myself permanently from their lives. . . . My major concern is the awkwardness of having them for neighbors. No, Laurie, you're too kind. Getting involved with the wife of a neighbor was inexcusable.''

"Do you think my getting involved with Jimmy was inexcusable?''

"Not in the least. He was an amiable and convenient summer romance. And it's ended with a minimum of ruckus, hasn't it?'' He turned sharply to face her, bringing his knee up on the seat.

"Not formally, Daddy. I have been seeing less of him. I didn't even tell him I was going to the city today.''

"There's no reason for a formal ending to what began casually enough. Why not simply let it wither on the vine? I know you're too sensible to consider bringing him to the city with you this fall, the way when you were a girl you sometimes insisted on bringing home turtles, who promptly crawled under a bed or breakfront and died.''

"I'm sure he has no desire to move to New York.'' That she did know to be true, although she had hoped to talk him into going. She had been plotting exactly how to do that. She was dismayed at Tyrone's seamless opposition.

"He's a sensible lad. If I need more renovations at the Cape, I'll surely use him. He's a good workman, a rare virtue nowadays.'' Tyrone beamed at her. "I know you're far too mature to let any occasion arise for a quarrel. Let things attenuate. Keep it civilized and gentle. I can't provide that kind of termination with Candida, unfortunately, because of the mess of the drowning.''

That meant to her that she could continue to see Jimmy at the pond, and that he could visit her in the city once she had her own apartment. Sally had turned up some possibilities and Donald was supposed to be working on the problem also. She hoped she would not have to take a large part in the search. It was tedious and unpleasant to have to call strangers and beg for favors and ask what felt like too intimate questions about rooms and prices. Talking about money always felt sticky.

Fortunately the next day Donald turned up a perfect condo in a new building just finishing. She would not be able to move in before October, but she could stay in the country (with Jimmy) until then, or she could live with Tyrone in the city. She still had a room in his duplex. She signed the papers at ten the next morning and then rushed off to LaGuardia to fly into Hyannis, where Sally met her to take her to the funeral. Tyrone would come Thursday night, so that he would be there when Sean arrived on Friday.

The service was held on the Great Beach, just over the dunes from their house where the path that led from the end of the pond road came out. Most of the people had parked at the nearest public beach and walked the half mile. She felt nervous about seeing Jimmy for the first time since his mother had died. He was wearing black jeans and a black linen jacket, which she thought rather informal attire; however half the mourners sported sundresses, short sleeved shirts, even shorts. The day was hot and dry, the sky cloudless and much higher than it usually looked over the Cape. The wind was smart and from the northwest.

Sally wore a navy linen suit that looked even more incongruous than her own navy and white dress against the backdrop of dunes. She was glad they hadn't had to walk past the sunbathers and splashing infants, past the lifeguard and the muscle boys at the public beach, but simply trotted over the dune, both carrying their shoes by the straps. It seemed a tacky funeral. Even Tom's service had been better than this, in spite of the shame. It was bizarre. She would miss Susan; she knew she would. It was hard to imagine summers without Susan to take care, to fuss over her, to arrange everything. What would they do without her? It would be bleak to arrive with no Susan to make everything warm and nice. She felt a sense of privation and a sadness that felt overwhelming at first; it made her remember that long ago di-

342

vorce, and that first summer she had come here without her mother, with Tyrone and the new wife, Janette. Susan had made that summer bearable.

"Susan found churches boring. I think it's daring and sweet of Willie to do it the way she would have wanted, don't you?" Burt said softly as he stood beside her. "I've become a connoisseur of funerals the past few years."

"Well, they held a regular lying in state at the funeral parlor," Leroy murmured. "So there was something for the straight friends, and now the kinky part for us."

"Oh, no," Burt said. "The kinky part is when Johnny throws the ashes out of an airplane."

"You're kidding," Laurie whispered.

"No we aren't," Burt said. "Ask your boyfriend. That was Susan's request. Willie's doing it exactly the way she wanted it. I find that moving. So often you get some minister who never saw the poor soul making up a eulogy that could have been read over their dog."

Tyrone was absolutely right, she thought, Susan had simply gone off the deep end. She had exploded parts of herself all over the landscape. It was like a weird hippie tea party on the sand, with everyone sitting in a circle and people rising one at a time to say something about Susan, to read a poem, to sing a song or play a melody on a guitar. Mary Lou, the woman who ran a real estate office in town, recited the Twenty-third Psalm with her voice quivering. Willie talked about how long they had been together and all the things they had loved to do, all the little pleasures they had shared. When he talked abut their life together with their friends and living in harmony with the land, giving and taking with it in the round of seasons, he almost broke down. For a moment Laurie thought he was about to cry. She had a strong sense of being violated by his emotions. At normal funerals, everything was controlled, muted. The widow or widower didn't stand up and tell you how ghastly they were feeling. She imagined herself rising at Tom's service and screaming how nasty it all was. People would really have loved that. Enough pain, enough scandal, enough ugliness! Had they no shame?

Jimmy read a poem she recognized halfway through as Mark Edelmann's. Dinah, dressed in a long lavender coat without sleeves, stood and played the flute, first alone and then with her

343

boyfriend Itzak. It was eerily beautiful, the two flutes weaving in and out like streamers in the air.

Johnny had built a strange object she said was intended as an honorary funeral pyre for her mother, because, Johnny asked rhetorically, why should Buddhists have all the pretty funerals? It was erected by Willie and Johnny together, while people were passing around wine and bread and fruit and cheese. Now it felt like a mad picnic. Finally the tower was finished, twenty feet tall and with a precarious grandeur to it, white and gilt and black and lavender, hung with streamers that the wind whipped toward the sea. Willie, Dinah, Jimmy and Johnny were walking about it chanting something she preferred not to hear. She felt partly moved, because Johnny did have talent and she had made this strikingly grotesquely pretty thing on the beach. Laurie wondered if she should relinquish her annoyance at Johnny. It would look great in a gallery. It would be highly salable. She could imagine it in a commercial context, perhaps in the lobby of a restaurant or a resort hotel. It was that festive.

But Johnny stopped and held a match and Willie, Dinah and Jimmy did the same. Soon streamers of flame were blowing out from the house of paper and plywood, and it was blazing away. Even on fire it was pretty, but it flared up very fast. In twenty minutes it had burned down to the sand. Jimmy and Willie brought buckets of seawater to douse the coals. Then everybody began to pick up and go home.

It was a good thing Tyrone had not come, she thought. He would have considered it a waste of time, for as it turned out, it wasn't a real service, not an event anybody could be expected to attend solemnly. Is this all that Susan would have for a funeral? She drifted uncertainly over to Jimmy. "Burt says that Johnny is going up in a plane to scatter the ashes?" She wanted to beg him to deny the rumor.

"Toby can fly. He's borrowing a plane."

"Does he have a license?"

Jimmy shrugged. "I didn't ask." He had not smiled at her, but she could not tell if that was because of the occasion or because he was irked. She had a couple of days before Tyrone arrived. She touched his arm, asking, "Do you want to come over tonight? We can have supper together."

"I'm eating with my family." He walked beside her however as she padded barefoot to Sally, who was sitting on the dune holding their shoes by the straps. They had never put them on.

344

Sally did not look pleased to see Jimmy going back with them. Laurie tried to make conversation but nobody wanted to chat. She would be alone with Jimmy in a few minutes and make up with him then. Indeed he followed her into her little house without invitation or comment. She headed for the bathroom to put in her diaphragm and use the toilet. Then she sprayed on Rive Gauche.

When she came out of the bathroom, the room was empty. She assumed he had gone outside to sit on the deck, but he was not there. Then she caught sight of him halfway along the pond, walking rapidly on the path toward his house. She wanted to fly after him. She started to call out, but realized her voice would be audible to everyone on the pond. She felt foolish standing there with the diaphragm inserted. Why had he left? He could not have felt insulted she had gone into the bathroom. He must have changed his mind. Perhaps he thought that making love after even such a silly ceremony was improper.

Sally gave her a little smile as she drifted up on the deck of the big house. "Don't be upset. It's all for the best. Your father would like it out of the way before Labor Day anyhow."

For a moment she missed Susan, because she would have run to Susan with her quandary; except that she couldn't have anyhow. She wondered for a moment, as she followed Sally's narrow navy clad back into the livingroom, if she could confide in Sally. But she did not think Sally would appreciate such an attempt. Sally knew everything about them, but kept it all cool and controlled and neat. Actually as Laurie got older and stronger and more confident, she had less need for someone warm to console her and share her troubles. Adults did not need that. Tyrone didn't. Nor did Sally herself. She would be strong and she would not miss Susan. If she did, anyhow, she would not say anything to Tyrone. She had the feeling he would find any display of emotion about Susan in bad taste. It had been such a tacky and disruptive event, Susan coming upon Tyrone and Candida, really, and then drowning. It embarrassed her to think about it. How could they all have continued together after that, gone on picnics or out to dinner? Susan had tried to take advantage of Tyrone, that was the secret hinge of the shameful ness. She was proud how they had all pulled together, Tyrone, Sally, Donald, herself, in efficient damage control. That she would say to Tyrone when he arrived. He would say how strong she was. He would be proud of her again.

What she had to do was to get herself together before Sean came. Perhaps she would even finish that painting she had been working on back in May and hang it where he might just happen to notice it. She wouldn't say anything about it, of course. She only had three days. Forget the painting. She would be seeing any amount of Sean in New York with them being partners.

No, it would be better to get her hair cut again, shorter. She had noticed how the girls around SoHo were wearing their hair. Back to the hairdresser's, fast. Rafael had been on vacation, so she would have to find someone on the Cape. In New York, she had bought a new outfit, but now she wasn't sure about it. She wondered if she could sneak over and try it on for Candida, if Tyrone wouldn't find out. Too bad about Candida. She would not have made a bad wife for Tyrone. Laurie would have preferred her to what she would probably get.

She must also have a serious talk with Celeste about the meals for Friday. They had to be perfect and extraordinary, while suggesting a minimum of fuss. As soon as Tyrone returned to the city, she would stay on for a while and get Jimmy back.

Actually she missed him strongly, especially in the evenings and at night. He was the only man she had ever really enjoyed making love with, not once or twice in the beginning, when everybody was trying hard and infatuated, but regularly. Jimmy made her feel attractive and generous. Surely it would not do any harm to continue with him once Tyrone had left her on her own.

FORTY-EIGHT

Dinah

Dinah flipped back and forth twice in each hour while they were in Edinburgh over whether it was a good or a completely lousy idea that she had come with Itzak. She was with him only two days of the festival followed by a five day vacation. She would then fly home from Prestwick, while he went on to Birmingham, Bristol, Brussels and finally London before returning. She disappeared in his radiance when he was the star. That made her itchily recall her own performer's days with the Wholey Terrors.

not her recent concert in Hartford. That had been a small audience who had responded well enough. No great high, no torrent of emotion. But she remembered igniting audiences as their arousal beat back at her in waves of sound and energy, feeling the room throb and the air sizzle. She remembered that hot fuss frothing about her. People adored performers and paid them and flocked to them the way they never did composers.

In a way she was jealous. He would be richly paid and receive more adulation for half an hour performing a piece she had written for him than she would receive for having spent six months writing it. On the other hand, he was generous with the money he had. He wanted her to come, so he paid for the tickets, lodging, car rental, food. Since to her money was time for working, she could not have afforded a vacation. Still the festival stimulated her. With him, she was surrounded by music and musicians. Plunging into a provocative atmosphere did her good. But when she felt properly stimulated, what she needed was home, the quiet space that was hers alone.

They went off to Galloway, to a country hotel where a five minute walk brought them onto a moor where grey sheep raised their heads to watch them warily, where the fog caught on the rocks like tufts of wool. Their room was large and light and looked out on a surprisingly subtropical walled garden, with a couple of scrubby palms among the box, the azaleas and huge old gnarled clematis vines. The chatty waitress explained it was the gulf stream that brought mildness this far north. Their room was rather formally furnished, with deep velvet chairs and high mahogany dressers, a king-sized bed and a bath as large as many hotel rooms she had been put up in.

The food was excellent and plentiful, lamb, salmon, trout, coarse oatmeal bread at breakfast. They walked and they ate and they made love and they talked. This was not an area that drew hordes of tourists. The hotel was full of professional men and their families come for the salmon or trout fishing. The villages were red brick or whitewashed stucco with near shutters, the fields divided into quilts by drywall stone fences subtly colored with lichens. Part of each day they both played the flute. He practiced two hours daily regardless of where he was, and she worked at the same time. What she was getting on with was a series of short pieces for solo flute or two flutes, or flute and taped flute, intended to explore the limits of the instrument's capacities and tentatively called, *What Manner of Bird Is This?*

She was enjoying the work, but she also was amused to realize rather cynically that probably this would be a success in publication, since the pieces would be attractive to students seriously engaged in learning the flute, an obvious strategem for teachers. Well done, this series would get a lot of use.

It was hard to call Willie, because doing so from the hotel room would put an additional strain on her relationship with Itzak, and because of the time difference. Most days when she had an opportunity to phone, it was the middle of the night in Massachusetts, or she did try and got no one. Finally she reached him. "Are you bearing up?" she asked.

He said something unintelligible. The connection was echoey. When they had made more noises at each other, she understood he was saying that he was depressed, that he could not work. "Jimmy and me are busting our humps on the Victorian in town, turning it into condos."

"I thought you'd lost that job when Tyrone sold the building?"

"Are you having a good time in Scotland?"

It was a conversation of non sequiturs. Obviously he blamed her for not being with him; but he too had gone away for a week. When she spoke to him, she wondered what she was doing in Scotland, indeed. Being happy with Itzak seemed unfeeling, almost gross. She was letting Willie down. He was not going to see much of her until she had been back a couple of days anyhow, because she was returning just in time for Rosh Hashonah and had promised Zee way back at Pesach that she would go to services both days with her, which meant a long drive. But Willie did have Jimmy, who had moved back into his house. It wasn't as if he were alone.

"How much longer are you going to be hanging around over there?" Willie asked, his voice quavering.

"I leave in two days. Come on, Willie, I'm not taking any longer than you did in Minneapolis."

"Did you think I shouldn't have gone?"

"No, no! I was delighted. I mean, I thought it was good. We both needed to get away."

"You could have come with me."

"Willie, I'll be back home soon. Good-bye. See you." She leaned against the wall of the hallway off the diningroom. She felt weak, guilty. Then she saw Itzak trapped halfway down the broad front stairs by a fan from London, and trotted off to his rescue.

"At least you're not a violinist or a pianist," she said as they walked that midmorning on the Mull of Galloway. It was a peninsula that rolled along to a rocky tip, cliff tops devoid of trees hundreds of feet above the crashing sea, sandstone cliffs tinged bronze and grey and mauve, splashed with white guano, seething with kittiwakes, razorbills and guillemots. It reminded her a little of Northern California, up near Mendocino, where the band had based itself for the first summer—the way the rocky pastures would roll lushly along until suddenly they left off in midair and the sea burst against the rocks far below. But the sky hung low here, like the Cape. "The hierarchy of instruments means that you aren't canonized, just overly adored."

"I don't feel overly adored," he said. "Not in any useful way. You know how it is with an audience." He gave a sort of wince of the body, not quite a shudder, more a ripple. It was a physical reaction on an animal level, like a movement of the powerful muscles of a horse under the shiny coat. It made her want to touch him. They both came from peasant stock, survivors in the larger sense, strong, stocky, vital. "What you experience is the music. They just amplify it." He grimaced. "Not a completely honest statement. Every performer needs applause."

"I wasn't thinking of the concerts themselves. I was thinking of the fans."

"Dinah, either I'm successful and I make money and people make a fuss, or I'm unsuccessful and I make a rotten living teaching in some dull place and having private students on the side, like your mother. Is that how you think I should live?"

No, she wanted to shout, remembering how glorious he was onstage. That wasn't what she meant, not at all. Who would want to deny herself the opportunity to watch him soar and dip acrobatic as a tern over the Bay. "There's nothing wrong with how you are with fans, Itzak. You don't wake up at night in a sweat craving more applause. I'm concerned with my own lumpy self, and how I take being around it when it's not directed at me."

"You don't have to go on the road with me. Usually it's a bum idea. I'm crazed and all I do is practice, perform and do the publicity they require." He sighed, for a moment looking suddenly weary, not because he was tired, but because he was remembering in his mind and his body a fatigue with which he was altogether too acquainted.

Once again she felt they shared a physical being, as if their bodies or their nervous systems had begun to overlap, to intermingle, like the root systems of two trees growing near each other. There was a bodily identification beginning with him that was new to her. That had not been an aspect of her intimacy with Mark: he was too much older, too lean and whiplike in his body, tight and taut and inturned.

As Itzak looked out to sea and then back to her, she took in at once the fine droplets on his dark curls, the somber beauty of his eyes, the almost silly and perfect cleft in his chin, and she realized in despair and relief that she loved him. It was something stronger than she was used to feeling. Still knowing that made her situation no easier. What did love striking hard mean? Destruction? The loss of autonomy? Terrible vulnerability? That she could be entered, occupied, crushed? Or that she would be truly companioned, an intimacy of ambiguous depths? That she would found a new family with him or that she would founder? Was this passion an irrelevant allurement?

A fine rain hung in the air, heavier than mist but not quite droplets. She stepped on a pad of cow dung and slipped. He caught her by the arm. They climbed up to the white Victorian lighthouse, walking separately but close together, their hands occasionally brushing. Whenever they touched, no matter how accidentally, desire rippled deep in her. For all the doubts that stirred her brain, her body no longer doubted him at all. Her body trusted him, responded to him more strongly than it ever had to anybody else or likely might again. How to weigh such a response?

"Have you ever thought that perhaps part of my appeal for you might be that I haven't jumped all over you?"

"Sure, in the beginning. By now, your unwillingness to commit is driving me to the brink. I want to get on with our life together or separately."

"Couldn't it be sometimes together and sometimes separately? It seems to me it would be that way anyhow."

"Of course. But the physical separation has nothing to do with commitment. Once a commitment is made, we can work on terms, on how to manage our lives, our careers, our needs.

350

That's the point we're failing to get to." He swung around and took hold of her shoulders, holding hard.

"I love you, Itzak. It has nothing to do with any lack of love."

"It has to do with how strong you really think you are."

"Oh, dirty pool!" She pulled away. She had said she loved him, and he had paid no attention at all. Had he noticed? She wanted an acknowledgment. She wanted him to answer her. Instead he took her hand as they walked on the brink of the cliff, the seabirds screeching below them, the sea smashing the rocks. Cows were pastured on the high center, and she wondered what kept them from walking off the cliffs. Perhaps just common sense. She said resentfully, "I'm supposed to have to prove how strong I am."

"It would test both of us. Can't you imagine how many easier relationships I could find? You're a gritty woman. Addictive but problematic."

"Now who's found the worm in the apple?"

"I don't miss seeing that we're going to have some hard times with each other, that it'll be raw and exhausting as often as it's warm and wonderful." He sat down on a rock, his hands on his spread knees, looking levelly at her. "I walk into a party like the one we went to Sunday. It's full of women more beautiful than you are, younger, more fashionable. Women I would enjoy fucking a couple of times and enjoy talking to maybe once. I know how rare it is to be able to get into that kind of conversation with a friend that goes on for years and years and just continues underneath everything the way the blood goes on through the arteries whatever you're doing, till you die." He rose and went past her, standing looking out to sea where dim shapes—Ireland, the Isle of Man—floated like fallen bluish clouds.

She ordered herself to listen and not to give way to the blip of jealousy and even pain that he could say other women were more attractive than herself to him in any way. It was absurd to feel such jealousy, and yet she did. He gazed down at the rocks far below. "In some ways we could be closer than I was to my wife. We have more in common. We communicate better. You and I could have an extraordinary intimacy."

"I was close to Susan. We talked every day for ten years. There's something in me that turned her off, that went numb to her, that couldn't really feel what she needed or wanted."

351

"How close were you? How close can you be to anybody if music is your life and they have no feeling for music?"

"Itzak, this death wasn't like Mark's. When Mark died, it was the culmination of a process of dying that had gone on for a year and a half. When it finally came, it was awful but merciful." She came to stand beside him, pressing herself to his side. "But Susan's death is abrupt and bizarre and stupid. I can't even believe it yet, let alone accept it."

He pulled away from her. "You'll end up living with Willie because you feel guilty about Susan."

"No!" she said. "I don't know. It still hurts to think about it."

"But it hurts me to be kept hanging. You have to commit or let go. I care about my music as much as you care about yours. I want a core relationship, I want solidity. I'm willing to work at it, but I want it in place. I don't find shopping around amusing. I'm sick to death of feeling uprooted."

She had a sudden premonition of him closing himself to her. He would be a stranger, someone whose discs she picked up in record stores, someone whose concerts she might attend every few years. She was afraid. "I'm used to behaving simply and I'm not very good at figuring out what I want when it isn't immediately clear. I'm trying!"

"Sorrow is a reasonable response when your friend dies, estranged from you. Guilt isn't. You're not the one who refused to reconcile."

"But I do feel guilty."

"Because of your father you feel you have to keep everyone alive."

"I feel as if my life is this vast amorphous pile of junk I can't straighten out, and I can't figure out where to begin."

"You'd better begin by figuring out whether you want me, because I'm not going to wait longer while you decide. When I get back—it'll be just after Yom Kippur, which I mean to spend in London—you're giving me an answer finally, no buts, no maybes. Commitment or good-bye."

He said that to her grimly and he meant it, she sensed how strongly he meant it, yet he did not sulk. A few minutes later they were scrambling up the path that rose and fell, swung around clefts, corkscrewed up, always keeping to the cliff tops or just a step back from the brink. On the plateau cows and calves were grazing in a rocky field. The wind was tattering the fog. Through

352

rents, a dark blue sky glittered briefly. They ate apples from his pockets and sucked butterscotch candies. When they cut inland to the Iron Age fort to sit on the low rounded overgrown ramparts and drink coffee from the small thermos the hotel had lent them, the grass was a green so deep and bright, it seemed to rub off on the eyeballs. Was she full of joy because she liked the landscape and liked walking and liked eating good food, or was she happy because she was doing so with this man? It was tedious always to be turning on herself and trying to figure it out. He was right, she must think clearly about her life, she must make decisions and put her house in order. That he did not withdraw when he gave her that ultimatum made it all the harder to believe she could continue to jolly him along. He wasn't to be got around or distracted.

Rosh Hashonah began the evening she got home. Between then and Yom Kippur, she must sort herself out. The task that Itzak had set her, the holidays emphasized. They would give her a framework for examination of her beliefs and her actions. For Itzak, for Willie, for all her dead, her father and Susan and Mark, for herself, she must strive to be clear. Her possibilities had irrevocably changed, and she must make choices that would result in a life necessarily different no matter which way she moved forward out of her long impasse. She must sit in rigorous judgment and put her mind and then her life in order, as the holiday season demanded.

FORTY-NINE

Willie

Willie stayed in Minneapolis for a week, but then he started feeling he had to get home. His daughter ate late—mostly take-out and snack foods—and stayed up late. Her loft offered little privacy, for it was one big room. He enjoyed going around with her and meeting other artists, he liked seeing a lot of her work. He helped her with framing and tried to cook for her and her boyfriend Aldo, who was awkward with him. He made sure to take long walks every day at a time he thought they might like to go to bed together, but it was uncomfortable. Even though he dreaded going home, he was getting tired and cranky. He needed his own things and his daily schedule. He had to figure out how to live now that Susan was gone. He could not remain with Johnny, peripheral, irrelevant, rootless.

His house felt dusty. The last of summer had passed. The Virginia creeper was crimson, the tomato plants hung with their last glut. Jimmy had finished Dinah's addition, but instead of moving into the new bedroom, he resumed sleeping in his old room. Bogey was sick. He had been throwing up and then refusing to eat. Willie took him to the vet, who said he was suffering from extreme depression. Willie began to bring Bogey upstairs at night, letting him sleep on the foot of the bed. He took the dog for long walks. Dealing with the dog's depression seemed some kind of tonic for his own. Dinah was off for a week in Scotland with Itzak Raab, whom she was still seeing.

Willie knew he had to do something about that guy, because he was taking up more and more of Dinah's time and attention, but he felt too low to mobilize himself. Jimmy was blue, just like him. Laurie had gone to the city and Jimmy said that was over. Willie knew Jimmy was missing Susan too, but they tried to steer away from mentioning her, as they might avoid a deep pothole that could break an axle. They were both lost souls. Most mornings they had taken to going into town for breakfast, but he tried to make a real supper every evening. Today he broiled sirloin steaks. They both needed little treats. "Laurie will be back. She'll come up holidays and summers."

"I am not some local helper you call up when you arrive. Call the plumber, the electrician, the housecleaners and the local stud service. No thanks. She's not that much fun."

He had a brief urge to tell Susan, See, I told you it would fade away by itself if we kept our mouths shut. "Are we really all done at Dinah's?"

"Sure. And now I don't need a room there anymore. I'd sooner live with you. What a boondoggle. Tyrone took us for a ride and I wasted the summer while we were in the permit process playing with Dinah's house."

Willie put his elbows on the table. "And what am I supposed to do with the thing in the yard?"

"Why don't we just finish it off in one story for a garage? We can't make it a rental unit. There's no plumbing, and we'd never get the permits."

"We did okay on Tyrone on the boathouse, but we got skinned on the gallery."

Jimmy was silent for a minute. Then he said smugly, "We may end up doing that renovation."

Willie took his head out of his hands and stared at Jimmy. "No way."

"Where there's a will. I have been getting to know the son, Bob Sampson."

"What does getting to know mean?"

"Come on, after all those years of Mother and Dinah in the sack, you're not going to turn homophobic on me."

"What about AIDS?"

"Have you ever heard of safe sex? I would have married Laurie. I really would have. I liked her just fine, and I knew how to make her happy. Bob is a hell of a lot easier. All he wants is a scene or two. He likes me. He likes you. He likes quality work."

"This wasn't necessary."

"Nobody else needs to be read into the picture. We were doing the renovation. We'll go on doing the renovation."

"You don't have to fuck any random landlord who might give us a job."

"You use what you've got. I need to get established here. I have plans. Getting blown by some rich kid a couple of times is a pretty easy way to get a job, frankly."

"But you just don't have to use yourself that way, Jimmy, you don't! We're not starving. We're not that hard up. We never would be."

"Bob's nice enough. Like everybody else, he wants people to care about him. You don't understand. If somebody's attracted to me and they show it, I tend to like them. After all, they're paying me a compliment."

"But you can't just roll over for everyone who whistles."

"Don't give me any trouble about it, Willie. I need that job. I saw how to get it back. Laurie acted like a creep. I'm a forgiving sort—I'd still take Lisa back if she asked me—but I'm no serf you can summon to the castle when you breeze in."

"She really hurt you."

"She pissed me off, royally. I hope I get a chance to make her feel like shit sometime. I would find that truly satisfying." Jimmy got up and whistled to Bogey. "I'll take him for a little extra romp around the pond. Didn't the vet say we should exercise him till he drops?"

"That's supposed to give him an appetite."

"It gives me one." Jimmy put on his leather jacket and went out, followed by the dog.

Willie cleaned up, scrubbing the plates. How could Jimmy sell himself for a damned carpentry job? Laurie was an idiot to have let Tyrone bust up her relationship. Jimmy was weird sometimes, but he was a good kid finally—fiercely loyal to his family. He was forgiving, as he said. Hardworking. But Jimmy's view of the world was not that different from Dinah's tomcat Figaro. He had the same level of morality.

Willie adored his daughter and his son, but they amazed him, how individual and spiky and strange they were. They seemed to him as exotic and as beautiful as adults as they had when he had first seen each of them, multicolored orchids waxy and squalling and blood-streaked. He realized he was so caught up in Jimmy that he had not thought to miss Susan for several hours. That was the longest he had gone without thinking about her.

He could imagine that some people would tend that pain, but he wanted only to close the door on it. It would not go away, but he wanted it to sink out of his awareness. He was afraid to feel as much pain as he did. He feared total disability, that his life would cease and he would lie limp and spent. He felt as if Susan had been dead for months instead of weeks and he was still treading in place. He wanted Dinah with him, not off in Scotland. It wasn't fair she had run away, run from his pain, from her own. Being alone just didn't work for him. It turned every day into a ghost town of the emotions, streets laid out, buildings erected for the use of those who had vanished.

A letter had come from a French curator, who had some kind of position with the Ministry of Culture or at least was putting together a show under their auspices, requesting slides. Now the curator was writing again, definitely interested in that South Africa piece Willie had done in the spring, the nation tree of death. The curator wanted it for a show in January. A big one. Hadcke would have a major installation in it; they were showing a huge new painting by Kiefer. The idea of arranging to ship sculpture that big to Paris made him want to go to sleep. It all seemed too difficult. He stuck the letter up on the refrigerator under a magnet in the form of a ceramic whale that Susan had bought at a crafts fair. He would think some other time about shipping a piece the size of a stuffed elephant across the Atlantic.

The next morning, he went out to his studio to look at the piece in question, stowed away since his show in August. His studio was cold and damp. He poked around for a few minutes. It hardly seemed worthwhile to start a fire. It was Saturday, but Allie Dove was out on the pond hauling in Tyrone's raft with the help of Ozzie. The day was silver grey, the pond like a puddle of melted lead. He found he did not much like to look at it. He turned his back on the Dove brothers and the raft and retreated to the kitchen. A lot of the summer people were up for the weekend, for the weather report had been overly optimistic, but Tyrone and Laurie had not appeared. He was glad of that, for he hoped Laurie would stay away until Jimmy had a new girlfriend. Jimmy needed to be married, there was no doubt of that. Of course, he still was. Willie often forgot that Jimmy was still married to Lisa and in fact had a child. A grandchild he had never seen. He had a sudden urge to see that child, but he was not about to inflict himself on Lisa. However, he thought to himself, maybe I will call her up. She always liked me. See how she's doing. Why not? I'm sure Jimmy never got around to writing her about Susan.

Jimmy popped in. "Want me to go into town for the mail, or do you want to do it this morning?"

Both of them liked that task, and sometimes they jockeyed for position, to be the one who was free at the optimum moment. It was eleven-thirty and the mail would be in the boxes. The advantage of going, besides being the one who opened the mail and read it first, the one who went through the catalogs and third class mail and tossed the ones he did not find attractive and brought home only the junk mail that intrigued him, was that the post office was always a social scene. He could count on running into two to four friends per trip.

"You go," Willie said, aware of his own generosity.

Jimmy went at once, before his father could change his mind. Willie smiled and looked up Lisa's number in the address book Susan had kept in the table under the phone.

She answered on the sixth ring, sounding a little harried. It took her a moment to place him or to figure out at any rate whether to go on talking, but she did. "Is something wrong?"

"Jimmy didn't think we should trouble you with it—he said

357

you couldn't possibly come out to the funeral anyhow—but I did want you to know that Susan's dead.''

"Dead? That's awful. Jimmy was so close to her. Was she sick?''

"She drowned in the pond swimming after dark," Willie said. "It was a big shock for all of us. He did take it hard.''

Lisa was silent for a while. "What's he doing these days?''

"Working construction. He's earning a decent living, although the work is hard, of course. But he's good at it. He has a good eye and a good hand.''

Someone spoke. A woman's voice. The roommate? Lisa covered the mouthpiece and said something back. When Lisa came on again, he asked. "How's my grandson? You wouldn't consider sending me a photo, would you?''

"I didn't know you wanted to see him. Of course I'll send you photos. We took some really cute ones just two weeks ago, when we went to the Locks for a picnic.''

"Your roommate and you?''

"She has a little baby boy. No father.''

"But your child does have a father and a grandfather," Willie said mildly. "Jimmy has never gotten over breaking up with you.''

"He ruined everything, Willie," Lisa said, and he could imagine her shaking her head, screwing her face up the way she did. "I hope he's sorry. I hope he's really sorry.''

"He is. He isn't even seeing anybody here. He's been concentrating on getting established as a builder.''

"I've been putting off getting the divorce straightened out. He's not going to start trouble over custody, is he?''

"I know he's been talking about wanting to see his son, but he said he thought he'd given you enough trouble.''

"I'm really sorry about Susan. She was such a lovely woman. She enjoyed things so much, like going out to dinner with us. . . . She was special. She gave me a dress last time she was here, one she made herself. . . . I am sorry about it. Maybe I'll write Jimmy. Of course I couldn't have come out. Besides, I'm barely surviving. Jimmy has been sending the money on time, but it isn't enough. Ask him if he can't send another twenty-five a week. Chris is too young for day care—''

Ah, Chris. That was the baby's name. He wrote it in the book beside Lisa's phone number. Then he wouldn't forget again.

". . . and my roommate can't baby-sit both kids except

weekends, so I can only work Saturday and Sunday unless I get a job that pays enough for a woman full time, but I don't think it's so good for them anyhow, for children that young when their mother's at work all the time. . . ."

When he got off the phone, he felt he had done his bit saving Jimmy. Feeling as dependent as he did on his son for getting through each day, he felt he owed him a little help, obvious or clandestine, whatever might do the most good. He did not think that Lisa was adamant any longer. Time and trouble and taking care of a four-month-old baby had softened her toward Jimmy somewhat, perhaps enough to be worked on. He did not think there was any danger Jimmy would go back to Seattle, but Lisa might be brought here. Maybe he would take care of the baby. He had enjoyed his own, after all. He had liked being a father. He still did like it. It would probably suit him, in the long run, better than it suited Jimmy. Willie was wanting that little grandson. Maybe Lisa would come, get a job, she and Jimmy would be busy and he would raise the little boy, whom he saw as something like Jimmy had been as a toddler, ruddy and plump.

That would give him something at the center of his life. It would be lively here again. He would call Lisa a couple of more times before he started working on Jimmy. Jimmy and he himself needed saving, badly, and maybe Lisa and Chris could rescue them. Something had to. He could not just drag on feeling hopeless.

FIFTY

Willie

The next morning Willie awoke to rain scratching on the roof, the rattling of sashes. The wind had come up strong during the night. He did not like to open his eyes, as there were Susan's things all in their places, and no Susan. The bed no longer gave up her scent—the sheets had been changed and changed again— but on the dresser her perfumes and powders stood, the top of her jewelry box open on the jumble of earrings. He was more camping in the room than living in it, most of his clothing still across the hall in the room Jimmy had moved back into. They lacked the energy to straighten themselves out. Order was losing to piles of unwashed clothes and casual dirt. He thought as he walked reluctantly down into his grey day, that the house was beginning to show that two men lived there and no woman. If only Dinah would hurry back. If only Dinah would move in and center his life. Why keep two houses open all winter?

As he stood just outside the door examining the harried clouds, letting Bogey do his business without a walk this morning, he could hear the surf pounding beyond the pond and over the dunes. An east wind was bringing rain and a sudden chill. The summer people had been fooled. They would start leaving by noon. The raft was gone and the pond stretched clear to the far shore, etched into short rough waves capped with froth. The gulls were passing low overhead on crooked wings, shrieking. He smelled salt and his skin stung slightly. This was the sort of morning he would have returned upstairs to Susan, wakened her with a pot of tea and they might have made love. Then she would go back to sleep and he would work.

He was not the sort of man who failed to appreciate what he had until he lost it. He had appreciated Susan strongly. Susan had felt he failed her by not having the kind of success she had hoped for, by not making as much money as she would have liked. Still he had not failed her in being loving, in being attentive, of that he was sure. He remembered his resolution to move Lisa and Chris, his unknown grandson, here to the pond, and while the idea seemed less powerful than the day before, it still had enough substance to give him a sense of momentum and hope.

Most mornings in the week he and Jimmy had taken to driving into town to breakfast at the Sandspit, where all the guys in the building trades ate. It was good networking, as Jimmy put it, because if you needed a mason or an electrician or an extra hand, you could find the man you wanted right over his cranberry muffin. It was where you heard about lots that might be available, subdivisions that might open up, who hadn't paid their bills. At the same time you could hear everything else worth knowing about everybody in town. Jimmy liked it for the contacts in the trade, but Willie did it for the company, so he wouldn't start the day lonely and blue.

However, on a Sunday, it was a different scene, family and couples and visitors. It would fill him with self-pity. He was puttering around the kitchen putting utensils away and wiping

360

the counters when Candida arrived in a bathrobe, with blood all over her face from a laid-open lip. It shook Willie to look at her. That bastard had to have hit her with all his might to cut her like that. She was crying so hard she could not speak at first. He set her down in a chair and this time he called Jimmy's good buddy George, the officer who had recovered Susan's body, and asked him if he could come by to take a look at what Candida's husband had done to her.

"Oh, you shouldn't have done that!" she said. "He'll be furious. He locked me out of the house."

"It's time for this to stop," Willie said. He felt purposeful. If his own life was over, he could still fix other people's, young people's lives. "You need help. They're used to domestic violence. It's not like ten years ago, when they'd tell you to go home and be a good wife. Even at town meeting, we talk about battering. Now I'm not going to clean you up until George gets here. He's on his way." He did not tell her that George remembered her all right, as the blond who wore the string bikini and even her pubic hair was blond. George would burn rubber getting there.

"It was so stupid! We started fighting about what to do about a leak in the roof—and it just exploded until he kept hitting me. I ran outside to get away from him and he locked the door and shouted from the upstairs window that I could stay out until I got down on my knees and begged him. He kept calling me names. I was sure everyone for miles could hear!"

"I didn't hear a thing," Willie said soothingly.

"I didn't know what to do! I was cold and wet and bleeding, and I just ran here."

He felt strong, competently dealing with Candida who was weeping and soaking wet. He wrapped a blanket around her and brought her hot tomato soup. George took her story and said it would be a good idea if she came into the station house to swear out a formal complaint. As Candida had been locked out in a robe and torn nightgown, Willie took her upstairs and found something of Susan's for her to wear. It was also clear she'd need stitches in her lip. He felt nervous as he waited for her to come downstairs in Susan's blue corduroy dress, but she did not look anything like Susan in it. She had belted it and unbuttoned the top three buttons, so it looked like a different dress.

George got her purse for her from the MacIvor house. He had words with Alec, who announced he was going back to Boston the next morning at six with or without Candida. George brought the purse with her keys and money and identification to Candida along with her raincoat, while she huddled in the truck beside Willie. Even with the two of them there, she seemed frightened that Alec would suddenly dash out of the house and hurt her.

"Why don't you leave him?"

"I have to, don't I? I've been putting things off. I was getting ready to this summer, I was thinking about it all the time, really I was." She had stopped crying but she held a bloody tissue to her cut lip. "I feel so embarrassed, everybody knowing how he treats me. I can't go on. In the city it's worse. There's nobody I can turn to. We live in a high-rise on the Jamaicaway, and nobody talks to me. We never see anyone but other doctors and their wives."

Willie waited with her through the whole process. In the emergency room at the hospital in Hyannis, she told him all about her mother, who had wanted to be an artist, her father who was a broker and had abused her mother, her brother who had cocaine problems and her sister, who had four children already. She told him about the boarding schools she had gone to. He told her about his family in turn and his civil rights days. By the time she was finally called, she was starting to tell him how she had met Alec. The doctor put three fine stitches in her lip, assuring her no one would be able to see his work. Then Willie brought her back home, since she did not want to go to her own house. "Alec has to return to the city. I'll just stay here, if you don't mind, till I can go over tomorrow, when I know he's gone. That's why I had that kind policeman get me the keys."

Willie said, "You're certainly safe here, I promise you. I'm not planning to go anyplace." It occurred to him he still had a key to her house, the duplicate he had made in May, but he did not tell her that.

"You really wouldn't mind if I stayed here tonight?"

"Jimmy and I would enjoy the company," he said genially. "The two of us rattle around over here."

"Of course . . . I noticed you have all her things still there. Do you want them? Or would you like some help?"

Right after Susan drowned, he had clung to the smell of the room, the traces of her. But he realized he was not comforted by that imitation presence any longer. Instead every gossamer

362

scarf, every earring tossed in a little dish gave him pain. "I can't do it. I can't get rid of anything."

"I could do it for you," she said. She no longer seemed to him the brittle pretty girl he had met that summer. He felt her vulnerability. She was thinner, slighter than Susan. She had smaller breasts and longer legs. He thought of her as just as fragile as Susan had been. "I could clear out her clothes and take them to the thrift shop or put them on consignment. That room is like a shrine to her."

He nodded. "I left it as it was." He did not bother telling her that it was particularly that way because Susan had cleared him out of the room and made him stay across the hall. "But could you really deal with her things?"

"You've done so much for me. Susan was my friend, and it would make me feel better if I could do something nice back for you."

"Then do it."

He put her in Johnny's room, still as it had been when she went away to college with old David Bowie and Blondie posters and masks she had made in high school. Candida seemed too mature for the room, but she acted glad to be there. She began working on the bedroom after supper. "Tomorrow I'll borrow your truck and get some boxes in town," she said calmly. Like him, obviously she felt better having a focus outside herself. It was therapeutic for her to help him, obviously, as it was for him to take on her troubles. It was right, he thought, right on all levels.

He decided to say as much, bluntly, out of curiosity about how she would respond. "I distract myself from my pain by helping you. You distract yourself from your pain by helping me. It's silly, but it works."

"I think it's beautiful," Candida said. "I think being open to each other and helping each other is what being human is all about."

She worked on the bedroom until ten, when she retired to Johnny's room. He fell asleep quickly. The day had been busy. When he woke, he was surprised to find her already downstairs. "You get up early," he said. "Susan thought nine was barely civilized."

"I haven't been sleeping well. But yes, I'm an early bird. The days here are so pretty in the morning." She put butter and jam on the table to go with the toast. "What do you have for breakfast, usually? Should I fry eggs? Or make an omelet?"

"Two sunny-side up," Willie said. "The pepper's in the grinder on the right."

Jimmy came down, his eyebrows rising. "Over lightly for me."

Monday morning. "Let's see how far we can get on the garage today. If the Sampsons are serious, when do we start?"

"They want six units, and of course they want it yesterday. Sure, let's get shut of the garage, put the windows in and close it up. Like you, I'm sorry we ever began." Jimmy reached for the small TV that sat on the kitchen table, looked again at Candida and thought better of turning it on. He would never have done so when Susan was alive. Turning on the TV at meals was a habit the two of them had got into lately.

"You won't be sorry in the winter," Candida said. "As soon as the stores open, I'll get some boxes. Willie, would you mind dreadfully walking by to see if Alec left for the city? I'm afraid to go over until I know he's gone."

"I'll take a walk with Bogey right after breakfast."

It was nice to have eggs. He didn't bother usually, just opened a box of cereal. She didn't make coffee as well as he did. He'd have to show her the way he liked it. It was soothing having a woman in the house. He felt less desolate. He didn't mind at all offering her refuge. When Jimmy had gone to the bathroom he asked her, "What happened to Tyrone? He got you into this."

"He's a bastard," she said tightly. "Got me into it and bailed out."

"He won't help?"

"He won't even take my phone calls. I'm too much trouble to bother with."

"He stuck it to us on the gallery we were renovating for him."

They exchanged Tyrone stories until Willie decided he should take Bogey and check on Alec. The MacIvor house was locked up and the blue Mercedes with the MD plates was gone. When Willie came home, Candida was on the phone with some lawyer. Jimmy was ready to roll on the garage, so they went to work, pushing themselves and each other. She drove to town for boxes, as she had promised.

When he knocked off and went upstairs to bathe and change, the room was a different place. She had put his clothes in the

364

closet and arranged his toiletries on the dresser top. His shoes were on the shoe rack. She had left some vases and bric-a-brac; other pieces she had removed. She had cut red chrysanthemums from Dinah's garden for the bedside table. He wandered from bed to dresser in a grateful daze. He could never have touched Susan's things, and he knew it. Candida had renewed the room for him and made it his.

The house smelled of pork chops. She must have bought them in town. Susan told him pork was too fatty, and Dinah wouldn't eat it. It smelled like home, like childhood. He was surprised that she could cook. She was not as good a cook as Dinah or as he himself was, but she did just fine. It was nice to have supper made for Jimmy and him. If he had realized she was going to do that, they could have worked an hour longer.

He was eager to be done with the garage, for the whole thing was unnecessary now, depressing. Tomorrow they would reach a point where they could leave it alone, indefinitely. Jimmy had got an advance from the Sampsons and left orders at the lumberyard. Still, Candida was right. In the winter, they would be glad for a garage. It was time to start on the job in town. He was thankful that he was a carpenter as well as an artist, if he was still a sculptor at all. What an irony that the request from the big show in France came just when he had lost his ability to work. Maybe he would never be able to create again, now that Susan was gone. Or maybe, when Dinah came back home, he would find himself again.

FIFTY-ONE

Dinah

Dinah always did tashlich on Rosh Hashonah day. It was a ritual she had performed with her father, journeying to the Chicago River—the casting off of sins, which Nathan had explained as attitudes, bad habits, heavy baggage she wanted to unload. She put crumbs into the pockets of her old suede jacket that had been Mark's. As the tide was turning outward, she crossed a covered sluice where a tidal river widened to enter the Bay. It was a place heavily used by fishers of all types, human and bird, great blue heron and kingfisher and gull, raccoon and fox and bluefish in a feeding frenzy. Beyond a fragile spit, the larger Bay stretched away, while the smaller bay before her curved along in a half moon shape, houses on one shore and the rest unspoiled, accessible only on foot or by small boat. The grass was still apple green in the marshes, tawny already on the hillsides. Enormous gulls croaked and mewed as they rose heavily or sat bobbing on the waves. On the marsh nearest the shellfish beds, a midden of oyster shells made a whitish mound.

What was she throwing away as she tossed the crumbs on the outgoing tide? I must discard the fear of intimacy, as if to know me is to eat me. I must abandon a self-absorption so great I can be surprised when one of the closest people in my life suddenly turns on me, for the suddenness is only in my perception. I must close with Itzak or let him go. I must stop trying to hold on to everybody, all options open, all promises half made. I must try to look clearly and closely and honestly at Willie and at Itzak, what I want, what they want and need—to choose. I must not throw away old commitments for new, but I must not cling to what is comfortable because I fear what is more challenging. It is time for me to decide whether to have a child, and if not, to be clear about that too. It is the year and the season to stop blundering and choose.

It was time to go to Dr. Bridey, her gynecologist, for her annual checkup. Almost a year had passed and she was still waffling. Slowly she walked home past fields of goldenrod not yet nipped by frost. Itzak had forbidden calls, so they would not speak till he returned, when their decision had to be ready. In the marshes, blackbirds were gathering in great flocks, about to fly south. One flock took two minutes to pass over her, walking under the beating of wings like a thousand tiny hand drums. All alive were heeding their biological imperatives.

She had been given her house back, for the work was finished and Jimmy had moved in with Willie. Her privacy was healing. She could work when and how she chose. She could traipse around in her underwear, hang her bras on the shower rod to dry, run downstairs rosy from her bath to put water on to boil. Yet she felt lonely. She was not sure if it was Itzak she missed, or just company.

In her absence, Willie and Jimmy had roofed the building in the yard as a one-story garage, shingled it and put on the side and garage doors. The truck still parked in the drive every night, however. The center of the garage, as she peered in, was occupied by sawhorses and an electric saw. A row of garden implements, some buckets and an opened sack of bone meal had accumulated there. Willie and Jimmy had driven off at seven that morning in the truck and had not yet come back.

This was the day she volunteered in the library from six to nine, so she ate a fast supper and rushed off. It was one more event that delayed her seeing Willie. She had left her car in Itzak's driveway, taking a taxi from Logan, so she had not even needed her plane met. She had hoped to surprise a decision out of herself, but she felt muddled and conflicted. Willie was being patient, which she appreciated. It made her feel indebted. He was less insistent than Itzak, certainly a virtue. What advantage was there in seeking the harder relationship over the easier?

Burt told her about Candida's flight from her husband. Willie and George were her champions. A divorce was in process. Neither partner wanted to stay married and indeed, Burt said, it was quickly apparent in talking to Candida or to Alec that their feelings about each other amounted to intense dislike, with a wash of fear on Candida's part and anger on Alec's. They would go the no fault route if their lawyers could negotiate a property settlement. If they had to fight it out in court, legal battles could cost thousands and get nasty. Tyrone was hiding in New York and had not been down since Labor Day. The local consensus was that he had acted like a creep. A rumor was going around that he had been having an affair with Susan too, and that when Susan discovered him with Candida, she had killed herself.

"That's pure horseshit, Burt," Dinah said. "Susan adored Tyrone, but an affair? He had absolutely no reason to have an affair with her. He might have fifteen years ago, when they first met, but then she had little kiddies."

"It's not my rumor, Dinah. But Mary Lou is convinced. She swears Susan was in love with Tyrone and that he promised to help her move to Manhattan to be near him, if she'd leave Willie."

"Does Willie know what people are saying?"

"Willie's too well-liked. Nobody would repeat it around him. But Jimmy must know. Construction workers gossip worse than a sewing circle."

That people should make up stories about Susan stung Dinah; but in a sense Susan had loved Tyrone: not the man, but the life

367

she made him represent. "I'll never believe it was suicide, but I can believe it was a fatigue of the will. A failure to want to fight through and survive."

"Too much psychologizing, dear. Even a good swimmer can tire and mistake her energy level or the distance. Muscles get cold and they cramp. Then you get a faceful of water and start sputtering and coughing. . . ."

"I still think if we'd all been together, she'd still be alive."

"You're brooding. Accepting death is hard when you just broke up with somebody. The pain of parting is there already and then comes worse pain." Burt spoke with the authority of someone who had lost half his friends to AIDS. At least once a month he had a funeral to attend.

When she got home, Nita had called leaving a message for her to turn on Channel 2, public TV, at nine. It was half past. She assumed that Nita was performing, perhaps the BSO. Instead there was Itzak halfway through a lush full orchestral arrangement of the Bachianas 6. It was like walking into the middle of an animated conversation; she felt left out, deprived of what she had missed. But it was disorienting, too, to see him in a concert taped before they had ever met. Was this their future, her watching him on TV, noticing his name in the paper?

The next day she stopped by the new house. Willie and Jimmy were off wherever they had been going every day. She left a note on the table inviting them both to supper. That was the coward's way, but in Jimmy's company, she should be able nonetheless to figure out what she ought to do about Willie: or what she wanted. Ought was one tangle she could not thread her way through, and want-to was a briar patch equally knotted and overgrown.

When she was with Itzak, she wanted to be with him and only with him. She felt right. She fought it and quarreled with it and fussed over it and analyzed it, but the connection was powerful. On the other hand, new relationships had a compulsion to them—infatuation and novelty. She had shared a decade with Willie. That was an old and honorable commitment she should not lightly discard for something newer, more compelling sexually or emotionally or intellectually.

With Susan dead, did she owe Willie her companionship? Might he not truly need her more than Itzak did? Itzak had his fame and his success. What did Willie have, besides the life she had helped him create?

368

Willie and Jimmy appeared for supper. "I was wondering what had happened to you," Willie complained with a big grin. "I was getting worried."

She went through her explanation, finding herself watching him carefully for his reaction to her going to services. Why was she suddenly sensitive? Being with Itzak made her feel her Jewishness more strongly, which no doubt was part of his appeal. But she could hardly give a lot of weight to his Jewishness, although it was important to her, for it was not Willie's fault he was a gentile. She remembered how sarcastic she had been to Burt about Joe, the Black fisherman who had gone out with Tyrone's maid Celeste that summer, when he decided after six years with his white girlfriend that he couldn't stay with her because she was white. "Did he just notice? I mean, one morning in bed, did he suddenly say, hey, that isn't makeup?" No, she could not in good faith suddenly decide that Willie's not being Jewish was a large flaw.

"Look at this." Willie pulled an envelope of photos out of his jacket pocket. "This is my grandson Chris."

The photos took Chris from turnip-shaped baldy to towheaded beaming infant. Willie wanted a fuss, needed it more than Jimmy did. Jimmy also looked at the photos, as if he were still curious about them. He stared, but then he handed them back to his father. Chris had not, Dinah noted, been introduced as Jimmy's son so much as Willie's grandson.

Willie was telling an elaborate story about Chris and a neighbor's poodle. Dinah asked, "So, you're on speaking terms with Lisa?" She addressed the question to both of them.

"I call her every Sunday," Willie said proudly. "I hear about Chris's week. Gosh, he looks like you did at his age," he added to Jimmy.

"Babies look more or less the same," Jimmy said mildly. "It was a little awkward when you put me on with Lisa. We've never been real fluent on the telephone."

"It's a beginning," Willie said.

Dinah looked from one to the other. Willie was playing some hand of his own. Jimmy looked to be just figuring that out. She couldn't abandon them. She was related to Jimmy, a surrogate but highly real aunt or stepmother.

They were working on the same Victorian house, but for a different owner. She could sense each of them had something to say about that they were not going to say in front of the other, so she cut short her questioning until she might see each privately. How could so much have happened in her brief absence? Fall had quickened the pace of life.

Once the summer people cleared out, her friends always seemed to be buzzing around at three times the rate of August. Many of the locals worked such long hours during the summer season, they had time for little else but sleep. Come September, they had shopping lists of things to do and people to see, a whole life to catch up on, money to spend. Susan had always gone into a mild depression in September, but Willie claimed to find life more invigorating when he didn't have to stand in line for half an hour to buy a quart of milk and a newspaper, when he didn't have to park a mile out of town and hike in to get his mail. If he wanted to experience a permanent traffic jam, he would have stayed in Manhattan, he said. People fell in love in fall, threw parties, changed careers, broke up, made the kind of decision that faced her.

Jimmy excused himself at ten, but Willie stayed put. She realized that he could actually sleep the night with her. That was something they had regretted not being able to do over the years, but she was used to that separation. At first she had had trouble sleeping with Itzak, unaccustomed as she was to another body and will in her private space. Then she had grown to enjoy his presence, although she did not think she would ever again be someone who wanted to share her bed every night. Sex and sleep had been forever divorced for her.

She had not decided whether she would resume making love with Willie. She had stopped sex as a temporary measure when she was waiting for him to tell Susan. Now Willie was assuming they were going upstairs together, and she could not figure out why they shouldn't. It seemed natural, and refusing felt rude and premature. She had not figured out what to do, so why hurt him? He put his arm around her and drew her toward the stairway. It did not seem the moment to argue. We are the survivors of that shipwreck, she thought climbing the steps ahead of him in a melancholy daze. We must comfort each other.

In her room they each undressed and got into bed before they began to caress each other. He felt bulky, immense after Itzak, coarser to the touch. She had trouble concentrating on the lovemaking. As she was kissing him, her mind was wandering over the situation. She felt ill at ease. He had been Susan's long before he became hers, and she was used to him as partially or mostly

Susan's. She could not quite get Susan out of her mind. She was slow to excite. Her body felt sluggish, her mind, hyperactive. But Willie was patient. That was his nature, and she was grateful to him. He never liked to rush lovemaking, and he did not mind taking it gradually.

By the time she was riding him, she had slipped into the act and she no longer thought about whether she was at ease or not because she no longer much thought. Instead her mind moved in rhythms, her heart drumming, the varied tempos of the fucking, the beat in his throat against her mouth, his pulse inside her. The rhythms moved in bursts of light across her clenched eyes and she felt carried forward as if on an immense wave of brasses. When she came, she lay a moment against his chest and then began again for him, shifting forward, going harder, faster for him, reaching down to grasp his balls.

She felt at peace when they lay side by side, still partially entangled and sticky. She should get up and wash before she dribbled all over the sheets, but she hated to ruffle the warm calm in which they lay. It was familiar with him, it was good still. She was so weary of comparing the two men, dissimilar and incomparable, that she felt like never thinking about either relationship again. Willie was more tolerant of Itzak than Itzak of Willie, which also seemed to argue in Willie's favor.

I am not a woman but a debating society, a conference full of workshops and controversies unable to hammer out a single resolution, doomed to remain in session until some final consensus is reached and beginning to feel like disbanding entirely. She decided she was on the verge of giving them both up. She would collect more cats and eschew the company of men.

At breakfast Willie was pondering too. He said suddenly, "It's silly to keep both houses open all winter. We should live in mine—it's bigger—and close this one up."

"Willie, I work on a piano or on my synthesizer. I'm not about to have all that apparatus moved. I have a dehumidifier installed behind the piano for wet weather. Moving Chester would put him hideously out of tune."

"Umm. I guess I could live here."

"Isn't that a lot of work just to cut oil and electric bills? What about Jimmy?"

"That's why I thought of my house. It's bigger. But Jimmy could use the room he was using."

"But I was delighted when Jimmy moved out. I work at home—I don't go off to a studio the way you do."

"I understand." He was silent for a while, eating his cereal. Then he said, "I like living with a woman. I miss it. When Candida stayed with us right after Alec beat her the last time, Jimmy and I really appreciated having a woman in the house."

"Why don't you ask Candida to move in?" Dinah suggested sarcastically. "She seems available."

"You think she'd like that?" Willie asked.

Dinah assumed he was joking back. "Ask her."

"She's finally getting a settlement worked out. For a while it seemed they'd have to take to the courts." He began telling her the tedious details of the struggle between Alec and Candida MacIvor. She tuned out, clearing the table. Time to get him moving. She wanted to sit down with the compositions she had begun in Scotland and see what her sketchy beginnings might lead toward. He was talkative. Finally she interrupted. "Willie, I need to get at my music. I don't like to talk in the mornings, and normally neither do you. Aren't you working?"

"Not on my sculpture. I haven't been able to since Susan died. Maybe I'll be able to buckle down soon." He did, however, at last get his jacket and head for town.

The next few evenings she ate at Willie's. Then she did not see any of them while she and Zee went off for Yom Kippur services. When she broke her fast, Toby was a supper guest too. He and Jimmy seemed thick. "We're going into business together," Jimmy said. "We're going to develop Toby's land."

Dinah said nothing. It was not what she would consider good news. She loved walking in the woods back there, and the last thing she longed for was a row of summer houses, a subdevelopment of four hundred thousand dollar aquariums for psychiatrists and lawyers. On the other hand, land was the only thing the Captain had, since the IRS had taken his house and his boat, and no doubt he was sick of camping in an old clam shack on what used to be his family's woodlot. He, too, wanted to make a buck and a living. It was the nature of development for summer people that after a while, if you were not serving them or selling to them, you were priced out.

"Where will you get the money to start?" Presumably they could finance the second house off the first and so on, but where would they get the cash for building the first on spec? Unless they had a buyer before they started or sold just the land. Nothing in that for Jimmy and not much for Toby.

"We're going to the bank Monday. And I know some guys who'll come in as partners. They have cash."

Why did she assume they were about to launder some money? That evening she spent with Willie in his house, so that she could get away in the morning. He had not brought up the idea of closing one of the houses again. In the morning she rose early, took a brisk walk with him around the pond and then went to work. It was Saturday. Willie decided to take the weekend off construction. He ambled toward his studio. "I'll give it a try," he said. "Might as well shake up the mice."

"If you have mice, I'll lend you Figaro," she said over her shoulder.

"I mean the ones in my head."

Dinah had a few in her own. It was not a good workday. Her life she liked to keep less interesting than her work, and right now her life was demanding too much attention. She was standing at the windows staring at the lightly ruffled water when Candida tripped by. She idly wondered if she should tell Candida where everybody was—Jimmy off with Toby walking over the land in question, Willie in his studio. Candida however reappeared from the house and flashed across the yard to the studio, gave a fast tap and passed inside. Dinah expected her to emerge swiftly, but Willie was obviously receiving—probably stuck—for Candida did not leave while Dinah was standing there.

Dinah played through the sketches trying to improvise a richer texture. Instead her eyes kept coming to rest on the calendar. Itzak had spent Yom Kippur in London. He had had in mind attending services in his old synagogue, seeing his ex-wife and establishing some sort of peace, swallowed up and off limits in the world he had lived in before they had met, a dense world of old friends and old lovers and old commitments. Tomorrow he would be returning, expecting resolution where she knew only moods and thoughts shifting like the surface of the pond. Time was closing in on her. Not to decide was to decide. He would give up on her.

She thought that quite likely from a rational point of view, but her body flinched. Her body gave her first a stomachache, then intestinal cramps. It said, you're trying to kill me. It said, oh sorrow! It said, I want Itzak. Her body was too hot and then too cold and then it made a false flu of aches and gripes.

She put down her flute and went to the windows again. Tosca planted herself right in front of her, putting her paws on Dinah's shoulders and staring into her face. "Right, Tosca," she muttered, "it's a hard knot to unravel." She did want Itzak. It was something fierce and heavy pulling on her. It was something she wanted to give way to, but that did not mean she should do so. Wanting comes and wanting goes, she thought, but truly she could not think of a time in her life when that had been true. Her years of casual sex had been governed more by others' desires for her than by any particular desperate wanting on her part. In fact most of those partners had been unmemorable, interchangeable, forgotten unless unusually proficient or inept. She had never stopped wanting Mark, even when he was too ill to make love. She had not stopped wanting Willie, although if she chose Itzak, she could control that desire. She had never stopped wanting Susan.

But choosing Itzak would disrupt her life. She would have to be in the city more, not something she would pick in itself. Would she refuse Itzak, because the relationship was less convenient? That would be cowardly, mean. Round and round she went, digging herself into a pit that just grew deeper. Her deadline had come. Tomorrow she must meet Itzak's plane at Logan.

At four she gave up her futile attempts to concentrate and went next door. She was surprised to find no one in the house. When she went to the studio, she was even more surprised to find Candida still there. Since eleven? Candida and Willie were building a large crate. Willie was ebullient. "Candy figured out how we can ship my piece to Paris. I was ready to forget about it, but she stayed on it. She talked to the curator—she speaks French."

"Oh, un peu," Candida said, rolling her eyes. "Anyhow he speaks English perfectly well. We'll take it into Boston and ship it through the port. It would be a terrible pity to pass up this exhibition. People from all over the world will see it. It's an important show."

Dinah wondered when Candida had become an expert on the art world. She had glanced at the letter on the refrigerator, then forgot it. She was too involved in her decision to be much use to Willie.

Candida stayed to supper, without anybody asking her as far as Dinah could tell. She seemed to do so by right. Willie was in the best of spirits. He kept telling Dinah little things about

374

Candida, as if commending them to each other. "Candy likes to cook. She has a wonderful touch with pastry. Wait till you taste her pies," Willie said. For some reason his accent was pronounced. Candida seemed to bring out the southern gentleman in him. "Doesn't she make a fine pie?" he asked Jimmy to stand witness. Toby came by for Jimmy soon after supper and they went off together.

"Candy likes to walk," he said. "You could take walks together."

"Oh yes," Candida said with too fervent enthusiasm. "I just love walking. I walk for miles, practically, whenever I get a chance."

As the evening wore on, she caught Candida staring at her with intense curiosity and wariness. What did Candida hope for? What did the woman fear from her? Never previously had Candida shown the least curiosity about her. Suddenly Dinah was a person Candida had decided was important for good or ill.

Willie's desire that she suddenly begin to like Candida worried at her. She began to suspect something more between them than his saving her from a punch in the nose. Could she ask Jimmy? Why not just wait and ask Willie? Why not go home and see what happened next? She stood and excused herself on the basis of fatigue and a long day's work tomorrow. Neither objected. They both saw her to the door.

She went into her house but did not turn on the lights. Instead, feeling a trifle ridiculous, an amateur theatrical gumshoe, she watched the new house. The lights went out downstairs, but for the hall light left on for Jimmy. The lights went on upstairs, in the master bedroom. Candida did not leave. With Tosca and Figaro curled together like improperly sized yin and yang, nose to tail and tail to nose in her lap as she rocked, she sipped cognac and watched for another two hours. Now it was after twelve. The house was dark except for the hall light, which Jimmy turned out as he went in. She could follow his progress to the bathroom and then to his bedroom. Finally his light too snapped off and the new house was completely dark.

FIFTY-TWO

Willie

Willie was trying to work, depressed and feeling it doubly because fall was his favorite season and he felt desperately alone. He had never grown bored with the colors of the Cape, never come to take them for granted. Every fall they burned for him, but this time, he did not catch fire with the Virginia creeper, the rum cherries. He avoided thinking how he was going to mail his enormous piece off to Paris, but it stood in the middle of the floor like a big awkward reproach whenever he entered his disused and dusty studio. He felt as if somebody else had created it and he was a fraud. While Dinah was in Scotland, he was marking time waiting for her; perhaps with her return his life would begin again. He was angry with her in a muted way for going, but she had been depressed too. They had pulled together getting through the funeral, the endless arrangements, but grief had separated as much as united them. It was a private emotion that each took off to brood over. He understood her running off to Scotland, at the same time he did not think it fair to desert him.

Therefore he was not irritated as he once would have been when Candida appeared just at twelve carrying a basket. "I had a roast beef, so I made sandwiches. I thought you might like lunch. I guess I'm so used to cooking for someone, I do it automatically, but the house felt empty." She was wearing a pale blue sweater and skirt the color of her eyes. It set off her pale hair and her remaining tan. She always wore a fair amount of makeup, but he was used to that by now. It was just her way of trying to please, a kind of flirtation. Perhaps she had begun applying lots of makeup to cover the bruises from Alec.

"No, I'm glad for the company. Should we go up to the house?"

"Let's picnic here. Your studio fascinates me. I'd never been in an artist's studio before yours."

"Are you chilly? I can make a fire in the stove."

"That would be just lovely."

He cleared a space on a card table and they pulled up straight chairs. She had brought sandwiches, a pasta salad and a bottle of Cabernet Sauvignon. In a short time he was feeling almost happy, with company and good food and wine to warm him. He just never went and bought wine. That was something Susan had taken care of, so he had never learned what to pick out. He and Jimmy drank beer. They tended to eat in front of Dan Rather. Then they watched a ball game, with the pennant race tightening. It was a good season for sports on TV to kill the time till he could crawl into bed.

It felt wonderfully comforting and civilized to sit down with a woman and eat real food face-to-face, even on a card table in his studio and to drink a good red wine, even out of coffee cups, and sit and smile and flirt a little. She was telling him her week's excitement with the lawyers and the settlement. She made funny stories of it, although he knew she found it upsetting and at times frightening. He was astonished to hear himself chuckling and then laughing. He could not remember the last time he had laughed out loud.

Then she got up, came around to him and put her arms around his neck. "Willie, you've been so good to me, I don't know what I'd do without you," she said and kissed him on the mouth.

The wine must have gone to both their heads, he thought, but it also felt very sweet that she would come to him that way. He was surprised, and he thought he should not take advantage of her if she was drunk. Then he decided she wasn't drunk and neither was he and so what? Her sweater was soft under his hands, more cloud than wool. Candida's clothes seemed evanescent. But not the body underneath. She took a good firm grip on him. She was tall and he liked that. He liked the way she felt rubbing against him forthrightly, to let him know what she wanted. He appreciated being let to know that directly, not to be guessing and making mistakes.

He was surprised but then not. It felt right and natural. She had good firm swelling hips and buttocks his hands slid down to. It was awkward getting the clothes off the first time. Her underwear too was pale blue and she smelled like nice soap. She was not wearing perfume. He realized he had told her he did not like it, that Susan's perfume used to give him a headache. He liked her having listened and taken note.

They made love on the cot in his studio. He had done that many times with Dinah, but never with Susan. Candida was hot

377

and wet and eager. From the first moment he touched her between the legs and found the clitoris, she began breathing heavily and wriggling her ass. A kind of blush spread over her cupcake breasts. He got so excited he came sooner than he wanted, but he got hard again in a while and came back into her. Oh, it tasted good. He felt himself alive through and through for the first time in weeks. He felt whole. He did not want to take his hands off her. It was getting to be late afternoon. Shadows the color of the backs of swallows barred the grass. He peed in the yard and came back to her, still spread on his couch like a Matisse odalisque. Her body was pear-shaped. He imagined doing a series of woman-fruit shapes in resin, to celebrate the way her body felt. Shapes that would seem to pulsate and yet *be* solidly, pulling him in toward them, pulling the eye and the hand into them. He saw a shape, woman and not, ripeness.

Afterward he made supper and she ate with Jimmy and him and spent the night. He felt a little awkward. There was no way to explain to Jimmy—what could he say? He slept better than he had in months. In the morning they made love again. She said she took the pill. She had not had any affairs ever, she said, not until she thought she was in love with Tyrone, but she wasn't. She had simply wanted to be in love so much she had talked herself into it. She had known she wanted him for a whole month already.

Sex made her cheerful, he could tell, just as it did him. She was growing more confident around him. She got out of bed in the mornings even more quickly than he did and ran downstairs in her blue robe to make breakfast. He could not get over how fast she got up and how she liked to make love in the mornings. It started the day out differently, on a high note.

When they got to the house in town that morning, Willie did not turn on his radio right away but said to Jimmy, "You know Candy stayed with me."

Jimmy shrugged. "I figured that was in the works."

"How come?" Willie cocked his head. "It surprised me."

"She's fine, Dad. We both need a woman. . . . What's Dinah going to think about it? That's more to the point."

Willie grunted. That had to be dealt with when Dinah got back. He said nothing during their couple of phone calls. He hated trying to talk to her across the Atlantic. It made him feel grumpy.

Candy was trying to get the legal work straightened out in the

378

city, so she had to keep running back and forth. In the settlement the lawyers were working out, Alec got the condo and she got the house on the pond. They each kept their own vehicles, the securities they had brought with them, and split the mutual funds and the bank accounts. Willie had never been through a divorce, so the details intrigued him. Alec's lawyer argued that his client should be compensated for the injury done him by Candida's infidelity. Candida's lawyer denied the infidelity, demanded compensation for the years she had spent supporting Alec emotionally and at times financially through medical school and internship, threatening to request a share of his lucrative practice. After much bobbing and weaving, a no fault divorce was worked out. In a way Willie was disappointed, for he had always loved courtroom dramas, but he could understand Candida's reluctance. Jimmy followed the proceedings with interest, like the pennant race.

At first, it wasn't clear to him how involved he and Candida were going to be. He assumed he would actually live with Dinah. They had been together all those years, but they had never lived in the same house. Then Dinah came back and said no right out. She wanted to live in her house and she did not want him to live there with her. He was disappointed, but Dinah obviously could see that. She immediately suggested to him that he find out if Candy wanted to live with him.

He was surprised she had guessed about them—or maybe Jimmy had dropped a hint? Maybe the change in himself was so apparent she could guess?—and pleased she accepted the relationship. He had expected to break it to her over the next week or so, but since she knew and didn't seem outraged, he brought the two women together as soon as he could, so they might commence getting to be friends. He worried a little how it would work out, who he would spend the night with, and decided probably he would spend it alone for the sake of getting them off to a good start. Dinah's running off with Zee to services had meant he had had some time to spend with Candida that week.

"You don't just expect them to, you know, get involved the way Mother and Dinah were," Jimmy asked cautiously in the kitchen the night Willie had them both to supper.

"Candy has never had a relationship with a woman—but then your mother hadn't either, before Dinah. I don't feel it's my

379

place to push that or to prevent it. I just want them to like each other."

Jimmy rolled his eyes upwards. "Lots of luck."

"Dinah's adaptable, and Candy really wants to get along with her."

Indeed Dinah was very tactful and excused herself, leaving them together. He felt as if he was finally getting his life pulled back into shape. He didn't come right out and ask Candy that evening if she wanted to live there, because he realized she had to keep her own residence while the divorce was in progress. But once they had become lovers, she never suggested that she go home at night. Now even when Candy didn't sleep over, he saw her things hanging there, her slippery satin dark blue robe, her velour slippers that matched it, her fuchsia nightgown and her flimsy royal blue. The room no longer felt bereft. Susan had liked Candida and brought her into their lives; they had been friends. Susan would have approved of Candida being with him.

That was good because Dinah was making herself scarce. He wanted to confront her, but she had vanished. Even the cats were off someplace with her.

Sunday Willie called Lisa, as he did every week. She was expecting his call. "Willie, I've been thinking about what you said, about us coming to visit. If you send tickets, we could come for Thanksgiving or Christmas."

"I'll do it. I'll buy the tickets and send them to you. How's my grandson Chris?"

When he got off the phone, Candy was open about the fact that she'd been listening. "You know, I was a travel agent. I worked in an agency in Boston while Alec was in med school. Let me make the arrangements."

He was happy to turn the travel plans over to her. He liked the way she saw problems and set out to solve them without making a fuss. Alec was an idiot, letting go a cute warm generous woman like Candy. Alec was too immature and too self-involved to appreciate her, that's what he told Candy. She had happened to him almost accidentally, like Susan running into him with her bicycle, but one of his strengths was that he could seize what was offered him, size it up quickly, instinctively, and take good strong hold. They were both earthy people who could make strong commitments without fuss.

"I was into security, Willie. How much further can you go than marrying a medical student? Obviously with Tyrone, I was

380

doing the same old thing, looking for a man to take care of me. But I don't need taking care of. I'm not a child. I have my own money. I've finally grown up and now I can be with a man who isn't safe and dull—a real artist. I wouldn't have dared to be with you when I was younger, because I was too scared."

"But you've taken charge. A lot of women don't have the guts to leave a man who beats them."

"You gave me the courage to leave. It was your support!" She shook back her hair in that way she had and beamed at him. She was letting her hair grow out for him—she knew he liked it softer.

The next day they took his piece into Boston to ship it to France. Alec had taken over the condo, so they stayed in a new hotel down on the harbor. They had an Italian supper in the North End and then walked along the docks, window shopping. The whole trip was a present she was giving him. She had made the reservations on her credit card, separate now from Alec's account, and she had chosen the hotel and the restaurant, places she wanted to share.

He felt special with Candy. He felt as if she was courting him, as if she saw him as this incredibly attractive and seductive man, as if his being simply the sculptor he was made him adorable to her. She kept asking him to teach her about art. She brought home books on Henry Moore and Hans Haacke, because he mentioned them casually. Maybe she was right, that he had saved her from Alec, from cruelty and abuse, from misery. Yes, they had saved each other. He had been paralyzed with grieving.

"Alec never had time for me. If we went to Cambridge and ate in a fern bar, it was a big event. Our social life was having bad dinners with proctologists and orthopedic surgeons and ob-gyn men. And their wacked out beaten down wives. My future."

He began to see them both as people who were more loving, more giving, more sexual and sensual than the partners they had been with appreciated or could use. With each other, they bloomed into what they were meant to be.

"You know what? My divorce will be settled long before the show. Let's go to France when it opens."

"To Paris? In February?"

"Why not? I've never been able to travel. I did during college, in fact I spent my junior year in Grenoble. But Alec was the world's worst traveler. He hated anyplace where he couldn't get a steak rare and Diet Pepsi, and he thought all those foreigners were jabbering that way just to annoy him.''

"I don't know what kind of traveler I am. Susan and I went to Europe the summer we married. But once we had kids, we rarely traveled. New York. My parents a couple of times.'' He had a moment of anxiety as he thought of his daughter. He wondered if he could get Dinah to break the news of his new relationship to Johnny; then he realized Jimmy would already have told Johnny. He could ask Jimmy how she was taking it.

"Will I meet your parents?''

"Do you want to?''

"Of course. Once I'm divorced. Not until then, naturally, it wouldn't be right.''

"They'll like you,'' he said immediately, then thinking about it knew that he was absolutely right. That, too, would be put back together. That, too, would be healed. They would go to North Carolina together in the spring. The desire to see it, to smell it again, made him ache with desire that focused him once more on her. He was starting a new growth cycle, like a big oak tree.

FIFTY-THREE

Laurie

Laurie was hungry and cold. They did not have the heat on yet in the gallery, nor had it been needed until today, when the temperature had decided to sink the way the stock market had been doing that week. She had sent Rudi, the kid Sean had hired to assist her, for sushi take-out. She was stuck waiting for a delivery of pedestals promised every day since Monday. It was two already; Rudi had disappeared in transit. She had spent the last three weeks trying to decide if Rudi had been hired so that (1) Sean could fuck him; (2) Sean thought Rudi decorative, which he was; (3) some obscure favor was being done or paid back.

Whatever was going on, Rudi was next to useless. He tied up the phone on personal calls. He chatted with everyone who came in, as if he were the hostess of a floating tea party. The only thing he did well was move heavy objects, for he certainly had he body of a weight lifter, displayed at every opportunity. She had been disarmed at first by his omnivorous flirtatiousness, his puppyish desire to be liked and admired, but his pursuit of attention was interfering with his getting work done. He had to be let go. Sean had hired him and Sean should fire him. She tried to view calmly and equably approaching Sean about that task, but her empty stomach clutched.

The initial supper on the Cape had gone splendidly, although she had been disappointed he did not in fact stay Friday night with them, but left for Provincetown and his friends after supper. Celeste had followed her instructions almost perfectly. The grilled fresh tuna with bitter orange sauce had been smashing. From the clam vol au vents to the fresh fruit sorbets, it had been exactly right. Sean had been charming, full of anecdotes about people she longed to meet, dropping gossip about artists and critics, just as she had imagined.

When Sean had arrived that afternoon, Daddy and he had closeted themselves for a couple of hours, hammering out the last details of the agreement for the gallery. While she was dressing for supper, Tyrone knocked at her door and slipped in to bring her up-to-date. It was truly going to happen. She had felt giddy with joy all evening, sorry only that Sean was granting them merely his company at supper and not staying that night as had been planned. Oh well, she had consoled herself, she would be seeing plenty of him in New York.

That at least had proved to be true. However, in the gallery that charm evident on the Cape had not been directed toward her. Perhaps Sean was nervous about the gallery succeeding. When she had briefly approached Tyrone about the tension she felt between Sean and herself, he had suggested that as a likely source and urged patience. She did not feel she could complain again. Tyrone had done so much for her, and with the market troubled, he was working long hours and on the phone most of the time he was home. She could not pester him about how Sean treated her, that was clear. She must deal with him on her own. Tyrone had a right to expect such an initiative, such responsibility from her. She had to justify his trust.

She found herself crunching the order for the pedestals to a amp ball in her hand. Carefully she spread it on the desk, rubbing out the wrinkles. She imagined exactly what she would say to Rudi when he finally walked in with her lunch. "Well, is that my supper? Or tomorrow's breakfast? Tell me, were you growing seaweed? How far did you go for that, Tokyo or just San Francisco? Did you pick out the rice grains one at a time?'

It would be a pleasure to fire him. She had friends too, including Evan, who could perfectly well move objects around just as heavy as Rudi could, but who was hardworking and would appreciate her throwing a gallery job his way. She had known Evan since art school. He was someone she would enjoy having around. She had always been kind of interested in him, but in school, he had been living with a woman, and then he had been married; only recently had he become available. He worked in the medium of painted photographs and painted color slides but he was built like an old-fashioned moving man. She had run into him at the Whitney, and when they had coffee afterward she sounded him out. He said he'd love to have a part-time job for the winter. It had been fun to hint around at her situation, to bring up the job possibility as if casually. It had given her fascinating little taste of power.

She would be moving into her apartment eventually, but in the meantime she was living in her old room at Tyrone's. He had been out of the country a great deal, in Tokyo twice, in London, in Saudi Arabia, in Bonn. He had returned Saturday and they had had a lovely supper together Sunday night, but he was frenetically busy. Betty had been restored to her position as Tyrone's usual dinner and theater partner, when he had visitors to entertain. She got on with Betty, who tended to glaze over as the evening progressed anyhow, but after her rapport with Candida, it was a comedown. She missed Candida. It had been pleasant to have a confidante to share her admiration for Tyrone.

Laurie's condo had been supposed to be ready in October. She had thought she'd be moved in by now. Now they were saying January. She would not have minded, really, since she liked having Celeste cook for her, having laundry taken care of and she'd certainly had the big duplex mostly to herself. The problem was that she still missed Jimmy. She kept getting strong subliminal message from Tyrone that he did not want her going to the Cape. He was worried, she could tell. Living at Tyrone's meant not having Jimmy as a guest, that was clear never stated. She was sensitive enough to know that the whole area of Susan Dewitt's death was extremely sore and touchy and that Candida was permanently off limits.

She was sure that if she only had the chance she could talk Jimmy into visiting. In the meantime, there was no one with whom she could talk about him, nothing to remind her they had been close. She could not even find the necklace he had given her. She thought she had worn it on the Cape, but then Labor Day weekend she could not find it, and she had not been able to put her hands on it since. She could not have lost it! She would certainly not let Jimmy discover she had, if she had been that careless.

Maybe Rudi's ineptitude particularly galled her because that was the job she had thought she could throw Jimmy's way, but there had not been an opportunity to do so. But she did feel that, as she was supposed to be in charge of all the practical and management side of the gallery, hiring the assistant should be her prerogative. That too she must bring up with Sean. Her demands seemed reasonable when she ran the list over in her mind. She walked to and fro on the newly laid floor, practicing feeling in charge. She *was* in charge. Why did she let Sean intimidate her?

Just then Sean walked in with Rudi and his old friend and former lover Carl, and Carl's friend Inga. Seeing her across the room at openings, it had taken Laurie a couple of times to realize Inga was female, for she was six feet two, lean, perfectly flat and dressed in tailored black worsted, pants and suit jacket, with a regimental tie. Inga was an ex-model who had moved into catering and was reputed to be doing extremely well. They were giddy and hilarious. They all disappeared into Sean's office—it had been supposed to be both of theirs, but he had taken it over and she was relegated to a corner of the storage room—without even a nod at her, except for Sean's query, "Order come? Tant pis."

They remained closeted with Sean until four, when the pedestals finally arrived. By the time she was done with the delivery men, Sean was alone in his office. She still had had no lunch. She decided the moment had come to beard him, for Rudi had not even apologized and had instead acted as if he were on intimate terms with Carl and Inga, while she twiddled her thumbs in the empty gallery waiting for the delivery men.

"Sean, I want to talk to you about Rudi."

Sean put down the catalog from a show in Milan. "What on earth is there to say about him?"

"He doesn't do his job. He's a nuisance. He was supposed to bring back my lunch today, and he never did. I was stuck here waiting for the delivery men to bring the pedestals—"

385

"The phone's working. Why didn't you call up and order something? Half the places around here deliver."

"But I was waiting for Rudi to bring me sushi."

"He was lunching with Carl, who, by the way, has agreed to jump ship from Manning Stanwyck and join us. Quite a coup." He preened, visibly.

"That's fantastic." She was particularly pleased because Manning had never been the least bit nice to her when she had worked for him. She didn't like Carl either, but he was certainly moving up, and his show would be widely reviewed. The last show at Manning's gallery had sold out. She was pleased she could remember without getting upset, since the day she had helped hang that show had been the day Tom died. "When should we schedule him?"

"It has to be after the first of the year, for legal reasons. February, I think. That's what I told him would be best. He's agreeable. He had a show last November, but he has good output. Oh, Inga's agreed to cater the opening party for the Steinmesser show."

How could he inform her about Carl's show last November, after she had hauled those canvases about when Sean had insisted it be rehung? She could not believe he did not remember. "You didn't even ask me! These are arrangements I'm supposed to be taking care of, and I already got estimates from four caterers—"

"I want Inga. I don't want some grubby salmon mousse or last year's canapés, blackened goldfish or burnt shark, no thank you. I will make those decisions. The taste of the gallery has to be evident in every detail. When I want you to arrange something, I'll tell you."

"Sean, we're supposed to be partners, but you don't treat me as a partner. You treat me worse than you treat Rudi. And I want him fired. He doesn't do anything useful."

"He's pleasant and decorative, which is considerably more than you add, Laurie. We are not partners. I'm in charge here. That's the way the agreement I signed with the backers states it, and that's the only terms on which I would come in. I run the whole show. You're my fifth wheel. I've put up with you in good faith and in good spirits, but let's be very clear about our situation."

"My father said I was to manage the practical side of the gallery. That's what he told me."

"I'm sure he put it nicely, but you're free to read the agreement. I had it all spelled out. Why shouldn't you take care of the details? You did a fine job having the pedestals delivered. Now you take care of getting somebody in from a temp service to put our mailing list on the computer so we can send out invites to the first opening. Have them here by Monday next. Oh, and find out why the heat isn't on." He picked up the Italian catalog he had been reading. "Arriverderci."

She shuffled out into the cold and empty gallery and sat on a pedestal that lay on its side preparatory to being sited. Rudi was chuckling on the phone. Her eyes burned, but tears would be too embarrassing. She was in exactly the same position here as she had been at Manning Stanwyck's gallery, the tweeny ignored and pushed around and used for whatever no one more important cared to bother with. She would call Tyrone and tell him she just couldn't go on this way. She would quit!

And do what? She could not quit. He had poured a huge amount of money into this gallery. She did not doubt Sean had the agreement he had described and that agreement had been part of his price. Tyrone had paid it for her. She must put up with Sean for him. Gradually she would take over. Wasn't she her father's daughter? She would show Sean what she could do. She was associated with an up and coming gallery that would start out visible and grow quickly important. That was still true.

Sean did not know her yet. Her being a woman was not the problem, because he obviously took Inga seriously. She had to prove herself. What could she do but try? At least unlike Manning, he did not have a string of overdressed girlfriends parading through the premises. There was room for her to take charge. She blew her nose.

She would have liked to leave early because she felt faint with hunger, but she did not want to seem to retreat after their confrontation. Moreover, she had better get on the phone as soon as Rudi relinquished it and try to deal with the heat problem. She hoped that Celeste would have a nice meal waiting for her. Once she got the phone, she could call the duplex and tell Celeste she wanted to eat on the early side—unless Tyrone was dining at home. She had a sudden image of the navy and white dress she had worn to the death party on the beach, Susan's bizarre funeral. She had not worn that dress since. She must have slipped the necklace in the pocket. Oh dear, had it gone to the cleaners? She must find out from Celeste where the dress

387

was. Celeste would never have sent out a dress without going through the pockets, surely she wouldn't have. As soon as she got home, she would have Celeste find it and there in the pocket would be the necklace Jimmy had given her. She could feel its weight in her hand. In the meantime, all she could do was balance on the pedestal shivering and wait for the phone to be free.

FIFTY-FOUR

Dinah

Dinah was to meet Itzak at Logan when he flew in from London. She had a lot of problems to solve with him, but if he wanted her, he was getting her. She danced down the steps that morning, happy to have decided at last. His plane landed at two, so she should get there by two-thirty or so, the earliest he might clear customs. She was not angry with Willie but relieved: they were sorting themselves out. Without Susan, things between them were too thin, and perhaps some such instinct had led him to Candida. Candida was hardly someone to draw Dinah. They would be fine as friends, but first she had to re-create her own life.

There had not yet been a frost, so her garden was rich in dahlias, marigolds and nasturtiums, late phlox and asters. She picked two baskets full while Figaro sang through the screen. Then she wrapped the stems in wet paper towels inside of aluminum foil and loaded them carefully in the trunk, along with an enormous salad, her last tomatoes and peppers and a vermilion kuri squash. She packed for a few days' stay.

At nine she left, the cats howling in the backseat, and drove to Brookline. All the way in she alternated between thinking how she would tell him and worrying about how they would live. It would demand flexibility on both their parts to make it work, a great deal of attention and effort. Nonetheless, she kept bursting into wordless song, bellowing at full stretch testing the resonances of the car, testing her own voice, whooping and sliding up and down, shifting into falsetto. The cats shut up. They were glad to get to Brookline. They had long ago claimed the house and ran at once to where their food dishes should be.

She was thinking she had not worked her voice since she had been in the Wholey Terrors. It was an instrument she had neglected, and that was stupid. After all, people carried their voice boxes around with them at all times.

She set out the flowers, filling every vase and half his glasses till bouquets stood on the diningroom table, in the kitchen, the livingroom, flowers on every available surface in the bedroom. She went shopping and stocked the refrigerator, picked up a bottle of champagne she considered essential for their evening. Then it was time to drive to the airport. Wouldn't she feel like an utter fool if he had changed his mind? Yet she could hardly blame him, for she had temporized all summer. She had not spoken to him since Scotland, so she had no idea what had been happening, what he was feeling. She did not fear the ex-wife, although his time in London made her a little uneasy. Who knows what loose ends might tie themselves about him there?

Several overseas flights arrived around the same time in the international terminal, so she bought and read through a *USA TODAY*, searched the terminal without success for reading matter, went to the women's room twice, combed her hair, stared at her familiar but suddenly dumb face, called Nita and left a banal message on the answering machine. Then she joined the crowd staring at the doors through which travelers exiting customs dribbled. She got up, she sat down, she got up again.

Finally he stumbled out with his flute case and his luggage, looking disheveled and dazed. She ran to him. He was gripping his flute case tightly, so she embraced him awkwardly and took one of his suitcases. "Welcome back," she said. "I missed you. I love you. Did you make a rapprochement with your ex-wife?"

"It was a bumpy crossing. There's a storm between England and here. I hate big planes when it's rough."

At first she thought he was putting her off, but he had that glazed look she recognized from her own gigs. "Are you all right?"

"Rapprochement not possible yet." In the parking garage he dropped his luggage beside her car and fell upon her, burying his sharp chin in her hair. He held her fiercely, his hands digging into her arms and back.

She got him into the car and back to Brookline without prying much out of him except that the meeting with his ex-wife had been a disaster, he had not felt at home in London, he had once again experienced his life as in shreds and he could not stand

389

that chaos. He thought he had played badly at Albert Hall, and the critics had been unkind about the Telemann. He was not used to bad reviews and took them seriously.

"You ought to be a composer! People are always calling your music fraudulent or boring or hideous or decadent or whatever they can think of. You get used to being attacked, believe me. It passes. You continue."

"I don't want to continue the way I have. I can't live all discombobulated. I need to be settled."

"Itzak, I'm absolutely ready to make the commitment you want—"

"Oh? Is this it? Or are you going to change your mind again tomorrow."

"Itzak, how often have I changed my mind?"

"You've certainly kept it wide open, swinging in the breezes."

Was he disappointed? Or just exhausted. He was certainly crabby. Now that she was willing to commit, had he withdrawn? She felt herself sinking. "But we have a huge amount of working out to do. How much settling can you really get from me?"

"What does that mean? You're still involved with Willie, or what?"

"Only as friends. I'm absolutely willing to be a couple with you."

"That's what matters most to me. That and to be sure you really love me."

"I can give you that, willingly, easily, joyfully. But I work on my own music. I travel too. I'm not prepared to live in the city. I'm prepared to go back and forth. I don't want to go on tour with you."

"What I want is a home to come back to. We can experiment with dividing our time between Brookline and the Cape."

She was almost dazed at the changes coming over them. "I'm ready to try."

"I love performing, but after a time, I lose myself."

Figaro ran to him in the front hall, which seemed to move him. "Do you remember me? You big rascal." He seemed a loosely packed bag of emotions with the bottom going. She was worried. What was she taking on? Well, him. About the flowers he said grumpily, "Did someone take me for a soprano? Who sent them?"

"I picked them. They're all from my garden."

"Oh. Thanks." He was hungry. He ate the salad at once,

two enormous plates of it with dark bread she had bought. As in afterthought he ate some Muenster and then took a bath, asking for coffee and balancing the cup on the rim of the tub. It will always be a big deal when he comes home, she thought, and felt oddly comforted. He will always be going out to tour and coming back trailing parts of himself. He lay in the tub in very hot water and washed himself again and again. She scrubbed his back, smooth, bony under her hands, hot and wet and sleek. His prick wavered underwater like pale seaweed.

He had never had a garden. He was a city person through and through. She felt defeated in advance. It looked grim, laborious. Willie and she shared a bounty of daily pleasures, walking, gardening, looking at trees and birds, a sense of the land, canning, clamming, all those country pleasures of the turning seasons. Maybe she was being too hasty in rejecting Candida. They did not have to be lovers. They could be friends. Maybe she was making a dreadful mistake.

He was staring at her. She helped him dry off and brought him more coffee. He dragged himself toward his king-sized bed, flung himself onto it. "It's time to move into this house. It's time to settle in," he said. "I kept thinking in the plane you'd have gone back to Willie and taken the easy way out." He seemed very vulnerable as he lay propped up. He kept himself in shape. He worked out on the road and at home, she knew, but he would always be a more fragile man than Willie.

She felt guilty for having wavered. He needed her more, he wanted her more than Willie ever would. "Willie isn't my lover, he's my friend now, and he has a new lover he'll marry once she's free. But I like him and I feel connected to his children. I helped raise them, and I can't throw them out of my life. Think of them as the children of a first marriage. Or as nephew and niece."

"I need to be connected. Deeply." Naked, he let himself down in the bed to lie on his elbow, facing her. His eyes were very dark under his wet hair, curling from the water.

"There's no ambiguity for me. I love you, I'm going to live with you, that's that. Everybody else are friends. I lived my life differently for a long time, but that's what we both need now."

"Do you need me?"

"I do. I need to go forward in my personal life the way I have in my work life. And I need both more integrated." What doubts I have are my own private business, she thought, for I have

391

equivocated long enough. I am marching off a cliff and any second thoughts will remain just that.

"Nobody thinks it will work. Everybody says you can't have a virtuoso and a composer together."

"I think if a woman and a man can live together, anybody can."

"I don't want to be on the road nine months out of twelve. I want to reduce to maybe three or four big tours a year. Beyond that just assorted gigs in the area, like Tanglewood in the summer."

"I know you can't imagine now that you might like the country, but you might. It was new to me too when I moved there."

"I do think your work is important. I'm sure it'll be a tug-of-war, but it has to stretch both of us." He put his hand on her shoulder. It was a gesture of assurance, but when the actual contact occurred, she could see his eyes change, darken. The hand seemed to grow warmer as he felt her, and the gesture turned from touch into caress. "I forget how much I want you. I forget when I'm away. I forget how strong it is."

"So do I. So do I." She sighed, holding him off with a braced hand.

He pulled her over onto him. "Let's see if we remember how to put it all together."

"Just one agreement, first. No condoms, no pills. We won't try and we won't prevent. We won't even think about it."

"That's the very last thing I want to worry about."

"What's the first?" She smiled into his shoulder, sleek, satiny.

He was exhausted and they made love in slow motion, as if underwater. Afterward he fell asleep at once. She gradually extracted her numbing arm and turned onto her side to face him. Tosca stepped gingerly across the pillow to sniff them both. Figaro curled into the bend of Itzak's knee and soon was softly snoring. She was not drowsy, but she could use the time just to think. With her decision finally made and ratified by his willingness, her life had become their lives together; now a great deal of massive construction and reconstruction was going on faster than she could grasp the implications.

She was beginning what was clearly her second marriage, whether or not they sought out a rabbi soon or in a couple of years. She was setting a different kind of roots, more traditional in one respect, less so in another. It would be very much a bonding of prickly equals. Although society would not judge it so, she was quite aware that this relationship was much riskier than her long triangle. It cut more deeply into her work, into her identity. It changed the nature of her journey, in some ways bringing her back onto an earlier course. It was a different alignment, in society, in family, in her work. If Itzak did not realize how profoundly they would be changing each other, he soon would; and they would continue or they would not, but each would be transformed.

And each time they made love, as just now, it would be an attempt to continue the line of survivors that pressed through her into the future. If she would be in the short run less of a composer, she accepted that risk, to be more fully who she was, Dinah bas Nathan, Dinah in history, Dinah the woman seizing her last chance at what she had finally decided she must have.

FIFTY-FIVE

Dinah

Dinah jumped back hastily as a centipede scuttled off the log she was shoving into the fireplace. "It isn't Christian, Itzak. It's pagan. And what the hell, I've been observing it with them for years and I can't start complaining now."

"But to go and steal a tree from someone's yard?"

"Willie and I have done it every year for the last decade. They don't count their trees or even notice."

"From murdering trees with him, what happens then?"

"Why don't you come with us? I'd like that." She knew he was as nervous as she was, because Dr. Bridey's office was supposed to have the results of her test by late afternoon. That knowledge was like a fire burning in the corner of the room each was conscious of and pretended not to notice every moment. She did not want to speak of it aloud, for that would be to admit her hope, and she was too superstitious to do that.

"What do I know about stealing trees?" But he put on his parka at once.

Dinah smiled. Another lump passed over. Theirs was a bumpy road, but they tooled along. Itzak, once he was persuaded into the woods, left off glowering and asked a hundred questions. Itzak was always forgetting how well he got on with Willie, for both men were curious about everything. Soon Willie was into his old shtick explaining pitch pines and Itzak told him stories back about planting trees in Israel, visiting his ex-wife's family. She walked in front of them enjoying her own silence and their discourse. She pinched off a leaf of wintergreen and crumbled it into brittle pieces under her nose, inhaling the clean odor.

Willie chopped at the trunk until he had it almost cut through—six quick masterful blows. Then he handed the ax to Itzak. "Want to take over?"

Itzak gave a wary swing. Then he warmed to the task. Whack, whack. He was grinning. The tree toppled. He stood over it, pleased with himself but disappointed the cutting was finished so quickly. "Do we need another?"

"One is usually enough," Willie said. "We have to set it up. That's harder than taking it down." Willie had taken to acting older brother with Itzak, and Itzak slid into playing the city Jew who couldn't tell a pine from an oak. They did not yet really see each other clearly, but those were comfortable poses for them, easy, companionable.

When they unloaded the tree from the truck, Willie was twitching with eagerness. "This is Chris's first tree. He'll be excited!" Lisa had arrived two days before for the long negotiated visit.

Chris was indeed excited. He cried hysterically for twenty minutes until Lisa carried him upstairs. The tree went up in the livingroom of the new house, where Candida too was living—her house being for sale.

Lisa was only a little shorter than Jimmy, a solidly built woman with maple-sugar blond-brown hair, a strong jaw and broad forehead, full cheeks. Judging from the fact that half her blouses and dresses seemed to need pinning across the chest, her breasts had probably grown with nursing. She was soft spoken, her eyelids often at half mast; she was obviously ill at ease, not sure of her position or her best direction. She gravitated toward Willie, as her strongest supporter. Dinah also noticed that she was wearing a necklace that looked exactly like the one Jimmy had given Laurie. She wondered if he could have bought two of them. "It's a present from Jimmy," Lisa said, fingering it. "He bought it for me last spring when the baby was born, but he just gave it to me. A friend of ours made it."

"It's not a Christmas present," Jimmy said smoothly. "It's a welcome present."

When Candida and Dinah were in the kitchen together getting the food out, Candida said, "Willie is very eager that Lisa and Jimmy get back together."

"I thought so. The grandson?"

"That, and he wants Jimmy settled. When Jimmy's on the loose, he's too loose, Willie says." She beamed at his cleverness. "*They* haven't been here at all this fall, none of them. I think Tyrone is terrified. It's bizarre to think he's scared of a woman like me."

"You seem happier with Willie anyhow."

"Willie is perfect for me. I've played it safe my whole life, and what did I get for it? Men with no respect or feeling for me. Willie has a heart." Candida was growing her hair out and had gained some weight. She looked less fashionable but healthier, with a glow to her skin and a gleam in her eyes. "I have a favor to ask you," she said in a husky whisper.

Dinah felt wild apprehension. What could Candida want?

"I wish you could say a word to Willie about his sculpture. He's taken to doing these lovely pieces in resins, he calls them odalisques. But this is a time when suddenly there's European interest in his more social work. A curator in Hamburg has approached us about a show. That would boost Willie's career, but there he is making these lovely sensuous women. Nice, but not what they're looking for." Candida stepped closer. "This is his chance, you see, for his work to take off."

Candida was a born manager, she thought. "Why don't you start buying all the papers? Get the left wing papers. Get the *Guardian*. Start reading *Mother Jones* and talking about articles. He'll be riled up in no time. He'll start doing the political sculptures again."

"Thank you!" Candida squeezed her forearm. She had a strong grip. "Politics, that's the ticket?"

"Take him to meetings about Central America and South Africa."

"Central America and South Africa," Candida repeated with enthusiasm.

"Nicaragua. El Salvador. Guatemala."

"Nicaragua. El Salvador. Guatemala. Central America and South Africa. Thank you so much!"

Dinah detached her arm. "I have to make a phone call now. I'll be back."

"Use the phone here."

"It's long distance." She did not bother putting on her coat but ran across the yard, dark already, Venus up. She had to call Dr. Bridey's office before five. Inside her house, the cold lay on her skin, numbing her. It felt like a second skin of scales. She fumbled with the phone, had to redial. It was Brookline she was calling, but she wanted to be alone. It was her private business, because the odds were her missed period was caused by wishful thinking or hormonal imbalance or a change of diet.

She asked the nurse for the results. The woman came back. "Was that Mrs. Asher?"

"No, Adler. Dinah Adler."

"Hold on, please. We're checking."

They had lost the results. The negatives fell through the cracks. False hopes. False promises. The house felt chilly. It needed a new furnace; this one dated from before Mark's and her arrival. Mark had a son he rarely saw, in whom he had taken only occasional interest. Even at the time she had thought that unfeeling of him, but she had been so young, it had been hard for her to challenge him.

"Miss Adler?" The voice sounded less cheery. "Your test was positive."

"Thank you. Thank you." Dinah thought she sounded exactly as inane and as grateful as Candida. She picked up Tosca, glaring from the top of the old refrigerator. "I won't let you get jealous or unhappy. Think of it as one more lap being born." She rocked Tosca and squeezed her. Then as she sometimes did, she felt her father. He was sitting in the old chair at the table nodding at her the way he did when she had played some difficult passage well. The sense of his presence faded.

She walked back across the yard, through the vast clean darkness. She heard an owl hunting across the pond. Eyes shone red as taillights near the truck. Raccoon? It was good to come in from the clear starry night to the kitchen that smelled of turkey roasting.

At the door to the livingroom she paused. Lisa had come down and she and Jimmy were helping Willie string lights. Itzak was sitting cross-legged before the fireplace watching. He saw her at once and raised his eyebrows quizzically. He glanced at the clock—he had obviously lost track of time—then jumped to his feet. "Did you call?"

She motioned for him to come into the hall, but he had forgotten everybody else. He had that capacity to concentrate utterly till nothing existed in this moment except the two of them and the news. It was the same concentration he had for his music. "The test was negative, of course? Of course."

She was not about to announce her condition in front of everyone. "Itzak, come outside."

He walked toward her, but he was not about to wait. "So what did the test say? Negative?"

She could feel the weight of his caring and now Willie and Jimmy and Lisa paused, turning. But Itzak was in unnecessary pain and apprehension: she could feel his emotions burning her. "It's positive."

"I didn't think there was any . . . what?"

"Positive," she said patiently. "I'm pregnant." Maybe she was wrong and his anxiety was the opposite of hers. Well, it was her pregnancy, and only his if he chose to claim it.

"Yes, a baby?"

"Unless it's a kitten and Figaro's responsible. Who else sleeps in the bed?"

"A baby? My god!" he whooped.

Everybody turned. Lisa was grinning. Willie looked as if somebody had punched him in the gut. Jimmy gave one of his bright smiles and went back to disentangling the lights. Dinah drew Itzak into the hall. "You're happy? It's all right?"

"If only my grandparents could know. Of course I'm glad—you think I'm crazy and I don't understand what this means to you? We'll work it out!"

Even if we can't, she thought, I'll have the baby. The one I had to have.

"Maybe I should cancel my tour."

"Itzak, it will still take us nine months like other people. We have seven and a half to go. I'm just starting that chorale for voices and percussion. I think January third is a lovely date for you to go on tour. I will hole up here and take care of myself and write like a maniac."

Jimmy sat on her left at supper. "You only got pregnant to have some use out of the room we put on. A frugal woman." Then he said to the table at large, "Toby's going to drop by after supper while we're trimming the tree."

"We always have just family," Willie said. "Why him?"

"I have to talk a little business with him."

"Tonight? Why does it have to be tonight?" Willie said sourly. "Here we all are together for once, finally." Willie and she had fallen into a brother-sister mode lately, lots of kidding, avoiding privacy. It would become easier over time as each of them went further into their couple.

Lisa was looking down into her lap, her hands kneading each other.

Jimmy said, "I want a lot in the subdivision. I'm going to build for my wife and kid. Toby and I have to work it out. They're all three quarters of an acre, but one of them is cut awkwardly—"

"A house?" Willie interrupted. "Are you staying?" he asked Lisa.

Her round cheeks visibly reddened, as did her throat. "Er, yes, we figured that would be best for Chris, at least to try it, yes."

Willie was beaming. As he leapt from his chair, his white hair seemed to rise like a mane. "That's splendid!" he sang out. "Let's have a toast! This is the greatest thing that's happened around here in ages! Where's my boy Chris?"

"It's his nap time at home. I think we should let him sleep," Lisa said firmly.

Jimmy looked quite pleased with himself. He had a gift for making do. He was happy with Laurie while she treated him decently; he was happy with Lisa if they didn't fight too much. He was an opportunist, but not for money or power. He wanted to be comfortable.

Toby came by after supper. He was looking portly in a three-piece suit made of good wool but tight across the back. He and Jimmy talked seriously in a corner. While Dinah was bringing in glasses and cordial, he caught her in the kitchen. "Just tonic for me. So you're with that musician these days. You like living in the city?"

"I'm back and forth."

"Well, you get tired of commuting and your flute player, you let me know. I never felt I had anything to offer a woman. But I'm straight these days, no drugs, no alcohol, and I've always had an eye out for you. I used to watch you in the spring."

She did not tell him how he had scared her. Instead she said, "You're a little late, Toby. I'm taken. And pregnant besides."

"If you change your mind, look me up." He took a card from his pocket, a printed business card, and presented it to her. She felt like giggling but tucked it in the pocket of her wool slacks and went back to the livingroom where Itzak was watching for her. The tree was being trimmed. This year she decided she could skip that ritual, for it reminded her too strongly of Susan. "I'm a little tired. Would you like to go home?"

"Home." Itzak nodded. He could enjoy visiting this house, but they would never engage him the way for instance Nita did. "To celebrate."

"To celebrate. And give the cats some supper." She had forgotten before. Time to talk, to sketch plans. She tried to tell as they crossed the yard slowly with arms around each other's waists whether she could feel the baby. Nothing physical was obvious. Nonetheless all the furniture of her mind had been turned around.

"I was just thinking how happy I am that we're going to have a baby, and how relieved I am it didn't happen with my first wife. I'd feel guilty. I'd probably have stayed and been miserable all my life."

My *first* wife, he said. She supposed they would start talking about marriage, gradually. She had a sudden take of all the members of the chorale crying like babies, crying at the top volume. Throttle full open. Stretched wide as the beaks of baby birds. That would be an interesting sound. Cry out loud but stop at the conductor's signal. Twenty-four bars of baby's crying. A chorus, a chorale of babies.

Or suppose right after that she divided the chorus into four parts, soprano babies and alto babies. Then tenor and baritone babies. Wah! Wah! Wah! Wah! The voice used percussively. Then drawn out long. Different rhythms of crying set against each other. It would be amusing. It would be fresh and fascinating in texture. That was another way she would celebrate continuance. Even her pregnancy would issue into music.

As a gardener she loved the seasons. She had resisted the changes in her life, but everything had changed anyhow into a different kind of loving, a different kind of ripeness, new ideas for her music. If she had a daughter, maybe they'd call her Shoshana. Finally she was growing the baby that carried on for her father and all the other dead whose memory spread over the sky like the smear of stars up in the cold black night. A seed of light grew in her. If she had never been a dutiful daughter, as her mother had often said (Shirley, whom she must call tomorrow), she at least was a daughter who was doing her duty to the dead. No doubt this child traveling on that long trajectory through her body toward birth was coming into trouble, into a bumpy and less than idyllic childhood. The choices we make resonate and redound, she thought. But mostly her own fierce self would be making what she had to, weaving traps of sound to catch the mind.

Bestselling author

Marge Piercy

has written several novels about
the devastating effects
of our changing society over the years.
Each is unique,
yet each finds hope
in the resilience of the human spirit
and courage from the strength of the human will

*Look for these classics in Fawcett paperback
wherever books are sold. . . .*

Marge Piercy

GONE TO SOLDIERS

The long overdue novel of the "other" World War II: not the war fought on the front lines, but the war, fought mostly by women, on the factory lines, the food lines and behind enemy lines in Europe.

Ten extraordinary people—six women and four men— move through the dizzying atmosphere of the world's wartime capitals: the impulsive couplings and bittersweet partings, the stultifying deprivations and the once-in-a-lifetime chances. Piercy shows how World War II became a crucible, where unformed young people were hardened into men and women, charged with saving civilization as no generation had before or has since.

"A literary triumph for Marge Piercy and a landmark volume in the literature of war."

—*USA Today*

"Not since John Dos Passos's *U.S.A.* trilogy has a group of individual portraits so seamlessly blended together into a single, broad canvas of human experience."

—*Chicago Sun-Times*

"Panoramic...This is a sweeping epic in the best sense."

—*The Philadelphia Inquirer*

Marge Piercy

WOMAN ON THE EDGE OF TIME

The fascinating story of Connie Ramos, a Chicana woman in her mid-thirties, living in New York and labeled insane, committed to a mental institution. But the truth is that Connie is overwhelmingly sane, heroically sane, and tuned in to the future.

Connie is able to communicate with the year 2137. Two totally different ways of life are competing. One is beautiful—communal, nonsexist, environmentally pure, open to ritual and magic. The other is a horror—totalitarian, exploitive, rigidly technological.

In Connie's struggle to keep the institution's doctors from forcing her into a brain control operation, we find the timeless struggle between beauty and terror, between good and evil... with an astonishing outcome.

"Both absorbing and exciting."
—*The New York Times Book Review*

"Chilling, provocative, and controversial."
—*Mademoiselle*

"An ambitious, unusual novel about the possibilities for moral courage in contemporary society."
—*The Philadelphia Inquirer*

"A stunning, even astonishing novel... Marvelous and compelling."
—*Publishers Weekly*

Marge Piercy

FLY AWAY HOME

Successful Boston cookbook author Daria Walker, whose greatest pleasures are her home and her family—and who loves her husband deeply—is devastated to learn he wants a divorce.

Now she must put her life back together. But as she strives to understand the husband she is losing, Daria must face the shocking truth behind the smooth facade of prominent real-estate attorney Ross Walker—and re-create her own values, her own sense of family, and herself.

"FLY AWAY HOME has the hallmark of true literature: It makes the reader think. . . . This is the kind of novel you'll probably pass on to a friend."
—*The Pittsburgh Press*

"A can't-put-it-down story that moves swiftly to its conclusion with a touch of intrigue and surprise."
—*Detroit Free Press*

"Daria is an endearing, complex mixture of vulnerability, sensuality, fear, courage, enthusiasm, and pride. Although Sara Davidson, Judith Rossner, and Nora Ephron have chronicled the revamped romantic professional and domestic roles of the American woman, with FLY AWAY HOME, Marge Piercy has bested them all."
—*Boston Herald*

Marge Piercy

GOING DOWN FAST

As a blighted neighborhood is invaded by a university—an institution that promises to bring new life—the people who live there are forced to go along with too many changes too fast. There is Anna, a woman living through a succession of losses—marriage, job, home, and lover. And Rowley, a blue-eyed soul singer whose greatest limitation is his belief that he is powerless. Together with Leon, an underground filmmaker, and Caroline, a beautiful woman with a dark and desperate secret, they all watch the progress of the wrecking ball, hoping as always, for something better... perhaps even for love.

DANCE THE EAGLE TO SLEEP

A passionate, powerfully imagined novel about young rebels driven underground by a tyrannical society. They call themselves the Indians. Through the experiences of four young revolutionaries—Shawn, a rock music celebrity; Corey, part Indian, whose heritage gave the movement its name; Billy, a brilliant young scientist; and Joanna, a pretty runaway "army brat" who survives on pot and sex—this macabre and moving adventure brings an all-too-possible future into shattering focus.

"Brilliant... A frightening, marvelous book."
—*The New York Times*

Marge Piercy

VIDA

She remembered the early fugitive days when half the police in the country seemed to have nothing to do but search for them. No time for false I.D., no time for anything but running, never sleeping in the same place two nights straight. The worst had been times when they had lost their contacts and been cast out, left to their own resources with no shelter and no money. That was when Jimmy tried selling his body on the streets of Chicago with only moderate success. That was when Kevin and she had robbed a liquor store at gunpoint. You gave up or you survived. She had been there.

Vida was their star—the charismatic red-haired beauty from the pages of *Life* magazine—the symbol of the passionate rebellion of the 60s. Now, years later, the shouting is over but Vida is still on the run. Staying in network hideouts, traveling disguised, she finds herself warming again toward a man, an outcast ten years younger than herself. VIDA is the most important novel about the 60s and the lengthy demise of the 70s, terrifying, harshly real, yet moving and sensual.

SMALL CHANGES

The explosive novel of women struggling to make their places in a man's world. Set against the early days of the feminist movement, SMALL CHANGES tells of two women and the choices they must face. Intelligent, sensual Miriam Berg trades her doctorate for marriage and security, only to find herself hungry for a life of her own—but terrified of losing her husband. Shy, frightened Beth ran away from the very life Miriam seeks, ran away to a new world, different ideas, and a different kind of love—the love of another woman.

"Beautiful, inspiring, realistic."

—*Boston Phoenix*

"Marge Piercy is a raw, tough, willful, magnificent novelist."

—*The Christian Science Monitor*

Marge Piercy

THE HIGH COST OF LIVING

For Leslie, the heroine of this searching novel, the cost of living
—and loving—is getting higher and higher. First of all, she is
miserable for having lost her lover, Valerie, to another woman.
And she has begun to doubt just about everything about her life.
Now she is involved in a strange erotic triangle with Honor,
adolescent virgin who has romantic ideals, and Bernie, a homo-
sexual street hustler trying to settle down. Leslie and Bernie both
want Honor. They also want each other. But all Honor wants is a
little spice in her life. A powerful, searing novel of three young
dreamers caught up in a life-style they can neither accept nor
change.

BRAIDED LIVES

Growing up in Detroit in the 50s and going to college when the
first seeds of sexual freedom are sown, Jill and Donna are two
young women coming of age in a turbulent time. Wry, independent Jill tells the story of BRAIDED LIVES, of her own social
and sexual awakening, as well as that of her beautiful cousin
Donna, who is desperately searching for a man to save her from
herself. In her odyssey, Jill falls in and out of love with Mike,
then Peter, confronts her relationship with her mother, and
builds a new relationship with her childhood friend Howie. But
love cannot overcome the fundamental differences in their lives,
inextricable though they are.

"Rings with passionate awareness... Honest and impressive."

—*The Washington Post Book World*

"From the first page... the reader is captivated, mesmerized. It is impossible to put down.... A rich, complex and
thoroughly satisfying examination of life."

—*Publishers Weekly*

Marge Piercy

These novels are available in bookstores, or use this coupon to order by mail. You can also call toll-free 1-800-733-3000 to order with your major credit card. Please mention interest code JOB 43.